W9-BWQ-748

THE COLLECTED STORIES

The
Collected
Stories

John
McGahern

Alfred A. Knopf
New York
1993

THIS IS A BORZOI BOOK
PUBLISHED BY ALFRED A. KNOPF, INC.

ISBN 0-679-41913-6
LC 92-54448

Manufactured in the United States of America

Published February 2, 1993
Second Printing, March 1993

For
Rosaleen, Breedge,
Margaret, Monica, Dymphna
and
Frank

Contents

The Collected Stories

Wheels

Grey concrete and steel and glass in the slow raindrip of the morning station, three porters pushing an empty trolley up the platform to a stack of grey mail-bags, the loose wheels rattling, and nothing but wait and watch and listen, and I listened to the story they were telling.

'Seven-eighths of his grave he'd dug in that place down the country when they went and transferred him up on promotion.'

'Took to fishing out beyond Islandbridge, bicycle and ham sandwiches and a flask of tea, till he tried to hang himself from a branch out over the river, but the branch went and broke and in he fell roaring for help.'

'No use drowning naturally if you'd meant to hang yourself in the first place.'

'Think there's any chance they'll have him up for attempted whateveritis?'

'Not nowadays – they'll give him a six-month rest-cure in the Gorman on full pay.'

They'd filled the trolley, the smile dying in the eyes as they went past, the loose wheels rattling less under the load, the story too close to the likeness of my own life for comfort though it'd do to please Lightfoot in the pub when I got back.

'Looked at with the mind, life's a joke; and felt, it's a tragedy and we know cursed nothing,' he'd said last night over pints of Guinness.

Flush of tiredness in my face after the drinking, the jug of water by the bed had been no use, rough tongue, dry roof of mouth, dull ache and throb of the poison along the forehead and on all the nerves, celebrating this excursion home; and always desire in the hot tiredness, the dull search about the platform for vacancy between well-fleshed thighs: may I in my relax-sirs slacks (Hackney, London) plunge into your roomy ripeness and forget present difficulties?

3

The train drew in. I got a table in the restaurant car facing a priest and a man in his fifties, a weathered face under a hat, the blue Sunday suit limp and creased.

A black woollen scarf inside the priest's gaberdine almost completely concealed the Roman collar. The waiter brought us tea and toast on trays and the priest broke the silence.

'Have you come far?' he asked the hatted man at his side.

'From London, on the nightboat.'

'You must work there, then,' the priest continued in an interested politeness.

'I do and fukken all, for the last twenty-eight years, on the buildings.'

The man hadn't seen the collar and was unaware of the shock of the swear-word. The priest looked anxiously about the carriage but asked, 'Is it tough on the buildings?' more to prove he could master the unsocial than out of any politeness now.

'Not if you use your fukken loaf like. You soon get wised-up that nobody'll thank you for making a fukken name for yourself by working. I'm a teaboy.' The man was relaxed, ready to hold forth.

'And are you going home on holiday?' the priest changed.

'Not effin' likely. I'm going home to bury the brother,' he announced importantly.

'I'm sorry. May he rest in peace,' the priest said.

'A release to himself and everybody else; been good for nothing for years.'

The priest rose. He'd risked enough.

'If you're ever in London,' the man held out his hand, 'you'll find me any Sunday morning in the Archway Tavern, in the door of the Public Bar facing the Gents.'

The priest thanked him, anxious to be gone, and as he turned to the door the man saw the round collar.

'That was a priest,' he murmured as if waiting for the certainty to sink in. 'Why didn't you tell me?'

'I got no chance.'

'Well I'll be fukken blowed.' He slumped.

'He didn't seem to mind too much. I wouldn't worry.'

'Still, he's a priest, isn't he? You have to draw the line fukken somewhere. I'll go and tell him I'm sorry.'

'I wouldn't worry,' I said, but he shambled to the door.

'He was all right about it, he said he understood,' he informed when he returned after minutes, relief of confession on the old face as he pondered, 'Tidy how a body can put his fukken foot in it.'

The train had crossed the Shannon. The fields were slowing. I took the suitcase and shook hands with the man.

The front door was open when I got to the house. She was on her knees in the hall, scrubbing the brown flagstones. She must have heard the iron gate under the yew at the road and the footsteps up the unweeded gravel but she did not stop or look up until I was feet away. All she said was my name, but all the tense emotion of the face, the tears just held back, went into the name, and it was an accusation. 'Rose,' I answered with her name.

I thought she was going to break, and there was the embarrassment of the waiting silence, the still brush in her hand beside her knees on the wet stone.

'Did you get the letter that I was coming?'

'Your father got a letter.' Her face hardened, and it was already a hard greying face, the skin stretched tight over the bones, under the grey hair.

'Was it all right to come?'

She still didn't rise or make any sign for me to enter, and when she dipped the brush in the water and started to scrub the stone again I put the suitcase down close to the wall of the house and said, 'I'll fool around till he comes.' She didn't answer and I could hear the rasp of the scrubbing brush on the stone till I'd gone the other side of the house.

They'd net-wired a corner of the orchard off for her hens, the wild nettles growing coarse and tall out of the bare scratched earth; henshit enriches the clay, I'd heard them say.

'Be quiet, trembling between timidity and the edges of violence as the rest of your race, and wait for him to come: life has many hours, it'll end.'

The bell without rope or tongue hung from the stone archway where the pear tree leaned; it used to call the workmen to their meals.

'Why don't you go to night lectures and try for promotion?' Lightfoot had asked, pints on the marble of the Stag's Head.

'I don't want to.'

'Wouldn't it be better for you to have some say in the world than

5

to have jumped-up jacks ordering you around all the time?'

'Drink your drink. They have piped music in the office now. They talk less.'

I saw my father come on the tractor, two creamery cans on the trailer, old felt on his head. I wondered if the sweat-band stank as it used to or if it was rotten now. I watched him take the cans off the trailer, then go inside, body that had started my journey to nowhere.

The suitcase was still against the wall of the house. I left it there, but went in. One place was laid on the table by the window, and she was bent over saucepans.

'Your father has come from the creamery. He's gone out again but he'll soon be in for his dinner.'

'Thanks. It's all right.'

As I grow older I use hardly anything other than these formal nothings, a conciliating waiter bowing backwards out of the room.

I took the newspaper, went through the daily calamities that spice the well-being or lighten trouble with news of worse, the turning of the pages loud above the sounds of cooking in the gnawing silence. At last she took the whistle from the nail on the wall and blew three short blasts from the flower garden.

Clay muffled his boots as he came in, leaving a trail on the washed stone. I stood but he turned past me to the table as if he hadn't seen me.

'Is the dinner ready, Rose?'

'In a second, Jim.'

He drummed an idle rhythm with the bone of the knife on the cloth until she put the plate before him, fried eggs and bacon, a yellow well of butter in the middle of the creamed potatoes.

'There, Jim.'

'Thanks, Rose.'

The knife and fork rang often on the plate to break the aggressive sucking and swallowing of the food, but he said nothing.

'I came on the train,' I offered, and had to smile at how foolishly it hung in the silence till he lifted his hat with the flourish of a man in a hurry, the sweat-band still apparently intact, and went in the direction of the timber-stack.

When he'd gone she put my plate on the table. 'There's some dinner.'

6

'Why didn't he speak? Does he not want me in the house?' I asked quietly as I ate.

She was stirring a mixture of meal and skim milk in a bucket for the calf with a stick.

'Do you know, Rose?' I'd to ask again.

'It's not my place to interfere. It'll only drag more trouble into it.'

'Well, I'll ask him myself.'

'What do you want to go and upset him for?' Her voice was sharp.

'No. I can't stay here without knowing whether he wants me or not. The place is his.'

'If you let it go today it'll calm down and tomorrow it'll be as if nothing happened,' she reasoned in her care, but I could feel the hatred. The disappointment and pain had hardened with the years, but she could mask them better now.

In the confidence of her first days in the house she'd taken down the brown studio photo of the old wedding, *Warner Artist Grafton Street*, replacing it with the confetti-strewn black and white of her own, the sensible blue costume in place of the long white dress to the silver shoes. She'd been too old for white.

Against her hopes, too old for children too, the small first communion and the confirmation photos stayed on the sideboard, replaced by no other, only disappearing when the youngest left and they were alone.

All remembered her near madness in the middle of her months as she felt the last years slip.

'For Chrisake don't you know there's children listening? I'm tired. Let me get to sleep.'

'You should have stuck with your children to the grave.'

The noise of the blow came, she escaping to the fields, losing herself between the tree trunks till she'd grown cold and come in to sit numbly in a chair over the raked fire till morning. Perhaps she'd hoped he'd come, but he hadn't, stiff with anger at the shouted insult to his maleness, more bitter since it echoed his own bitterness at growing old. The next day he'd dug the potatoes where the sheets hung on the line between two trees above the ridge, scattering clay on the sheets she'd scrubbed white for hours on the wooden scrubbing-board.

The years had gone by and now they were alone and he was her child and everything. I could understand her care and hatred, but it was getting late, and I didn't want to stay.

I found him splitting lengths of beech beside the useless pier he'd built to absorb the glass about the house, dangerous with jagged bits. He held the length steady with his boot against the pier while he drove the wedge into the timber. I waited until it split and the wedge fell loose.

'Can I speak to you?'

As he turned to put another length of beech into position, I said, 'If you don't answer I'll just leave.'

'Well, I'm not in America as you can no doubt see.' He suddenly turned.

'I can't understand why you've not spoken to me since I came.'

'You're joking surely. Do you mean to tell me that you don't know why?'

'I don't. I'd not ask you if I knew.'

'You mean to say you know nothing about that letter you wrote in the spring?' he accused, the voice breaking under the whole day's resentment. 'I had to wait till near the end of my days for a right kick in the teeth.'

There was the treacherous drag to enter the emotion, to share and touch, the white lengths of beechwood about his boots and the veins swollen dark on the back of the old hands holding the sledge. With his sleeve he wiped away tears.

'The one important thing I ever asked you couldn't even be bothered,' he accused.

'That's not true. When you wrote you wanted to move to Dublin I went round the auctioneers, sent you lists, looked at places.'

'And you said if I did get a place and moved that you wanted no room in it.'

'I want to live on my own. I didn't want you to come thinking differently.'

'I didn't come under illusions. You took good care of that,' he accused bitterly. 'And I was foolish enough to think there might be more than pure selfishness.'

I knew the wheel: fathers become children to their sons who repay the care they got when they were young, and on the edge of dying the fathers become young again; but the luck of a death and a second marriage had released me from the last breaking on this ritual wheel.

'You are married,' I said. It was a washing of hands.

'Yes, I'm married,' he said in a bitterness close to regret. 'What's that got to do with it?'

'What did she think of you leaving?'

'She'd be hardly likely to stay here on her own if I went.' He resented the question.

'It's your life and her life, for me to enter it would be simple intrusion. In the long run it'd cause trouble for everybody.'

I could hear the measured falseness of my own voice, making respectable with the semblance of reason what I wanted anyhow.

'I'd give anything to get out of this dump,' he changed.

'It's quiet and beautiful.' The same hollowness came, I was escaping, soothing the conscience as the music did the office.

'Quiet as a graveyard,' he took up. 'And stare at beauty every day and it'll turn sicker than stray vomit. The barracks shut now, a squad car in its place. Sometimes children come to the door with raffle tickets, that's all. But there's plenty of funerals, so busy Mrs McGreevy's coffin last month came out roped on the roof of the bread van, and the way they talked about her was certain proof if proof was needed that nobody seriously believes in an after-life. They were sure they'd never hear the edge of her tongue again either in hell or heaven or the duck-arsed in-between. I'd give anything to get out,' he said with passion.

There was silence but it was easier after he'd spoken. Then he asked, 'Are you down for long?'

'I'll stay till tomorrow if it's all right.'

'That's about as long as you can stand us I suppose.'

'It's not that. I have to be at work.'

I helped him gather the tools.

'I think Rose is giving you your old room. I want to get the last things done before night.'

'I've left your case in your old room, the bed is aired,' she said when I came in.

'There's no trouble any more but I have to go tomorrow, it's to be back at the office,' I explained.

'The next time you must come for longer.' It was easy in the lies that give us room.

'I'll do that and thank you.'

Quietly the dark came, the last tasks hurried, a shift of hens on the roost of the hen-house before the bolting of the door. Inside, the lamp was lit and he said, 'That's another day put down,' as he took off his boots and socks, reek of feet and sweat as he draped socks over the boots on the floor.

'Rose, the corns were tormenting me no end today. Any chance you'd give them a scrape with the razor?'

'You better soak them first,' she answered.

She placed a basin of steaming water by his chair on the floor, the water yellowing when she added Dettol. She moved the lamp closer.

He sat there, her huge old child, soaking his feet in water, protesting like a child. 'It's scalding, Rose,' and she laughed back, 'Go on, don't be afraid.' And when she knelt on the floor, her grey hair falling low, and dried the feet that dripped above the lighted water, I was able to go out without being noticed as she opened the bright razor.

Cattle and a brown horse and sheep grazed on the side of the hill across the track. The sun came and went behind white cloud, and as it did the gravel shone white or dulled on the platform.

'The train won't go without you unless I tell it,' the one official said to an anxious passenger pressing him to open the ticket office and he went on stacking boxes on the gravel where the goods van would come in. When he did open the office and sold tickets there was still time left and the scrape of feet changing position on the gravel grew more frequent.

I had no hangover and no relax-sirs desire and as much reason to go back as come. I'd have hangover and desire in the morning and as much reason then as now. I was meeting Lightfoot in the bar beside the station and would answer 'How did it go?' with how it went, repetition of a life in the shape of a story that had as much reason to go on as stop.

I walked through the open carriages. There was nobody I knew. Through the windows the fields of stone walls, blue roofs of Carrick, Shannon river. Sing for them once First Communion Day *O River Shannon flowing and a four-leaved shamrock growing*, silver medal on the blue suit and white ankle socks in new shoes. The farther flows the river the muddier the water: the light was brighter on its upper reaches. Rustle of the boat through the bulrushes as we went to Moran's well for spring water in dry summers, cool of watercress and bitterness of the wild cherries shaken out of the whitethorn hedge, black bullrush seed floating in the gallons on the floorboards, all the vivid sections of the wheel we watched so slowly turn, impatient for the rich whole that never came but that all the preparations promised.

Why We're Here

Gillespie tested the secondhand McCullagh chainsaw as soon as he came from the auction, sawing some blown-down branches stacked against the wall of the house into lengths for firewood. The saw ran perfectly.

'Now to get rid of the evidence. For it'll not be long till he's up with his nose smelling unless I'm far out,' he said to the sheepdog when he'd finished. He carried the saw and sawn lengths into the shed, scattering the white sawdust wide into the grass with his boot. Then he farted. 'A great release that into the evening, thank God,' he sighed, as he waited for the aroma of the decomposing porter he'd drunk in Henry's after the auction to lift to his nostrils, his eyes going over the ground beside the stack of blown-down branches again. 'Not much evidence left that I can see. Nothing to do now but wait for him to arrive up.'

He was waiting at the gate when Boles came on the road, the slow tapping of the cattle cane keeping time to the drag of the old feet in slippers, sharply calling 'Heel' to his dog as a car approached from Carrick, shine of ointment over the eczema on his face as he drew close.

'Taking a bit of a constitutional, Mr Boles?'

'The usual forty steps before the night,' Boles laughed.

The two dogs had started to circle, nosing each other, disturbing the brown droppings of the yew. They stood in its shade, where it leaned above the gateway.

'Lepping out of your skin you are, Mr Boles. No holding the young ones in these days.'

'Can't put the clock back. The old works winding down, you know.'

'No future in that way of thinking. You're good for ten Beechers yet, if you ask me.'

They watched the dogs trying to mount each other, circling on the dead droppings of the yew, their flutes erect, the pink flesh unsheathed, and far off a donkey braying filled the evening with a huge contentment.

'At much, this weather?' Boles asked.

'The usual foolin' around. Went to the auction.'

'See anything there?'

'No, the usual junk, the Ferguson went for a hundred. Not fit to pull you out of bed.'

'Secondhand stuff is not the thing, a risk, no guarantee,' Boles said, and then changed to ask: 'Did I hear an engine running up this way an hour ago?'

'None that I know of.'

'I'd swear I heard an engine between the orchard and the house an hour ago.'

'Country's full of engines these days, Mr Boles. Can't believe your ears where they come from.'

'Strange.' Boles was dissatisfied, but he changed again to ask: 'Any word of Sinclair this weather?'

'The crowd up for Croke Park saw him outside Amiens Street with an empty shopping bag. They said he looked shook. Booked close enough to the jump.'

'Never looked very healthy.'

'*The ignorance and boredom of the people of this part of the country is appalling, simply appalling,*' Boles mimicked an English accent quietly. 'That's the speech he'll make to Peter at the gate. A strange person.'

'Touched, that's all. I got to know his form well, the summer I bought this place from him and was waiting for him to shunt off. Especially when I was close to the house, mowing with the scythe there between the apple trees, he used to come out and spout to the end of the world. The ignorance and the boredom but nothing about his own, bad, manners and the rain, speaking as one intelligent man if you don't mind to another, O Saecula Saeculorum world without end Amen the Lord deliver us. He even tried to show me how to put an edge on the scythe.'

'I knew him fifteen years here.'

'Fifteen too long, I'd say.'

'No, he was a strange person. He suffered from the melancholy.'

'But he had a pension, hadn't he, from that cable in Valencia?'

'No, it wasn't money troubled him.'

'*No reason why we exist, Mr Boles. Why we were born. What do we know? Nothing, Mr Boles. Simply nothing. Scratching our arses, refining our ignorance. Try to see some make or shape on the nothing we know,*' Boles mimicked again.

'That was his style, no mistaking, nature of the beast. The way he used to treat that wife of his was nobody's business.'

'In Valencia he met her, a girl in the post office. He used to cut firewood in the plantation, I remember, and he'd blow a whistle he had when he'd enough cut. She'd come running with a rope the minute she'd heard the whistle. It was a fair sight to see her come staggering up the meadow with a backload of timber, and him strolling behind, golfin' at the daisies with the saw, shouting *fore*.'

'Poor soft bitch. I knew a few'd give him fore, and the size of him in those plus fours. He should have stayed where he belonged.'

'*I am reduced to the final ambition of wanting to go back to look on the green of the billiard table in the Prince of Wales on Edward Road. They may have taken it away though. Sign of a misspent youth, proficiency at billiards,*' Boles mimicked again.

'On the same tack to me in the orchard. A strange coot. Luther's idea about women. The bed and the sink. *As good to engage a pig in serious conversation as a woman. All candles were made to burn before the high altar of their cunts. It was no rush of faith, let me tell you good sir, that led to my conversion. I was dragged into your Holy Roman Catholic Apostolic Church by my male member.* I'll not forget in a hurry how he came out with that spiff.'

'He had a curious blend of language sometimes,' Boles said.

'And he ends up after all his guff with an empty shopping bag outside Amiens Street Station.'

'A lesson, but I liked him. Great smell of apples in the evening.'

'Rotting on the ground. Wouldn't pay you to gather. Except a few hundredweight for Breffni Blossom. They don't mind the bruises.'

'Better than wastin' in the grass.'

The passing cars had their headlamps on now. A mile away, over fields of stone walks, the lighted windows of the nine-twenty diesel rattled past.

'Train to Sligo.'

'Empty, I suppose.'

'I suppose . . . Time to be moving in the general direction of the bed.'

'No hurry, long enough lying down in the finish. How is the eczema?'

'Stays quiet long as I don't go near timber. I've got this stuff on to keep the midges off.' He brushed his finger lightly along his cheek.

'If everything was right we'd appreciate nothing.'

'Still, I'd have sworn I heard a chainsaw up this way today,' Boles said as he turned to the road.

'Must have been from elsewhere,' Gillespie contradicted. 'What the wind can do with sounds is no joke.'

'There was hardly a puff of wind today.'

'Surprising what even a little can do, as the woman said when she pissed in the sea.' Gillespie laughed aggressively.

'I was certain, but time to go,' Boles said and called his dog.

'No use detaining you if you have, though it's young, the night, yet.'

'Goodnight, then.'

''Night, Mr Boles.'

He watched him go, the light tapping of the cattle cane in time to the drag of feet in slippers, calling 'Heel' to the dog as headlamps flooded the road from Boyle.

'That's what'll give him something to think about,' Gillespie muttered as he called his own dog back and turned towards the house.

Coming into his Kingdom

'They're in love, they're in love, they're in love! Nora's in love with Stevie,' the crowd of children cried at the fallen girl and boy.

They'd been struggling to sit in the Chair, a little hollow in the roadside ditch, on their way home from school. In one of the struggles Stevie had managed to get hold of the Chair, but before he could grip the grass or dig his heels into the clay Nora had jerked him out with all her weight. And when he came so easily with her she overbalanced on to the road, her grip tightening desperately on his arm to drag him down on top of her. His forehead struck heavily against her jaw, and they lay stunned together on the road for a moment, his mouth on the flesh of her side-face between the ear and outer roots of the hair, his body solidly on her, his legs thrown between her opened thighs.

There was an anxious silence, fear of the injury that'd ruin their game, till someone shouted, 'They're in love.' The cry went through the crowd, raggedly taken up at first, though soon it grew to almost a chant.

'They're in love! They're in love! They're in love! Nora's in love with Stevie!'

Nora, a blonde girl of thirteen, quickly woke to what the shouting was about and pushed the stunned boy loose with her palms. His knee caught her dress as he rolled and bared the white young flesh of her thighs from the brown as far as the knees to the legs of a faded blue knickers.

'Nora has blue drawers,' the jeer changed as the girl rose to her feet, instinctively smoothing her dress down, taut with shame and anger that broke in violent sobbing. She lifted her school-bag, burst through the circle of children, and began to run. They chased her down the earthen road between the sloe bushes to call, 'Nora's mad in love! Nora has blue drawers! Nora's goin' to marry Stevie'; but when someone shouted, 'Nora's goin' to have a baby,' it stopped as suddenly as it began. They'd gone too far. They slowed. Nora went out of sight at the next turn of the road. The stragglers and Stevie caught up with the main group. They looked about the fields and road, afraid they'd been observed. The whole thing could easily lead to trouble. They began to go quickly home, little conversation now, the group thinning as children said goodbye to each other till the next day and turned up the lanes to their farmhouses. After a mile only Stevie and a girl as old as Nora were left. They had to walk another whole mile of road to the village, climb Cox's Hill on the way.

Their canvas shoes dragged rustling through the dead leaves as they walked in the frozen loneliness of the country in October. Men dug potatoes alone in fields of long ridges where only the weeds were green, the sea of stalks on which blossoms swayed in June dead and grey as matchwood. Neither of them spoke as they climbed Cox's Hill, their eyes bent on the drag-drag of their canvas shoes uphill through the leaves, the noise of someone shouting angrily at a horse beginning to drift from the woods across the river. There was only this silence between them, and he had longed for the moment they'd be alone as now, hurt and shamed by the shouting that he couldn't understand. He was waiting for her to speak but the only sound that came was the rustling of her canvas shoes uphill through the leaves.

'They cheered and shouted,' he had to fumble at last. 'They cheered and shouted when I fell on Nora.'

The girl's eyes stayed on the leaves that she was now kicking uphill as she walked.

'They cheered and shouted,' he said definitely. 'Teresa, they cheered and shouted when I fell on Nora.' This time she did look up and stared so coldly at him that he flinched.

'They cheered and shouted,' she admitted.

'But why? I only fell on Nora.'

'What does it matter why? They cheered and shouted, that's all.'

'But there must have been some reason?'

'You fell on Nora.'

'But why did they shout?'

'That's the why,' she laughed.

'But that's the why is no answer. Was there some reason for it?'

'There's a raisin for everything. And a currant for the cake.'

'But why, Teresa? Why did they shout?'

'Why should I tell you?'

'No why. Just tell me.'

'You're too young. You'll have to wait to find out. Why should I be the one to tell you? Answer me that and I'll tell you.'

'You're not that much older than me,' he argued painfully and doggedly and without much hope.

They'd reached the top of the hill. Before them, against the lake with its swaying barrels and Oakport Wood turning to rust beyond great beech trees, was the village where they lived; the scattered shops and houses and humble sycamores of the roads dwarfed by the church in its graveyard of old yew and cypress trees. Past it the Shannon flowed, under the stone bridge at its end, flinting river of metal moving endlessly out into the wastes of pale sedge that waited for its flood waters to rise.

'I don't see what harm it would do you to tell,' he pleaded.

'You'll have to grow up.' She laughed the animal laugh of her superiority. Soon she'd be a woman in her prime. Already her body was changing. She laughed again without turning her head and started to run downhill. He moved to keep up with her, but he was too sick at heart, he let her run. He felt the same futility and confusion of everything as when his mother had gone away for ever, the terror and pain of his whole life draining away. Then something frighteningly alluring in the running girl's stride stirred him to follow her, but he was again bewildered by the memory of the softness of Nora's body, the shame of the shouting ringing in his ears. 'They're in love! They're in love! They're in love!' and he began to weep with anguish.

All through the next morning the schoolroom was tense. They waited for what Master Kelly would say after prayers. It was with such relief they heard him say what he said every morning, 'Open your home exercises and come up in your proper order, the fourth class first, and leave them on the table.' They watched the road and concrete steps down to the school for someone to come and complain, but no one came. Every move of Nora's was watched, every move of Stevie's, every hand that went up to ask to go to the lavatory. The growing tension followed them to the playground, the boys in one group, the girls apart in another, Nora strung tight and eating her lunch alone by the wall. Then suddenly and unnaturally, as if she was the mouthpiece of a decision, one of the older girls called a game and declared, 'Nora must be Queen. Come on, Nora, we're making you the Queen,' and they gathered round her, and soon the air was filled with the excited noises of their play. The boys started to kick an old rag ball made from corks and the wool of ripped socks about at the other end of the yard. Stevie watched the tenseness go in the play, connected in some way to the fit of shrieking at the Chair the evening before. 'They're in love! They're in love! They're in love!' still haunting him with his own helplessness, but he'd try once more to get behind the mystery. He would offer Teresa a penny toffee bar on their way home.

Quickly they chased past the Chair that evening, they didn't even think of stopping. 'It was nearly winter, the summer had gone, the ground was gettin' too damp for playin' on,' and in ones and twos and threes they branched up their laneways till the girl and boy were left alone on the road to the village again. No rain had fallen, and their canvas shoes rustled through the dead leaves as they set to climb Cox's Hill as on every other school evening of their lives.

'Why were they all so quiet today? Was it because of the Chair, Teresa?' he began at last.

She didn't answer for a long time and then she smiled, inwardly, sure of her superiority. 'It might be.'

'But why, why did they cheer?' Her playful nonchalance was enough to rouse his anxiety to desperation.

'You don't know very much, do you?' she said.

'No, but can't you tell?'

'You don't know how you come into the world, do you?' she said, and he was shocked numb. He'd been told so many ways. He couldn't risk making a greater fool of himself before Teresa. There was so much confusion.

'No,' he admitted. 'Do you know?'

'Of course I know. Mammy explained everything to me and Maura ages ago, a day we were over at the bathing place in the lake. When we were drying ourselves with the towels after swimmin' she told us everything.'

In his mind he could see the picture of the lake and bathing suits and the woman talking mysteriously to the girls while they dried their naked bodies with the towels, but he was again bewildered when she added, 'That's the cause they shouted when you fell on Nora.'

They shouted, 'You're in love,' when he fell on Nora, he grasped back, desperate. What had the fall on Nora got to do with the way he'd been born? If they were the same thing, all Teresa had to do was to tell, a few words, and everything'd be explained. The cries at the Chair, the fear he'd felt around him all day would be explained – everything would.

If he'd been quiet and had pretended not to care she'd probably have told him then, but immediately he produced the toffee bar, she drew away.

'If you tell me, I'll give you the bar,' he told her softly.

'Tell you what?'

'How we be born, why they shouted.'

'Why should I tell you? Tell you for a toffee bar and commit a mortal sin by telling you?' and she strode quickly ahead.

'It can't be that much harm to tell and the toffee bar is new. I got it in Henry's yesterday,' he pleaded, more fearful now, the halo of sin over everything.

'Have you anything else to give? A toffee bar isn't enough.' She began to relent and his heart beat faster. Her eyes were greedy on the bar in his hand, tiny scarlet crowns on its wrapping. He had one thing more, the wheel of a clock, the colour of gold, and it could spin.

'There's nothing else,' he warned anxiously.

'Give them to me first.'

'And then you won't tell?'

'I'll cross my heart.'

She thumbed the rough shape of a cross on her dress and he gave her the bar and wheel.

'Now,' he urged when she seemed reluctant to begin.

'I don't know how to start,' she said.

'You crossed your heart.'

'You have to try and guess first.'

'You crossed your heart to tell.'

'Can you not think?' she ignored. 'Do you not remember as we came to school Monday? Moran's bull and Guinea Ryan with the cow? Can you not think?' she urged impatiently.

The black bull in the field last Monday as they came to school, the chain hooked to his nose, dragging Moran towards the cow that Guinea held on a rope halter close to the gate. The cow buckling to her knees under the first savage rise of the bull. He shuddered at what he'd watched a hundred times related to himself: all the nights his father had slept with his mother and done that to her; he'd been got that way between their sheets; he'd come into the world the way the calf came.

'Can you not think?' the girl urged.

'Is it like the bull and the cow?' he ventured. It couldn't be, it would be too fantastic, and he waited for her to laugh.

Instead, she nodded her head vigorously: he had struck on how it was.

'Now you've been told,' she said. 'That was why they cheered when you fell on Nora.'

Suddenly, it was so simple and so sordid and so all about him that it seemed he should have discovered it years before.

They were silent now as they went downhill home, a delicate bloom on the clusters of blue sloes along the road, the sudden gleam of the chestnut, the woollen whiteness of the inside of a burst pod in the dead leaves their shoes went rustling through. 'They're in love! 'They're in love!' coming again to his ears but it was growing so clear and squalid that there was hardly anything to see.

The whole world was changed, a covering torn away; he'd never be able to see anything the same again. His father had slept with his mother and done that to her, the same father that slept with him now in the big bed with the broken brass bells and rubbed his belly at night, saying, 'That's what's good for you, Stevie. Isn't that what you like, Stevie?' ever since it happened the first night, the slow labouring voice explaining how the rubbing eased wind and relaxed you and let you sleep.

He'd come out of his mother's body the way the calf came – all at school had seen the calves born on their farms. And in Aughoo churchyard, at the back of the sacristy and under the shade of the boundary ash tree, his mother's body was now buried; the body his father had done that to, out of which he'd come; the body in a rotting coffin, under the clay, under the covering gravel. NT was after her name on the limestone cross they'd bought in Smith's for thirty pounds. They'd lifted three withered daffodils out of the jam jar when they'd visited it last July, weeded the daisies and dandelions out of the white gravel. And there had been trouble too over the shrub of boxwood their aunt had planted on the grave. It had already taken root, and their father had torn it up in anger. He had called to their aunt's house on their way home, shouting that she had no business interfering with his wife's grave and he didn't want to have them rooting up a stupid tree when it came to his own turn to go the way of all flesh.

His eyes followed his feet as they went through the leaves. He had been shattered by his mother's going, the unexpected mention of her name could still break him, but even that was growing different. His mother had lain down naked under his naked father years ago, his beginning: it was good to stand in the daylight of the others for once and not to be for ever a child in the dark.

While he walked, his wondering changed to what it would be like to rise on a girl or woman as the bull rose; if he could know that everything would be known. If he could get Teresa to lie down for him some evening on their way, behind the covering of some sloe bushes – could he ever bring himself to ask her to do that for him? His body was tingling and hot as the night in convalescence he'd watched his mother undress and get into the bed that she'd moved into his room at the height of his illness, snowflakes drifting round the windows that winter evening and robins about the sills, the room warm and bright later with the fire and low nightlight, and he'd ached to creep into her bed and touch every part of her body with his lips and the tips of his fingers. Teresa was now walking very fast ahead on her own.

He shuddered as the vision of the animals coupling came again, his father doing that to his mother years ago, out of which he'd come, her body in the clay of Aughoo now with worms and the roots of dandelions, and his father rubbing his belly at nights in the iron bed with the broken brass bells.

'Our Father, who art in Heaven, hallowed be thy name; thy kingdom come: thy will be done on earth,' broke suddenly on his lips as he gathered himself to catch up with the girl so as not to have to come into the village on his own.

Christmas

As well as a railway ticket they gave me a letter before I left the Home to work for Moran. They warned me to give the letter unopened to Moran, which was why I opened it on the train; it informed him that since I was a ward of state if I caused trouble or ran away he was to contact the guards at once. I tore it up, since it occurred to me that I might well cause trouble or run away, resolving to say I lost it if asked, but he did not ask for any letter.

Moran and his wife treated me well. The food was more solid than at the Home, a roast always on Sundays, and when the weather grew hard they took me to the town and bought me wellingtons and an overcoat and a cap with flaps that came down over the ears. After the day's work when Moran had gone to the pub, I was free to sit at the fire while Mrs Moran knitted, and listen to the wireless – what I enjoyed most were the plays – and Mrs Moran told me she was knitting a pullover for me for Christmas. Sometimes she asked me about life at the Home and when I'd tell her she'd sigh, 'You must be very glad to be with us instead,' and I would tell her, which was true, that I was. I usually went to bed before Moran came back from the pub, as they often quarrelled then, and I considered I had no place in that part of their lives.

Moran made his living by buying cheap branches or uncommercial timber the sawmills couldn't use and cutting them up to sell as firewood. I delivered the timber with an old jennet Moran had bought from the tinkers. The jennet squealed, a very human squeal, any time a fire of branches was lit, and ran, about the only time he did run, to stand in rigid contentment with his nostrils in the thick of the wood smoke. When Moran was in good humour it amused him greatly to light a fire to see the jennet's excitement at the prospect of smoke.

There was no reason this life shouldn't have gone on for long but for a stupid wish on my part, which set off an even more stupid wish in Mrs Grey, and what happened has struck me ever since as usual when people look to each other for their happiness or whatever it is called. Mrs Grey was Moran's best customer. She'd come from America and built the huge house on top of Mounteagle after her son had been killed in aerial combat over Italy.

The thaw overhead in the bare branches had stopped the evening we filled that load for Mrs Grey. There was no longer the dripping on the dead leaves, the wood clamped in the silence of white frost except for the racket some bird made in the undergrowth. Moran carefully built the last logs above the crates of the cart and I threw him the bag of hay that made the load look bigger than it was. 'Don't forget to call at Murphy's for her paraffin,' he said. 'No, I'll not forget.' 'She's bound to tip you well this Christmas. We could use money for the Christmas.' He'd use it to pour drink down his gullet. 'Must be time to be moving,' I said. 'It'll be night before you're there,' he answered.

The cart rocked over the roots between the trees, cold steel of the bridle ring in the hand close to the rough black lips, steam of the breath wasting on the air to either side. We went across the paddocks to the path round the lake, the wheels cutting two tracks on the white stiff grass, crush of the grass yielding to the iron. I had to open the wooden gate to the pass. The small shod hooves wavered between the two ridges of green inside the wheeltracks on the pass, the old body swaying to each drive of the shafts as the wheels fell from rut to rut.

The lake was frozen over, a mirror fouled by white blotches of the springs, and rose streaks from the sun were impaled on the firs of Oakport across the bay.

The chainsaw started up in the wood again. He'd saw while there was light. 'No joke to make a living, a drink or two for some relief, all this ballsing. May be better if we stayed in bed, conserve our energy, eat less,' but in spite of all he said he went on buying the branches cheap from McAnnish after the boats had taken the trunks down the river to the mill.

I tied the jennet to the chapel gate and crossed to Murphy's shop. 'I want Mrs Grey's paraffin.'

The shop was full of men. They sat on the counter or on wooden fruit boxes and upturned buckets along the walls. They used to trouble me at first. I supposed it little different from going into a shop in a strange country without its language, but they learned they couldn't take a rise out of me, that was their phrase. They used to lob tomatoes at the back of my head in the hope of some reaction, but they left me mostly alone when they saw none was forthcoming. If I felt anything for them it was a contempt tempered by fear: I was here, and they were there.

'You want her paraffin, do you? I know the paraffin I'd give her if I got your chance,' Joe Murphy said from the centre of the counter where he presided, and a loyal guffaw rose from around the walls.

'Her proper paraffin,' someone shouted, and it drew even more applause, and when it died a voice asked, 'Before you get off the counter, Joe, throw us an orange.'

Joe stretched to the shelf and threw the orange to the man who sat on a bag of Spanish onions. As he stretched forward to catch the fruit the red string bag collapsed and he came heavily down on the onions. 'You want to bruise those onions with your dirty awkward arse. Will you pay for them now, will you?' Joe shouted as he swung his thick legs down from the counter.

'Everybody's out for their onions these days.' The man tried to defend himself with a nervous laugh as he fixed the string bag upright and changed his seat to an orange box.

'You've had your onions: now pay for them.'

'Make him pay for his onions,' they shouted.

'You must give her her paraffin first.' Joe took the tin, and went to the barrel raised on flat blocks in the corner, and turned the copper tap.

'Now give her the proper paraffin. It's Christmas time,' Joe said again as he screwed the cap tight on the tin, the limp black hair falling across the bloated face.

'Her proper paraffin,' the approving cheer followed me out of the door.

'He never moved a muscle, the little fucker. Those homeboys are a bad piece of work,' I heard with much satisfaction as I stowed the tin of paraffin securely among the logs of the cart. Ice over the potholes of the road was catching the first stars. Lights of bicycles – it was a confession night – hesitantly approached out of the night. Though exposed in the full glare of their lamps I was unable to recognize the bicyclists as they pedalled past in dark shapes behind their lamps, and this made raw the fear I'd felt but had held down in the shop. I took a stick and beat the reluctant jennet into pulling the load uphill as fast as he was able.

After I'd stacked the logs in the fuel shed I went and knocked on the back door to see where they wanted me to put the paraffin. Mrs Grey opened the door.

'It's the last load until after Christmas,' I said as I put the tin down.

'I haven't forgotten.' She smiled and held out a pound note.

'I'd rather not take it.' It was there the first mistake was made, playing for higher stakes.

'You must have something. Besides the firewood you've brought us so many messages from the village that we don't know what we'd have done without you.'

'I don't want money.'

'Then what would you like me to give you for Christmas?'

'Whatever you'd prefer to give me.' I thought *prefer* was well put for a homeboy.

'I'll have to give it some thought, then,' she said as I led the jennet out of the yard, delirious with stupid happiness.

'You got the paraffin and logs there without trouble?' Moran beamed when I came in to the smell of hot food. He'd changed into good clothes and was finishing his meal at the head of the big table in tired contentment.

'There was no trouble,' I answered.

'You've fed and put in the jennet?'

'I gave him crushed oats.'

'I bet you Mrs Grey was pleased.'

'She seemed pleased.'

He'd practically his hand out. 'You got something good out of it, then?'

'No.'

'You mean to say she gave you nothing?'

'Not tonight but maybe she will before Christmas.'

'Maybe she will but she always gave a pound with the last load before,' he said suspiciously. His early contentment was gone.

He took his cap and coat to go for a drink or two for some relief.

'If there's an international crisis in the next few hours you know where I'll be found,' he said to Mrs Moran as he left.

Mrs Grey came Christmas Eve with a large box. She smelled of scent and gin and wore a fur coat. She refused a chair saying she'd to rush, and asked me to untie the red twine and paper.

A toy airplane stood inside the box. It was painted white and blue. The tyres smelled of new rubber.

'Why don't you wind it up?'

I looked up at the idiotically smiling face, the tear-brimmed eyes.

'Wind it up for Mrs Grey,' I heard Moran's voice.

I was able to do nothing. Moran took the toy from my hand and wound it up. A light flashed on and off on the tail and the propellors turned as it raced across the cement.

'It was too much for you to bring,' Moran said in his politic voice.

'I thought it was rather nice when he refused the money. My own poor boy loved nothing better than model airplanes for Christmas.' She was again on the verge of tears.

'We all still feel for that tragedy,' Moran said. 'Thank Mrs Grey for such a lovely present. It's far too good.'

I could no longer hold back rage: 'I think it's useless,' and began to cry.

I have only a vague memory afterwards of the voice of Moran accompanying her to the door with excuses and apologies.

'I should have known better than to trust a homeboy,' Moran said when he came back. 'Not only did you do me out of the pound but you go and insult the woman and her dead son. You're going to make quick time back to where you came from, my tulip.' Moran stirred the airplane with his boot as if he wished to kick it but dared not out of respect for the money it had cost.

'Well, you'll have a good flight in it this Christmas.'

The two-hour bell went for Midnight Mass, and as Moran hurried for the pub to get drinks before Mass, Mrs Moran started to strip the windows of curtains and to set a single candle to burn in each window. Later, as we made our way to the church, candles burned in the windows of all the houses and the church was ablaze with light. I was ashamed of the small old woman, afraid they'd identify me with her as we walked up between the crowded benches to where a steward directed us to a seat in the women's side-altar. In the smell of burning wax and flowers and damp stone, I got out the brown beads and the black prayerbook with the gold cross on the cover they'd given me in the Home and began to prepare for the hours of boredom Midnight Mass meant. It did not turn out that way.

A drunken policeman, Guard Mullins, had slipped past the stewards on guard at the door and into the women's sidechapel. As Mass began he started to tell the schoolteacher's wife how available her arse had been for handling while she'd worked in the bar before assuming the fur coat of respectability, 'And now, O Lordy me, a prize rose garden wouldn't get a luk in edgeways with its grandeur.' The stewards had a hurried consultation whether to eject him or not and decided it'd probably cause less scandal to leave him as he was. He quietened into a drunken stupor until the Monsignor climbed into the pulpit to begin his annual hour of the season of peace and glad tidings. As soon as he began, 'In the name of the Father and of the Son and of the Holy Ghost. This Christmas, my dearly beloved children in Christ, I wish . . .' Mullins woke to applaud with a hearty, 'Hear, hear. I couldn't approve more. You're a man after my own heart. Down with the hypocrites!' The Monsignor looked towards the policeman and then at the stewards, but as he was greeted by another, 'Hear, hear!' he closed his notes and in a voice of acid wished everybody a holy and happy Christmas and climbed angrily from the pulpit to conclude the shortest Midnight Mass the church had ever known. It was not, though, the end of the entertainment. As the communicants came from the rails Mullins singled out the tax collector, who walked down the aisle with closed, bowed head, and hands rigidly joined, to shout, 'There's the biggest hypocrite in the parish,' which delighted almost everybody.

As I went past the lighted candles in the window, I thought of Mullins as my friend and for the first time felt proud to be a ward of state. I avoided Moran and his wife, and from the attic I listened with glee to them criticizing Mullins. When the voices died I came quietly down to take a box of matches and the airplane and go to the jennet's stable. I gathered dry straw in a heap, and as I lit it and the smoke rose the jennet gave his human squeal until I untied him and he was able to put his nostrils in the thick of the smoke. By the light of the burning straw I put the blue and white toy against the wall and started to kick. With each kick I gave a new sweetness was injected into my blood. For such a pretty toy it took few kicks to reduce it to shapelessness, and then, in the last flames of the straw, I flattened it on the stable floor, the jennet already nosing me to put more straw on the dying fire.

As I quietened, I was glad that I'd torn up the unopened letter in the train that I was supposed to have given to Moran. I felt a new life had already started to grow out of the ashes, out of the stupidity of human wishes.

Hearts of Oak and Bellies of Brass

'If Jocko comes today I'll warm his arse for this once.' Murphy laughed fiercely. The hair on the powerful arms that held the sledge was smeared to the skin with a paste of dust and oil. The small blue eyes twinkled in the leather of the face as they searched for the effect of what he'd said. There was always the tension he might break loose from behind the mixer with the sledge, or, if he didn't, that someone else would, with shovel or with sledge.

'A disgrace, worse than an animal,' Keegan echoed. He wore a brown hat that stank with sweat and dust over his bald head. Keegan was very proud he had a second cousin who was a schoolmaster in Mohill.

'I want to be at no coroner's inquest on his head,' Murphy said and started to beat the back of the steel hopper out of boredom as the engine idled over.

Jocko came every day, crazed on meths and rough cider, and usually made straight for the pool of shade and water under the mixer.

'He'd be just a ham sandwich if you brought down the hopper with him lying there and we'd all be in the fukken soup,' Murphy continued.

'Likes of him coming on the site anyhow would give it a bad name in no time,' Keegan tiraded, while Galway rested on his shovel, watching the breasts of the machinists lean above their sewing in the third-floor windows of Rose and Margols, gown manufacturers on Christian Street. Galway was youngest of us all. I'd worked the whole of the hot summer with Galway and Keegan behind the mixer Murphy drove like some royal ape, and in the last two weeks Jocko had come every day. The mixer idled away. On the roof they were changing the bays.

'Talkin' about given the site a bad name, the way you came in this morning was disgrace to the livin' daylight,' Keegan said to me.

'I wouldn't lose any sleep about it if I were you.' My grip

tightened on the handle of the shovel, its blade was silver-sharp from a summer of gravel and of sand.

'I come in with a decent jacket and tie, and then I change. I don't come in with work clothes on. If people see you looking like shit they'll take you for shit. I don't know and I don't care what the king of the monkeys wears but we who are Irish should always be tidy when we sit down to tea,' he quoted in support from a forgotten schoolbook.

'You and your fucking monkeys,' I said. I kept a tight grip on the shovel as I remembered the lightning change of the face from its ordinary foolishness to viciousness when in horseplay Galway had knocked off the hat to betray the baldness. The blade of Keegan's shovel just missed Galway's throat.

'King of the fukken monkeys,' Galway guffawed as a breast leaned out of sight above her machine, but before Keegan's attack had time to change to Galway, Barney whistled from the scaffolding rail on the roof. The bay was ready. The mixer, in smoke and stink of diesel, roared in gear.

'Come on: shovel or shite, shite or burst,' Murphy shouted above the roar.

The shovels drove and threw in time into the long wooden box, tipped by handles at each end into the steel hopper when full, two boxes of gravel to the one of sand, and as the sand was tipped on the gravel Keegan came running from the stack with a cement bag on his shoulder to throw it down on top. Galway's shovel cut the bag in two and the grey cloud of fallout drifted away as the ends were pulled free.

The hopper rose. We could rest on shovels for this minute. When it stopped Murphy took the sledge to beat the back of the hopper, and the last of the sticking sand or gravel ran into the revolving drum where the water sloshed against the blades.

As he hammered he shouted in time, 'Our fukker who art in heaven bought his boots for nine-and-eleven,' the back of the hopper bright as beaten silver in the sun.

As the hopper came down again he shouted in the same time, 'Shovel or shite, shite or burst,' and the shovels mechanically drove and threw, two boxes of gravel to one of sand, and the grey fallout from the hundredweight of cement as the bag was cut in two, and the ends pulled free. It'd go on like this all day.

Murphy ran the mixed concrete from the drum down a shoot into a metal bucket. With a whine of the lift engine the bucket rose to Sligo, a red-faced old man with a cap worn back to front, who tipped it into a cylindrical metal container fixed to the scaffolding, and then ran the bucket down again. The barrows were filled from a trapdoor in the container, and they ran on planks to toss the concrete on the steel in the bays. The best of the roof on a hot day was that wind blew from the Thames.

In the boredom of the shovelfuls falling in time into the wooden box I go over my first day on the site a summer before.

They'd said to roll my jacket in the gutter before I went in, and when I got on the site to ask for the *shout*.

'Who has the *shout* here?' I asked. They pointed Barney out. He wore the same black mourning suit in wellingtons that he now leaned in against the scaffolding rail, watching the concreting on the roof, the black tie hanging loose from the collar of the dirty white shirt.

'Any chance of a start?' I asked.

His eyes went over me – shoulders, arms, thighs. I remembered my father's cattle I had stood for sale in the Shambles once, walking stick along the backbone to gauge the rump, lips pulled back to read the teeth; but now I was offering to shovel for certain shillings an hour: shovel or shite, shite or burst.

'Have you ever done any building work before?' Barney had asked.

'No, but I've worked on land.' They'd said not to lie.

'What kind of work?'

'The usual – turf, oats, potatoes.'

'You've just come over on the boat, then?'

'Yesterday . . . and I heard you might give me the start.'

'Start at twelve, then,' he said in his slow way and pointed to the wooden hut that was the office. 'They'll give you the address of the Labour. Get back with your cards before twelve.'

There was no boredom those first days, though time was slower and there was more pain, drive to push the shovel in blistered hands with raw knee in the same time as the others, a shovel slyly jabbed against a thigh as if you've stumbled, and the taunt, 'Too much wankin' that's what's wrong,' in the way fowl will peck to death a weakened hen; fear of Thursday, Barney's tap on the shoulder. 'You're not strong enough for this job. You'll have to look for something lighter for yourself. Your cards'll be ready in the office at payout.'

No fear of the tap on the shoulder on this or any Thursday now, shut mouth and patience and the hardening of the body. My shovel drove and threw as mechanically as any of theirs by now.

'What time is it?' I asked Keegan. He fumbled in his pocket for the big silver watch wrapped in cloth to protect it against the dust. He read the time.

'Another fukken twenty minutes to go,' Galway said in the exasperation of the burden of the slow passing of the minutes, a coin for each endured minute.

'Another fukken twenty minutes,' I repeated, the repetitious use of fukken with every simple phrase was harsh at first but now a habit. Its omission here would cause as much unease as its use where 'Very kind. Thank you, Mr Jones' was demanded.

'There's no fukken future in this job,' Keegan complained tiredly. 'You get old. The work is the same, but you're less able for it any more. In other jobs as you get old you can put the work over on others.'

'No sign of Jocko yet.' Galway tried to change to Murphy. Galway wore a white handkerchief knotted at both ends to keep the dust out of his Brylcreemed black hair.

'I'll give him his future when he comes,' Murphy said as he sledged the back of the hopper.

'The childer go to school and they'll have better than me,' Keegan kept on at what was felt as nagging rebuke. 'They'll have some ambition. That's why I work behind this bloody mixer and the woman chars. So that they can go to school. They'll have some ambition. They'll wear white collars.'

'Pork chops, pints of bitter, and a good old ride before you sleep, that's fukken ambition,' Murphy left off sledging to shout, and when he finished he laughed above the mixer.

'That's right,' Galway agreed. 'Come on, Keegan: shovel.'

'I'll shovel with a jumped-up brat any day,' Keegan answered with the same antagonism, but fell behind, sweat running down from under the hat.

'Shovel or shite, shite or burst,' Murphy trumpeted as he saw the competition, and then at last the hooter blew.

We passed the Negro demolition crew as we went to the canteen, the wood from the houses burning fiercely behind the bulldozer. On the roof two Negroes hacked away slates with pickaxes. The prostitutes lived in the condemned row, moving from empty house to empty house ahead of the demolition. Limp rubbers floated in the gutters Monday mornings while they slept in the daylight.

Through the hatch in the canteen Marge handed out ham or tomato rolls and mugs of tea.

'Ta ta, Pa,' she said as I gave her coins. This had been hardest of all to get used to, to have no name at all easier than to be endlessly called *Pa*.

'Thanks, Marge.' It angered me that there was still the bitterness of irony in my smile, that I was not yet completely my situation; this ambition of mine, in reverse, to annul all the votes in myself.

I sat with the rest of the mixer gang at a trestle table. Behind us the chippies played cards. The enmity glowed sullenly between Galway and Keegan, but Galway ate his rolls and gulped tea without lifting his head from the racing paper, where he marked his fancies with a stub of pencil.

I read aloud out of the local *Herald* my mother sent me each week from home that prayers had been ordered in all the churches in Ireland for good weather. It had rained all summer, and now the harvest was in danger.

'That it may rise higher than for fukken Noah. That they may have to climb trees,' Murphy answered, laughing, vicious.

'They never did much for us except to starve us out to England. You have to have the pull there or you're dirt,' Keegan advanced.

The familiar tirade would continue, predictable as the drive and throw of their shovels. I went outside to sit on a stack of steel in the sun until the hooter blew, but even there it wasn't possible to be alone, for Tipperary followed to sit too on the steel. He'd been taken away to the Christian Brothers when he was eleven but hadn't been able to pass the exams that would have qualified him as a teacher, and when they put him to work in the kitchens he'd left and come to England. He fixed steel in the bays. The cheeks were hollow, infantile puzzlement on the regular face from which sensuality, if it had ever been there, had withered.

'Do you think Shakespeare's all he's bumped up to be?' he asked.

He'd heard that I had gone two years to Secondary School, and he believed that we could speak as one educated man to another.

He was sometimes called the *Professor*, and baited mercilessly, though there was a purity in his dogged stupidity that troubled them towards a certain respect. His attention made me uncomfortable. I had no desire to be one of his thieves at these occasional crucifixions, or to play Judas for them to his Christ.

I told him that I didn't know if Shakespeare was all that he was bumped up to be, but people said so, and it was people who did all the bumping up or bumping down.

'But who is people?' he pursued.

'People is people. They praise Shakespeare. Pull your beer. Give you the start. They might even be ourselves.' I laughed, and watched the door of the canteen, and listened for the hooter, and longed to hurt him away. He touched something deeper than my careful neutrality. I hadn't any wish to live by anything deeper.

'And do you consider George Bernard Shaw all that he's bumped up to be?' he asked, perhaps puzzling over his failure to answer satisfactorily the questions put to him at exams before they'd sent him to the kitchens.

'I know nothing about George Bernard.' I got up off the steel.

'But you went to Secondary School?'

'For two years.'

'But why didn't you go on? You passed the exams.'

'Forget it. I didn't go on.' I was disturbed and hated Tipperary for the disturbance.

'But why, you'd have learned things. You'd have learned whether things are what they're bumped up to be or not.'

'I'd have learned nothing. I might have got a better job but my ambition is wrong way round anyhow. Almost as good behind the mixer as anywhere else.'

While Tipperary meditated another question there was a motionless silence between us on the stack of rusted steel in the sun.

'Murphy says he's going to do Jocko if he comes today,' I changed.

'Sligo has some plans, too, up top,' he answered slowly. 'It's not fair.'

'It'll happen though – if he comes.'

The hooter blew. Nobody came from the canteen. They'd sit there till Barney stormed in. 'Come on. You don't get paid sittin' on

34

your arses five minutes after the hooter's gone. Come on. Out.'

'How's it going, Paddy Boy?' the lorry driver asked as he got me to sign for the load of gravel he'd tipped behind the mixer.

'Dragging along,' I answered as I scrawled a few illegible letters on the docket; it never mattered who signed.

'Keep it going, that's it.' He touched my shoulder before turning to shout a few friendly obscenities at Murphy who'd started the mixer.

The heat grew worse. Jocko didn't come. Nobody spoke much. Even on Galway's face the sweat streaked the white coating of cement dust.

'Anyone volunteer to go for lemonade?' Keegan asked when more than an hour had gone. I said I'd go to Greenbaum's; it was some minutes escape from the din of the engines and diesel and dust in the airless heat.

'Walkin' kills me these days.' Keegan was grateful.

I went through the gap in the split stakes linked with wire into Hessell Street, green and red peppers among the parsley and fruit of the stalls. It smelled of lice and blood and fowl, down and feathers stamped into the blood and henshit outside the Jewish poulterers, country air after the dust of the mixer.

'Six Tizers,' I asked Greenbaum, old grey Jew out of Poland. 'Put them on the slate.'

'Everything on the slate and then one day you jack and go and Greenbaum is left with the baby.'

'You'll get paid. Today is payday.'

'And Greenbaum charges no deposit on the bottles. You just throw them away. And who loses? Greenbaum loses,' he complained as he put the bottles on the counter, as much in love with complaint as the cripple with crutches he goes on using after he is cured.

The bottles were passed around from mouth to mouth behind the mixer as the bucket climbed to Sligo at the top.

'You shouldn't gurgle,' Keegan ragged at Galway. 'We who are Irish –'

'Should always be tidy when we sit down to tea,' Galway took up viciously. 'Come on: shovel, you old bollocks.'

'Shovel or shite, shite or burst. It's payday,' Murphy shouted as if *shovel* had set an alarm off in his head, and without break the

35

shovels drove and threw, two boxes of gravel to one of sand, the small grey puff of cement in the airless heat as we pulled the cut ends of the bag loose, till the hooter blew for payout.

Tipperary joined me at the end of the queue outside the payout window.

'Jocko didn't arrive yet,' I said to keep his conversation easy.

'No. Sligo's going to put the water on him from up top when he comes. It's not fair.'

'It'll probably happen though.'

'But it's not fair.'

We each held the thin brass medal on which our number was stamped, a hole in the medal for hanging it on the nail in the hut at night.

At the window we called our name and number and showed the brass medal and the timekeeper handed us our pay in a small brown packet.

On the front of the pack was written the number of hours we had worked, the rate per hour, the amount we'd earned minus the various deductions.

As the men stood around checking their money, the large hands counting awkwardly and slowly, a woman's voice cried, 'Come and get them while they're hot.'

Their eyes lifted to search for the voice, towards the condemned row of houses ahead of the bulldozer and the burning wood, where from an upper window old Kathleen leaned out, shaking her large loose breasts at the men.

'Cheap at the price,' she cried. A cheer went up; and some obscenities were shouted like smallarms fire.

'Even better downstairs,' she cried back, her face flushed with alcohol.

'A disgrace. Terrible,' Tipperary said.

'It's all right. She just got excited by the money.' He disturbed me more than she did.

'This evening after pints of bitter they'll slink round,' he said.

As I did once. A Christmas Eve. She'd told me she'd all her Christmas shopping done except to buy the turkey. She said she hoped to get one cheap at Smithfield. They dropped the prices before the market closed to get rid of the surplus, and she was relying on a customer who was a porter there.

Only for her practised old hands it would have been impossible to raise desire, and if it was evil when it happened, the pumping of the tension of the instinct into her glycerined hole, then nothing was so extraordinarily ordinary as this evil.

'Why not? Let them go round, and what's so fucking special about what's between your legs anyhow?' I shouted at him, and turned my back so as not to have to see the hurt on the dim acolyte's face in its confusion of altars. I started to count out the money from the small brown packet.

I love to count out in money the hours of my one and precious *life*. I sell the hours and I get money. The money allows me to sell more hours. If I saved money I could buy the hours of some similar bastard and live like a royal incubus, which would suit me much better than the way I am now, though apparently even as I am now suits me well enough, since I do not want to die.

Full of beer tonight after the Rose and Crown we'll go round to Marge and Kathleen like dying elephants in the condemned row.

Before I'd finished counting, Tipperary tapped my shoulder and I shouted, 'Fuck off,' and did not turn to see his face.

The hooter went. The offered breasts withdrew. A window slammed.

'The last round,' someone said.

The mixer started. The shovels drove and threw: gravel, sand, gravel; gravel, sand, gravel; cement.

Murphy sledged on the beaten steel of the hopper, vocal again now that the brown packet was a solid wad against his arse. 'Our fukker who art in heaven bought his boots for nine-and-eleven,' he sang out as he sledged. 'Come on: shovel or shite, shite or burst.'

Jocko came so quietly that he was in the pool of shadow under the hopper before he was noticed, the pint bottle of violet-coloured spirit swinging wide from one pocket, crawling on all fours towards the pool of water in the sand beneath the drum of the mixer.

'Out,' Murphy shouted with a curse, angered that Jocko had got so far without being noticed. 'Out. I'll teach your arse a lesson. Out.'

He took the shovel that leaned against the mixer, and drove at Jocko, the dull thud of the blade on cloth and flesh or bone, buttocks that someone must have bathed once, carried in her arms.

'I warned you if you tried this stunt again I'd warm your arse. I want to be at no coroner's inquest on your head. Out.'

We stood and watched Murphy drive him out of the pool of water, then push him out of the shadow of the hopper into the evening glare. We said nothing.

The eyes in the hollow sockets, grey beard matted about the scabs of the face, registered no pain, no anything: and when they fell on the barrow of wet concrete that the surveyor had used to test the strength of the mix he moved mechanically towards it, sat in, and started to souse himself up and down in the liquid concrete as a child in a bath.

'Jesus, when that sets to his arse it'll be nobody's business,' Galway said between dismay and laughter.

'Out of the fukken barrow,' Murphy shouted, and lifted him out by the neck, pushing him down the tyre-marked yellow slope. He staggered but did not fall. The wet clothes clung to his back and the violet-coloured bottle in the pocket was clouded and dirty with wet concrete.

Sligo, his cap back to front, leaned across the scaffolding rail on top, the black rubber hose in his hands. The jet of water started to circle Jocko, darkening the yellow sand. Sligo used his thumb on the jet so that it sprayed out like heavy rain.

When Jocko felt the water, he lifted his face to its coolness, but then, slowly and deliberately, he took a plastic coat and faded beret from the opposite pocket to where the bottle swung, and in the same slow deliberate way put them on, buttoning the plastic coat to the throat and putting the collar up. The jet followed a few yards of his slow walk and then fell back, but he still walked in the evening sun as if it was raining.

Greenbaum, old grey rat searching for Tizer bottles among the heaps of rubble, lifted his head to watch him pass through the gap in the fence of split stakes into Hessell Street but immediately bent again to search and complain. 'Greenbaum charges no deposit on the bottles, and then what do they do, throw them away, throw them away, never return. Greenbaum's an old fool.'

Strandhill, the Sea

The street in front of Parkes' Guest House, grains of sand from the street coming on the grey fur of the tennis ball, the hopping under my hand idle as the conversations from the green bench before the flowerbed, red bells of the fuchsia vivid behind them and some roses and gillyflowers, the earth around the roots of everything speckled with sea shells, overhead the weathered roughcast of the wall of the house.

The sky was filling. Rain would come, and walls close around the living evening, looking towards the bleared windows, no way to get out from the voices.

'There was great stuff in those Baby Fords and Austins. The cars going nowadays are only tin compared,' Mr McVittie said, the heavy gold watch chain across the waistcoat of the brown suit, silver hair parted in the centre, knobbed walking stick in his hand. He could have stepped out of a yellowed wedding photo.

'Only they weren't so fast as now,' Mr O'Connor added, following McVittie all the week in the way stray dogs at night will stick to any pair of heels that seem to go home.

'Before the war, before I got married, I used to have one of the old Citroëns, and it could go for ever, only it was very hard on petrol,' Mr Ryan said, feel of his eyes on the up and down of the tennis ball on the street.

Conversations always the same: height of the Enfield rifle, summer of the long dresses, miles to the gallon – from morning to the last glows of the cigarettes on the benches at night, always informations, informations about everything. Having come out of darkness, they now blink with informations at all the things about them, before the soon when they'll have to leave.

The sky filled over Sligo Bay, the darkness moving across the links and church, one clear strip of blue between Parkes' and Knocknarea, and when that would fill – the rain, the steamed windows, the informations, till the dark settled on their day.

Fear of the sky since morning had kept them on the benches away from the strand a mile downhill they'd come to enjoy, fear of the long trudge past the golf links and Kincora and Central in rain; but they'd still the air here, sea air, it was some consolation. Even the strand, reached in good weather, the mile downhill accomplished, the mile home uphill yet out of mind, and in possession of strand of Strandhill, long and level for miles, the cannon on its rotting initial-covered carriage pointed towards the Atlantic as if on guard over the two ice-cream parlours; women at the tideline, with a child in one hand and skirt held tight between thighs with the other, whinnying at each spent rush of water at their feet before it curled in a brown backwash round their heels; all this time envy of the buckets and beach ball of others to gladden a royal stay.

Cars ran miles to the gallon, still on the bench: twenty-five, thirty-two, thirty-nine with careful timing and more use of clutch than brake. Another guest, Mr Haydon, marked the racing columns of the newspaper on the edge of the same bench; hairnet of purple threads on the face, commercial traveller. 'Never made the grade,' McVittie had pronounced. 'Soon for the jump.' On the next bench a pattern for a Fair Isle pullover lay open between Mrs O'Connor and Mrs Ryan, and around them children in all postures. Ingolsby was the one guest who sat alone, retired lecturer of English, while the tennis ball hopped or paused.

'What part of the world is Lagos in?' Haydon stirred out of the newspaper to interrupt the wear and tear on clutches. 'You should know that, Mr Ryan. You're a teacher.'

'I think Africa,' the uncertain reply came, and his sudden flush and blanching brought Ingolsby in.

'Because somebody happens to be a teacher is no reason why they should know where Lagos is.'

'If teachers don't know that sort of thing who can know?' Haydon was angered. 'Don't they have to teach the stuff to kids?'

'If a teacher has to teach a geography lesson he simply looks up his information in a textbook beforehand. A doctor doesn't go round with all his patients' ailments in his head. He has files,' Ingolsby explained with solid satisfaction.

'But it's not getting us any nearer to where the hell Lagos is?'

'It's in Nigeria,' Ingolsby said.

'It's in Nigeria, in Africa.' Ryan tried to smooth over the antagonism.

Strandhill, the Sea

'That was what I wanted to know. Thank you, Mr Ryan,' Haydon said pointedly and buried his head in the newspaper again.

'Amazing the actual number of places there is in this world, when you come to think,' O'Connor added.

'A man could spend his whole life learning the names of places and they'd still be as many as the sands of the seashore left,' McVittie said.

The ball was idle in my hand. The tide was full, a coal boat moving out from Sligo in the channel. There were no blue spaces against Knocknarea.

Small annual calvary of the poor, mile downhill and uphill between Parkes' and the cannon. The Calm Sea closer, inlet that ran to Ballisodare past the lobster pool, no envy there, deserted except the one day they put flags down and held the races at low tide, but still in the dead quiet the pain of voices coming across the golf links, and Jane Simpson with others there.

The first rain was loud on Haydon's newspaper, and it was followed by a general rising and gradual procession indoors between the still sparse drops.

'Imagine the name they called this.' Ingolsby paused to hold a blood-orange rose towards Ryan as they went along the flowerbed.

'I'm not so well up on flowers,' Ryan apologized.

'*Climbing Mrs Sam McGredy. Climbing Mrs Sam McGredy,*' Ingolsby enunciated.

'Names are a funny thing,' Ryan said without thought.

'Names are a funny thing, as you put it,' Ingolsby repeated sarcastically. '*Peace* or *Ena Harkness* or even the *Moulin Rouge* but *Climbing Mrs Sam McGredy*! That's an atom bomb,' then he lowered his voice. 'Never feel you have to know anything because you happen to teach. Never let them bully you with their assumptions of what you should be. Say you don't know, that it can be discovered in books, if they're interested. It's only pretending to know something that's embarrassing.'

The counsel roused impotent deeps of hatred in Ryan's eyes as they went the last steps to the door.

A Miss Evans was the one addition to the company over lunch, and when the litter was cleared away with the sheets that served as cloth, and the old varnish of the big elliptical table shone dully about the bowl of roses put back on its centre, Mrs Parkes set a small coal

41

fire to burn in the grate as an apology for the gloom of rain. All the bars of the evening had fallen into place. 'The rain anywhere is bad, but at the sea, at the sea, it's the end,' rose as a constant sighing in the conversations. The need to escape to some other world grew fiercer, but there was no money.

'Steal, steal, steal,' was the one way out.

Raincoat and southwester and outside – without them noticing. Mist halfway down the slopes of Knocknarea, rain and mist blurring the sea. Past Huggards, past the peeling white swan sailing on the signboard of the Swan Hotel, steady drip from the eaves louder than the distant fall of the sea and gull cries, glow of the electric light burning inside through the mist on Peebles' window, stationer and confectioner: shock of the warning bell ringing as you opened the door.

A girl in blue overalls behind the counter was helping a man choose postcards and they were laughing.

'Can I help you?' She turned.

'I want to look round.' It was the only possible thing, and it was lucky she was busy with the man.

Rows of comics were on the counter, hours of insensibility to the life in Parkes', *Wizard* and *Hotspur* and *Rover* and *Champion*, whole worlds.

Put a *Hotspur* on top of the *Wizard*, both on top of the yellow pile of *Rovers*, and draw breath. The man was paying for the postcards. Lift the three free, put them inside the open raincoat, the elbow holding them tight against the side. Walk.

'Any chance of seeing you in the Silver Slipper tonight?' the man asked.

'Stranger things happened in the world,' she answered, and they both laughed again.

It was impossible to walk loose and casual to the door, it was one forced step after the other, having to think to walk, waiting all the time for the blow from behind. 'Excuse me,' it'd probably begin, and then the shame, the police. To get caught the one reason not to steal. In the next world it was only a venial sin, purgatory, and the saints alone got the through express to heaven.

Step after step and rigid step and no blow, a cash register ringing and then the warning bell above the door and the breathing relief of the wet out-of-doors to the sea blurred beyond the golf links, rain coming down same as ever before. Past Huggards and over the sodden sand of the street, raindrops brilliant in the red ruffles of the roses by the wall.

'Where did you get the money from for that trash?' came once I was in the room.

'Sixpence I found down at the front yesterday.'

'Why have you to be always stuck in that trash? Why can't you read something good like Shakespeare that'll be of some use to you later?'

The old tune: some use to you later.

'I don't imagine the comics'll do much harm. Good taste isn't cultivated in a day. We rise on stepping stones to greater things,' Ingolsby intervened.

'I suppose there's some consolation in that.' Ryan was anxious to escape, knowing the hostility the themes of Ingolsby's ponderous conversations roused. They were felt as a slur or rebuke. This time he'd not escape easily. Ingolsby needed to live through his own voice too this wet evening.

'What's your opinion of Shakespeare's validity for the modern world?'

'It's not so easy to say,' he deferred again, his eyes anxious about the room, his wife on the sofa with Mrs O'Connor, measuring a sleeve of a pullover on their daughter; soon she'd be knitting silently and patiently again while the night came the same as every other coming into her patient life, while McVittie said to O'Connor, 'The shops out in the country were hard hit by emigration. But we managed to survive. We branched into new lines. We got Esso to put down a petrol pump for instance. We changed with the times.'

'It's a cardinal law of nature that every man should have his head firmly screwed on to know how to change with the times and survive,' O'Connor agreed.

The people in the room had broken up into their separate groups, and when Miss Evans raised her arms in a yawn out of the chair Haydon leaned forward to say, 'There must have been right old sport last night.'

'I beg your pardon, Mr Haydon,' she laughed, pleased.

'The way all women are, all on their dignity till the business gets down to brass tacks and then an almighty turn of events. And who'd object to an old roll between the sandhills after the dancing anyhow?' he raised his voice, as if to irritate Ingolsby, who was pressing a reluctant Ryan on Wordsworth.

She laughed softly, a hint of defiance against the unconcealed hostility of the married women with their children in the laugh, smiling a little as she looked towards the windows streaming with rain.

'The sandhills won't be much of a temptation tonight, Mr Haydon.'

'No,' he said, laughing gently with her, 'but where there's an old will there's always an old way.' In a voice gentle with what sounded like regret he inquired, 'It was at the Silver Slipper you were last night, wasn't it, a bird told me?'

'The bird was right,' she said. 'The Blue Aces were playing there.'

'The rain, the rain at the sea, is deadly.' He turned absently in tiredness or memory and reached and took a white shell from the mantelpiece and held it to his ear to listen to it roar.

'It makes everything miserable,' McVittie said, tired of his complete possession of O'Connor, but all Haydon did was nod heavily as he replaced the shell and turned again to the girl.

The wash of rain on the windows, the light through their mist going dull on the blue sea of the wallpaper, the red and yellow hollyhocks like tall flowering masts of sailing ships; and when a child wiped a clearing on the glass, cabbages showed between the apple trees in the garden, and the green cooking apples were bright and shining in the leaves with rain.

'Education comes from the Latin *educo*, to lead forth. People seem to have forgotten that in the modern interpretation of education,' Ingolsby laboured.

It was some consolation to Ryan that he'd abandoned the poets, but his eyes still apologized to the room. He'd make his position even clearer yet, in his own time.

The turning of the pages without reading, pleasure of delaying pleasure to come. Heroes filled those pages week after week. Rockfist Rogan and Alf Tupper and Wilson the Iron Man. The room, the conversations, the cries of the seagulls, the sea faded: it was the world of imagination, among the performing gods, what I ashamedly desired to become.

Alf Tupper put aside welder and goggles, changed into his country's singlet to leave the whole field standing in that fantastic last lap, and Wilson, *Wilson, the Iron Man, simply came alone into Tibet and climbed to the top of Everest.*

The Key

They cut the tongues out of the dead foxes brought to the barracks and threw them out to the grey cat or across the netting wire into the garden. They cut the tongues out of the foxes so that they couldn't be brought back again for the half-crown the government gave for each dead fox in its campaign for the extermination of foxes. Dry mornings they put out the 'Recruitment' and 'Thistle Ragwort Dock' posters on their boards and took them in again at nightfall and when it rained.

The Sergeant and his policeman, Bannon, had other such duties, for the last crime had been four years before when Mike Moran stole the spare wheel of Guinea McLoughlin's tractor, but as he threw it in the river they'd not enough evidence to obtain a conviction. As an army in peacetime their main occupation was boredom, and they had similar useless exercises. The Sergeant inspected the solitary Bannon on parade at nine each morning. They'd spent a certain number of hours patrolling local roads on their bikes. One or other of them had always to be on BO duty in the dayroom beside the phone that seldom rang. These regulations the Superintendent in the town tried to enforce by surprise inspections. These inspections usually found the Sergeant at work in his garden. As he'd almost certainly have been signed out in the books on some fictitious patrol, he'd have to run for cover of the trees along the river and stay hidden until the car left. Then he'd saunter in nervously chewing a grass stalk to inquire what had taken place.

All this changed the day he bought one of the lucky dips at Moroney's auction. The lucky dips was a way to get rid of the junk at the end of the auction. They came in large sugar bags. His bag concealed two canisters of nuts and bolts and a yellowed medical dictionary.

Bannon was now sent out on the bike to patrol the local roads. The Sergeant sat all day in the dayroom poring over the yellowed pages detailing diseases and their remedies. The weeds in the garden

45

started to choke the young lettuce, the edges of the unsprayed potato leaves to fritter black, and when the summer thunder with its violent showers made the growth more rapid he called me down to the dayroom.

'Sit down.' He offered a chair by turning it towards the empty fireplace. The dictionary was open among the foolscap ledgers on the table, *Patrick Moroney MD 1893* in faded purple copperplate on its flyleaf.

'You're old enough to know that nobody can be expected to live for ever?' he began.

'Yes.'

'If you expect something it's only common intelligence to prepare for it, isn't that right?'

'Yes.'

'Our ages being what they are, it's no more than natural to expect me to be the first to go?'

'That'll be years yet.'

'We thought that once before and we were wrong. One never knows the day or the hour. The foolish virgins are our lesson.'

I sat stiffly on the wooden chair.

'If I go you're the oldest and you'll have to look after the others. I think now is the time to begin to learn to fend for yourselves. This summer I expect you to look after the garden and timber as if I no longer existed. That way there'll be no danger you'll be caught napping when the day comes.'

'But you do exist.'

'Have I to spell it out?' he suddenly shouted. 'As far as the garden and timber goes I won't exist. And I'll see to the best of my ability that you'll learn not to depend on me for ever. It's no more than my Christian duty. Is that clear now?'

'Yes.'

'Begin by informing the others of the state of affairs. There has to be some beginning somewhere. Is that clear now?'

'Yes.'

I left to go up the long hallway to the living quarters, the noise of the children at play on its stone floor growing louder. 'I exist, I don't exist,' repeated itself over and over as I tried to find words to tell them the state of affairs, bewildered as to what they were.

They laughed when I tried to explain, and then I shouted, 'I'm no longer joking. He said he'd give us no help. He said we'd have to learn to live without him. That's what he said we'd have to do.'

It took long tedious hours to weed the garden, our hands staining black with the weeds. The excitement of bringing the timber down by boat from Oakport compensated for the tedium of the gardens and when the stack grew by the water's edge he approved: 'The hard way is the only way.'

On hot days he sat outside on one of the yellow dayroom chairs with the dictionary, the young swallows playing between their clay nests overhead under the drainpipe. The laughter from the garden disturbed him. The children were pelting each other with clay. He put down the book to come out where I was backing up the matted furrows, pumping half-canfuls of spray out on the potato stalks.

'It's not enough for you to work. You have to keep an eye on the others as well,' he said.

'What'll I do if they won't heed?' I was wet and tired backing up the rows of dripping stalks.

'Get a stick to them, that's what you'll do,' he said and left, anxious to return to the book. 'I have to get some peace.'

The circuit court saw him in Carrick, and he took home a thermometer in a shining steel case, senna leaves, sulphur, cascara, various white and grey powders, rose-water, and slender glass flagons, in which he began to keep samples of his urine, each morning holding the liquid in the delicate glass to the window light to search for trace of sediment. His walk grew slow and careful.

From the autumn circuit he brought a cow's head, blood staining the newspaper, and a bomb box, the colour of grass and mud, war surplus. He showed us how to open the head down its centre, scrape out the brains, cut the glazed eye out of the sockets and the insides of the black lips with their rubber-like feelers.

Before going to bed we put it to stew over a slow fire. The next morning he remained in bed. He knocked with his shoe on the boards and told us to inform Bannon that he was going sick. After signing the ledgers at nine Bannon climbed the stairs to see how he was, and on coming down rang Neary, the police doctor.

Neary called on his way to his noon dispensary. Bannon climbed with him to the bedroom door. Only the low murmur of question and answer, the creak of moving shoes on the boards, came at first, but then the voices rose. They lulled again, while the doctor apparently made some additional examination, only to rise again worse than ever. The voices brought Bannon to the open door at the foot of the stairs to listen there with hands behind his back. Each time the voices died he returned to his patient surveyal of the road from the dayroom window, only to be brought back to the foot of the stairs by a fresh bout of shouting. He was visibly uneasy, straightening down the front of his tunic, stuffing the white hankie farther up his sleeve, when the bedroom door opened and closed sharply, and the doctor's quick steps were on the stairs. Bannon waited out of sight inside the open doorway until the doctor was at the foot of the stairs, then appeared obsequiously to unbolt the heavy front door of the porch, and followed Neary out on the gravel. The examination had lasted well past the noon of the doctor's dispensary.

'I hope there's nothing serious?' Bannon ventured on the gravel.

'As serious as it can be – apparently mortal,' the doctor answered with angry sarcasm as he put his satchel on the passenger seat of his car. 'And he knows all about it. Why he needs to see me is the one puzzlement.'

'How long will I mark him in the sick-book for?' Bannon shied away.

'Till kingdom come,' the doctor answered; but, before he closed the car door, changed: 'Till Wednesday. I'll come on Wednesday.'

We brought him broth of the cow's head and milk pudding, the air stale in the room with the one window shut tight on the river and half blinded; and Bannon, morning and evening, brought him local gossip or report, in which he took no interest. Every hour he spooned a concoction he'd made for himself from the juice of senna leaves and white powders.

On Wednesday Neary appeared well before his dispensary hour. This time the room upstairs was much quieter, though the door did close on, 'What I want is to see a specialist, not a bunch of country quacks.' The doctor was more quiet this time as he came down to the waiting Bannon at the foot of the stairs. When they passed through the heavy door on to the gravel, thick-veined sycamore leaves blowing towards the barrack wall from the trees of the avenue, Neary tentatively asked, 'Had you noticed any change in the Sergeant before he took to bed?'

'How do you mean, Doctor?' Bannon was as always cautious.

'Any changes in his behaviour?'

'Well, there was the book.'

'The book?'

'The book he spent the whole summer poring over, a book he bought at the auction.'

'What kind of book?'

'Medical book, it was.'

'Medical book' – the doctor moved stones of the gravel slowly with his shoes as he repeated. 'I might have known. Well, I won't deny him benefit of specialists if that's what he needs,' and in the evening the doctor rang that a bed was available in the Depot Hospital. The Sergeant was to travel on the next day's train. A police car or ambulance would meet him off the train at Amiens Street Station.

When Bannon climbed the stairs with the news, the Sergeant immediately rose and dressed.

'It took him a long time to see the light,' he said.

'I hope they won't keep you long there,' Bannon answered carefully.

'Tell the girls to get my new uniform out of the press,' he asked the policeman. 'And to get shirts and underwear and pyjamas out for packing.'

When he came down he told Bannon he could go home for the night. 'You'll have to mind this place for long enough on your own. I'll keep an eye on the phone for this evening,' he said with unusual magnanimity.

The packing he supervised with great energy, only remembering later that he was ill, and then his movements grew slow and careful again, finally shutting himself away with the silent phone behind the dayroom door. Before he did, he told me he wanted to see me there after the others had gone to bed.

A low 'Come in' answered my knock.

His feet rested on the bricks of the fireplace, a weak heat came from the dying fire of ash, and beside him, on another yellow chair, was the bomb box, the colour of mud and grass. A tin oil-lamp was turned low on the trestle table, on the black and red ink-stains, on the wooden dip pens standing in their wells, on the heavy ledgers and patrol books, on an unsheathed baton. A child muttering in its sleep from the upstairs room came through the door I'd left open. 'Shut it. We're not in a field,' he said.

'Early, in the summer, we talked about you managing without me.

And you did a good job in the garden and bringing the timber down. Well, it looks as if we prepared none too soon.'

'How?'

'You know what clothes and feeds you all – my pay. The police own the roof above your head. With my death that comes to a full stop. We all know how far your relatives can be depended on – as far as the door.'

He'd his greatcoat on over his uniform, the collar turned up but unbuttoned, his shoulders hunched in a luxury of care as if any sudden movement might quench the weak flame of life the body held.

'Fortunately I have made provisions for the day,' he said, turning to the bomb box on the chair, and with the same slow carefulness unlocked it. Inside, against the mud and grass camouflage over the steel, was a green wad of money in a rubber band, two brown envelopes and a large package.

'You see this money,' he said. 'It's one hundred pounds. That's for the immediate expenses when they take the body home. It won't cross the bridge, it'll go to Aughoo, to lie with your mother, no matter what your relatives try.

'Then open this envelope, it has your name,' he lifted the thin brown envelope, 'all instructions for the immediate death, what to do, are down there one by one.

'This other envelope has the will and deeds,' he continued. 'Lynch the solicitor in Boyle has the other copy, and the day after the funeral take this copy into him.

'I have discussed it all with Lynch, he'll help you with the purchase of a small farm, for after the death you'll have to get out of the barracks if you don't all want to be carted off to the orphanage, and if you dither the saved money'll go like snow off a rope. Paddy Mullaney wants to sell and Lynch and I agreed it's ideal if it comes at the right price. After the farm the first thing to get is a cow. You'll have to work from light to dark on that farm to keep these children but it'll be worth it and you have my confidence,' he said with great authority.

He locked the box, and handed me one of the keys.

'You have a key and I have a key. When news of the death comes you'll go first thing and open the box with your key. Is that clear?' he demanded.

The Key

What was to happen was taking clearer outline as I listened, eyes fixed on the bright metal of the key in the sweat of my palm. 'The bigger package is not for the time being of any importance. It's for when you grow older. Old watches, your mother's rings, photos, locks of hair, medals, albums, certificates. It's for when you all grow older.' Then he remembered again that he was ill, and sank back at once into the dark blue greatcoat.

What he'd been saying was that he was going to die. He'd be put in a coffin. The coffin would be put in the ground and covered with clay. He'd give no answer to any call.

Mullaney's farm where we'd go to live, small slated house of the herd, fields sloping uphill to the mound, wet ground about the mound where once they'd startled a hare out of its form in the brown rushes; it had paused in the loop of its flight as the shot blasted its tense listening into a crumpled stillness.

Stone walls of those fields. Drudge of life from morning to night to feed the mouths, to keep the roof above their heads. The ugly and skin shapes of starlings, beaks voracious at the rim of the nest, days grown heavier with the burden of the carrying.

'But you're not going to die.'

'All the symptoms point to the one fact that it's certain.'

'But the symptoms may be wrong.'

'No. It's as certain as anything can be in this life.'

'Don't, don't . . .'

'Do you love me, then?'

'Yes.'

'If you love me then you must do your best for the others. We can't order our days. They are willed. We have to trust in the mercy of God.'

'I'll have nobody.'

'You have the key. You'll open the box with the key when the news comes? Now we have to go to bed. It matters not how long the day.' He lifted the box by its handle, moved towards the stairs, its weight dragging his right shoulder down. 'Blow out the lamp. I'll wait for you.'

Painfully the slow climb of the stairs began. His breathing came in laboured catches. He leaned on the banister rail. Three times he paused, while I kept pace below, the key in my palm, weak moonlight from the window at the top of the stairs showing the hollowed wood in the centre of the steps, dark red paint on the sides of the way.

51

'I want you to come to my room to show you where to find it when the news comes.'

He opened the door of his room that stank from the stale air and senna leaves and sweat. The moon from the river window gave light enough, but he gave me matches to light the glass lamp, and grew impatient as I fumbled the lighting.

'Under the wardrobe,' he said as he pushed the box between the legs of the plywood wardrobe, its brass handle shining and the silver medallions of the police caps on its top.

'You'll pull it out from under the wardrobe when the news comes. You have the key?'

'But I don't want you to die.'

'Now,' he put his hand on my head, 'I love you too, but we can't control our days, we can only pray. You have the key?'

The key lay in the sweat of the palm.

'You'll open the box with the key when the news comes.'

The train took him to the hospital the next day but before the end of the same week he was home again. He asked at once if his room was ready and immediately went there. He said he didn't want anything to eat and didn't want to be called the next morning. No one ventured near the door till Bannon climbed the stairs. When no answer greeted the timid twice-repeated knock he opened it a small way.

'You're home, Sergeant. Are you any better?'

The Sergeant was sitting up in bed with spectacles on, going through the medical dictionary. He looked at Bannon over the spectacles but didn't answer.

'I just came up to see if there was anything I could do for you? If you wanted me to ring Neary or anything?'

'No. I don't want you to do anything. I want you to get to hell down to the dayroom and leave me in peace,' he shouted.

A scared and bewildered Bannon closed the door, came down the stairs, and there was no sound from the bedroom for several hours till suddenly a loud knocking came on the floorboards.

'He wants something.' 'You go up.' 'No, you go up.' 'No.' It spread immediate panic.

The next knock was loud with anger, imperative.

'Nobody'll do anything in this house.' I spoke almost in his voice as I went up to the room.

It had been relief to see him come home, even joy in the release. None of us knew what to make of him shutting himself away in the upstairs room. The shouts at Bannon had been loud. I still had the key.

'It took you long enough to come.'

He was lying down in the bed, and the medical book was shut on the eiderdown to one side.

'I was in the scullery.'

'You weren't all in the scullery.'

'They didn't want to come.'

'I want something to eat,' he said.

'What would you like?'

'Anything, anything that's in the house.'

'Bacon and egg or milk pudding?'

'Bacon and eggs'll do.'

I held the key in my hand. I wanted to ask him what to do with the key, if he wanted it back; and my eyes kept straying under the plywood wardrobe where the bomb box must be; but the face in the bed didn't invite any questions.

That day and the next he stayed in the room, but at five o'clock the third morning he woke the whole house by clattering downstairs and even more loudly opening and closing cupboard doors and presses, muttering all the time. When we came down he'd gone out. We saw him outside examining the potato and turnip pits, the rows of winter cabbage.

After his breakfast he shaved at the old mirror and carefully combed his receding hair over the bald patches of the scalp, polished his boots, gathered the silver buttons and medallions of the tunic on the brass stick and shone them with Silvo.

On the stroke of nine he went down to the dayroom. I heard his raised voice within minutes. 'Nothing done right. I've told you time in and time out that these records must never be let fall behind,' and the unfortunate Bannon's low excuses.

For several weeks I kept the key in my pocket, but each time I tried to ask him what to do with it and if he wanted it back, I wasn't able. Eventually, one warm evening, with some anxiety, I threw it as far away towards the river as I was able, watching its flight curve between the two ash trees to fall into the sedge and wild nettles a few feet from the water.

Korea

'You saw an execution then too, didn't you?' I asked my father, and he started to tell as he rowed. He'd been captured in an ambush in late 1919, and they were shooting prisoners in Mountjoy as reprisals at that time. He thought it was he who'd be next, for after a few days they moved him to the cell next to the prison yard. He could see out through the bars. No rap to prepare himself came to the door that night, and at daybreak he saw the two prisoners they'd decided to shoot being marched out: a man in his early thirties, and what was little more than a boy, sixteen or seventeen, and he was weeping. They blindfolded the boy, but the man refused the blindfold. When the officer shouted, the boy clicked to attention, but the man stayed as he was, chewing very slowly. He had his hands in his pockets.

'Take your hands out of your pockets,' the officer shouted again, irritation in the voice.

The man slowly shook his head.

'It's a bit too late now in the day for that,' he said.

The officer then ordered them to fire, and as the volley rang, the boy tore at his tunic over the heart, as if to pluck out the bullets, and the buttons of the tunic began to fly into the air before he pitched forward on his face.

The other heeled quietly over on his back: it must have been because of the hands in the pockets.

The officer dispatched the boy with one shot from the revolver as he lay face downward, but he pumped five bullets in rapid succession into the man, as if to pay him back for not coming to attention.

'When I was on my honeymoon years after, it was May, and we took the tram up the hill of Howth from Sutton Cross,' my father said as he rested on the oars. 'We sat on top in the open on the wooden seats with the rail around that made it like a small ship. The sea was below, and smell of the sea and furze-bloom all about, and then I looked down and saw the furze pods bursting, and the

54

way they burst in all directions seemed shocking like the buttons when he started to tear at his tunic. I couldn't get it out of my mind all day. It destroyed the day.'

'It's a wonder their hands weren't tied?' I asked him as he rowed between the black navigation pan and the red where the river flowed into Oakport.

'I suppose it was because they were considered soldiers.'

'Do you think the boy stood to attention because he felt that he might still get off if he obeyed the rules?'

'Sounds a bit highfalutin' to me. Comes from going to school too long,' he said aggressively, and I was silent. It was new to me to hear him talk about his own life at all. Before, if I asked him about the war, he'd draw fingers across his eyes as if to tear a spider web away, but it was my last summer with him on the river, and it seemed to make him want to talk, to give of himself before it ended.

Hand over hand I drew in the line that throbbed with fish; there were two miles of line, a hook on a lead line every three yards. The licence allowed us a thousand hooks, but we used more. We were the last to fish this freshwater for a living.

As the eels came in over the side I cut them loose with a knife into a wire cage, where they slid over each other in their own oil, the twisted eel hook in their mouths. The other fish – pike choked on hooked perch they'd tried to swallow, bream, roach – I slid up the floorboards towards the bow of the boat. We'd sell them in the village or give them away. The hooks that hadn't been taken I cleaned and stuck in rows round the side of the wooden box. I let the line fall in its centre. After a mile he took my place in the stern and I rowed. People hadn't woken yet, and the early morning cold and mist were on the river. Outside of the slow ripple of the oars and the threshing of the fish on the line beaded with running drops of water as it came in, the river was dead silent, except for the occasional lowing of cattle on the banks.

'Have you any idea what you'll do after this summer?' he asked.

'No. I'll wait and see what comes up,' I answered.

'How do you mean *what comes up*?'

'Whatever result I get in the exam. If the result is good, I'll have choices. If it's not, there won't be choices. I'll have to take what I can get.'

'How good do you think they'll be?'

'I think they'll be all right, but there's no use counting chickens, is there?'

'No,' he said, but there was something calculating in the face; it made me watchful of him as I rowed the last stretch of the line. The day had come, the distant noises of the farms and the first flies on the river, by the time we'd lifted the large wire cage out of the bulrushes, emptied in the morning's catch of eels, and sunk it again.

'We'll have enough for a consignment tomorrow,' he said.

Each week we sent the live eels to Billingsgate in London.

'But say, say even if you do well, you wouldn't think of throwing this country up altogether and going to America?' he said, the words fumbled for as I pushed the boat out of the bulrushes after sinking the cage of eels, using the oar as a pole, the mud rising a dirty yellow between the stems.

'Why America?'

'Well, it's the land of opportunity, isn't it, a big, expanding country? There's no room for ambition in this poky place. All there's room for is to make holes in pints of porter.'

I was wary of the big words. They were not in his own voice.

'Who'd pay the fare?'

'We'd manage that. We'd scrape it together somehow.'

'Why should you scrape for me to go to America if I can get a job here?'

'I feel I'd be giving you a chance I never got. I fought for this country. And now they want to take away even the licence to fish. Will you think about it anyhow?'

'I'll think about it,' I answered.

Through the day he trimmed the brows of ridges in the potato field while I replaced hooks on the line and dug worms, pain of doing things for the last time as well as the boredom the knowledge brings that soon there'll be no need to do them, that they could be discarded almost now. The guilt of leaving came: I was discarding his life to assume my own, a man to row the boat would eat into the decreasing profits of the fishing, and it was even not certain he'd get renewal of his licence. The tourist board had opposed the last application. They said we impoverished the coarse fishing for tourists – the tourists who came every summer from Liverpool and Birmingham in increasing numbers to sit in aluminium deck-chairs on the riverbank and fish with rods. The fields we had would be a bare living without the fishing.

I saw him stretch across the wall in conversation with the cattle-dealer Farrell as I came round to put the worms where we stored them in clay in the darkness of the lavatory. Farrell leaned on the bar of his bicycle on the road. I passed into the lavatory thinking they were talking about the price of cattle, but as I emptied the worms into the box, the word *Moran* came, and I carefully opened the door to listen. It was my father's voice. He was excited.

'I know. I heard the exact sum. They got ten thousand dollars when Luke was killed. Every American soldier's life is insured to the tune of ten thousand dollars.'

'I heard they get two hundred and fifty dollars a month each for Michael and Sam while they're serving,' he went on.

'They're buying cattle left and right,' Farrell's voice came as I closed the door and stood in the darkness, in the smell of shit and piss and the warm fleshy smell of worms crawling in too little clay.

The shock I felt was the shock I was to feel later when I made some social blunder, the splintering of a self-esteem and the need to crawl into a lavatory to think.

Luke Moran's body had come from Korea in a leaden casket, had crossed the stone bridge to the slow funeral bell with the big cars from the embassy behind, the coffin draped in the Stars and Stripes. Shots had been fired above the grave before they threw in the clay. There were photos of his decorations being presented to his family by a military attaché.

He'd scrape the fare, I'd be conscripted there, each month he'd get so many dollars while I served, and he'd get ten thousand if I was killed.

In the darkness of the lavatory between the boxes of crawling worms before we set the night line for the eels I knew my youth had ended.

I rowed as he let out the night line, his fingers baiting each twisted hook so beautifully that it seemed a single movement. The dark was closing from the shadow of Oakport to Nutley's boat-house, bats made ugly whirls overhead, the wings of ducks shirred as they curved down into the bay.

'Have you thought about what I said about going to America?'

he asked, without lifting his eyes from the hooks and the box of worms.

'I have.'

The oars dipped in the water without splash, the hole whorling wider in the calm as it slipped on the stern seat.

'Have you decided to take the chance, then?'

'No. I'm not going.'

'You won't be able to say I didn't give you the chance when you come to nothing in this fool of a country. It'll be your own funeral.'

'It'll be my own funeral,' I answered, and asked after a long silence, 'As you grow older, do you find your own days in the war and jails coming much back to you?'

'I do. And I don't want to talk about them. Talking about the execution disturbed me no end, those cursed buttons bursting into the air. And the most I think is that if I'd conducted my own wars, and let the fool of a country fend for itself, I'd be much better off today. I don't want to talk about it.'

I knew this silence was fixed for ever as I rowed in silence till he asked, 'Do you think, will it be much good tonight?'

'It's too calm,' I answered.

'Unless the night wind gets up,' he said anxiously.

'Unless a night wind,' I repeated.

As the boat moved through the calm water and the line slipped through his fingers over the side I'd never felt so close to him before, not even when he'd carried me on his shoulders above the laughing crowd to the Final. Each move he made I watched as closely as if I too had to prepare myself to murder.

Lavin

When I knew Lavin he was close to the poorhouse but he'd still down mallet and cold chisel to limp after the young girls, crooked finger beckoning, calling, 'Come, give us a peep, there must be a few little hairs beginning,' and that strange inlooking smile came over the white stubbled face while the girls, shrieking with laughter, kept backing just fast enough to stay outside his reach.

When I heard people speak of Lavin it was in puzzlement that when young and handsome he had worked such cruel hours at his trade, though he had no need because his uncle had left him Willowfield, the richest farm around; and he had taken no interest in girls though he could have had his pick; and at a threshing or in a wheatfield he'd be found at nightfall gathering carelessly abandoned tools or closing gaps after the others had gone drinking or to dress for the dances. Neither could they understand his sudden heavy drinking in Billy Burns's. Before that if he had to enter a pub he'd accept nothing but lemonade. Burns was blamed for giving him credit when his money ran out, and after he seized and held in the house the gypsy girl who sold him paper flowers with wire stems, it was the same Burns who gave him the money to buy the gypsies off in return for Willowfield. The gypsies had warned him that if he didn't pay what they wanted they'd come and cut him with rusted iron. What money he was able to earn afterwards was from his trade, and that steadily dwindled as machinery replaced the horse. All of his roof had fallen in except above the kitchen, where oats and green weeds grew out of the thatch. Whatever work he got he did outside on the long hacked bench, except when it was too cold or wet.

The first time I stopped to watch him it was because of the attraction of what's forbidden. He was shaping a section of a cart wheel, but he put down mallet and chisel to say, that strange smile I'll always remember coming over his face, 'Those sisters of yours are growing into fine sprigs. Have you looked to see if any of them have started a little thatch?'

'No.' His smile frightened me.

'It should be soft, light, a shading.' His voice lingered on the words. I felt his eyes did not see past the smiling.

'I haven't seen,' I said and started to watch the roads for anybody coming.

'You should keep your eyes skinned, then. All you have to do is to keep your eyes skinned, man.' The voice was harder.

'I don't sleep in their rooms.'

'No need to sleep in the same room, man. Just keep your eyes skinned. Wait till you hear them go to the pot and walk in by mistake. It'll be cocked enough to see if it has started to thatch.' The voice had grown rhythmical and hard.

It was more a desire to see into the strangeness behind his smile than this constant pestering that made me give him the information he sought.

'The two eldest have hair but the others haven't.'

'The others have just a bald ridge with the slit,' he pursued fiercely.

'Yes.' I wanted to escape but he seized me by the lapels.

'The hair is fairer than on their heads?'

'Yes.'

'Fair and soft? A shade?'

'Yes, but let me go.'

'Soft and fair. The young ivy covering the slit.' He let me go as the voice grew caressing and the smile flooded over the face. 'So fair you can see the skin through it yet. A shading,' he gloated, and then, 'Will you come with me a minute inside?'

'I have to go.'

He turned as if I was no longer there and limped, the boot tongueless and unlaced, to the door, and as I hurried away I heard the bolt scrape shut.

I avoided Lavin all that winter. I'd heard his foot was worse and that he was unlikely to see another winter outside the poorhouse. It should have assuaged my fear but it did not, and besides I'd fallen in love with Charley Casey.

Charley Casey was dull in school, but he was good at games, and popular, with a confident laugh and white teeth and blue-dark hair. He had two dark-haired sisters of seventeen and nineteen, who were both beautiful, and a young widowed mother, and there hung about him that glamour of a house of ripe women. I helped him at his exercises, and in return he partnered me in handball. We started to skate in the evenings together on the shallow pond and to go to the river when the days grew warmer. I was often sick with anxiety when he was absent, able to concentrate on nothing but the bell that would set me free to race to his house.

I tried to get him to read *David Copperfield* so that we could share a world, but always he had excuses. When the school closed and I had to go to the sea, he promised that he'd have it read by the time I got back. At the sea I spent most of my time alone among the sandhills imagining the conversations we'd have about *David Copperfield* on the riverbank when the slow week by the sea would be over.

The morning we got back I rushed to his house without waiting to eat. As I pursued him with questions it grew depressingly clear that he'd not read a word and he admitted, 'I did my best to read it but I fell asleep. It's too hot. I'll read it when it rains.'

'You promised,' I accused.

'Honest, I'll read it when it rains. Why can't we go to the river same as before!'

'I don't want to go to the river. Why don't we go to see Lavin?' I said in thirst for some perversity.

'That's a great idea.' I was taken aback by his enthusiasm. 'Why don't we see old John?'

I walked slowly and sullenly to Lavin's, resentful that he had fallen so easily in with my proposal.

Tools beginning to rust were outside on the old bench and the door was open. Lavin sat inside, his foot upon a footrest. The foot was wrapped in multicoloured rags that included red flannel and stank in the heat. Casey crossed the shavings-littered floor to the empty fireplace to ask, 'How's the old foot, John?'

'Playing me up, Charley Boy, but Himself was never in better order.'

'I've no doubt,' Charley laughed loudly.

I stood close to the door in smouldering anger.

'How are the two beauties of sisters? The thatch must be good and black and thick, eh? Brimmin' with juice inside, or have they shaved?' The smile came instantly, the repetitious fondling voice lingered on each word.

'No. They didn't shave it, John. It's as thick as thatch. Not that thatch is going to be all that thick above your head for long,' Casey laughed.

'Never mind the roof now. How is little John Charles coming along? Sprouting nicely?' He touched Casey's fly gently with his fingertips.

'You have to show me yours first. You never saw such a weapon as old John has.' Casey laughed and winked towards me at the door.

'No sooner said than done.' Suddenly Lavin opened his trousers.

'A fair weapon and as stiff as a stake.' Casey gripped it in his fist.

'Know the only place the stiffs get in – the cunt and the grave,' Lavin joked, his mouth showing black stumps of teeth as he laughed.

'I bet you put it stiff and hard into the gypsy, old Johnny Balls,' Casey teased.

'Yeah, and what about seeing little John Charles now?'

'Fire ahead,' Casey laughed. I wanted to shout but couldn't as Lavin unbuttoned Casey's fly and gently started to play with it in his fingers.

'Sprouting along royal, fit for milking any day.'

He fondled the penis until it was erect and then stretched to take a heavy carpenter's rule from the mantel.

'An increase of a good inch since the last time, upon my soul,' he said. 'Why don't you come up from the door to see which little John Charles is farthest advanced?'

'No.' I fought back tears of rage.

'Come on,' Casey said challengingly. 'Let old John compare them.'

'I don't want.'

'Have it your own way, so,' he said, and as he took the rule to measure Lavin I left and waited outside. He soon followed.

'Why did you do it?' I attacked immediately.

'Oh, I like to take a hand at old John every now and then and get him all worked up,' he said casually.

'Why did you let him fool around with you?'

'What does it matter? It gets him all worked up.'

'It's disgusting,' I said, disturbed by feelings that had never touched me so fiercely before.

'Oh, what does it matter? He'll soon be in the poorhouse. Why don't we go for a swim?'

I walked in sullen silence by his side across the bridge. I wanted to swim with him but I wanted to reject him, and in my heart I hated him. I calmed as we walked. At the boathouse I helped him lift someone's night line. It had no fish though the hooks had been cleaned of bait. We started to talk again as we went to where the high whitethorns shielded the river from the road. We stripped on the bank and swam and afterwards lay on the warm moss watching the bream shoal out beyond the reeds, their black fins moving sluggishly above the calm surface, white gleam of the bellies as they slowly rolled, until harness bells sounded on the road behind the whitethorns.

At the iron gate where the whitethorns ended two gypsy caravans and a spring cart came into our view. The little round curtained window in the back glittered in the sun, and two dogs roped to the axle trotted heads low, mechanically, between the red wheels. Now and then a whip cracked above the horses' heads into the jingling of the harness bells.

'Do you think Lavin did what he was supposed to do to the gypsy girl?' I asked.

'He'd hardly have to pay with the farm if he didn't,' Casey answered with quiet logic. The image of the monstrous penis being driven deep into the guts of the struggling gypsy girl made me shiver with excitement.

'It'd be good if we had two caravans, you and me, like the caravans gone past. You and me would live in one caravan. We'd keep four women in the other. We'd ride around Ireland. We'd make them do anything we'd want to.' If Casey had been more forward with Lavin early on, I was leading now.

'It'd be great,' he answered.

'They'd strip the minute we said strip. If they didn't we'd whip them. We'd whip them with those whips that have bits of metal on the ends. We'd whip them until the blood came and they'd to put arms round our knees for mercy.'

'Yes, we'd make them get down on their hands and knees, naked, and do them from behind the way the bull does,' Casey said, and dived sideways to seize a frog in the grass. He took a dried stem of reed and began to insert it in the frog. 'That's what'll tickle him, I'm telling you.'

'Why couldn't we do it together?' I tentatively asked, stiff with excitement. He understood at once.

'I'll do it to you first,' he said, the dead reed sticking out of the frog in his hand, 'and then you'll do it to me.'

'Why don't you let me do it to you first, and then you can have as long as you like on me?'

'No.'

The fear was unspoken: whoever took his pleasure first would have the other in his power and then might not surrender his own body. We avoided each other's eyes. I watched the dead reed being moved in and out of the frog.

'They say it hurts,' I said. There was relief now of not having to go through with it.

'It'd probably hurt too much.' Charley Casey was eager to agree. 'It'd be better to get two women and hurt them. They say a frog can live only so long under water.'

'Why don't we see?'

I found a stone along the bank and we tied one of the frog's legs with fishing line to the stone. We took it some hundred yards up the bank to where a shallow stream joined the river. We dropped the stone and watched the frog claw upwards, but each time it was dragged back by the line, until it weakened, and it drowned.

We crossed the bridge in silence, already changing. I helped him at school for some time afterwards but in the evenings we avoided each other, as if we were aware of some shameful truth we were afraid to come to know together.

I never saw Lavin again. They took him to the poorhouse that October when the low hedges were blue with sloes, though by then the authorities referred to it as the Resthome for Senior Citizens.

Casey is now married, with children, and runs a pub called the Crown and Anchor somewhere in Manchester, but I've never had any wish to look him up. In fact he seldom enters my mind. But as I grow older hardly a day passes but a picture of Lavin comes to trouble me: it is of him when he was young, and, they said, handsome, gathering the scattered tools at nightfall in a clean wheatfield after the others had gone drinking or to change for the dances.

My Love, My Umbrella

It was the rain, the constant weather of this city, made my love inseparable from the umbrella, a black umbrella, white stitching on the seams of the imitation leather over the handle, the metal point bent where it was caught in Mooney's grating as we raced for the last bus to the garage out of Abbey Street. The band was playing when we met, the Blanchardstown Fife and Drum. They were playing *Some day he'll come along/The man I love/And he'll be big and strong/The man I love* at the back of the public lavatory on Burgh Quay, facing a few persons on the pavement in front of the Scotch House. It was the afternoon of a Sunday.

'It is strange, the band,' I said; her face flinched away, and in the same movement back, turned to see who'd spoken. Her skin under the black hair had the glow of health and youth, and the solidity at the bones of the hips gave promise of a rich seed-bed.

'It's strange,' she answered, and I was at once anxious for her body.

The conductor stood on a wooden box, continually breaking off his conducting to engage in some running argument with a small grey man by his side, but whether he waved his stick jerkedly or was bent in argument seemed to make no difference to the players. They turned their pages. The music plodded on, *Some day he'll come along/The man I love/And he'll be big and strong/The man I love*. At every interval they looked towards the clock, Mooney's clock across the river.

'They're watching the clock,' I said.

'Why?' her face turned again.

'They'll only play till the opening hour.'

I too anxiously watched the clock. I was afraid she'd go when the band stopped. Lights came on inside the Scotch House. The music hurried. A white-aproned barman, a jangle of keys into the quickened music, began to unlock the folding shutters and with a resounding clash drew them back. As the tune ended the conductor

65

signalled to the band that they could put away their instruments, got down from his box, and started to tap the small grey man on the shoulder with the baton as he began to argue in earnest. The band came across the road towards the lighted globes inside the Scotch House, where already many of their audience waited impatiently on the slow pulling of the pints. The small grey man carried the conductor's box as they passed in together.

'It is what we said would happen.'

'Yes.'

The small family cars were making their careful way home across the bridge after their Sunday outings to their cold ham and tomato and lettuce, the wind blowing from the mouth of the river, gulls screeching above the stink of its low tide, as I forced the inanities towards an invitation.

'Would you come with me for a drink?'

'Why?' She blushed as she looked me full in the face.

'Why not?'

'I said I'd be back for tea.'

'We can have sandwiches.'

'But why do you want me to?'

'I'd like very much if you come. Will you come?'

'All right I'll come but I don't know why.'

It was how we began, the wind blowing from the mouth of the river while the Blanchardstown Fife and Drum downed their first thirst-quencher in the Scotch House.

They'd nothing but beef left in Mooney's after the weekend. We had stout with our sandwiches. Soon, in the drowsiness of the stout, we did little but watch the others drinking. I pointed out a poet to her. I recognized him from his pictures in the paper. His shirt was open-necked inside a gabardine coat and he wore a hat with a small feather in its band. She asked me if I liked poetry.

'When I was younger,' I said. 'Do you?'

'Not very much.'

She asked me if I could hear what the poet was saying to the four men at his table who continually plied him with whiskey. I hadn't heard. Now we both listened. He was saying he loved the blossoms of Kerr Pinks more than roses, a man could only love what he knew well, and it was the quality of the love that mattered and not the accident. The whole table said they'd drink to that, but he glared at them as if slighted, and as if to avoid the glare they called for a round of doubles. While the drinks were coming from the bar the poet turned aside and took a canister from his pocket. The inside of the lid was coated with a white powder which he quickly licked clean. She thought it was baking soda. Her father in the country took baking soda for his stomach. We had more stout and we noticed, while each new round was coming, the poet turned away from the table to lick clean the fresh coat of soda on the inside of the canister lid.

That was the way our first evening went. People who came into the pub were dripping with rain and we stayed until they'd draped the towels over the pump handles and called 'Time' in the hope the weather would clear, but it did not.

The beat of rain was so fierce when we came out that the street was a dance of glass shapes, and they reminded me of blackened spikes on the brass candleshrine which hold the penny candles before the altar.

'Does it remind you of the candlespikes?' I asked.

'Yes, now that you mention it.'

Perhaps the rain, the rain will wash away the poorness of our attempts at speech, our bodies will draw closer, closer than our speech, I hoped, as she returned on the throat my kiss in the bus, and that we'd draw closer to a meal of each other's flesh; and from the bus, under the beat of rain on the umbrella, we walked beyond Fairview church.

'Will I be able to come in?' I asked.

'It would cause trouble.'

'You have your own room?'

'The man who owns the house watches. He would make trouble.'

Behind the church was a dead end overhung with old trees, and the street lights did not reach as far as the wall at its end, a grey orchard wall with some ivy.

'Can we stay here a short time, then?'

I hung upon the silence, afraid she'd use the rain as excuse, and breathed when she said, 'Not for long, it is late.'

We moved under the umbrella out of the street light, fumbling for certain footing between the tree roots.

'Will you hold the umbrella?'

She took the imitation leather with the white stitching in her hands.

Our lips moved on the saliva of our mouths as I slowly undid the coat button. I tried to control the trembling so as not to tear the small white buttons of the blouse. Coat, blouse, brassière, as names of places on a road. I globed the warm soft breasts in hands. I leaned across the cold metal above the imitation leather she held in her hands to take the small nipples gently in teeth, the steady beat on the umbrella broken by irregular splashes from the branches.

Will she let me? I was afraid as I lifted the woollen skirt; and slowly I moved hands up the soft insides of the thighs, and instead of the 'No' I feared and waited for, the handle became a hard pressure as she pressed on my lips.

I could no longer control the trembling as I felt the sheen of the knickers, I drew them down to her knees, and parted the lips to touch the juices. She hung on my lips. She twitched as the fingers went deeper. She was a virgin.

'It hurts.' The cold metal touched my face, the rain duller on the sodden cloth by now.

'I won't hurt you,' I said, and pumped low between her thighs, lifting high the coat and skirt so that the seed fell free into the mud and rain, and after resting on each other's mouth I replaced the clothes.

Under the umbrella, one foot asleep, we walked past the small iron railings of the gardens towards her room, and at the gate I left her with, 'Where will we meet again?'

We would meet at eight against the radiators inside the Metropole.

We met against those silver radiators three evenings every week for long. We went to cinemas or sat in pubs, it was the course of our love, and as it always rained we made love under the umbrella beneath the same trees in the same way. They say the continuance of sexuality is due to the penis having no memory, and mine each evening spilt its seed into the mud and decomposing leaves as if it was always for the first time.

Sometimes we told each other stories. I thought one of the stories she told me very cruel, but I did not tell her.

She'd grown up on a small farm. The neighbouring farm was owned by a Pat Moran who lived on it alone after the death of his mother. As a child she used to look for nests of hens that were laying wild on his farm and he often brought her chocolates or oranges from the fairs. As she grew, feeling the power of her body, she began to provoke him, until one evening on her way to the well through his fields, where he was pruning a whitethorn hedge with a billhook, she lay in the soft grass and showed him so much of her body beneath the clothes that he dropped the billhook and seized her. She struggled loose and shouted as she ran, 'I'll tell my Daddy, you pig.' She was far too afraid to tell her father, but it was as if a wall came down between her and Pat Moran who soon afterwards sold his farm and went to England though he'd never known any other life but that of a small farmer.

She'd grown excited in the telling and asked me what I thought of the story. I said that I thought life was often that way. She then asked me if I had any stories in my life. I said I did, but there was one story that I read in the evening paper that interested me most, since it had indirectly got to do with us.

It was a report of a prosecution. In the rush hour at Bank Station in London two city gents had lost tempers in the queue and assaulted each other with umbrellas. They had inflicted severe injuries with the umbrellas. The question before the judge: was it a case of common assault or, much more serious, assault with dangerous weapon with intent to wound? In view of the extent of the injuries inflicted it had not been an easy decision, but eventually he found for common assault, since he didn't want the thousands of peaceable citizens who used their umbrellas properly to feel that when they travelled to and from work they were carrying dangerous weapons. He fined and bound both gentlemen to the peace, warned them severely as to their future conduct, but he did not impose a prison sentence, as he would have been forced to do if he'd found the umbrella to be a dangerous weapon.

'What do you think of the story?'

'I think it's pretty silly. Let's go home,' she said though it was an hour from the closing hour, raising the umbrella as soon as we reached the street. It was raining as usual.

'Why did you tell that silly story about the umbrellas?' she asked on the bus.

'Why did you tell the story of the farmer?'

'They were different,' she said.

69

'Yes. They were different,' I agreed. For some reason she resented the story.

In the rain we made love again, she the more fierce, and after the seed spilled she said, 'Wait,' and moving on a dying penis, under the unsteady umbrella in her hands, she trembled towards an inarticulate cry of pleasure, and as we walked into the street lamp I asked, we had so fallen into the habit of each other, 'Would you think we should ever get married?' 'Kiss me.' She leaned across the steel between us. 'Do you think we should?' I repeated. 'What would it mean to you?' she asked.

What I had were longings or fears rather than any meanings. To go with her on the train to Thurles on a Friday evening in summer and walk the three miles to her house from the station. To be woken the next morning by the sheepdog barking the postman to the door and have tea and brown bread and butter in a kitchen with the cool of brown flagstones and full of the smell of recent baking.

Or: fear of a housing estate in Clontarf, escape to the Yacht Sunday mornings to read the papers in peace over pints, come home dazed in the midday light of the sea front to the Sunday roast with a peace offering of sweets. Afterwards in the drowse of food and drink to be woken by, 'You promised to take us out for the day, Daddy,' until you backed the hire-purchased Volkswagen out the gateway and drove to Howth and stared out at the sea through the gathering condensation on the semicircles the wipers made on the windshield, and quelled quarrels and cries of the bored children in the back seat.

I decided not to tell her either of these pictures as they might seem foolish to her.

'We'd have to save if we were to think about it,' I heard her voice.

'We don't save very much, do we?'

'At the rate the money goes in the pubs we might as well throw our hat at it. Why did you ask?'

'Because', it was not easy to answer then, when I had to think, 'I like being with you.'

'Why, why,' she asked, 'did you tell that stupid story about the umbrellas?'

'It happened, didn't it? And we never make love without an umbrella. It reminded me of you.'

'Such rubbish,' she said angrily. 'The sea and sand and a hot beach at night, needing only a single sheet, that'd make some sense, but an umbrella?'

It was the approach of summer and it was the false confidence it brings that undid me. It rained less. One bright moonlit night I asked her to hold the umbrella.

'For what?'

She was so fierce that I pretended it'd been a joke.

'I don't see much of a joke standing like a fool holding an umbrella to the blessed moonlight,' she said.

We made love awkwardly, the umbrella lying in the dry leaves, but I was angry that she wouldn't fall in with my wish, and another night when she asked, 'Where are you going on your holidays?' I lied that I didn't know. 'I'll go home if I haven't enough money. And you?' I asked. She didn't answer. I saw she resented that I'd made no effort to include her in the holiday. Sun and sand and sea, I thought maliciously, and decided to break free from her. Summer was coming and the world full of possibilities. I did not lead her under the trees behind the church, but left after kissing her lightly, 'Goodnight.' Instead of arranging to meet as usual at the radiators, I said, 'I'll ring you during the week.' Her look of anger and hatred elated me. 'Ring if you want,' she said as she angrily closed the door.

I was so clownishly elated that I threw the umbrella high in the air and laughing loudly caught it coming down, and there was the exhilaration of staying free those first days; but it soon palled. In the empty room trying to read, while the trains went by at the end of the garden with its two apple trees and one pear, I began to realize I'd fallen more into the habit of her than I'd known. Not wanting to have to see the umbrella I put it behind the wardrobe, but it seemed to be more present than ever there; and often the longing for her lips, her body, grew, close to sickness, and eventually dragged me to the telephone.

'I didn't expect to hear from you after this time,' she said.

'I was ill.'

She was ominously silent as if she knew it for the lie that it was.

'I wondered if we could meet?'

'If you want,' she answered. 'When?'

'What about tonight?'

'I cannot but tomorrow night is all right.'

'At eight, then, at the radiators?'

'Say, at Wynn's Hotel instead.'

The imagination, quickened by distance and uncertainty, found it hard to wait till the eight of the next day, but when the bus drew in, and she was already waiting, the mind slipped back into its old complacency.

'Where'd you like to go?'

'Some place quiet. Where we can talk,' she said.

Crossing the bridge, past where the band had played the first day we met, the Liffey was still in the summer evening.

'I missed you a great deal.' I tried to draw close, her hands were white gloved.

'What was your sickness?'

'Some kind of flu.'

She was hard and separate as we walked. It was one of the new lounge bars she picked. It had piped music and red cushions. The bar was empty, the barman polishing glasses. He brought the Guinness and sweet sherry to the table.

'What did you want to say?' I asked when the barman had returned to polishing the glasses.

'That I've thought about it and that our going out is a waste of time. It's a waste of your time and mine.'

It was as if a bandage had been torn from an open wound.

'But why?'

'It will come to nothing.'

'You've got someone else, then?'

'That's got nothing to do with it.'

'But why, then?'

'I don't love you.'

'But we've had many happy evenings together.'

'Yes, but it's not enough.'

'I thought that after a time we would get married.' I would grovel on the earth or anything to keep her then. Little by little my life had fallen into her keeping, it was only in the loss I had come to know it, life without her, the pain of the loss of my own life without the oblivion the dead have, all longing changed to die out of my own life on her lips, in her thighs, since it was only through her it lived.

'It wouldn't work,' she said, and, sure of her power, 'All those wasted evenings under that old umbrella. And that moonlit night you tried to get me to hold it up like some eejit. What did you take me for?'

'I meant no harm and couldn't we try to make a new start?'

'No. There should be something magical about getting married. We know too much about each other. There's nothing more to discover.'

'You mean . . . our bodies?'

'Yes.'

She moved to go and I was desperate.

'Will you have one more drink?'

'No, I don't really want.'

'Can we not meet just once more?'

'No.' She rose to go. 'It'd only uselessly prolong it and come to the same thing in the end.'

'Are you so sure? If there was just one more chance?'

'No. And there's no need for you to see me to the bus. You can finish your drink.'

'I don't want to,' and followed her through the swing-door.

At the stop in front of the Bank of Ireland I tried one last time. 'Can I not see you home this last night?'

'No, it's easier this way.'

'You're meeting someone else, then?'

'No.'

It was clean as a knife. I watched her climb on the bus, fumble in her handbag, take the fare from a small purse, open her hand to the conductor as the bus turned the corner. I watched to see if she'd look back, if she'd give any sign, but she did not. All my love and life had gone and I had to wait till it was gone to know it.

I then realized I'd left the umbrella in the pub, and started to return slowly for it. I went through the swing-door, took the umbrella from where it leaned against the red cushion, raised it and said, 'Just left this behind,' to the barman's silent inquiry, as if the performance of each small act would numb the pain.

I got to no southern sea or city that summer. The body I'd tried to escape from became my only thought. In the late evening after pub-close, I'd stop in terror at the thought of what hands were fondling her body, and would, if I had power, have made all casual sex a capital offence. On the street I'd see a coat or dress she used to wear, especially a cheap blue dress with white dots, zipped at the back, that was fashionable that summer, and with beating heart would push through the crowds till I was level with the face that wore the dress, but the face was never her face.

I often rang her, pleading, and one lunch hour she consented to see me when I said I was desperate. We walked aimlessly through streets of the lunch hour, and I'd to hold back tears as I thanked her for kindness, though when she'd given me all her evenings and body I'd hardly noticed. The same night after pub-close I went – driven by the urge that brings people back to the rooms where they once lived and no longer live – and stood out of the street lamps under the trees where so often we had stood, in the hope that some meaning of my life or love would come, but the night only hardened about the growing absurdity of a man standing under an umbrella beneath the drip from the green leaves of the trees.

Through my love it was the experience of my own future death I was passing through, for the life of the desperate equals the anxiety of death, and before time had replaced all its bandages I found relief in movement, in getting on buses and riding to the terminus; and one day at Killester I heard the conductor say to the driver as they sat downstairs through their ten-minute rest, 'Jasus, this country is going to the dogs entirely. There's a gent up there who looks normal enough who must umpteen times this last year have come out here to nowhere and back,' and as I listened I felt like a patient after a long illness when the doctors says, 'You can start getting up tomorrow,' and I gripped the black umbrella with an almost fierce determination to be as I was before, unknowingly happy under the trees, and the umbrella, in the wet evenings that are the normal weather of this city.

Peaches

I

The shark stank far as the house, above it the screech of the sea birds; it'd stink until the birds had picked the bones clean, when the skeleton would begin to break up in the sun. The man reluctantly closed the door and went back to making coffee. He liked to stare out the door to the sea over coffee in the mornings. After he made the coffee he put the pot with bread and honey and a bowl of fruit on the table in the centre of the red-tiled floor. The windows on the sea were shuttered, light coming from the two windows looking out on the mountain at the back and a small side window above the empty concrete pool without. He was about to say that breakfast was ready when he saw the woman examining the scar under her eye in the small silver-framed mirror. Her whole body stiffened with intensity as she examined it. He cursed under his breath and waited.

'It makes me look forty.' He heard the slow sobs. He lifted and replaced a spoon but knew it was useless to say anything.

'If we get the divorce I'll sue you for this,' she said with uncontrolled ferocity in a heavy foreign accent. She was small but beautifully proportioned, with straight wheaten hair that hung to her shoulders.

'It wasn't all my fault.' He lifted the spoon again.

'You were drunk.'

'I had four *cervezas*.'

'You were drunk. As you're always drunk except some hours in the mornings.'

'If you hadn't loosened that rope to put in the cheese it wouldn't have happened.'

He'd bought a fifteen-litre jar of red wine in Vera, it was cheaper there than in the local shops, and had roped it in the wooden box behind the Vespa. When he was drinking at the bar, she'd loosened the rope to put some extra cheese and crystallized almonds in the box. He hadn't noticed the loose rope round the wickerwork of the

75

jar when leaving; it had made no difference on the tar but the last mile was a rutted dirt-track. The Vespa had to be ridden on the shoulders of the road not much wider than the width of the wheels. Drowsy with the beer and the fierce heat, he drove automatically until he found the wheels losing their grip in the dust on the edge of the shoulder. When he tried to pull out to the firm centre of the shoulder the fifteen litres started to swing loose, swinging the wheels further into the loose dust.

There was all the time in the world to switch off the engine so that the wheels wouldn't spin and to tell her to hold his body as soon as he knew he was about to crash, and he remembered the happiness of the certainty that nothing he could do would avert the crash. Shielded by his body she would have been unhurt, but her face came across his shoulder to strike the driving-mirror. Above him on the road she'd cried out at the blood on his face. It was her own blood flowing from the mirror's gash below her eye.

'I'm ugly, ugly, ugly,' she cried now.

'The doctor said the scar'd heal and it doesn't make you ugly.'

'You want to kill me. Once it was Iris.' She ignored what he'd said and started to examine two thin barely visible scars down her cheek in the mirror. 'She tore me with her nails when she wanted to kill me. Both of you want to kill me.'

'All children fight.'

'Jesus,' she swore. 'You even want to take her side. You want to pretend that nothing happened. Jesus, Jesus.'

'No.' The man raised his voice, angry now. 'I know all children fight. That they're animals. And I do know I didn't want to kill you.'

'Everything I say or do you criticize. Always you take the others' side.' She was again close to crying.

'Earlier it starts in the morning and earlier,' he said about the fighting.

'Who was its cause? If we ever get a divorce . . .'

'O Jesus Christ,' the man broke in, he clasped his head between his hands, and then steps sounded on the hard red sandstone that led from the house to the dirt-track. The woman at once moved out of sight to a part of the L-shape of the room where the cooker was, whispering fiercely, 'Don't open the door yet,' and began quickly drying her face, powdering, drawing the brush frantically through her wheaten hair. He made a noise with the chair to let whoever was outside know he was coming as she whispered, 'Not yet. Do I look all right?'

'You look fine.'

The man moved with exaggerated slowness to the door. Outside in the sun-hat and flowered shirt and shorts stood Mr McGregor with an empty biscuit tin and a bunch of yellow roses.

'I thought your wife might like these,' he proffered the yellow roses, 'and that you might find this useful for bread or something.'

He was their nearest neighbour, a timber millionaire who'd built the red villa with its private beach a few hundred metres up the road for his retirement, and now lived with his two servants and roses there. Even his children wouldn't come to him on visits because of his miserliness. He got round the villages in a battered red Renault, but once a month the grey Rolls was taken out of the garage for him to drive to the bank in Murcia. Money and roses seemed to be his only passions, and out of loneliness he often came to them with roses and something like the empty biscuit tin which otherwise he'd have to throw away.

'Would you like to have some coffee?' the man asked when his wife had accepted the roses.

Over the tepid coffee they listened for an hour to the state of his garden, the cost of water, and the precariousness of the world's monetary system.

When he'd gone they examined the empty biscuit box. Huntley and Palmer figrolls it had once held, and suddenly they both started to laugh at once. The woman came into the man's arms and lifted her mouth to be kissed.

'We won't fight, will we?'

'I don't want to fight.'

'Don't worry about the eyes. We'll never have the divorce?'

'Never.'

She started to clear the dishes from the table, humming happily as she did. 'It's bad to fight. It's good to be brisk. Do you know who loves you?'

He said, 'I think you're very beautiful,' glad of a respite he knew wouldn't last for long.

II

'Why did we come here to this shocking country in the first place?' the woman accused.

'It was cheap and there was sea and sun and we thought it would be a good place to work,' he enumerated defensively.

'And you know how much work has been done?'

'Yes. None.'

'We could have stayed in hotels as cheaply as it costs to rent here. Neither of us wanted to leave Barcelona when we did. But because those phoney painter bastards had to have a taxi because of their baby you came when you did. They wanted you to come to get you to pay half of their taxi fare. When we could have travelled slowly and cheaply we had that terrible fourteen-hour drive, with the baby slobbering and crying.'

He remembered the scent of orange blossom coming through the open window, small dark shapes of the orange trees outside the path of the headlights and Norman, the painter, saying, 'Smell the orange blossom, sweetie, isn't it marvellous, isn't it marvellous to be here in Spain?'; and then turning back to yell into the darkness of the taxi, 'For Christ's sake, sweetie, can't you get him to shut up for one minute?'

'Yes. It was horrible but we were dependent on them for the language,' the man said.

'*We would have managed.*' The woman enunciated each word separately, in slow derision.

'They put us up after the crash,' the man said.

'Yes, but even you insisted on leaving, with him strutting naked round our beds with an erection, going on about the marvels of nudity and bringing those awful paintings up for us to see when we had no choice but to look at them.'

'We've finished with those people.'

'They practically had to shit all over you before you did anything.'

One day they came with their child to the house to swim in the sea and Norman had behaved as if in his own house. He'd gone upstairs after swimming and started to shower without asking. The man had asked them to leave. It had been the last straw.

'They'd practically to shit all over the house before you asked them to leave,' the woman taunted.

'Can't you shut up and give me some peace?'

'And now we can't even open doors or windows because of the shark. I don't know what brought us to this country. Why did I ever leave my own birches?' She started to cry.

'Can't you, can't you shut up!' the man said. 'And you're not going to provoke me into hitting you. That's too easy.'

An image came of blood streaming down her finger from the splinters of a wine glass he'd swept once from her hand, the look of triumph on her face as she said, 'Now we see the street angel in his royal colours – nothing but a mean, mean bully.'

'You're going to have to accept the fact of your own hatred. There's no use absolving it temporarily by provoking me to violence.'

'Bah,' she said, 'I laugh at that. I wouldn't even bother to answer that.'

III

The man swept the dead spiders and scorpions and lizards across the floor of the empty pool and shovelled them out on to the bank. The dry scorpions broke into sections but the spiders and lizards lay stiff as in life on the bank of old mortar and gravel.

The clean floor of the pool was ready for the waterman when he came. He backed up his small tanker, originally designed to carry petrol or fuel oil, to the edge of the pool. He'd saved the money to buy the tanker by working for one year in a steel works in Düsseldorf. He connected the ragged pipe to the end of the tanker, and when he turned the brass handle the water started to run into the pool with several small jets leaking out on the way. The woman came out in a blue bathrobe trimmed with white on the edges, and the three started to watch, in the simple fascination of water filling an empty pool.

'The fish, the fish it stinks.' The man pointed to the shore.

'Yes, it stinks,' the man answered.

'What did you think of Germany?'

'The roads, great roads, much speed.'

Then suddenly he stiffened, gave a sharp cry of fear, and seized the shovel by the side of the pool, pointing to a scorpion between two stones close to the wall of the house. In a panic he started to beat it with the shovel until he made paste of it against the bone-hard ground. When he'd put the shovel aside he caught his ankle in his hand, miming gestures of pain.

'Bad, bad,' he said. 'I've seen men made babies by the stings.'

'It's the only thing outside the humans that commits suicide,' the woman said.

It was a favourite subject of hers, the parallels between animal and human behaviour. It bored him.

Mention of suicide suddenly brought back the early days of their relationship in that country of snow and birch trees and white houses rising out of red granite against a frozen sea, a light of metal that made the oranges and lemons shine like lamps in the harbour market. It was before they married. He was waiting for his papers to come and they were living in one of the houses along the shore close to the middle of the city.

'It's owned by the Actors' Union for the actors when they get too old to act,' she'd explained to him.

'But how does it happen that you who are young and successful can get a room here?'

'There's not enough old ones. They have empty places.'

'But where are the old, then?'

'They've gone to the seaside.'

He at once accepted that the Actors' Union had two houses, and the elderly had a choice of a house in the city or a house by the seaside, until an evening over brandies and coffee with a friend of hers, the quiet Anselm, who was more interested in the history of rocking chairs than in his legal practice, had remarked, 'It is extraordinary that the Actors' Union give the retired a choice of a house in the city or by the sea.'

'Why?'

'She said that the reason she had a room in the old actors' house was that there were vacant rooms because some of the retired preferred to live in another house at the seaside, that they had choice.'

'No, no.' She'd overheard from the kitchen. 'No, no. I meant that they'd gone to the suicide.'

He grew aware of her hostile stare at the pool's edge. Perhaps he was neglecting the waterman. Quickly he asked him if he'd have something to drink. He wanted water. When they'd given him the drink and paid him, the waterman told them he'd to hurry away to bring two loads of water for the Canadian's roses before lunch.

IV

As soon as the tanker moved towards the dirt-track the man started to pump the water up to the tank on the roof, though he knew the woman was staring at his back with arms folded. The wooden handle of the pump had split, was held together with a rope, and was loose and awkward about the iron spike.

'I want to speak to you about something.' Her voice was cold.

'What?' he stopped.

'When I was talking to the waterman you never listened to one word.'

'I did.'

'What?'

'About the scorpion.'

'Anybody'd see you were miles away but you want to be listened to yourself. And you start to pump to avoid having to listen to anything.'

'I want to get the water up.'

'Be honest. You're either pumping water up. Or oiling the floor. Or walking on the beach. Or drunk in the rocking chair staring at the sea. Or running to the village for one thing or another.'

'Someone has to get the things.'

'Not that much. The child doesn't always have to be running messages for Mammy.' Her voice mimicked the singsong of a child's voice.

'Can't you shut up?'

'And you've done no work for more than a year now. Except run messages for Mammy.' She continued the mimicry.

'So I haven't done any work. Well, I haven't. And I want to pump the water up.'

'That's what you're running from – your work and from me. I am married to a man who can neither talk nor work.'

'You have to wait for work to come. Why don't you do the work if you're so keen on it, then?'

'I've done the translations for the theatre.'

He was about to say in irritation that translation wasn't work but drew it back; there had been enough quarrelling for one morning.

'I want to pump the water up,' he said.

'All right, pump the water up,' she said and went in. As he pumped, both hands on the loose rope, he heard the sharp precise taps of her typewriter through the creak of the pumping and the water falling in the tank from the upstairs room.

When the tank was full, the overflow spilling down on the crushed scorpion, he went towards the fig trees in the hollow between the house and mountain. He sat under the trees to save water. He picked a place between the blackened and dried turds under the trees. When his own smell started to rise above the sharksmell and the encircling flies, he heard the typewriter stop, and when he was close to the house the lavatory upstairs flushed.

A rush of anger came, a waste of water: and then he remembered his father's nagging over lights left on. 'You burn enough electricity in this house to run a power station.' He was ashamed that the instinct to save a few pence of light had become a resentment against the waste of water.

V

He climbed the stairs in the hope of making some amends. It was not an easy life with him in this place and she had followed him from her own country. He'd offered her little, he thought, the day they married: a morning waking into electric light, left on because of the bedbugs.

She had to be at rehearsals at nine. Over breakfast they arranged to meet in the bookshop beside the theatre a half-hour before the wedding. He remembered watching her stand in the sealskin cap and white lambswool coat at the bus stop until the bus came. In less than three hours they'd be married. A man is born and marries and dies, it'd be the toll of the second bell, one more to come; and there'd be no ceremonies, no ring, no gold or silver, no friends, no common culture or tongue: they'd offered each other only themselves.

It was All Souls' Day and the candles shone against the snow on the graves between the avenues of birches through the bus windows after crossing the bridge past the Alko factory.

Her hands were trembling on the magazine in the bookshop

when he arrived. 'I thought you'd taken the plane.'

'I am sorry I'm a bit late.'

'You didn't want to come?'

'We better hurry.'

The hall was like an unemployment exchange. She'd taken the script she had been working on at breakfast and made notes on the margins as they waited on the chairs.

'It's for the afternoon rehearsal,' she explained.

A couple in their early fifties, a bald man in a grey suit and a woman in pink taffeta, heavily made-up and carrying a sheaf of roses, were chatting and laughing with another couple.

'What kind of people are they?' he asked.

'Probably married so often already that the church has refused them and they have to come here.' She continued writing on the margins of the script.

When they were called she asked the two porters to act as witnesses, tipped them when they agreed, and they followed sheepishly to the doorway of the room and remained there during the ceremony neither fully in nor out. The mayor stood with the chain of his office on his breast behind a leather-topped desk.

When the mayor asked the man to put the wedding ring on her finger, they had none, and he looked on in disapproval as she took the silver ring with the green stone the sculptor killed in the car crash had given her, and the man put it on her wedding finger. It was with the same distaste that the mayor called the porters from the doorway to sign the certificate – but they were married. As he paid the fee she joked, 'The divorce will cost much more.'

They had coffee close to the harbour.

'It seems as if nothing has happened,' they said as she went back to rehearsal. He brought wine and meat and returned by bus past the glimmer of candles in the graveyard to switch on all the electric lights in the flat; two-thirty on the clock and already dusk deepening fast.

It was the night of the Arts Ball their wedding quarrel began in the depression of bands and alcohol.

'You didn't want to marry me,' she said.

'I was there, wasn't I?'

'You deliberately left your passport behind.'

'I wouldn't have gone back for it if I had.'

'You resented being married to me – it was unconscious.'

'I hate this house of bugs. We needn't ever have moved from the actors'.'

'Never have moved when they were asking me at the theatre every day if I had the sailor in their flat yet!'

It grew, until she threw the glass of whiskey, stinging his eyes, and they ran from each other in the snow, big snowflakes drifting between the trees. She went to a hotel and he back past the candles, now covered under snow, to the electric-lit room.

Was this whole day to be the shape of their lives together?

VI

The door to the roof balcony was open at the head of the stairs, and on the balcony she lay naked on the yellow bands of the collapsible deck-chair, a bundle of old press cuttings by her head. She was examining an article about herself in a woman's magazine. It had coloured pictures of her and had been written three years before.

'You are taking sun?'

'Why don't you come and take sun too?' she asked.

'I will later. You are reading about yourself?'

'It's by Eva who used to live with me. She wanted to put in that I always slept under the pillow. She thought that'd be of much interest to her readers. I didn't let her.' She was happy and laughing.

'Do you ever want to go back to the theatre?'

'No, no. I married you to get out of the theatre. It's a system of exploitation.'

'How?'

'Everybody is abused and kicked, down to the actor who is the most kicked of all. It's pure fascism.'

'You'd never get anything done if someone didn't impose his will.'

'That's what we've been taught and we must unlearn. There should be complete participation for everybody.'

'It wouldn't work.'

He turned towards the sea. A woman was riding side-saddle past on the dirt-track on a mule. She was all in black against the sea, shaded by a black umbrella she held above her head with the same hand as held the reins.

'That's nothing but capitalistic propaganda,' she said. The conversation was already boring the man.

'What would you replace them with?' he inquired, concealing his irritation.

'Machines.'

'And, say, if I didn't want to go to see machines? If I want to go to see people?'

'The machines will replace them so well as to make actors obsolete.'

'Do you know what I remember?' he said to avoid a quarrel. 'The night you came from the theatre, first night of *The Dragon*, with all the roses, and we had to search among the roses for the one bottle of champagne.'

'Do you love me as much as you did then?' she asked.

'Yes. I love you as much,' and he knew less and less what love was.

'It'd be nice if we could have birches and lakes and snow and the white white houses here as well as sun and sea.'

'It'd be nice,' he agreed.

'And no sharksmell,' she laughed.

VII

'The cabbages,' she cried. 'I didn't see to the cabbages. The day he was killed he wrote from the front for me to see to the cabbages.'

'Why did he ask you?'

'I was the farmer, I had the blonde hair, he wrote to me to look after the cabbages. I didn't see to the cabbages.'

'Why cabbages?' The man tried to rock her quiet in his arms, stroking the straight blonde hair.

'He was starting to grow cabbages, Father did, it was his plan, he wanted to spread out the earning, so as not to have to depend for all the money on the trees.'

'How was he killed?' The man realized he'd made a mistake in asking, the crying worsened, but perhaps it was better for her to cry the disturbance completely away.

'In the forest. The soldiers were nervous. He was coming back

85

from reconnoitring the Russian lines. The men were nervous. There were Russians in the forest. His Sergeant was killed too, but the two soldiers behind escaped.

'They took the coffin out from the other coffins when the lorry brought him to the farm. And I didn't see to the cabbages.'

'If it wasn't the cabbages it would be something else,' he said. 'All lives are so fragile that when they go for ever we feel as if we have betrayed them in some way.' He tried to soothe.

'I didn't see to the cabbages,' she sobbed, but more quietly, and then, 'I'm sorry to break down like this.'

'It doesn't matter. It's all right. Why don't we go for a swim?'

'Let's go for a swim.' She suddenly smiled. 'Let's go for a swim.'

Everybody got the same blows in some way or other, he thought as they changed into bathing costumes. Now in this house they were busy making miserable their passing lives, when it should be as easy to live together in some care or tenderness.

'I didn't see to the cabbages. I didn't see to the cabbages,' would not leave his head.

VIII

The bus passed them in a cloud of white dust, trussed fowl and goats and rabbits hanging out of the sides, as they walked away from the house and rotting shark. All the seats in the bus were full and men were standing. On the shore, oil and tar started to cling to their ropesoles.

'It'll be nice when the shark disappears and we can swim down from the house again,' the woman said. She'd begun to hum.

'We won't have this oil and tar.' His words seemed to hang on the air in their ineffectiveness.

They swam far out. The woman was the better swimmer, and twice she swam under the man, laughing as her yellow cap surfaced, and then they lay on their backs and let the waves roll against them, closing their eyes because of the fierceness of the light. They started touching each other until the woman said, 'It's so long since we had a fuck! Why don't we go in and have a fuck now?'

'Why not,' he said. 'We'll go in.'

They took the rope-soled sandals off the rock and walked unsure now in the knowledge of what they were about to do. Beyond the house and shark, the Canadian's grey Rolls was being polished for its monthly outing to the bank in Murcia.

In the play on the white sheet of the bed when the man went to part the lips of the woman's sex she pushed him away.

'Your fingers don't excite me. It's your penis I want. It makes me feel like being – curse it, it's another word I don't know.'

She was about to reach for the dictionary when the man said, 'No,' and drew her to him. He tried to make up what each gallon cost of the load of water that had been put in the pool that morning to postpone his coming, but he still came long before her; and then, afraid he'd go limp, held her close for her to pump him until she came with a blind word in her own language, and as he listened to her panting it seemed that their small pleasures could hardly have happened more separately if they'd each been on opposite ends of the beach with the red house of the Canadian between.

It had not seemed as hopeless as this once though there had always been trouble, and there'd been less talk of rights and positions, less talk of the fashionable psychologists in paperback on the floor by her side of the bed.

'Do you think I could go to an analyst when we get back to London?' She turned towards him from the white sheet washed at the stone trough of the fontana by old Maria's hands. He started: it was as if she'd touched too close to his thought.

'Why do you want?'

'Our relationship would get much better.'

'But how would it do you good?'

'All this summer I've got insights into myself and they'd come much quicker and clearer with an analyst.'

'You get these insights from your reading?'

'Yes. Much, much insights.'

'It'd cost a lot of money to go to an analyst.'

'I'd be brisker and do many more translations. It'd be easier for you to work too since the relationship would be much better.'

'Our relationship was good once without benefit of analysis.'

'But it was built on a false foundation,' she said fiercely and the man turned his face away towards the sea to conceal his bitterness.

'Maybe we could both go to the analyst,' she said.

If he had to go to an analyst he would return to the Catholic

Church and go to confession, which would at least be cheaper. He cursed secretly but answered, 'No, I won't go but you can go to an analyst if you think it'd do good.'

'Much, much good,' she said, 'and our lives'll be much happier. I won't spend any more times in bed depressed and crying. We'll be happy.'

'We'll be happy,' the man said.

Later, as he got the Vespa out of the garage, he heard the clean taps of her typewriter come from the upstairs room.

IX

He drank beer in the café on the square and watched El Cordobés fight in Madrid on the television as he waited for the *correo* to come up from Garrucha. When the mule passed the café with the postman and grey *correo* bags, he looked at the clock. It would take them more than half an hour to sort the mail.

He didn't pay for the beer but motioned to the barman that he'd be back at the end of the half-hour. It was a recognized habit by this time and the barman nodded back. If there was mail he'd come back to read it over a last beer at the café.

Ridges of rock were stripped on the road that ran uphill between low white houses to the post office. The mule was tethered to the black bars of the window and he'd to wait outside with the mule since the small room was crowded with black-shawled women. A muttering came from behind the closed grille where the postman and drunken postmaster were sorting the mail. When the grille was drawn noisily back the postmaster stared out at the women over spectacles and shouted, '*Extranjeros.*' The women made way for the man to go up to the grille.

'English,' the postmaster shouted, reek of garlic and absinthe on his breath. He continued loudly in a garbled imitation of English, and started to slowly count out the letters for the foreigners of the place. As he counted each letter he shouted his imitation English but he counted slowly so that the man could read the names and take any letter addressed to him; he could have taken any letter he wished, for all the postmaster would know, but there was only one letter for him, it was from London, and a letter for his wife from her old theatre. The postmaster's performance was meant to impress the women with his knowledge of English, but they winked and laughed throughout. As the man left he heard a woman shout some bawdry at the postmaster and his threats to clear the post offfice.

He went back over the stripped rock and clay to the café and waited until the beer came before opening his letter, a letter from his publisher enclosing reviews of his last book. It was never easy to read reviews, and he read through them quickly when the beer came. It was much like listening to talk about yourself from another room, and the listener cares little about the quality of the talk as long as it is praise. Always the poor reviews rankled and remained, they were probably nearer the truth in the long run. To publish was to expose oneself, naked, in an open market, and if the praise was acceptable he could hardly complain of the ridicule, since one always had the choice to stay in original obscurity.

The editor's letter was an inquiry about how the new book was coming along; in the sun of Spain it should ripen into something exciting. In the sun of Spain not a line had been written or was likely to be.

'I have known writers who failed. Who stopped writing. And they stank to themselves and to everybody else,' had once been said to him when he hadn't written for a long time.

'Why don't you stink, then?' he'd asked.

'I have no talent. I never began.'

'Couldn't I become a doctor and do a great deal more good in the world?'

'Yes, but you'd rot.' He remembered the argument had grown rancorous.

'I'll rot anyhow.'

'I know writers who failed. It's a failure worse than any other. But if it happened our friendship wouldn't change. That is separate.'

'Why should it be worse than any other?'

'I don't know. It's more personal than any other. Perhaps the egotism is so fierce to begin with.'

'It's a load of balls in my opinion.'

'Besides, you're too old to change.'

That was true. He was too old. He paid at the counter. He would fill the red plastic container at the fontana and go down to Garrucha and drink cognac until the fishing boats came in.

X

The man had two friends: Tomás who owned the café on the harbour, and José, an old sailor with whom he drank, buying almost all the drinks; and in return José insisted on helping him buy fish when the boats came in. The day José's small pension came each month was the one day he bought the drinks.

The café was open but deserted, not even Tomás's son was behind the bar, so he sat outside at the red iron table and stared out on the sea that showed no sign of the returning fishing boats. He was glad to have to delay drinking; he had too great a want of cognac to sink this day out of sight.

No one passed in the white dust of the harbour, the starved greyhounds panted with lolling tongues in the shade, and he sat for half an hour until the slow flop-flop-flop of Tomás's slippers, the heels trodden down, came from the room behind the bar.

After shaking hands Tomás yawned out towards the empty sea, and then laid his head on his palm in a gesture that he'd been sleeping.

'*Mucho calor.*' The man nodded.

'*Mucho, mucho calor.*'

Tomás clapped his hands and his son came from the back of the café. He shouted an order and lowered his short stout body, the eyes puffed from sleep, into a chair at the table. The boy brought two cognacs, a beer and coffee on a tray.

They were on the second drink when José came. He wore a black beret and white shoes and a threadbare but neat blue suit. Cognac and coffee were brought for him by the boy and he started to talk to the man in English.

'Is the *señora* not well?' he asked.

'She's well but she doesn't like to go out so much since the accident.'

'*Malo*, that accident, *malo*.' Both of them nodded. Then Tomás started to speak very rapidly to José. The man could not follow all the words. One fishing boat, a black speck, had appeared far out.

'Tomás wants to know if that President Kennedy who was shot in America was a rich man?' José turned to translate after rapid speech in Spanish.

'Very rich.'

'Richer than El Cordobés?'

'Much, much richer than El Cordobés.'

'He had someone to leave his money to?'

'He had a large family.' José translated the answers for Tomás.

There were now three boats coming home and pale flashes of gulls were visible behind the first boat. Both men nodded with satisfaction at the information that President Kennedy had a large family to leave his money to.

'Tomás says it is a very good thing that a rich man has a large family to leave his money to when he dies,' José said.

The gulls flashed in the late sun as they dived for the guts behind the boats as they came in, and when the fish boxes were landed José bought a kilo of gambas. They'd a last drink at the bar before the man left. Once he came to the dirt-track he drove very slowly, his reactions slow and stiff from the alcohol.

XI

A candle burned between the two wine glasses, and onion and parsley were already sprinkled on the sliced tomatoes in the long yellow dish on the table. She was humming at the stove, making notes on papers scattered between the cooking utensils. She moved towards him when he came in with the white string bag of gambas and the plastic container of water.

'I'm so happy,' she said. 'If one is energetic and works one doesn't want to stay in bed and cry.'

He poured the water equally into the clay jars, jars carried on women's heads in pictures of Egypt, that stood in a wooden stand beneath the stairs.

'The table and house look very beautiful,' he said.

'One can work at the same time as cook so that one isn't just a domestic animal.'

'You are doing the translations, then?'

'I was afraid of it but now I feel well and started it after you left.'

'I saw Tomás and José and got this letter for you.' He was at a loss how to respond to her happiness. He would not show her his letter or the reviews. The chances were they would disturb her too much. He knew she had a dread that her life would be lost in his, and it would break this peace.

'They want as much translation as I can do for them. They say I am the best translator they have.' She burst out of the intensity of her reading, once or twice gloating like a child.

They ate with the door closed because of the sharksmell, but they could hear the sea, and they drank white local wine with the shellfish and tomatoes and bread. She was full of plans and happy all through the meal, but after they'd eaten footsteps sounded on the path to the door, and a bicycle scraped against the wall. When he opened the door it was one of the local *guardia*. He asked for water. The man invited him in and offered him a chair. He laid his rifle against the stairs and sat at the table. They spoke in stumbling Spanish, the sea filling each silence, the drops of water sweating through the porous clay of the jars into the dish beneath the stand. As the *guardia* finished each cigarette, he ground it under his boot, twisting the heel until he'd ground it into the tiles in some misguided idea of courtesy. The last time he'd come they'd to scrape the tobacco from the tiles.

His boots were large and broken, the tops rising well above the ankles.

'Are the boots not too heavy for the heat?' the man asked after following the crushing of another cigarette butt.

'Much, much too heavy.'

'Why do you wear them, then?'

'It's regulations.'

'Do they cost much?'

'They cost very much.' He named an exorbitant price.

'Why don't you buy a cheaper, lighter pair in the shop?'

'It's not allowed. The government has given the monopoly to this man. All the *guardia* have to buy off the monopoly. They can charge what they like.'

'It's horrible,' the woman said in indignation.

'It's not fair but it is the way it is,' the man answered.

'It is the way it is,' the *guardia* said as he rose, screwing his last cigarette butt carefully into the floor and taking the gun from where it leaned against the stairs. The man saw him to the door, watched his bicycle light waver into the night, before he shut the door on the sharksmell.

'This country is horrible. It is a crime to live here,' the woman said as soon as he came back to the table.

'The people are not.'

'They are if they accept it. As the German people were with the Nazis.'

'Maybe they don't have much choice.'

'You are one of them. And you give me no support. You let that man come in and ruin the evening. Don't you know that there are some people who cannot live if they have to think about the possibility of someone always being about to enter their room? I am one of these. And you give me no protection.' She was sobbing as she went towards the stairs.

The man watched her go. He said or did nothing but refill his wine glass to the brim from the Soberano bottle.

XII

'Will you come with me to Garrucha?' he asked.

'There's no solutions going places,' she retorted. 'You buy me five postcards that you say I might like to send to my friends or you ask me to come to Garrucha and you think things are as good as they can be. Why don't you go back to yourself? Do you know that remorse originally meant going back to oneself before the word was poisoned by the popes?'

'I don't believe there are solutions.'

'There are solutions if one tries hard enough. It's the same old negativism you've been drilled to accept.'

'It'd be nice for me if you came to Garrucha.' He wanted to avoid argument at any cost. 'I thought it'd be nice to sit at the café and watch the sea and wait for the boats to come in to buy fish.'

'You want me to come with you, then?'

'I do.'

'That's different.' She was suddenly lit with pleasure. 'I don't want to go to Garrucha but I want you to want me to go to Garrucha. You'll wait for me to get ready?'

She took a half-hour to change into yellow sandals and a dress of dark blue denim that buttoned down the front and had a pocket over each breast. She asked many times as she changed if the make-up concealed the scar below the eye, but she was happy on the Vespa and sang a marching song in her own language.

José sat at the red table outside the café and was awkward in the

The Collected Stories

woman's presence until the talk came round to the Civil War.
'Yes. We shot the two priests at Garrucha. We took them out and
shot them against the wall of the church. And we'd shoot them
again if we got the chance,' José confided.
'Good, good.' The woman nodded vigorously.
'They say the communists lost the war,' José's excitement
brought Tomás out of the café. 'The communists did not lose the
war. The people of Spain lost the war. The fascists won it.'
José translated what he'd said for Tomás who nodded in his lazy
way.
'Tomás is communist too but he has to be careful since he has a
café,' José explained.
'I'm communist as well.' The woman pulled vigorously at her
cigarette.
'How did you escape, José?' the man asked. 'When it ended?'
'I got to Valencia, travelling at night, and got on a boat there.'
'Why don't the Spanish do something, overthrow that fascist
government?' the woman asked in nervous indignation. José
spread his hands.
'The people of Spain are tired,' he said.
A jeep came along the harbour. The magistrate and his glandular
son and two farmhands were in the jeep. When the magistrate saw
the woman he stopped and got out.
'You are the foreigners in Casa Smith.' He introduced himself.
'I've been looking for you. I've heard about you.'
Tomás melted back into the café, and José went stiff on the chair.
'I know English. I like foreigners. I hate Spanish scum,' the
magistrate said. He was grey and lean, a glare in the eyes that sees
nothing but his own obsessions.
'You will have a drink with me? Yes?' He waved and without
waiting for answer he ordered three cognacs, shouting the order
into the bar. Tomás's son came with the three cognacs on a tray.
'I like foreigners. I hate Spanish scum.' The magistrate drank.
'These are my friends,' the man said, and was about to move his
cognac towards José when the old sailor's hand forbade it. José sat
in petrified dignity on the chair.
'You do not know enough about Spain,' the magistrate shouted.
'Drink.'
The man looked at José who made no movement and when the

magistrate shouted again, 'Drink,' they both drank in bewilderment. 'We drink and now we go to see my peaches. I give you the first and finest peaches of the summer.'

'I have the Vespa,' the man said.

'There's plenty of place.' He gestured towards the jeep.

'I have to be back for the boats.'

'The jeep will take you back for the boats. Come. I give you the first and finest peaches of the summer.'

XIII

A large spraying machine on metal wheels stood inside the gate of the peach orchard, and the rows of trees ran farther than the eye could follow, the loose red earth of the irrigation channels between the rows.

'Thousands of trees.' The magistrate waved an arm, and when he shouted at the two workmen they ran and turned several water taps on. Water is magic in the south of Spain. As it gushed into the channels, the red clay drinking it as fast as it ran, the magistrate's frenzy increased. The glandular son sat bored and overcome in the jeep.

'I have water for my trees,' he shouted as he waved an arm towards the white moorish village that hung on the side of the mountain, 'and these scum do not have water for their houses,' he laughed in crazy triumph. 'You like my peach trees?'

'They are very fine,' the man said.

'All over the world they go. To London. To Berlin. To New York. They go from Valencia,' he shouted, his eyes on the woman's body under the blue denim dress.

'Come. I'll give you first peaches.'

They followed him, mesmerized, to a tree of ripening peaches, the rose blushes on the yellow in the green sheltering leaves, and he drew down a branch and started to tear free the ripe peaches. Before they could move – two, three, four, five, six – he was ramming the peaches into the breast pockets of the blue dress.

'I give you the first peaches of the summer,' he kept saying, and at seven, eight, when the fruit started to crush, the juice turning the denim dark as it ran down inside the dress, the man stepped between them.

95

'It's enough. I'll take any more you want,' and the magistrate's eyes reared like a mad dog at a gate and then drew back.

'You can have plenty more peaches. Any time you want. All summer.'

'Thank you,' the man said.

'I have even more water for my house than I have for the trees,' he went on, a white froth on his lips. 'I have a swimming pool full of water at my house. You come and see my pool full of water?'

'No. We have to get back for the boats.'

'But tomorrow, Sunday, you come to my pool and swim.' He made the breast-stroke movement. 'We can swim naked in my pool. No one can see like at the sea, and after we eat peaches at a table by the pool's edge and drink white wine, wine of my grapes.'

The man looked towards the woman in desperation but she stood dazed with shock or bewilderment. He didn't know how to get out of this, and he'd heard that the magistrate was dangerous if crossed.

'I come at twelve in the jeep and pick you up.'

'No,' the man said, desperate for time. 'We'll come later on the Vespa.'

'It's easier if I pick you up.'

'No. I have to work first. We'll come about two on the Vespa.'

'At two we'll swim and eat the peaches and drink white wine.'

'Yes. We want to get back.'

'I'll drive you back to the boats.'

The man saw that the juice stains were wider now on the blue denim as they got into the jeep.

At the café, where José still sat motionless as any lizard, the magistrate said as he stopped the jeep, 'You soon don't see those scum any more.'

'They are my friends,' the man interrupted.

'It is because you don't know. Soon you know you have better friends. Tomorrow we swim and eat peaches and drink wine,' he said, his eyes openly fondling the woman's body.

'At two,' the man said.

XIV

José was stiff with dignity at the red café table.

'You have been my friend, but if I see you again with that bastard

. . . Kaput.' He made a chopping stroke with his hand as if breaking the back of a rabbit's neck.

'It seemed to all happen as if I had no choice.'

'This time yes but not the next time.'

The woman, who had remained more blank than silent, sobbed and turned. 'You see what he did, José?'

'He put the peaches in your pocket?' José looked anxiously at the man; he did not want to get involved.

When the man moved to take the peaches from the breast pockets she stopped him. 'I am able to take them out myself.'

She took them out one by one. The skins were broken and the flesh crushed. She set them on the table, where three rolled to the outer rim.

'You don't want his peaches.' José quietly swept the peaches from the table and they tumbled out into the dust of the roadway.

'No, no,' the woman affirmed angrily. 'I don't.'

She no longer sobbed but her face was firm against the man, who was more in despair than shame.

The flop-flop of Tomás's slippers came down the café to the red tables outside. When he heard the story of the orchard, José translated what he said.

'He said he wouldn't serve that bastard. He sent his son out with the cognacs'; and added, 'He has to be careful though. He has a café.'

'Why is he so hated?' the man asked.

'His family were always fascists. We shot his two brothers, and when the fascists won he went into the Murcia jail with a bundle of birches. And he went from cell to cell till he broke every birch he had on the prisoners' backs. My brother was a prisoner there but not even a fascist pig beats shackled prisoners.' José was clinched in hatred even when he broke off to translate for Tomás who nodded that it was true.

When the woman asked Tomás if she could use his back room to wash the peach juice from her dress he came with her to show her where it was, and while they were away José leaned towards the man, 'If you are not careful you will lose wife. That fascist pig doesn't want to give you peaches. He wants your wife. He wants to fuck your wife.'

'I know,' the man said. 'Will you have a drink?'

'I'll have a cognac.'

The boy came with the cognacs and as the man paid he flinched at the look he thought he saw on the boy's face. The fishing boats with their flotilla of gulls flashing in the late sun were closing on the harbour. When the woman came from the back room her hair was combed so that it shone gold and her face was made-up.

'You want me to come and get some fish for you?' José asked.

'No. Not this evening,' the man said. 'I think we should go.'

'I am ready,' the woman said coldly.

As they turned away from the harbour the small figure of José got up from the table and made his way out of habit, the black beret at its usual angle, towards the incoming boats, as the greyhounds, their legs wavering under the cages of their ribs, started to come out of their porches to search for garbage in the cool.

XV

They rode in silence on the tar but when they came to the dirt-track the woman said, 'Please stop.' She got off the pillion seat. 'I'm walking to the house. If I have to look for another husband I don't want any more scars on my face,' and she looked hard and cold and tense, the profile lifted. The man drove ahead without speaking. The shark stank less in the cool, the bones wore little flesh, but he'd not be here, he thought, to see them bleach and break up in the sun. The light was good enough for him to see the flash of the lizards on the path move from a point of complete stillness to the next, out of way of the Vespa.

He sat in the rocking chair with the door open waiting for her to come up the path. Her mood had not changed.

'I'd like to leave tomorrow,' he said when she put down the crocheted woollen bag with the silver clasp and chain. He counted five drops of water from the clay jars drip into the bowls before she said, 'Where to?' in a tense voice.

'To London. You said you wanted to go back to London.'

'Running is no solution. We've always been moving. And what'll you do about your white wine and peaches?'

'We won't be here. It is why I played for two o'clock.'

'Why didn't you do something when he started to push in the

98

peaches?' she said fiercely, and then the first dry sob came between the slow drips of water.

'If I hit him and wound up in a Spanish jail it'd do us all a lot of good,' he said.

'You always have some excuse. You never give me any support. You know how awful it is to be married to a weak man. If I was married to a strong man like my father it would be different.'

'It would be some other way but you'd be the same.'

'I'd have support then. And what'll we do after London?' she stopped crying to ask, sudden demanding aggression in the voice.

'We can decide that when we get there.'

'It may be decided for you this time,' she threatened.

'Well, then it'll be decided for me,' he said.

With an explosive word he couldn't catch she climbed the stairs. He heard her turning on the bed as he got the suitcases out of the garage.

He hurriedly and raggedly got them out. When he'd the gas lamp lit and was looking about for what to put first in the suitcases open on the floor, he heard her loudly at the closet as if she'd started to take out her dresses.

Later, when the man went upstairs to the room, he found she'd taken all her clothes out of the wardrobe and had arranged them on the bed ready for packing, and she was muttering, 'Yes. It was no more than I deserved. I didn't see to the cabbages.'

Her face was hard and tense and she was not crying.

The Recruiting Officer

Two cars outside the low concrete wall of Arigna School, small and blue-slated between the coal mountains; rust of iron on the rocks of the trout stream that ran past the playground; the chant of children coming through the open windows into the rain-cleaned air: it was this lured me back into the schoolroom of this day – to watch my manager, Canon Reilly, thrash the boy Walshe; to wait for the Recruiting Officer to come – but a deeper reason than the quiet picture of the school between mountains in bringing me back, can only be finally placed on something deep in my own nature, a total paralysis of the will, and a feeling that any one thing in this life is almost as worthwhile doing as any other.

I had got out of the Christian Brothers, I no longer wore the black clothes and white half-collar, and was no longer surrounded by the rules of the order in its monastery; but then after the first freedom I was afraid, it was that I was alone.

I had come to visit one of my married sisters, when I saw the quiet school. I said I too would live out my life in the obscurity of these small places; if I was lucky I'd find a young girl. To grow old with her among a people seemed ambition enough, there might even be children and fields and garden.

I got a school immediately, without trouble. The newly trained teachers wanted places in the university towns, not in these back-waters.

Now I am growing old in the school where I began. I have not married. I lodge in a pub in Carrick-on-Shannon. I travel in and out the seven miles on a bike to escape the pupils and their parents once the school is shut, to escape from always having to play an expected role. It is rumoured that I drink too much.

With mostly indifference I stand at the window and watch Canon Reilly shake a confession out of the boy Walshe, much as a dog shakes life out of a rat; and having nothing to do but watch I think of the sea. We went to the sea in summer, a black straggle in front

100

of Novicemaster O'Grady, in threes, less risk of buggery in threes than pairs, the boards of the bridge across to the Bull hollow under the tread of our black sandals, and below us the tide washing against the timber posts. Far out on the Wall we stripped, guarding our eyes on the rocks facing south across the bay to the Pidgeon House, and when O'Grady blew the whistle we made signs of the cross on ourselves with the salt water and jumped in. He blew it again when it was time for us to get out. We towelled and dressed on the rocks, guarding our eyes, glad no sand could get between our toes, and in threes trooped home ahead of O'Grady and past the wired-down idiotic palm trees along the front.

The bell for night prayers went at nine-thirty, the two rows of pews stretching to the altar, a row along each wall and the bare lino-covered space between empty of all furniture, and we knelt in the long rows in order of our rank, the higher the rank the closer to the altar. On Friday nights we knelt in the empty space between the pews and said: My very dear Brothers, I accuse myself of all the faults I have committed since my last accusation, I broke the rule of silence twice, three times I failed to guard my eyes. After a certain rank and age the guarding of the eyes wasn't mentioned, you were supposed to be past all that by then, but I never reached that stage. I got myself booted out before I became impervious to a low view of passing girls, especially on windy days.

The sea and the bell, nothing seems ever ended, it is such non-senses I'd like written on my gravestone in the hope they'd sow confusion.

'You admit it now after you saw you couldn't brazen your way out of it,' Reilly shouts at the boy, holding him by the arm in the empty space between the table and the long benches where the classes sit in rows.

'Now. Out with what you spent the money on.'

'Lemonade,' the low answer comes, the white-faced boy starting to blubber.

'Lemonade, yes, lemonade, that's how you let the cat out of the bag. The Walshes don't have shillings to squander in the shops on lemonade every day of the week.'

Still gripping the boy by the arm he turns to the rows of faces in the benches.

'What sins did Walshe commit – mind I say *sins*, not one sin – but I don't know how to call it – this foul act?'

I watch the hands shoot up with more attention than I'd given to the dreary inquisition of the boy. I was under examination now.

'The sin of stealing, Canon.'

'Good, but mind I said sins. It is most important in an examination of conscience before confession to know all the sins of your soul. One foul act can entail several sins.'

'Lies, Canon.'

'Good, but I'm looking for the most grievous sin of all.'

He turned from the blank faces to look at me: why do they not know?

'Where was the poorbox when it was broken open?' I ask, having to force the question out. Even after the years of inspectors I've never got used to teaching in another's presence, the humiliation and the sense of emptiness in turning oneself into a performing robot in a semblance of teaching.

'In the church, sir.'

'An offence against a holy person, place or thing – what is that sin called?'

'Sacrilege.' The hands at once go up.

'Good, but if you know something properly you shouldn't need all that spoonfeeding.' The implied criticism of me he addresses to the children.

'Stealing, lies, and blackest of all – sacrilege.' He turns again to the boy in his grip.

'If I hand you over to the guards do you know where that will lead, Walshe? To the reformatory. Would you like to go to the reformatory, Walshe?'

'No, Canon.'

'You have two choices. You can either take your medicine from me here in front of the class or you can come to the barracks. Which'll you take?'

'You, Canon.' He tries to appease with an appearance of total abjection and misery.

'It's going to be no picnic. You'll have to be taught once and for all in your life that the church of God is sacred.' He raises his voice close to declamation, momentarily releases his grip on the arm, takes a length of electric wire from his pocket. The boy whimpers quietly as the priest folds it in two before taking a firm grip on the arm again.

'It's going to hurt, Walshe. But if you're ever again tempted to steal from the church you'll have something to remember!'

In a half-circle the beating moves, the boy trying to sink to the floor to escape the whistle and thud of the wire wrapping round his bare legs but held up by the arm, the boy's screaming and the heavy breathing of the priest filling the silence of the faces watching from the long benches in frightened fascination. When he finally lets go of the arm the boy sinks in a heap on the floor, the moaning changing to an hysterical sobbing.

'Get up and go to your place and I hope that's the last lesson you'll have to be ever taught.' He puts the length of wire back in his pocket and takes out a blue cloth to wipe his forehead.

The boy cowers as he rises, arms automatically protecting his torn legs, moves in a beaten crawl to his place, plunges his face in rage and shame into the folds of his arms and continues sobbing hysterically.

'Open your geographies and get on with your study of the Shannon,' I say as the heads turn towards Walshe. There's the flap of the books being opened. They find the page, stealing a quick furtive look towards the boy as they bend their heads. In the sobbing silence the clock ticks.

'An example had to be made to nip that blackguardism in the bud.' He turns to me at the window.

'I suppose.'

'How do you mean *suppose?*' The eyes are dangerous.

'I suppose it was necessary to do.'

'It *was* necessary,' he emphasizes, and after a pause, 'What I'd like to see is religious instruction to counteract such influences after Second Mass every Sunday. Mr McMurrough always took it.'

'It's too far for me to come from the town to take.'

'I can't see any justification for you living in the town. I can't see why you can't live in the parish. The Miss Bambricks at the post office have mentioned to me that they'd be glad to put you up.'

The Miss Bambricks were two church-mad old maids who grew flowers for the altar and laundered the linen.

Old McMurrough, whom I had replaced and who now lay in the Sligo madhouse reciting poetry and church doctrine, had taken catechism in the church each Sunday, while the Canon waited at the gate to bear any truant who tried to escape with the main congregation back in triumph by the ear to the class in the sidechapel.

'I am happy where I am,' I say.

'And there are many in the parish who think a public house in town is no lodgings for a person who has charge of youth.'

'I conduct myself there.'

'I'd sincerely hope so, but, if I may say so, it's not very co-operative.'

'I am sorry but I do not want to change,' I answer doggedly. With bent heads the class follows each word with furtive attention, but he changes in frustration at last, 'The Christian Brother will come after lunch today.'

'I'll take the other children outside, then, while he speaks to the boys. Luckily, the day is fine.'

'They're getting it very tough to get vocations. Even tougher still to keep those they do get. They're betwixt and between, neither priests nor laymen,' he volunteers but I don't want discussion.

'They may be lucky.'

'The backward rural areas are their great standby. Even if they don't stay the course they'll get an education which they'd not get otherwise.'

'That's how I got mine.'

The hurt from my own mouth was not as great if it had come from his.

'Well, it was some use, then.'

'Yes. It was some use.'

I watch him on his way. At the door he shouts a last warning to the sniffling Walshe, 'I hope that'll be one lesson your life will never forget and you can count yourself lucky that there was no guards on the job.'

There'd be no repercussions from the beating except Walshe'd probably get beaten again when the news travelled home, and, in a few days, if asked who'd scored his legs, he'd answer that he fell in briars.

I watch the black suit shiny from car leather climb the last steps to the road gate, pausing once to inspect a crack in the concrete, and I turned to wipe the blackboard, afraid of my own hatred.

'Now, I'll see what you've learned about the Shannon.'

Papers rustle in the benches, there's a quick expectant buzz.

Outside, the three stone walls of the playground run down to the lake, the centre wall broken by the concrete lavatory, above it the rapid sparkle of pinpoint flashes of sunlight on the wings of the blackdust swarm of flies; and on the windowsill in a jam jar a fistful of primroses some child has gathered from the May banks. In the stream of sunlight across the blackboard the chalkdust floats, millions of white grains, breathed in and out all day, found at night in the turnups of trousers, all the aridity of this empty trade.

'You, Murphy, tell me where the Shannon rises?'

A blank face answers in a pretence of puzzled concentration, and why should he know, his father's fields and cattle will see him through.

'Please, sir.'

The room is full of hands.

'Tell Murphy where the Shannon rises, Handley.' A policeman's son who'll have to put his trust in his average wits.

'Shannon Pot, sir, in the Cuilceach Mountains.'

'Can you tell the class now, Murphy, where it rises?'

'Shannon Pot, sir, in the Cuilceach Mountains.' A look of triumph shows on his well-fed face as he haltingly repeats it.

'Where does it flow, Mary?'

'Southwards into Lough Allen close to the town of Drumshambo,' the quick answer comes.

'What factory have they there?'

'Breffni Blossom jams.'

'Anybody's father send apples there?'

Three hands.

'Prior? Tell about the sending of the apples.'

'We pick them, sir. Put them in a heap, same as potatoes, but on the ground we cover them with straw.'

'Why do you cover them with straw?'

'Frost, sir.'

A low knock comes on the door that leads to the infant classroom, and my one assistant, Mrs Maguire, appears. She is near retirement: the slack flesh fills the ample spaces of the loose black dress, but the face in contrast is curiously hard, as if all the years of wrestling with children had hardened it into an intransigent assurance.

'When Mrs Maguire says something Mrs Maguire means what

she says.' The third-person reference punctuates everything she says. Now a look of anxious concern shows in the unblinking eyes.

'What happened with the Canon?'

'He thrashed Walshe for breaking into one of the poorboxes.'

I didn't want her to stay, though I too had often used the glow of fabricated concern to hurry or escape the slow minutes of the school day.

'Terrible. Awful.' She echoes a dull safety, hers and mine.

'We'll talk about it at lunch, then.'

'The world, the world,' she ponders as she withdraws to her own room.

I look at the clock, the crawl of the minutes, never the happiness of imagining it two o'clock and looking up and finding it half past three.

'Will you be an absorbed teacher? Will your work be like a game? Or will you be a clockwatcher?' Jordan, the Professor of Education, asked, more years ago than I care to remember, after a lecture. It was his custom to select one student to walk with him through the corridor, gleaming with wax and the white marble busts of saints and philosophers on their pedestals along the walls.

'I hope I'll be absorbed, sir.'

'I hope so too for your sake. I can imagine few worse hells than a teacher who is a clockwatcher, driven to distraction by the children, while the day hangs about him like lead.'

I could answer him now. I was a clockwatcher. The day hung mostly like lead, each morning a dislocation of your life in order to entice or bend the children's opposing wills to yours, and the day a concentration on this hollow grapple. It seems to be as good as anything else and easier to stay than move.

'We'll leave the apples for a time and go on with the Shannon.'

The class drags on until the iron gate on the road sounds. A woman comes down the concrete steps.

A mother coming to complain, I think, and instinctively start to marshal the reassuring clichés. 'The child is sensitive and when it loses that sensitivity will surprise us all. To force the child now can only cause damage. You have nothing to worry about.'

'That was my trouble too at that age. I was too sensitive. I was never understood,' she'd reply.

'Thank you for coming to see me.'

'I feel less worried now.'

In the beginning everybody was sensitive and never understood, but hides hardened.

This time, no mother, a Miss Martin: she lived with her brother across the empty waste of wheat-coloured sedge and stunted birch of the Gloria Bog. Her brother made toys from used matchsticks in the winter nights.

'I wonder if I could take young Horan from his lessons for a few minutes, sir. It's the ringworm.'

'Luke, see Miss Martin in the porch.' The boy goes quietly out to the porch, already charmingly stolid in the acceptance of his power, Luke, magical fifth in a line of male children unbroken by girls; and while he wailed under the water of his baptism at the stone font in Cootehall church a worm was placed in his hand – either the priest didn't see or was content to ignore it – but the Horans rejoiced, their fifth infant boy would grow up with the power of healing ringworm.

On Tuesdays and on Fridays, days of the sorrowful mysteries, he touched the sores thrice in the name of the Father and Son and Holy Ghost, power of magic and religion killing the slow worm patiently circling.

'Did you wash your hands, Luke?'

'Yes, sir. I used the soap.'

'Show them to me.'

'All right. You can get on with your work.'

The last to come before lunch was the tinker, with pony and cart, the brass shining on the harness, to clean out the lavatory, and as I give him the key we make polite professional remarks about the flies and heat.

'Ah, but not to worry, sir, I'll bury it deep.' He touches his cap.

Soon, soon, they'll come and flush him and me into the twentieth century, whatever the good that will do, and I grow ashamed of the violence of the thought, and, as if to atone, over lunch, give Mrs Maguire a quiet account of the beating young Walshe received for rifling the poorbox.

After lunch he comes, dressed all in black, with a black briefcase, the half-collar of the Christian Brother on the throat instead of the priest's full collar, a big white-haired man, who seemed more made to follow ploughing horses than to stand in classrooms. The large hand lifts the briefcase on the table.

'My name is Brother Mahon and Canon Reilly kindly gave me permission to speak to the senior boys about a vocation to the Irish Christian Brothers.' I wonder if he knows that I too had been once as he is now, if he looks at me as a rotten apple in the barrel; but if he does he says nothing, all glory to the power of the Lie or Silence that makes people easy in the void, all on our arses except the helping hand they give us on our way.

'I told Canon Reilly I'd take the other children out to the playground while you spoke.'

'Lucky to have such a fine manager as the Canon, takes a great interest in schools.'

'Couldn't ask for a better manager,' I answer. The brick supports the brick above it. I'm a rogue and you're another. 'I'll just take them outside now.'

'All except the boys of the sixth class take your English book and follow me outside,' and again, because I feel watched, the voice is not my own, a ventriloquist's dummy that might at any minute fall apart.

The Brother motions the scattered boys closer to the table, 'It'll only be just a man to man chat,' as I take the others out, to sit against the white wall of the school in the sun, facing the lake, where the tinker is putting the green sods back above the buried shit, the flies thick above the cart and grazing pony.

Through the open window the low voice drifts out into the silence of the children against the wall in the sun, and I smile as I listen. If one could only wait long enough everything would be repeated. I wonder who'll rise to the gleaming spoon and find the sharpened hooks as I did once.

'I want you to imagine a very different lake shore to your own little lake below your school.'

'Hot sands.' His words drift out. 'Palm trees, glittering sea, tired after fishing all the night and washing their nets. A tall dark man comes through the palms down to the water.'

'We have laboured all the night and have taken nothing, the fishermen answer. The two boats were so full of fish that they began to sink. They fall on their knees on the sand, and the tall man, for it was Jesus, lifted them up and said to them follow me. From henceforth you will catch men.

'In this schoolroom two thousand years later I bring you the same message. Follow me and catch men. Follow me into the Irish Christian Brothers, where as teachers you will lead the little children He so loved to Christ.

'For death comes as a thief in the night, the longest life is but a day, and when you go before the Judgement Seat can you without trembling say to Jesus I refused the call even the tired fishermen answered, and what if He refuses you as you refused Him?'

He sends them out into the porch, and brings them back one by one to interview them alone, while the tinker hands me back the key. 'I've buried it deep, sir. There'll be no flies,' and the rise and fall of voices comes from Mrs Maguire's infant prison house, *Eena, meena, mina moo, capall, asal agus bo.*

Name, age, your father's farm? he asks, and more to silence my own memory than the low chatter of the children I force, 'Come on now, get on with your reading,' but after they grow silent, to covertly read my real mood, the chatter grows loud again.

'You have listened to all that I've said?' I'd been asked once too.

'Yes, Brother,' I'd answered.

'Do you think you could spend your life as a Christian Brother?'

'I'm not sure, Brother.'

'Do you think your parents would have any objection?'

'I don't know, Brother.'

'What do you say we go and have a little talk with them after I've seen the rest of the boys?'

It was finished then, my mother's face had lighted when he drove me home. 'It'd be an honour to have a Christian Brother in the family.' 'He'll get a free education too, the best there is'; and that August I was in the train with the single ticket, fear of the unknown rooms and people. My brother inherited the bare acres in my place, and married, and with the same strength as she had driven me away he put her in a back room with the old furniture of her marriage while his new wife reigned amid the new furniture of the best rooms. Now each summer I take her to her usual small hotel at the sea, and I walk by her side on the sand saying, 'Yes and yes and yes' to her complaints about my brother and his wife, until she tires herself into relief and changes, 'Do you think should I go to the baths after lunch?' 'Go to the baths, it'll do your arthritis good.'

'I think I'll go, then.'

I want to ask her why she wanted the acres for my brother, why she pushed me away, but I don't ask. I walk by her side on the sand and echo her life with 'Yes and yes and yes,' for it is all a wheel.

A light tap comes on the classroom window, a gesture of spread hands that he is finished, and I take the children in. Two of the boys have been set apart, with their school-bags.

'I'm driving John and Jim to their houses. We'll talk over everything with their parents.'

'I hope it'll be all right.'

'We'll see that everything is made clear. Thank you for your help.'

After the shaking of hands I turn to the board but I do not want to teach.

'Open your English books and copy page forty-one in your best handwriting.'

I stand at the window while the nibs scrape. Certainly nothing I've ever done resembles so closely the shape of my life as my leaving of the Holy Brothers. Having neither the resolution to stay on nor the courage to leave, the year before Final Vows I took to bed and refused to get up.

'The doctor says you're in perfect health. That there's nothing the matter with you,' old Cogger, the boss, had tried to reason. 'So why can't you get up when we are even shortstaffed in the school?'

'I can't get up.'

'What's wrong with you that you can't get up?'

'Nothing.'

'If you don't get up I have no option but to report you to General Headquarters.'

I did not get up, he had no option, and the result was an order for my dismissal, but as quietly as possible so as not to scandalize my brothers in JC or the good people of the town. Old Cogger showed me the letter. I was to get a suit of clothes, underwear, railway ticket and one pound. It revived me immediately. I told him the underwear I had would do and he raised the one pound to five.

The next hurdle was how to get my fit in clothes in a small town without causing scandal. Old Cogger dithered till the day before I had to leave, but at nightfall brought home two likely fits. I picked one, and packed it, and off we set by bus for Limerick, to all appearances two Christian Brothers going on some ordinary business, but old Cogger would come back alone. We did not speak on the way.

Behind a locked door and drawn curtains I changed in the guest room of the house in Limerick. I've wondered what happened to the black uniform I left behind, whether they gave it to another CB or burned it as they burn the clothes of the dead. Cogger showed me to the door as I left for the train but I can't remember if he wished me luck or shook hands or just shut the door on my back. I had a hat too. Yes a brown hat and a blue suit, but I didn't realize how bloody awful they looked until I met my sisters on O'Connell Bridge. They coloured with shame. Afraid to be seen walking with me they rushed me into a taxi and didn't speak until they had me safely inside the front door of the flat, when one doubled up on the sofa unable to stop laughing, and the other swore at me, 'In the name of Jasus what possessed the Christians to sail you out into the world in a getup the like of that or you to appear in it?' Though what I remember most was the shock of *sir* when the waiter said 'Thank you, sir,' as I paid him for the cup of tea I had on the train.

Even if the memories are bitter they still quicken the passing of time. It is the sly coughing of the children that tells me the hands have passed three.

'All right. Put your books away and stand up.'

In a fury the books are put away and they are waiting for me on their feet.

'Bless yourselves.'

They bless themselves and chant their gratitude for the day.

'Don't rush the door, it's just as quick to go quietly.'

I hear their whoops of joy go down the road, and I linger over the locking up. I am always happy at this hour. It's as if the chains of the day were worth wearing to feel them drop away. I feel born again as I start to pedal towards the town. How, how, though, can a man be born again when he is old? Can he enter a second time his mother's bag of tricks? I laugh at last.

Was it not said by *Water* and the *Holy Spirit*?

Several infusions of whiskey at the Bridge Bar, contemplation of the Shannon through its windows: it rises in the Shannon Pot, it flows to the sea, there are stranger pike along its banks than in its waters, will keep this breath alive until the morning's dislocation.

The Beginning of an Idea

The word Oysters was chalked on the wagon that carried Chekhov's body to Moscow for burial. The coffin was carried in the oyster wagon because of the fierce heat of early July.

Those were the first sentences in Eva Lindberg's loose notes, written in a large childish hand, and she started reading them at the table again as she waited for Arvo Meri to come to the small flat. The same pair of sentences was repeated throughout the notes in a way which suggested that she leaned on them for inspiration. *The word Oysters was chalked on the wagon that carried Chekhov's body to Moscow for burial. The coffin was carried in the oyster wagon because of the fierce heat of early July.* There was also among the notes a description of Chekhov's story called 'Oysters'.

The father and son were on the streets of Moscow in that rainy autumn evening. They were both starving. The father had failed to find work after trudging about Moscow for five months, and he was trying to muster up enough courage to beg for food. He had drawn the tops of a pair of old boots round his calves so that people wouldn't notice that his feet were bare under the galoshes. Above father and son was a blue signboard with the word *Restaurant* and on a white placard on the wall was written the word *Oysters*. The boy had been alive for eight years and three months and had never come across the word oysters before.

'What does oysters mean, Father?'

The father had touched a passerby on the sleeve, but not being able to bring himself to beg he was overcome with confusion and stammered, 'Sorry.' Then he swayed back against the wall. He did not hear the boy's voice.

'What does oysters mean, Father?' the child repeated.

'It's an animal . . . it lives in the sea,' the father managed.

The boy imagined something between a fish and a crab, delicious made into a hot fish soup, flavoured with pepper and laurel, or with crayfish sauce and served cold with horseradish. Brought from the market, quickly cleaned, quickly thrown into the pot, quick-quick-quick, everyone was starving. A smell of steaming fish and crayfish soup came from the kitchen. The boy started to work his jaws, oysters, blessed oysters, chewing and slugging them down. Overcome by this feeling of bliss he grabbed at his father's elbow to stop himself from falling, leaned against the wet summer overcoat. His father was shivering with the cold.

'Are oysters a Lenten food, Father?'

'They are eaten alive . . . they come in shells, like tortoises but . . in two halves.'

'They sound horrible, Father.' The boy shivered.

A frog sat in a shell, staring out with great glittering eyes, its yellow throat moving – that was an oyster. It sat in a shell with claws, eyes that glittered like glass, slimy skin; the children hid under the table, while the cook lifted it by its claw, put it on a plate, and gave it to the grown-ups. It squealed and bit at their lips as they ate it alive – claws, eyes, teeth, skin and all. The boy's jaws still continued to move, up and down; the thing was disgusting but he managed to swallow it, swallowed another one, and then another, hurriedly, fearful of getting their taste. He ate everything in sight, his father's galoshes, the white placard, the table napkin, the plate. The eyes of the oysters glittered but he wanted to eat. Nothing but eating would drive this fever away.

'Oysters. Give me some oysters,' he cried, and stretched out his hands.

'Please help us, sir. I am ashamed to ask but I can't stand it any more,' he heard his father's voice.

'Oysters,' the boy cried.

'Do you mean to say you eat oysters? As small a fellow as you eats oysters?' He heard laughter close. A pair of enormous men in fur coats were standing over him. They were looking into his face and laughing. 'Are you sure it's oysters you want? This is too rich. Are you sure you know how to eat them?' Strong hands drew him into the lighted restaurant. He was sat at a table. A crowd gathered round. He ate something slimy, it tasted of sea water and mould. He kept his eyes shut. If he opened them he'd see the glittering eyes and claws and teeth. And then he ate something hard.

'Good Lord. He's eating the bloody shells! Here, waiter!'

The next thing he remembered was lying in bed with a terrible thirst, he could not sleep with heartburn, and there was a strange taste in his parched mouth. His father was walking up and down the small room and waving his arms about.

'I must have caught cold. My head is splitting. Maybe it's because I've eaten nothing today. Those men must have spent ten roubles on the oysters today and I stood there and did nothing. Why hadn't I the sense to go up to them and ask them, ask them to lend me something? They would have given me something.'

Towards evening the child fell asleep and dreamt of a frog sitting in a shell, moving its eyes. At noon he was woken by thirst and looked for his father. His father was still pacing up and down and waving his arms around.

The word Oysters was chalked on the wagon that carried Chekhov's body to Moscow for burial. The coffin was carried in the oyster wagon because of the fierce heat of early July. She found she had written it down once more. Chekhov was that boy outside the restaurant with his father in the autumn rain, was that starving boy crunching the oysters in the restaurant while they laughed, was the child in the bed woken by thirst at noon, watching the father pace up and down the small room waving his arms around. She wanted to write an imaginary life of Chekhov, from the day outside the restaurant to the day the body of the famous writer reached Moscow in the oyster wagon for burial. It would begin with oysters and end with oysters, some of the oysters, after the coffin had been taken away for burial, delivered to the same restaurant in which the child Chekhov had eaten shells. She wasn't yet sure whether she would write it as a novel or a play. The theatre was what she knew best, but she was sure that it would probably never get written at all unless more order and calm entered her life than was in it now. She closed the folder very quietly on the notes and returned it to a drawer. Then she showered and changed into a blue woollen dress and continued to wait for Arvo Meri to come.

That morning Arvo's wife had rung her at the theatre, where she was directing the rehearsals of Ostrovsky's *The Dragon*. At the end of the abusive call she shouted, 'You're nothing but a whore,' and then began to sob hysterically. Eva used the old defence of silence and put down the receiver and told the doorman that no matter how urgent any call claimed to be she was not to be interrupted in rehearsal. She was having particular difficulty with one of the leads, an actress of some genius who needed directing with a hand of iron since her instinct was to filch more importance for her own part than it had been allotted. She had seen her ruin several fine plays by acting everybody else off the stage and was determined that it wasn't going to happen in this production. Once she began to rehearse again she put the call out of her mind but was able to think of nothing else during the midday break, and rang Arvo at his office. He was a journalist, with political ambitions on the Left, who had almost got into parliament at the last election and was almost certain to get in at the next. When he apologized for the call and blamed it on his wife's drinking she lost her temper.

'That makes a pair of you, then,' and went on to say that she wanted a life of her own, preferably with him, but if not – without him. She had enough of to-ing and fro-ing, of what she called his Hamlet act. This time he would have to make up his mind, one way or the other. He countered by saying that it wasn't possible to discuss it over the phone and arranged to call at her flat at eight. As she waited for him in the blue woollen dress, she determined to have that life of her own. The two sentences *The word Oysters was chalked on the wagon that carried Chekhov's body to Moscow for burial. The coffin was carried in the oyster wagon because of the fierce heat of early July* echoed like a revenant in her mind and would not be still.

There was snow on Arvo Meri's coat and fur hat when he came and he carried a sheaf of yellow roses. Once she saw the flowers she knew nothing would change. She laid them across a sheepskin that covered a large trunk at the foot of the bed without removing their wrapping.

'Well?'

'I'm so sorry about this morning, Eva . . .'

'That doesn't matter,' she stopped him, 'but I do want to know what you propose to do.'

'I don't know what to do,' he said guiltily. 'You know I can't get a divorce.'

'I don't care about a divorce.'

'But what else is there to do?'

'I can take a larger flat than this. We can start to live together,' she said, and he put his head in his hands.

'Even though there's nothing left between us she still depends on the relationship. If I was to move out completely she'd just go to pieces.'

'That's not my problem.'

'Can't we wait a little longer?'

'More than two years seems long enough to me. You go to Moscow by going to Moscow. If you wait until all the conditions are right you can wait your whole life.'

'I've booked a table at the Mannerheim. Why don't we talk it over there?'

'Why not?' She shrugged with bright sarcasm, and lifted the yellow roses from the sheepskin. 'I ask you for a life and you offer me yellow roses and a dinner at the Mannerheim,' but he did not answer and started to dial for a taxi. She let the roses drop idly down on the sheepskin and pulled on her fur coat and boots and sealskin cap.

Charcoal was blazing in two braziers on tall iron stems on either side of the entrance to the Mannerheim. They hadn't spoken during the taxi drive and she remarked as she got out, 'They must have some important personage tonight.' As the lift went up, she felt a sinking as in an aeroplane take-off. A uniformed attendant took their furs and they had a drink in the bar across from the restaurant while they gave their order to the waiter. The restaurant was half empty: three older couples and a very large embassy party. They knew it was an embassy party because of a circle of toy flags that stood in the centre of the table. Through the uncurtained glass they could see out over the lights of the city to the darkness that covered the frozen harbour and sea. He had drunk a number of vodkas by the time the main course came, and she was too tense to eat as she nibbled at the shrimp in the avocado and sipped at the red wine.

'You don't mind me drinking? I have a need of vodka tonight.'

'Of course not . . . but it won't be any use.'

'Why?' He looked at her.

'When I was pregnant you took me to the Mannerheim and said, "I don't know what to do. It's not the right time yet. That is all I know," and drank vodka. You were silent for hours, except every now and then you'd say, "All I'm certain of is that it's not the right time yet for us to have a child." I had some hard thinking to do when I left the Mannerheim that night. And when I arranged for and had the abortion without telling you, and rang you after coming out of the clinic, you said the whole week had been like walking round under a dark cloud, but that I had made you so happy now. I was so understanding. One day we'd have a child when everything was right. And you came that evening with yellow roses and took me to the Mannerheim and later we danced all night at that place on the shore.'

She spoke very slowly. He didn't want to listen, but he didn't know what to say to stop her, and he ordered more vodka.

'And now when we spend three days in a row together your wife rings up and calls me a whore. You bring me yellow roses and take me to the Mannerheim. The vodka won't do any good . . . '

'But what are we to do?'

'I've given my answer. I'll take a larger flat. We'll live together as two people, from now on.'

'But can't we wait till after the elections?'

'No. It's always been "wait". And there will always be something to wait for. They say there's no good time to die either. That it's as difficult to leave at seventy as at twenty. So why not now?'

'But I love you, Eva.'

'If you loved me enough you'd come and live with me,' and he went silent. He had more vodka, and as they were leaving she noticed the attendant's look of disapproval as he swayed into the lift. The tall braziers had been taken in, and as they waited while the doorman hailed a taxi he asked, 'Can I come back with you tonight?' 'Why not? If you want,' she laughed in a voice that made him afraid. He was violently ill when he got to the flat and fell at once into a drugged sleep sprawled across the bed. She looked at him a moment with what she knew was the dangerous egotism of the maternal instinct before she made up a bed on the carpet and switched off the lights. He woke early with a raging thirst and she got him a glass of water. 'Was I sick last night?' 'Yes, but don't worry, in the bathroom.' 'Why didn't you sleep in the bed?' 'I'd have to wake you, the way you were in bed.' 'I'm sorry.' 'It doesn't matter.' 'Why don't you come in now?' 'All right.' She rose from the blankets on the floor. The night conversation seemed to her like dialogue from a play that had run too long, and the acting had gone stale. He drew her towards him in the bed, more, she knew, to try to escape through pleasure from the pain of the hangover than from desire. She grew impatient with his tired fumbling and pulled him on top of her, provoking him with her own body till he came. Afterwards they both slept. She shook her head later when he asked her, 'When will we meet?' 'It's no use.' 'But I love you.' She still shook her head. 'I'm fond of you but you can't give me what I want.' As he moved to speak she stopped him, 'No. I can't wait. I have work I want to do.' 'Is it that damned Chekhov's body?' 'That's right.' 'It'll never come to anything,' he said in hatred. 'I don't care, but I intend to try.' 'You're nothing but a selfish bitch.' 'I am selfish and I want you to go now.'

That morning there were several calls for her during rehearsals but she had left strict instructions that she wasn't to be disturbed, and when she got home that evening she took the phone off the hook.

She was surprised during the following days how little she yearned for him, it was as if a weight had lifted. She felt an affection for him that she felt for the part of her life she had passed with him, but she saw clearly that it was for her own life and not for his that she yearned. She would go on alone, and when he demanded to see her she met him with a calm that was indifference which roused him to fury. She had not built a life with him, she had built nothing: but out of these sentences *The word Oysters was chalked on the wagon that carried Chekhov's body to Moscow for burial. The coffin was carried in the oyster wagon because of the fierce heat of early July* she would build, and for that she had to be alone. She would leave this city that had so much of her past life, the theatre where she had worked so long. She would leave them like a pair of galoshes in the porch, and go indoors. She rang rich friends: was their offer of the house in Spain still open? It was. They only used it in July. They would be delighted to loan it to her. She went and offered her resignation to the old manager.

'But you can't leave in the middle of a production.'

'I'm sorry. I didn't explain properly. Of course I'll see the production through, but I won't be renewing my contract when it expires at the end of the year.'

'Is it salary?' He sat down behind his big desk and motioned to her to sit.

'No. I am leaving the theatre. I want to try to write,' she blurted out to save explanation.

'It's even more precarious than the theatre, and now that you've made your way there why throw it over for something worse still?' He was old and kindly and wise, though he too must have had to be ruthless in his day.

'I must find out whether I can or not. I'll only find out by finding out. I'll come back if I fail.'

'You know, contrary to the prodigal son story, few professions welcome back their renegades?'

'I'll take that risk.'

'Well, I see you're determined.' He rose.

As soon as a production begins to take shape it devours everybody around it so that one has no need for company or friends or anything outside it, and in the evening one takes a limp life home with no other idea than to restore it so that it can be devoured anew the next day. As she went home on the tram two days before the dress rehearsal she hadn't enough strength to be angry when she saw her photo in the evening paper and read that she was leaving the theatre to write. She was leaving to *try* to write. She should have been more careful. Kind as he was she should have known that the old manager would use any publicity in any way to fill the theatre. *To write* was better copy than the truthful *try to write*. She wondered tiredly if there was a photo of the coffin being lifted out of the oyster wagon or of the starving man in his summer coat in the rain outside the restaurant while the boy crunched on the oyster shells within; and whether it was due to the kindness usually reserved for the dear departed or mere luck, no production of hers had ever opened before to such glowing notices.

She left on New Year's Eve for Spain, by boat and train, passing through Stockholm and Copenhagen, and stopping five days in Paris where she knew some people. She had with her the complete works of Chekhov, and the two sentences were more permanently engraved than ever in her mind: *The word Oysters was chalked on the wagon that carried Chekhov's body to Moscow for burial. The coffin was carried in the oyster wagon because of the fierce heat of early July.*

She stayed five days in the Hôtel Celtique on the rue Odessa, and all her waking hours seemed taken up with meeting people she already knew. Most of them scraped a frugal living from translation or journalism or both and all of them wrote or wanted to be artists in one way or another. They lived in small rooms and went out to cheap restaurants and movie houses. She saw that many of them were homesick and longed for some way to go back without injuring their self-esteem and that they thought her a fool for leaving. In their eyes she read contempt. 'So she too has got the bug. That's all we need. One more,' and she began to protect herself by denying that there was any foundation to the newspaper piece. On the evening before she took the train to Spain she had dinner in a Russian restaurant off the Boulevard St Michael with the cleverest of them all: the poet Severi. He had published three books of poems, and the previous year she had produced a play of his that had been taken off after a week though it was highly praised by the critics. His threadbare dark suit was spotless, and the cuffs and collar of the white shirt shone, the black bow knotted with a studied carelessness. They were waited on by the owner, a little old hen of a Russian woman who spoke heavily accented French and whose thinning hair was dyed carrot. A once powerful man played an accordion at the door.

'Well, Eva Lindberg, can you explain to me what you're doing haring off to Spain instead of staying up there to empty that old theatre of yours with my next play?' The clever mordant eyes looked at her through unrimmed spectacles with ironic amusement.

'I was offered a loan of a house.' She was careful.

'And they inform me you intend to write there. You know there's not room for the lot of us.'

'That's just a rumour that got into a newspaper.'

'What'll you do down there, a single woman among hordes of randy Spaniards?'

'For one thing I have a lot of reading to catch up on.' She was safe now, borrowing aggression from his aggression.

'And why did you leave the theatre?'

'I felt I was getting stale. I wasn't enjoying it any more.'

'Have you money?'

'I have enough money. What about your own work?'

He started to describe what he was working on with the mockery usually reserved for the work of others. The accordion player came round the tables with a saucer, bullying those who offered him less than a franc. They had a second carafe of red wine and finished with a peppered vodka. Warmed by the vodka, he asked her to sleep with him, his face so contorted at having to leave himself open to rejection that she felt sorry for him.

'Why not?' he pushed; soon he would begin to mock his own desire.

'I've told you,' she said gently. 'I've had enough. I want to be alone for a time.'

She was alone for the whole of the journey the next evening and night, going early to her sleeper, changing at the frontier the next morning into the wider Spanish train, which got into Barcelona just before noon. A taximan took her to the small Hotel New York in the Gothic quarter and it proved as clean and cheap as he said it would be. She stayed five days in Barcelona and was happy. Like an army in peacetime she was doing what she had to do by being idle and felt neither guilt nor need to make a holiday.

She walked the narrow streets, went to a few museums and churches, bought a newspaper on the Ramblas, vivid with the flower stalls under the leafless trees in the cold dry weather, and ate each evening at the Casa Agut, a Catalan restaurant a few minutes walk from the hotel. She sat where she could watch the kitchen and always had gaspacho, *ensalada* and a small steak with a half-bottle of red Rioja, enjoying the march of the *jefe* who watched for the slightest carelessness, the red and white towel on his shoulder like an epaulet. After five such days she took the train to Valencia where she got the express bus to Almería. She would get off at Vera and get a taxi to the empty house on the shore. It was on this bus that she made her first human contact since leaving Paris, a Swedish homosexual who must have identified her as Scandinavian by her clothes and blonde hair and who asked if he could sit beside her. 'How far are you going?' she asked when she saw she was stuck with him for the journey. 'I don't know. South. I can go as far as I want.' Though the hair was dyed blond the lines in the brittle feminine face showed he was sixty or more. He spoke only his own language and some English and was impressed by her facility for acquiring languages. She wondered if the homosexual love of foreignness was that having turned away from the mother or been turned away they needed to do likewise with their mother tongue. 'Aren't you a lucky girl to find languages so easy?' She resented the bitchiness that inferred a boast she hadn't made.

'It's no more than being able to run fast or jump. It means you can manage to say more inaccurately in several languages what you can say better in your own. It's useful sometimes but it doesn't seem very much to me if that's all it achieves.'

'That's too deep for me.' He was resentful and impressed and a little scared. 'Are you on a holiday?'

'No. I'm going to live here for a time.'

'Do you have a house?'

'Yes. I've been loaned a house.'

'Will you be with people or alone?' His questioning grew more eager and rapid.

'I'll be alone.'

'Do you think I could take a room in the house?'

She was grateful to be able to rest her eyes on the blue sea in the distance. At least it would not grow old. Its tides would ebb and flow, it would still yield up its oyster shells long after all the living had become the dead.

'I'm sorry. One of the conditions of the loan is that I'm not allowed to have people to stay,' she lied.

'I could market for you and cook.'

'It's impossible. I'm sorry.' He would cling to any raft to shut out of mind the grave ahead.

'You? Are you going far?'

'The bus goes to Almería.'

'And then?'

'I don't know. I thought to Morocco.'

She escaped from him in Alicante where they had a half-hour break and changed buses. She saw the shirtsleeved porters pat the Swede's fur coat in amusement, '*Mucho frío, mucho frío,*' as they transferred it to the boot of the bus returning to Almería. She waited till she saw him take the same seat in the new bus and then took her place beside an old Spanish woman dressed in black who smelled of garlic and who, she learned later, had been seeing her daughter in hospital. She felt guilty at avoiding the Swede so pointedly. She did not look at him when she got off at Vera.

The house was low and flat-roofed and faced the sea. The mountain was behind, a mountain of the moon, sparsely sprinkled with the green of farms that grew lemon trees and often had vine or olive on terraces of stone built on the mountain side. In the dried-up beds of rivers the cacti flourished. The village was a mile away and had a covered market built of stone, roofed with tiles the colour of sand. She was alarmed when the old women hissed at her when she first entered the market but then she saw it was only their way of trying to draw people to their stalls. Though there was a fridge in the house she went every day to the market and it became her daily outing. The house had four rooms but she arranged it so that she could live entirely in the main room.

She reread all of Chekhov, ate and drank carefully, and in the solitude of the days felt her life, for the first time in years, in order. The morning came when she decided to face the solitary white page. She had an end, the coffin of the famous writer coming to Moscow for burial that hot July day; and a beginning, the boy crunching on the oyster shells in the restaurant while the man starved in his summer coat in the rain outside. What she had to do was to imagine the life in between. She wrote in a careful hand *The word Oysters was chalked on the wagon that carried Chekhov's body to Moscow for burial. The coffin was carried in the oyster wagon because of the fierce heat of early July*, and then grew agitated. She rose and looked at her face in the small silver-framed mirror. Yes, there were lines, but faint still, and natural. Her nails needed filing. She decided to change into a shirt and jeans and then to rearrange all her clothes and jewellery. A week, two weeks, passed in this way. She got nothing written. The early sense of calm and order left her.

She saw one person fairly regularly during that time, a local *guardia* whose name was Manolo. He had first come to the house with a telegram from her old theatre, asking her if she would do a translation of a play of Mayakovsky's. She offered him a drink when he came with the telegram. He asked for water and later he walked with her back to the village where she cabled her acceptance of the theatre's offer, wheeling his rattling bicycle, the thin glittering barrel of his rifle pointing skyward. The Russian manuscript of the play arrived by express delivery a few days afterwards, and now she spent all her mornings working on the translation; and how easy it was, the good text solidly and reliably under her hand, play compared with the pain of trying to pluck the life of Chekhov out of the unimaginable air.

Manolo began to come almost daily, in the hot, lazy hours of the afternoon. She would hear his boots scrape noisily on the gravel to give her warning. He would leave his bicycle against the wall of the house in the shade, his gun where the drinking water dripped slowly from the porous clay jars into catching pails. They would talk for an hour or more across the bare Scandinavian table and he would smoke and drink wine or water. His talk turned often to the social ills of Spain and the impossibility of the natural division between men and women. She wondered why someone as intelligent as he had become a *guardia*. There was nothing else to do, he told her. He was one of the lucky ones in the village, he got a salary, it was that or Germany. And then he married, and bang-bang, he said – two babies in less than two years. A third was on its way. All his wife's time was taken up with the infants now. There was nothing left between them but babies, and that was the way it would go on, without any money, seven or eleven, or more . . .

'But that's criminal in this age,' she said.

'What is there to do?'

'There's contraception.'

'In Spain there's not.'

'They could be brought in.'

'If you can I'll pay you,' he said eagerly.

When she sent back the completed translation she asked the theatre's editor if he could send the contraceptives with the next commission. She explained why she wanted them, though she reflected that he would think what he wanted anyhow. The contraceptives did get through with the next commissioned play. They wanted a new translation of *The Seagull*, which delighted her. She felt it would bring her closer to Chekhov and that when she had finished it she would be able to begin what she had come here to try to do in the first place. The only objection the editor had to sending the contraceptives was that he was uneasy for her safety: it was against the law, and it was Spain, and policemen were as notorious as other people for wanting promotion.

She thought Manolo was nervous and he left her quickly after she handed him the package that afternoon, but she put it out of mind as natural embarrassment in taking contraceptives from a woman, and went back to reading *The Seagull*. She was still reading it and making notes on the margins when she heard boots and voices coming up the gravel and a loud knock with what sounded like a gun butt on the door. She was frightened as she called out, 'Who's there?' and a voice she didn't know called back, 'Open. It's the police.' When she opened the door she saw Manolo and the *jefe* of the local *guardia*, a fat oily man she had often seen lolling about the market, and he barged into the house. Manolo closed the door behind them as she instinctively got behind the table.

The *jefe* threw the package she had given Manolo earlier in the day on to the table. 'You know this?' As she nodded she noticed in growing fear that both of them were very drunk. 'You know it's against the law? You can go to prison for this,' he said, the small oily eyes glittering across the table. She decided there was no use answering any more.

'Still, Manolo and myself have agreed to forget it if we can try them out here.' His oily eyes fell pointedly on the package on the table but the voice was hesitant. 'That's if you don't prefer it Spanish style.' He laughed back to Manolo for support, and started to edge round the table.

They were drunk and excited. They would probably take her anyhow. How often had she heard this problem argued. Usually it was agreed it was better to yield than to get hurt. After all, sex wasn't all it was cracked up to be: in Paris the butcher and the baker shook hands with the local whores when they met, as people plying different trades.

'All right. As long as you promise to leave as soon as it's done.' Her voice stopped him. It had a calm she didn't feel.

'Okay, it's a promise.' They both nodded eagerly. They reminded her of mastered boys as they asked apprehensively, 'With the . . . or without?'

'With.'

The *jefe* followed her first into the room. 'All the clothes off,' was his one demand. She averted her face while it took place. A few times after parties, when she was younger, hadn't she held almost total strangers in her arms? Then she fixed completely on the two sentences *The word Oysters was chalked on the wagon that carried Chekhov's body to Moscow for burial. The coffin was carried in the oyster wagon because of the fierce heat of early July,* her mind moving over them from beginning to end, and from beginning to end, again and again. Manolo rushed out of the room when he had finished. They kept their word and left, subdued and quiet. It had not been as jolly as they must have imagined it would be.

She showered and washed and changed into new clothes. She poured herself a large glass of cognac at the table, noticing that they must have taken the condoms. Then she began to sob, dry and hard at first, rising to a flood of rage against her own foolishness. 'There is only one real sin – stupidity. You always get punished for behaving stupidly,' the poet Severi was fond of repeating.

When she quietened she drank what was left of the cognac and then started to pack. She stayed up all night packing and putting the house in order for her departure. Numbed with tiredness she walked to the village the next morning. All the seats on the express that passed through Vera were booked for that day but she could take the *rápido* to Granada and go straight to Barcelona from there. She arranged for the one taxi in the village to take her to the train. The taximan came and she made listless replies to his ebullient talk on the drive by the sea to meet the train. The *rápido* was full of peasants and as it crawled from station to small station she knew it would be night before it reached Granada. She would find some hotel close to the station. In the morning she would see a doctor and then go to Barcelona. A woman in a black shawl on the wooden seat facing her offered her a sliver of sausage and a gourd of wine. She took the sausage but refused the wine. She wasn't confident that her hands were steady enough to direct the thin stream into her mouth. Then she nodded to sleep, and when she woke she thought the bitter taste of oysters was in her mouth and that an awful lot of people were pacing up and down and waving their arms around. She had a sudden desire to look out the window to see if the word *Oysters* was chalked on the wagon; but then she saw that the train had just stopped at a large station and that the woman in the black shawl was still there and was smiling on her.

A Slip-up

There was such a strain on the silence between them after he'd eaten that it had to be broken.

'Maybe we should never have given up the farm and come here. Even though we had no one to pass it on to,' Michael said, his head of coarse white hair leaning away from his wife as he spoke. What had happened today would never have happened if they'd stayed, he thought, and there'd be no shame; but he did not speak it.

'Racing across hedges and ditches after cattle, is it, at our age. Cows, hens, pigs, calves, racing from light to dark on those watery fields between two lakes, up to the tips of our wellingtons in mud and water, having to run with the deeds to the bank manager after a bad year. I thought we'd gone into all this before.'

'Well, we'd never have had to retire if we'd stayed.' What he said already sounded lame.

'We'd be retired all right. We'd be retired all right, into the graveyard long years ago if we'd stayed. You don't know what a day this has been for me as well.' Agnes began to cry and Michael sat still in the chair as she cried.

'After I came home from Tesco's I sorted the parcels,' she said. 'And at ten to one I put the kippers under the grill. Michael will have just about finished his bottle of Bass and be coming out the door of the Royal, I said when I looked at the clock. Michael must have run into someone on his way back, I thought, as it went past one. And when it got to ten past I said you must have fell in with company, but I was beginning to get worried.'

'You know I never fall in with company,' he protested irritably. 'I always leave the Royal at ten to, never a minute more nor less.'

'I didn't know what way to turn when it got to half past, I was that paralysed with worry, and then I said I'll wait five minutes to see, and five minutes, and another five minutes, and I wasn't able to move with worry, and then it was nearly a quarter past two. I couldn't stand it. And then I said I'll go down to the Royal. And I'll never know why I didn't think of it before.

'Denis and Joan were just beginning to lock up when I got to the Royal. "What is it, Agnes?" Denis said. "Have you seen Michael?" I asked. "No." Denis shook his head. "He hasn't been in at all today. We were wondering if he was all right. It's the first time he's not showed up for his bottle of Bass since he had that flu last winter." "He's not showed up for his lunch either and he's always on the dot. What can have happened to him?" I started to cry.

'Joan made me sit down. Dennis put a brandy with a drop of port in it into my hand. After I'd taken a sip he said, "When did you last see Michael?" I told him how we went to Tesco's, and how I thought you'd gone for your bottle of Bass, and how I put on the kippers, and how you never showed up. Joan took out a glass of beer and sat with me while Denis got on the phone. "Don't worry, Agnes," Joan said, "Denis is finding out about Michael." And when Denis got off the phone he said, "He's not in any of the hospitals and the police haven't got him so he must be all right. Don't rush the brandy. As soon as you finish we'll hop in the car. He must be nearhand."

'We drove all round the park but you weren't on any of the benches. "What'll we do now?" I said. "Before we do anything we'll take a quick scout round the streets," Denis said, and as soon as we went through the lights before Tesco's he said, "Isn't that Michael over there with the shopping bag?"

'And there you were, with the empty shopping bag in front of Tesco's window. "Oh my God," I said, "Michael will kill me. I must have forgot to collect him when I came out of Tesco's," and then Denis blew the horn, and you saw us, and came over.'

Every morning since he retired, except when he was down with that winter flu, Michael walked with Agnes to Tesco's, and it brought him the feeling of long ago when he walked round the lake with his mother, potholes and stones of the lane, the boat shapes at intervals in the long lake wall to allow the carts to pass one another when they met, the oilcloth shopping bag he carried for her in a glow of chattering as he walked in the shelter of her shadow. Now it was Agnes who chattered as they walked to Tesco's, and he'd no longer to listen, any response to her bead of talk had long become nothing but an irritation to her; and so he walked safely in the shelter of those dead days, drawing closer to the farm between the lakes that they had lost.

When they reached Tesco's he did not go in. The brands and bright lights troubled him, and as she made all the purchases he had no function within anyhow. So on dry days he stayed outside with the empty shopping bag if it wasn't too cold. When the weather was miserable he waited for her just inside the door beside the off-licence counter. When he first began to come with her after retiring, the off-licence assistants used to bother him by asking if they could help. As he said, 'No thanks,' he wanted to tell them that he never drank in the house. Only at Christmas did they have drink in the house and that was for other people, if they came. The last bottles were now three Christmases old, for people no longer visited them at Christmas, which was far more convenient. They went round to the Royal as usual Christmas Day. Denis still kept Sunday hours on Christmas Day. Though it was only the new assistants in the off-licence who ever noticed him on bad days now, he still preferred to wait for her outside with the shopping bag against the Special Offers pasted in the glass. By that time he would have already reached the farm between the lakes while walking with her, and was ready for work.

The farm that they lost when they came to London he'd won back almost completely since he retired. He'd been dismayed when he retired as caretaker of the Sir John Cass School to find how much the farm had run down in the years he'd been a school caretaker. Drains were choked. The fields were full of rushes. The garden had gone wild, and the hedges were invading the fields. But he was too old a hand to rush at things. Each day he set himself a single task. The stone wall was his pride, perhaps because it was the beginning. There were no limits before the wall was built. Everything looked impossible. A hundred hands seemed needed. But after the wall was built he cleared the weeds and bushes that had overgrown the front garden, cut away the egg bushes from the choked whitethorns, pruned the whitethorns so that they thickened. Now between wall and whitethorn hedge the front garden ran, and he'd gone out from there, task by single task.

This morning as he walked with Agnes he decided to clear the drinking pool which was dry after the long spell of good weather. First he shovelled the dark earth of rotted leaves and cowshit out on the bank. Then he paved the sides with heavy stones so that the cattle would not plough in as they drank and he cleared the weeds from the small stream that fed it. When he followed the stream to the boundary hedge he found water blocked there. He released it and then leaned on his shovel in the simple pleasure of watching water flow. For all that time he was unaware of the shopping bag, but when all the water flowed down towards the pool he felt it again by his side. He wondered what was keeping Agnes. He'd never finished such a long job before outside Tesco's. Usually he'd counted himself lucky if he was through with such a job by the time he'd finished his bottle of Bass in the Royal by ten to one.

The drain was now empty and clean. All the water had flowed down to the pool. He'd go to the field garden. The withered bean and pea stalks needed pulling up and the earth turned. A wren or robin sang in the thorns, faithful still in the bare days. He opened the wooden gate into the garden, enclosed on three sides by its natural thorn hedges, and two strands of barbed wire ran on posts to keep the cattle out on the fourth. Each year he pushed the barbed wire farther out, and soon, one of these years, the whole field would be a garden, completely enclosed by its own whitethorns. He pulled up the withered bean and pea stalks with the thorn branches that had served as stakes and threw them in a heap for burning. Then he began to turn the soil. The black and white bean flower had been his favourite, its fragrance carried on the wind through the thorns into the meadow, drawing the bees from the clover. Agnes could keep all her roses in the front garden . . . and then he felt himself leaning over the fork with tiredness though he hadn't half the ridge turned. He was too weak to work. It must be late and why had she not called him to his meal? He stuck the fork in the ground and in exasperation went over to the barbed wire. The strands were loose. A small alder shoot sprouted from one of the posts. He walked up the potato furrows, the dried stalks dead and grey in the ridges. This year he must move the pit to higher ground. Last winter the rats had come up from the lake – but why had she not called him? Had she no care? Was she so utterly selfish?

He turned and stared in the window, but the avenues of shelves were too long and the lights blinding. It was in this impotent rage that he heard the horn blow. Denis was there and Agnes was in the car. He went towards them with the empty shopping bag. They both got out of the car.

'Why did you leave me there?' he asked angrily.

'Oh don't be mad at me, Michael. I must have forgot when I came out.'

'What time is it now?'

'Five after three, Michael.' Denis was smiling. 'You've missed your bottle of Bass, but hop in and I'll run you home.'

It wouldn't have happened if we'd kept the farm. At least on the farm we'd be away from people, he thought obstinately as he put the food aside that he should have eaten hours before. He flushed like a child with shame as he heard again, 'Five after three, Michael. You've missed your bottle of Bass, but hop in and I'll run you home,' and thought that's how it goes, you go on as usual every day, and then something happens, and you make a mistake, and you're caught. It was Agnes who at last broke this impossible silence.

'I can see that you're tired out. Why don't you lie down for a turn?' she said, and began to clear the plates.

'Maybe I will lie down, then,' he yielded.

He slept lightly and restlessly. Only a fraction of what was happening surfaced in his dream. A herd of panting cattle was driven past him on a dirt road by a man wheeling a bicycle, their mouths slavering in the heat. Agnes passed by holding bread-crumbs in her apron. A white car came round the lake. As it turned at the gate a child got out and came towards him with a telegram. He was fumbling in his pocket for coins to give to the child when he was woken by Agnes.

'We'll be late getting to the Royal if you don't get up now,' she was saying.

'What time is it?'

When she told him the time, he knew they should be leaving in twenty minutes.

'I don't know if I want to go out tonight.'

'Of course you'll go out tonight. There's nothing wrong with you, is there?'

When she said that he knew he had to go. He rose and washed, changed into his suit, combed his coarse white hair, and at exactly twenty to nine, as on every evening of their lives, they were closing the 37B door in Ainsworth Road behind them.

All the saloon regulars looked unusually happy and bright as they greeted the old couple in the Royal, and when Michael proffered the coins for the Guinness and pint of Bass, Denis pushed them away. 'They're on the house tonight, Michael. You have to make up for that missed bottle of Bass tonight.'

Blindly he carried the drinks towards Agnes at the table. When he turned and sat and faced the room with his raised glass the whole saloon rang with, 'Cheers, Agnes. Cheers, Michael.'

'You see it was all in your mind, Michael. Everybody's the same as usual. Even happier,' Agnes said afterwards in the quiet of the click of billiard balls coming from the Public Bar.

'Maybe. Maybe, Agnes.' Michael drank.

All the people were elated too on the small farms around the lakes for weeks after Fraser Woods had tried to hang himself from a branch of an apple tree in his garden, the unconcealed excitement in their voices as they said, 'Isn't it terrible what happened to poor Fraser?' and the lust on their faces as they waited for their excitement to be mirrored.

'We'll go early to Tesco's in the morning. And then you can come down for your bottle of Bass. And it'll be the same as if nothing ever happened. What was it anyhow?' Agnes said, warmed by the Guinness.

'I suppose it was just a slip-up,' Michael answered as he sipped slowly at his pint, trying to put off the time when he'd have to go up to the counter for their next round.

All Sorts of Impossible Things

They were out coursing on Sunday a last time together but they did not know it, the two friends, James Sharkey and Tom Lennon, a teacher and an agricultural instructor. The weak winter sun had thawed the fields soft enough to course the hare on, and though it still hung blood-orange above the hawthorns on the hill the rims of the hoof tracks were already hardening fast against their tread.

The hounds walked beside them on slip leashes, a purebred fawn bitch that had raced under the name of Coolcarra Queen, reaching the Final of the Rockingham Stakes the season before, and a wire-haired mongrel, no more than half hound, that the schoolmaster, James Sharkey, borrowed from Charlie's bar for these Sundays. They'd been beating up the bottoms for some hours. An odd snipe, exploding out of the rushes before zigzagging away, was all that had risen.

'If we don't rise something before long we'll soon have to throw our hats at it,' Tom Lennon said, and it was a careless phrase. No one had seen the teacher without his eternal brown hat for the past twenty years. 'I've been noticing the ground harden all right,' the dry answer came.

'Anyhow, I'm beginning to feel a bit humped.' Tom Lennon looked small and frail in the tightly belted white raincoat.

'There's no use rimming it, then. There'll be other Sundays.'

Suddenly a large hare rose ahead, bounded to the edge of the rushes, and then looped high to watch and listen. With a 'Hulla, hulla,' they slipped the hounds, the hare racing for the side of the hill. The fawn bitch led, moving in one beautiful killing line as she closed with the hare, the head eel-like as it struck; but the hare twisted away from the teeth, and her speed carried the fawn past. The hare had to turn again a second time as the mongrel coming up from behind tried to pick it in the turn. The two men below in the rushes watched in silence as the old dance played itself out on the bare side of the hill: race, turn, race again; the hounds hunting well together, the mongrel making up with cunning what he lacked in grace, pacing himself to strike when the hare was most vulnerable – turning back from the fawn. But with every fresh turn the hare gained, the hounds slithering past on the hard ground. They were utterly beaten by the time the hare left them, going away through the hedge of whitethorns.

'They picked a warrior there.'

'That's for sure,' Tom Lennon answered as quietly.

The beaten hounds came disconsolately down, pausing at the foot of the hill to lap water from a wheelmark and to lick their paws. They came on towards the men. The paws were bleeding and some of the bitch's nails were broken.

'Maybe we shouldn't have raced her on such hard ground,' the teacher said by way of apology.

'That's no difference. She'll never run in the Stakes again. They say there's only two kinds to have – a proper dud or a champion. Her kind, the in-between, are the very worst. They'll always run well enough to tempt you into having another go. Anyhow, there's not the money for that any more,' he said with a sad smile of reflection.

Coolcarra Queen was a relic of his bachelor days that he hadn't been able to bear parting with on getting married and first coming to the place as temporary agricultural instructor.

They'd raced her in the Stakes. She'd almost won. They'd trained her together, turn and turn about. And that cold wet evening, the light failing as they ran off the Finals, they'd stood together in the mud beside the net of torn hares and watched this hare escape into the laurels that camouflaged the pen and the judge gallop towards the rope on the old fat horse, and stop, and lift the white kerchief instead of the red. Coolcarra Queen had lost the Rockingham Silver Cup and twenty-five pounds after winning the four races that had taken her to the Final.

'Still, she gave us a run for our money,' the teacher said as they put the limping hounds on the leashes and turned home.

'Well, it's over now,' Tom Lennon said. 'Especially with the price of steak.'

'Your exams can't be far off now?' the teacher said as they walked. The exams he alluded to were to determine whether the instructor should be made permanent or let go.

'In less than five weeks. The week after Easter.'

'Are you anxious about it at all?'

'Of course,' he said sadly. 'If they make me permanent I get paid whether I'm sick or well. They can't get rid of me then. Temporary is only all right while you're single.'

'Do you foresee any snags?'

'Not in the exams. I know as much as they'll know. It's the medical I'm afraid of.'

'Still,' the teacher began lamely and couldn't go on. He knew that the instructor had been born with his heart on the wrong side and it was weak.

'Not that they'll pay much heed to instruction round here. Last week I came on a pair of gentlemen during my rounds. They'd roped a horse-mower to a brand new Ferguson. One was driving the Ferguson, the other sitting up behind on the horse machine, lifting and letting down the blade with a piece of wire. They were cutting thistles.'

'That's the form all right.' The teacher smiled.

They'd left the fields and come to the stone bridge into the village. Only one goalpost stood upright in the football field. Below them the sluggish Shannon flowed between its wheaten reeds.

'Still, we must have walked a good twelve miles today from one field to the next. If we'd to walk that distance along a straight line of road it'd seem a terrible journey.'

'A bit like life itself.' The teacher laughed sarcastically, adjusting the brown hat firmly on his head. 'We might never manage it if we had to take it all in the one gasp. We mightn't even manage to finish it.'

'Well, it'd be finished for us, then,' the instructor countered weakly.

'Do you feel like coming to Charlie's for a glass?' he asked as they stood.

'I told her I'd be back for the dinner. If I'm in time for the dinner she might have something even better for me afterwards,' Tom Lennon joked defensively.

'She might indeed. Well, I have to take this towser back to Charlie anyhow. Thanks for the day.'

'Thanks yourself,' Tom Lennon said.

Above the arms of the stone wall the teacher watched the frail little instructor turn up the avenue towards the Bawn, a straggling rectangular building partly visible through the bare trees where he had rooms in the tower, all that was left of the old Hall.

Charlie was on his stool behind the bar with the Sunday paper when the teacher came with the mongrel through the partition. Otherwise the bar and shop were empty.

'Did yous catch anything?' he yawned as he put aside the paper, drawing the back of his hands over his eyes like a child. There was a dark stain of hair oil behind him on the whitewash where sometimes he leaned his head and slept when the bar was empty.

'We roused only one and he slipped them.'

'I'm thinking there's only the warriors left by this time of year.' He laughed, and when he laughed the tip of his red nose curled up in a way that caused the teacher to smile with affection.

'I suppose I'll let the old towser out the back?'

Charlie nodded. 'I'll get one of the children to throw him some food later.' When the door was closed again he said in a hushed, solicitous voice, 'I suppose, Master, it'll be whiskey?'

'A large one, Charlie,' the teacher said.

In a delicious glow of tiredness from the walking, and the sensuous burning of the whiskey as it went down, he was almost mindless in the shuttle back and forth of talk until he saw Charlie go utterly still. He was following each move his wife made at the other end of the house. The face was beautiful in its concentration, reflecting each move or noise she made as clearly as water will the drifting clouds. When he was satisfied that there was no sudden danger of her coming up to the bar he turned to the shelves. Though the teacher could not see past the broad back, he had witnessed the little subterfuge so often that he could follow it in exact detail: the silent unscrewing of the bottle cap, the quick tip of the whiskey into the glass, the silent putting back of the cap, and the downing of the whiskey in one gulp, the movements so practised that it took but seconds. Coughing violently, he turned and ran the water and drank the glass of water into the coughing. While he waited for the coughing to die, he rearranged bottles on the shelves. The teacher was so intimate with the subterfuge that he might as well have taken part in the act of love. 'If I'm home in time for the dinner she might have something even better for me afterwards,' he remembered with resentment.

'Tom didn't come with you?' Charlie asked as soon as he brought the fit of coughing under control.

'No. He was done in with the walking and the wife was expecting him.'

'They say he's coming up for permanent soon. Do you think he will have any trouble?'

'The most thing he's afraid of is the medical.'

Charlie was silent for a while, and then he said, 'It's a quare caper that, isn't it, the heart on the wrong side?'

'There's many a quare caper, Charlie,' the teacher replied. 'Life itself is a quare caper if you ask me.'

'But what'll he do if he doesn't get permanent?'

'What'll we all do, Charlie?' the teacher said inwardly and, as always when driven in to reflect on his own life, instinctively fixed the brown hat more firmly on his head.

Once he did not bother to wear a hat or a cap over his thick curly fair hair even when it was raining. And he was in love then with Cathleen O'Neill. They'd thought time would wait for them for ever as they went to the sea in his baby Austin or to dances after spending Sundays on the river. And then, suddenly, his hair began to fall out. Anxiety exasperated desire to a passion, the passion to secure his life as he felt it slip away, to moor it to the woman he loved. Now it was her turn to linger. She would not marry him and she would not let him go.

'Will you marry me or not? I want an answer one way or the other this evening.' He felt his whole life like a stone on the edge of a boat out on water.

'What if I don't want to answer?' They were both proud and iron-willed.

'Then I'll take it as No.'

'You'll have to take it whatever way you want, then.' Her face was flushed with resentment.

'Goodbye, then.' He steeled himself to turn away.

Twice he almost paused, but no voice calling him back came. At the open iron gate above the stream he did pause. 'If I cross it here it is the end. Anything is better than the anguish of uncertainty. If I cross here I cannot turn back even if she should want.' He counted till ten and looked back, but her back was turned, walking slowly uphill to the house. As she passed through the gate he felt a tearing that broke as an inaudible cry.

No one ever saw him afterwards without his brown hat, and there was great scandal the first Sunday he wore it in the body of the church. The man kneeling next to him nudged him, gestured with his thumb at the hat, but the teacher did not even move. Whispers and titters and one hysterical whinny of laughter that set off a general sneeze ran through the congregation as he unflinchingly wore it through the service.

The priest was up to the school just before hometime the very next day. They let the children home early.

'Have you seen Miss O'Neill recently, Jim?' the priest opened cautiously, for he liked the young teacher, the most intelligent and competent he had.

'No, Father. That business is finished.'

'There'd be no point in me putting in a word?'

'There'd be no point, Father.'

'I'm sorry to hear that. It's no surprise. Everything gets round these parts in a shape.'

'In a shape, certainly, Father.' There was dry mockery in the voice.

'When it gets wild it is different, when you hear talk of nothing else – and that's what has brought me up. What's going the rounds now is that you wore your hat all through Mass yesterday.'

'They were right for once, Father.'

'I'm amazed.'

'Why, Father?'

'You're an intelligent man. You know you can't do that, Jim.'

'Why not, Father?'

'You don't need me to tell you that it'd appear as an extreme form of disrespect.'

'If the church can't include my own old brown hat, it can't include very much, can it, Father?'

'You know that and I know that, but we both know that the outward shows may least belie themselves. It'd not be tolerated.'

'It'll have to be tolerated, Father or . . .'

'You can't be that mad. I know you're the most intelligent man round here.'

'Thanks, Father. All votes in that direction count round here. "They said I was mad and I said they were mad, and confound them they outvoted me,"' he quoted. 'That's about it, isn't it, Father?'

'Ah, stop it, Jim. Tell me why. Seriously, tell me why.'

'You may have noticed recently, Father,' he began slowly, in rueful mockery, 'a certain manifestation that my youth is ended. Namely, that I'm almost bald. It had the effect of *timor mortis*. So I decided to cover it up.'

'Many lose their hair. Bald or grey, what does it matter? We all go that way.'

'So?'

'When I look down from the altar on Sunday half the heads on the men's side are bald.'

'The women must cover their crowning glory and the men must expose their lack of a crown. So that's the old church in her wisdom bringing us all to heel?'

'I can't understand all this fooling, Jim.'

'I'm deadly serious. I'll wear my hat in the same way as you wear your collar, Father.'

'But that's nonsense. It's completely different.'

'Your collar is the sublimation of *timor mortis*. What else is it, in Jesus Christ? All I'm asking is to cover it up.'

'But you can't wear it all the time?'

'Maybe not in bed but that's different.'

'Listen. This joking has gone far enough. I don't care where you wear your hat. That's your problem. But if you wear it in church you make it my problem.'

'Well, you'll have to do something about it then, Father.'

The priest went very silent but when he spoke all he said was, 'Why don't we lock up the school? We can walk down the road together.'

What faced the priest was alarmingly simple: he couldn't have James Sharkey at Mass with his hat on and he couldn't have one of his teachers not at Sunday Mass. Only late that night did a glimmer of what might be done come to him. Every second Sunday the teacher collected coins from the people entering the church at a table just inside the door. If the collection table was moved out to the porch and Sharkey agreed to collect the coins every Sunday, perhaps he could still make his observances while keeping his infernal hat on. The next morning he went to the administrator.

'By luck we seem to have hit on a solution,' he was able to explain to the teacher that evening.

'That's fine with me. I never wanted to be awkward,' the teacher said.

'You never wanted to be awkward,' the priest exploded. 'You should have heard me trying to convince the administrator this morning that it was better to move the table out into the porch than to move you out of the school. I've never seen a man so angry in my life. You'd have got short shrift, I'm telling you, if you were in his end of the parish. Tell me, tell me what would you have done if the administrator had got his way and fired you?'

'I'd have got by somehow. Others do,' he answered.

And soon people had got so used to the gaunt face under the brown hat behind the collection table every Sunday that they'd be as shocked now to see him without it after all the years as they had been on the first Sunday he wore it.

'That's right, Charlie. What'll we all do?' he repeated as he finished the whiskey beside the oil heater. 'Here. Give us another drop before the crowd start to come in and I get caught.'

My brown hat and his heart on the wrong side and you tippling away secretly when the whole parish including your wife knows it. It's a quare caper indeed, Charlie, he thought as he quickly finished his whiskey to avoid getting caught by the crowd due to come in.

There was no more coursing together again after that Sunday. The doctor's car was parked a long time outside the white gate that led to the Bawn the next day, and when Tom Lennon's old Ford wasn't seen around the roads that day or the next or the next the teacher went to visit him, taking a half-bottle of whiskey. Lennon's young wife, a warm soft country girl of few words, let him in.

'How is he?' he asked.

'The doctor'll be out again tomorrow,' she answered timidly and led him up the creaky narrow stairs. 'He'll be delighted to see you. He gets depressed not being able to be up and about.'

All Sorts of Impossible Things

From the circular room of the tower that they used as a living room he could hear happy gurgles of the baby as they climbed the stairs, and as soon as she showed him into the bedroom she left. In the pile of bedclothes Tom Lennon looked smaller and more frail than he usually did.

'How is the patient?'

'Fed up,' he said. 'It's great to see a face after staring all day at the ceiling.'

'What is it?'

'The old ticker. As soon as I'd eaten after getting home on Sunday it started playing me up. Maybe I overdid the walking. Still, it could be worse. It'd be a damned sight worse if it had happened in five weeks' time. Then we'd be properly in the soup.'

'You have oodles of time to be fit for the exam,' the teacher said, hiding his dismay by putting the whiskey down on the dressing table. 'I brought this little something.' There was, he felt, a bloom of death in the room.

'You never know,' the instructor said some hours later as the teacher took his leave. 'I'm hoping the doctor'll have me up to-morrow.' He drank only a little of the whiskey in a punch his wife made, while the hatted man on the chair slowly finished his own half-bottle neat.

The doctor did not allow him up that week or the next, and the teacher began to come every evening to the house, and two Sundays later he asked to take the hounds out on his own. He did not cross the bridge to the Plains as they'd done the Sunday together but went along the river to Doireen. The sedge of the long lowlands rested wheaten and dull between two hills of hazel and briar in the warm day. All winter it had been flooded but the pale dead grass now crackled under his feet like tinder. He beat along the edges of the hills, feeling that the hares might have come out of the scrub to sleep in the sun, and as he beat he began to feel Tom Lennon's absence like his own lengthening shadow on the pale sedge.

The first hare didn't get more than halfway from where it was lying to the cover of the scrub before the fawn's speed caught it, a flash of white belly fur as it rolled over, not being able to turn away from the teeth in the long sedge, and the terror of its crying as both hounds tore it began. He wrested the hare loose and stilled the

141

The

weird childlike crying with one blow. Soon afterwards a second hare fell in the same way. From several parts of the river lowland he saw hares looping slowly out of the warm sun into the safety of the scrub. He knew they'd all have gone in then, and he turned back for Charlie's. He gave one of the hares to Charlie; the other he skinned and took with him to Tom Lennon's.

'Do you know what I'm thinking?' he said that night. 'I'm thinking that I should take the bitch.'

He saw sudden fear in the sick man's eyes.

'You know you're always welcome to borrow her any time you want.'

'It's not that,' he said quickly. 'I thought just to take her until you're better. I could feed her. It'd be no trouble. It'd take some of the weight off the wife.' When he left that evening he took the bitch, which was excited, thinking that she was going hunting again, though it was dark, and she rose to put paws on his shoulders and to lick his face.

She settled in easily with the teacher. He made a house for her in the garden out of a scrapped Ford but he still let her sleep in the house, and there was a lighter spring in his walk each evening he left school, knowing the excitement with which he would be met as soon as he got home. At night he listened to Tom Lennon's increasingly feverish grumblings as the exam drew closer, and he looked so angry and ill the night after the doctor had told him he could put all thought of the exam out of his mind that the suspicion grew stronger in the teacher's mind that his friend might not after all be just ill.

'What are you going to do?' he asked fearfully.

'Do the exam, of course.' There was determination as well as fear in the sunken eyes.

'But you can't do it if the doctor said you weren't fit.'

'Let's put it this way,' the sick man laughed in harsh triumph, 'I can't *not* do it.'

The night before the exam he asked the teacher to bring up the clippers. He wanted a haircut, and that night, as the teacher wrapped the towel round the instructor's neck and took the bright clippers out of their pale green cardboard box, adjusting the combs, and started to clip, the black hair dribbling down on the towel, he felt for the first time ever a mad desire to remove his hat and stand bareheaded in the room, as if for the first time in years he felt himself in the presence of something sacred.

'That's a great job,' Tom Lennon said afterwards. 'You know, while we're at it, I might as well go the whole hog and shave as well.'

'Do you want me to get you some hot water?'

'That wouldn't be too much trouble?'

'No trouble at all.'

Downstairs as they waited for the water to boil, the wife in her quiet voice asked him, 'What do you think?'

'He seems determined on it. I tried to talk him out of it but it was no use.'

'No. It doesn't seem any use,' she said. A starched white shirt and blue suit and tie were draped across a chair one side of the fire.

The teacher sat on the bed's edge and held the bowl of water steady while the instructor shaved. When he finished, he examined himself carefully in the little hand-mirror, and joked, 'It's as good as for a wedding.'

'Maybe it's too risky. Maybe you should send in a certificate. There'll be another chance.'

'No. That's finished. I'm going through with it. It's my last chance. There'll be no other. If I manage to get made permanent there'd be a weight off my mind and it'd be better than a hundred doctors and tonics.'

'Maybe I should give the old car a swing in readiness for the morning, so?'

'That'd be great.' The instructor fumbled for his car keys in his trouser pockets on the bed rail.

The engine was cold but started on the sixth or seventh swing. In the cold starlit night he stood and listened to the engine run.

'Good luck, old Tom,' he said quietly as he switched it off and took the car keys in.

'Well, good luck tomorrow. I hope all goes well. I'll be up as soon as I see the car back to find out how it went,' he said in a singsong voice he used with the children at school in order not to betray his emotion after telling him that the Ford was running like a bird.

Tom Lennon rose the next morning as he said he would, dressed in his best clothes, had tea, told his wife not to worry and that he'd be back about six, somehow got as far as the car, and fell dead over the starting handle the teacher had left in the engine the previous night.

When word was brought to the school, all the hatted man did was bow his head and murmur, 'Thanks.' He knew he had been expecting the death for some days. When he went to the Bawn a last time he felt no terror of the stillness of the brown habit, the folded hands, but only a certain amazement that it was the agricultural instructor who was lying there and not he. Two days later his hat stood calmly among the scarved women and bareheaded men about the open grave, and when it was over he went back to Charlie's. The bar was filled with mourners from the funeral-making holiday. A silence seemed to fall as the brown hat came through the partition, but only for a moment. They were arguing about a method of sowing winter wheat that the dead man used to advocate. Some thought it made sense. Others said it would turn out to be a disaster.

'Your old friend won't hunt again,' Charlie said as he handed him the whiskey. The voice was hushed. The eyes stared inquiringly but respectfully into the gaunt face beneath the hat. The small red curl of the nose was still.

'No. He'll not hunt again.'

'They say herself and the child is going home with her own people this evening. They'll send a van up later for the furniture.' His voice was low as a whisper at the corner of the bar.

'That makes sense,' the teacher said.

'You have the bitch still?' Charlie asked.

'That's right. I'll be glad to keep her, but the wife may want to take her with her.'

'That'll be the least of her troubles. She'll not want.'

'Will you have something yourself?' the teacher invited.

'All right, then, Master.' He paused suddenly. 'A quick one, then. We all need a little something in the open today,' and he smiled an apologetic, rueful smile in his small eyes; but he downed the whiskey, as quickly running a glass of water and drinking it into the coughing as if it hadn't been in the open at all.

The fawn jumped in her excitement on her new master when he finally came home from the funeral. As he petted her down, gripping her neck, bringing his own face down to hers, thinking how he had come by her, he felt the same rush of feeling as he had felt when he watched the locks of hair fall on to the towel round the neck in the room; but instead of prayer he now felt a wild longing to throw his hat away and walk round the world bareheaded, find some girl, not necessarily Cathleen O'Neill, but any young girl, and go to the sea with her as he used to, leave the car at the harbour wall and take the boat for the island, the engine beating like a good heart under the deck boards as the waves rocked it on turning out of the harbour, hold her in one long embrace all night between the hotel sheets; or train the fawn again, feed her the best steak from town, walk her four miles every day for months, stand in the mud and rain again and see her as Coolcarra Queen race through the field in the Rockingham Stakes, see the judge gallop over to the rope on the old fat horse, and this time lift high the red kerchief to give the Silver Cup to the Queen.

And until he calmed, and went into the house, his mind raced with desire for all sorts of such impossible things.

Faith, Hope and Charity

Cunningham and Murphy had worked as a team ever since they'd met on a flyover site outside Reading. They dug trenches and were paid by the yard. The trenches were in places where machines could not easily go, and the work was dangerous, the earth walls having to be shuttered up as they went along, the shutters held apart by metal bars with adjustable flat squares on both ends. Both men worked under assumed names to avoid paying income tax.

This money that they slaved for all the year in the trenches they flashed and wasted in one royal month each summer in Ireland. As men obsessed with the idea that all knowledge lies within a woman's body, but having entered it find themselves as ignorant as before, they are driven towards all women again and again, in childish hope that somehow the next time they will find the root of all knowledge, and the equally childish desire for revenge since it cannot be found, the knife in the unfathomable entrails. They became full of hatred. Each year, as Murphy and Cunningham dug trenches towards their next royal summer, their talk grew obsessional and more bitter. 'It's a kind of a sort of a country that can't even afford a national eejit so they all have to take turns.'

What slowed them up the most was not the digging but the putting up of the shuttering behind them. As August drew close they grew careless and their greed for money grew in order to make an even bigger splash this summer than ever before. Little by little the spaces between the metal bars lengthened. They felt invulnerable: no matter how careless they were the bad accident was bound to happen elsewhere.

Murphy was standing on top of the trench watching Cunningham wield the pick below, behind him the fence of split stakes on Hessell Street. The midday sun beat mercilessly down on the trench, and they worked it turn and turn about, coming up every five minutes or so to cool in whatever air stirred from the Thames.

The only warning given was a sudden splintering of timber before

146

the trench caved in. Murphy fell backwards from the edge but Cunningham had no time. The boards and clay caught him. His head and shoulders remained above the earth.

He stayed alive while they dug him out, but as soon as they released the boards he died. The boards had broken his back.

All that got through Murphy's shock as he rode with the body in the ambulance to the London Hospital was, 'The police'll be in on this. The assumed names will come out. I might have to have an earlier holiday than I expected.'

The men stood about the site in small silent groups after the ambulance had gone, the different engines idling over, until Barney, the old gangerman, stormed about in his black suit and tie and dirty white shirt, as if he'd suddenly gone epileptic. 'What the fuck are yous all doing? Come on. Get a move on. Do yous think you get fukken paid for standin' about all day?'

As the site reluctantly moved back to life, a sudden gust of wind lifted an empty cement bag and cartwheeled it across the gravel before wrapping it against the fence of split stakes on Hessell Street.

It was a hot day in Ireland too when the phone rang in the village post office to relay the telegram of the death. The hired girl Mary wrote it down on the official form, closed it in the small green envelope with the black harp and then wondered how to get it delivered. Because of the hot weather everybody was in the hay-fields two miles away, and she couldn't leave the place unattended to go that far. She decided to cross the road to see if James Sharkey was still in the school. The schoolhouse door was unlocked, and she found the hatted man alone in the classroom. He had stayed behind correcting exam papers.

'What is it, Mary?' He lifted his head from the desk as she tapped on the glass of the classroom door.

'It's Joe Cunningham from Derrada.' She held up the small green envelope. 'He's been killed in an accident in England. They're all at the hay.'

'Joe Cunningham.' The child's face came to him. A dull average boy, the oldest of the Cunninghams, two of them still at school. He'd been home last summer, boasting and flashing his money in the bars. 'What'll you have, Master? I'm standin' today. We

147

mightn't have been all geniuses but we got on toppin',' what looked like bits of tinfoil glittering in his jacket.

'I'll take it, Mary. It's just as well I take it. They know me a long time now. I suppose they took the car to the fields?'

'No, they went in the van.'

'I'll take the car, then.'

All the doors of the house were open when he got to Cunningham's but there was nobody in. He knew that they must be nearhand, probably at the hay. There is such stillness, stillness of death, he thought, about an empty house with all its doors open on a hot day. A black and white sheepdog left off snapping at flies to rush towards him as he came through the gate into the meadow. It was on the side of the hill above the lake. In the shade, a tin cup floated among some hayseed in a gallon of spring water. Across the lake, just out from a green jet of reeds, a man sat still in a rowboat fishing for perch. They were all in the hayfields, the mother and father and four or five children. The field had been raked clean and they were heading off cocks. All work stopped as the hatted man came over the meadow. The father rose from teasing out hay to a boy winding it into a rope. They showed obvious discomfort as they waited, probably thinking the teacher had come to complain about some of the children, until they saw the pale green envelope.

'I'm sorry,' the hatted man said as he watched the father read. 'If there's anything I can do you have only to tell me.'

'Joe's been killed in England. The Lord have mercy on his soul,' the father said in dazed quiet, handing the envelope to the mother, all his slow movements heavy with toil.

'Oh my God. My Joe,' the mother broke.

The older children began to cry, but two little girls lifted fistfuls of hay and began to look playfully at one another and the whole stunned hayfield through wisps of hay and to laugh wildly.

'I'll have to go to London. I'll have to take him home,' the father said.

'If there's anything I can do,' the teacher said again.

'Thanks, Master. Shush now,' he said to his wife. 'We'll all go in now. The hay can be tidied up after. Shush now, Bridget. We have to do the best by him the few days more he'll be with us,' the father said as they trooped out of the hayfield.

'Is there anything – a small drop of something – we can offer you, Master?' They paused at the open door.

'Nothing, thanks, Joe. What I'll do is let you get tidied up and I'll come round for you in about two hours. I'll take you into the town so that you can see to things.'

'Are you sure that won't be putting you to too much trouble, Master?'

'No trouble at all. Why don't you go in now?'

Before he switched on the engine he heard from the open door, 'Thou, Oh Lord, wilt open my lips,' in the father's voice. The leaves of the row of poplars along the path from the house were beginning to rattle so loudly in the evening silence that he was glad when the starting engine shut out the sound.

The father went to London and flew back with the coffin two days later. A long line of cars met the hearse on the Dublin road to follow it to the church. After High Mass the next day young people with white armbands walked behind the hearse until it crossed the bridge, where it gathered speed, and it did not slow until it came in sight of Ardcarne, where they buried him.

Some weeks later the Dance Committee met round the big mahogany table in the front room of the presbytery: the priest, the hatted teacher, the Councillor Doherty, Owen Walsh the sharp-faced postman, and Jimmy McGuire who owned the post office.

'We seem to be nearly all here.' The priest looked round when it had gone well past the time of the meeting.

'We are,' the postman answered quickly. 'Paddy McDermott said he was sorry he couldn't come. It's something to do with sheep.'

'We might as well begin, then,' the priest said. 'As we all know why we're here I'll just go over it briefly. Young Cunningham was killed in England. The family insisted on taking the body home. Whether it was wise or foolish it is done now and the only thing we know is that the Cunninghams can't afford to fly a coffin home from England. The talk is that old Joe himself will have to go to England this winter to pay off the expense of the funeral. We all feel, I think, that there's no need for that.' There was a low murmur of approval.

'So we've more or less decided to hold a dance,' the teacher took up quietly. 'Unless someone here has a better idea?'

'Have we thought about a collection?' the Councillor Doherty asked because he felt he should ask something.

'The dance more or less covers that as well,' the priest said, and the Councillor nodded comprehendingly. 'Anybody not going will be invited to send subscriptions.'

'I can manage that end of it,' the postman said. 'I can put the word out on my rounds so that it can be done without any fuss.'

'There's no question of getting a big band or anything like that. "Faith, Hope and Charity" will bring in as much and they'll play for a few crates of stout. We'll let people pay whatever they can afford,' the priest said.

'Faith, Hope and Charity' were three old bachelor brothers, the Cryans, who played at local functions. They had been known as 'Faith, Hope and Charity' for so long that nobody now knew how their name began. Faith played the fiddle. Hope beat out the rhythm on the drums. Charity was strapped into an old accordion that was said to have come from America.

'Well, everything seems settled, then, so, except the date.' The priest rose when everybody murmured agreement and unlocked the cabinet. He took out five heavy tumblers and a cut-glass decanter of whiskey. There was already a glass jug of water beside the vase of roses in the centre of the big table.

The dance was held on a lovely clear night in September. A big harvest moon hung over the fields. It was almost as clear as day coming to the dance and the hall was full. Most of the older people came just to show their faces and by midnight the dance belonged completely to the young. The Committee left after counting the takings. The postman and the teacher agreed to stay behind to close the hall. They sat on the table near the door watching the young people dance. The teacher had taught nearly all the dancers, and as they paired off to go into the backs of cars they showed their embarrassment in different ways as they passed the table.

'Now that "Faith, Hope and Charity" are getting into right old playing form,' the postman nodded humorously towards the empty crates of stout between the three old brothers playing away on the stage, 'they seem to be losing most of their customers.'

'Earlier and earlier they seem to start at it these days,' the teacher said.

'Still, I suppose they're happy while they're at it.' The postman smiled, and folded his arms on the table at the door, always feeling a bit of an intellectual in these discussions with the hatted teacher, while 'Faith, Hope and Charity' launched into the opening bars of 'A Whistling Gypsy'.

'No, Owen. No. I wouldn't be prepared to go as far as that with you, now,' James Sharkey began.

The Stoat

I was following a two-iron I had struck just short of the green when I heard the crying high in the rough grass above the fairway. The clubs rattled as I climbed towards the sound, but it did not cease, its pitch rising. The light of water from the inlet was blinding when I climbed out of the grass, and I did not see the rabbit at once, where it sat rigidly still on a bare patch of loose sand, crying. I was standing over the rabbit when I saw the grey body of the stoat slithering away like a snake into the long grass.

The rabbit still did not move, but its crying ceased. I saw the wet slick of blood behind its ear, the blood pumping out on the sand. It did not stir when I stooped. Never before did I hold such pure terror in my hands, the body trembling in a rigidity of terror. I stilled it with a single stroke. I took the rabbit down with the bag of clubs and left it on the edge of the green while I played out the hole. Then as I crossed to the next tee I saw the stoat cross the fairway following me still. After watching two simple shots fade away into the rough, I gave up for the day. As I made my way back to the cottage my father rented every August, twice I saw the stoat, following the rabbit still, though it was dead.

All night the rabbit must have raced from warren to warren, the stoat on its trail. Plumper rabbits had crossed the stoat's path but it would not be deflected; it had marked down this one rabbit to kill. No matter how fast the rabbit raced, the stoat was still on its trail, and at last the rabbit sat down in terror and waited for the stoat to slither up and cut the vein behind the ear. I had heard it crying as the stoat was drinking its blood.

My father was reading the death notices on the back of the *Independent* on the lawn of the cottage. He always read the death notices first, and then, after he had exhausted the news and studied the ads for teachers, he'd pore over the death notices again.

'Another colleague who was in Drumcondra the same year as

The Stoat

myself has gone to his reward,' he said when he looked up. 'A great
full-back poor Bernie was, God rest him.'
I held up the rabbit by way of answer.
'Where did you get that?'
'A stoat was killing it on the links.'
'That's what they do. Why did you bring it back?'
'I just brought it. The crying gave me a fright.'
'What will we cook for dinner? You know Miss McCabe is coming
tonight?'
'Not the poor rabbit anyhow. There's lamb chops and cheese and
wine and salad.'
My father had asked me to come to Strandhill because of Miss
McCabe. They'd been seeing one another for several months and
had arranged to spend August at the ocean. They seemed to have
reached some vague, timid understanding that if the holiday went
well they'd become engaged before they returned to their schools in
September. At their age, or any age, I thought their formality
strange, and I an even stranger chaperon.
'Why do you want me to come with you?' I had asked.
'It'd look more decent – proper – and I'd be grateful if you'd
come. Next year you'll be a qualified doctor with a life of your own.'
I had arranged to do postgraduate work for my uncle, a surgeon
in Dublin, when my father pleaded for this last summer. I would
golf and study, he would read the *Independent* and see Miss
McCabe.
The summer before he had asked me, 'Would you take it very
much to heart if I decided to marry again?'
'Of course I wouldn't. Why do you ask?'
'I was afraid you might be affronted by the idea of another
woman holding the position your dear mother held.'
'Mother is dead. You should do exactly as you want to.'
'You have no objections, then?'
'None whatever.'
'I wouldn't even think of going ahead if you'd any objections.'
'Well, you can rest assured, then. I have none. Have you some-
one in mind?'
'No, I don't,' he answered absently.
I put it aside as some wandering whim until several weeks later
when he offered me a sheet of paper on which was written in his

153

clear, careful hand: *Teacher, fifty-two. Seeks companionship. View marriage.* 'What do you think of it?' he asked.

'I think it's fine.' Dismay cancelled a sudden wild impulse to roar with laughter.

'I'll send it off, then, so.'

After about a month he showed me the response. A huge pile of envelopes lay on his desk. I was amazed. I had no idea that so much unfulfilled longing wandered around in the world. Replies came from nurses, housekeepers, secretaries, childless widows, widows with small children, house owners, car owners, pensioners, teachers, civil servants, a policewoman, and a woman who had left at twenty years of age to work at Fords of Dagenham who wanted to come home. The postman inquired slyly if the school was seeking a new assistant, and the woman who ran the post office said in a faraway voice that if we were looking for a housekeeper she had a relative who might be interested.

'I hope they don't steam the damn letters. This country is on fire with curiosity,' he said.

Throughout the winter I saw much of him because he had to meet many of the women in Dublin though he had to go to Cork and Limerick and Tullamore as well. In hotel lounges he met them, hiding behind a copy of the *Roscommon Herald*.

'You've never in your life seen such a collection of wrecks and battleaxes as I've had to see in the last few months,' he said, a cold night in late March after he had met the lady from Dagenham in the Ormond. 'You'd need to get a government grant before you could even think of taking some of them on.'

'Do you mean in appearance or as people?'

'All ways,' he said despairingly. 'I have someone who seems a decent person, at least compared to what I've seen,' and for the first time he told me about Miss McCabe.

Because of these interviews I was under no pressure to go home for Easter and I spent it with my uncle in Dublin. I wasn't able to resist telling him, 'My father's going to get married.'

'You must be joking. You'd think boring one poor woman in a lifetime would be enough.'

'He's gone about it in a curious way. He's put an ad in the papers.'

'An ad!' Suddenly my uncle became convulsed with laughter and

154

was hardly able to get words out. 'Did he get . . . replies?'

'Bundles. He's been interviewing them.'

'Bundles . . . God help us all. This is too much.'

'Apparently, he's just found someone. A schoolteacher in her forties.'

'Have you seen this person?'

'Not yet. I'm supposed to see her soon.'

'My God, if you hang round long enough you see everything.'

My uncle combed his fingers through his long greying hair. He was a distinguished man and his confidence and energy could be intimidating. 'At least, if he does get married, it'll get him off your back.'

'He's all right,' I replied defensively. 'I'm well used to him by now.'

I met Miss McCabe in the lobby of the Ormond Hotel, a lobby that could have been little different to the many lobbies he had waited in behind a copy of the *Roscommon Herald*. They sat in front of me, very stiffly and properly, like two well-dressed, well-behaved children seeking adult approval. She was small and frail and nervous, a nervousness that extended, I suspected, well beyond the awkwardness and unease of the whole contrived meeting. There was something about her – a waif-like sense of decency – that was at once appealing and troubling. Though old, she was like a girl, in love with being in love a whole life long without ever settling on any single demanding presence until this late backward glance fell on my bereft but seeking father.

'Well, what was your impression?' he asked me when we were alone.

'I think Miss McCabe is a decent, good person,' I said uncomfortably.

'You have . . . no objections, then?'

'None.'

We had been here a week. I had seen Miss McCabe three or four times casually. She looked open-eyed and happy. She stayed in the Seaview Hotel beside the salt baths on the ocean front and went for walks along the shore with my father. They had lunches and teas together. Tonight she was coming to the house for the first time. In all his years in the world my father had never learned to cook, and I offered to take care of the dinner.

She wore a long blue printed dress, silver shoes, and silver pendants, like thin elongated pears, hung from her ears. Though she praised the food she hardly ate at all and took only a few sips from the wine glass. My father spoke of schools and curricula and how necessary it was to get to the sea each August to rid oneself of staleness before starting back into the new school year, and her eyes shone as she followed every heavy word.

'You couldn't be more right. The sea will always be wonderful,' she said.

It seemed to discomfort my father, as if her words belonged more to the sea and air than to his own rooted presence.

'What do you think?' he asked predictably when he returned from leaving her back to the Seaview.

'I think she is a very gentle person.'

'Do you think she has her feet on the ground?'

'I think you are very lucky to have found her,' I said. The way he looked at me told me he was far from convinced that he had been lucky.

The next morning he looked at me in a more dissatisfied manner still when a girl came from the Seaview to report that Miss McCabe had a mild turn during the night. A doctor had seen her. She was recovering and resting in the hotel and wanted to see my father. The look on his face told me that he was more than certain now that she was not near rooted enough.

'Will you come with me?' he asked.

'It is yourself she wants to see.'

When he got back from the hotel he was agitated. 'She's all right,' he said. 'She had a mild heart attack. She still thinks we'll get engaged at the end of the month.'

'I thought that was the idea.'

'It was. If everything went well,' he said with emphasis.

'Did you try to discuss it with her?'

'I tried. I wasn't able. All she thinks of is our future. Her head is full of plans.'

'What are you going to do?'

'Clear out,' he said. 'There is no other way.'

As if all the irons were suddenly being truly struck and were flowing from all directions to the heart of the green, I saw that my father had started to run like the poor rabbit. He would have been better off if he could have tried to understand something, even though it would get him off nothing. Miss McCabe was not alone in her situation.

'Where'll you go to?' I asked.

'Home, of course. What are you going to do?'

'I'll stay here a while longer. I might go to Dublin in a few days.'

'What if you run into her and she asks about me?'

'I'll tell her you had to go home. How soon are you going?'

'As soon as I get the stuff into the boot of the car.'

Because I was ashamed of him I carried everything he wanted out to the car.

'I hope you don't mind,' he said as he prepared to drive away.

'No. I don't mind.'

I watched the car climb the hill. When it had gone out of sight I had the clear vision again of hundreds of irons being all cleanly struck and flowing from every direction into the very heart of the green.

All night the rabbit must have raced from warren to warren, the stoat on its trail. Plumper rabbits had crossed the stoat's path but it would not be deflected; it had marked down this one rabbit to kill. No matter how fast the rabbit raced, the stoat was still on its trail, and at last the rabbit sat down in terror and waited for the stoat to slither up and cut the vein behind the ear. I had heard it crying as the stoat was drinking its blood.

Doorways

I

There are times when we see the small events we look forward to – a visit, a wedding, a new day – as having no existence but in the expectation. They are to be, they will happen, and before they do they almost are not: minute replicas of the expectation that we call the rest of our life.

I used to panic when I saw my life that way, it brought the blind and overmastering desire to escape, and the religious life had seemed for long the one way out: to resign this life, to take on the habit of unchanging death-like days, the sweet passion; and when death came it could hold no terror. I had already died in life.

I no longer panic when I see that way: nature, having started to lose interest in me, is now content to let me drift away, and no longer jabs me so sharply that I must lose myself in life before it is too late.

And I have found Barnaby and Bartleby. All day and every day they are in the doorways of Abbey Street. I call them Barnaby and Bartleby but I do not know their names. They must have some shelter to go to for they disappear from the doorways about eight in winter, an hour later in the summer. I have never seen them leave. They seem to be there one moment and gone the next. I have never watched them go. I feel it would be an intrusion to draw too close and that they mightn't leave if watched. The early morning is the one time they are busy, searching the bins with total concentration before the garbage trucks come by. They never search the same bin together or stand in the same doorway. Only in freezing weather do they come close, just inside the door of the public lavatory, and even there they keep the red coinslot weighing machine between them, their backs to the wall, above their heads the black arrow pointing to the urinal stalls within.

They seem to change doorways every two hours or so and always to the same doorway at the same time. I thought at first they might be following the sun but then noticed they still changed whether the

158

sun was in or out. They wear long overcoats, tightly belted, with pleats at the back, that had been in fashion about fifteen years before. Often I want to ask them why have they picked on this way to get through life, but outside the certainty of not being answered I soon see it as an idle question and turn away. They never answer strangers who ask about the times of the buses out of Abbey Street. They have their different ways, too, of not answering. Bartleby, the younger and smaller, just moves his boots and averts his face sideways and down; but Barnaby stares steadily over his steel-rimmed spectacles into his interlocutor's eyes. Otherwise, they seem to take a calm and level interest in everything that goes on outside their doorway. They must be completely law abiding, for the police hardly glance at them as they pass on patrol.

II

The same winter that I began to follow Barnaby and Bartleby I met Kate O'Mara. We met at Nora Moran's.

Nora Moran was a painter who gave parties round people she hoped would buy her paintings or get her grants from foundations to advance her career or self-esteem; in some way they were all intertwined. We used to make fun of Nora. 'I ran into Nora Moran today. She's in a bad way. She's down to her last three houses,' after listening to her money worries in some coffee shop off the Green for hours as the coffee went cold and the cups were taken away. In our eyes she was a rich and successful woman. Still, we went to her parties, knowing we were being used as butcher's grass or chopped-down rhododendron branches to cover up the dusty margins of the processional ways in June. We went out of respect for Nora's early work and, less honourably, because it took a greater energy to stay away once Nora had made up her mind that we should go. As young women were not Nora's idea of either butcher's grass or rhododendrons, it was with surprise that I found myself facing a tall and lovely young woman at a party close to Christmas.

'Hi,' she said at once. 'My name is Kate O'Mara.'

'How do you happen to be at Nora's?' I asked as soon as the courtesies were over.

'I used to work on a magazine in New York,' she said. 'The editor is a friend of Nora's. We did a profile of her last year. When I was coming to Dublin everybody said I must see her.'

'You're here on holiday?'

'No,' she said, laughing. 'I guess you won't believe it. I came here to write.'

There are so many voices here already, and so little room. Who will hear all the voices, I thought. When I saw Nora Moran coming towards us I asked quickly, 'Will you let me take you out some evening?'

'Sure,' she answered uncertainly, surprised.

I had just time to write down the telephone number before Nora came between us. 'Well, what are you two getting up to here?' and when the social laughter ceased, I said, 'Kate was telling me about this profile of you . . .'

There was no need to say more. Nora was launched on her favourite subject.

III

'Why were you so anxious to keep from Nora that we were going out?' were the first words Kate asked the following Saturday when we were seated in a restaurant.

'She'd want to come.'

'I don't believe it.'

'It's true. She'd control the whole world if she could,' and then I asked, looking at her ringless fingers, 'Were you ever married?'

'No. Why do you ask?' The soup spoon paused at her lips.

'No why. It's probably stupid. We think of Americans as much married.'

'My mother would have a fit if she heard that. We're Catholics from way back. Nuns and priests galore. "No one was ever divorced in *my* family," my mother is fond of boasting.'

'Has that anything to do with your coming here?'

'In a way. The whole family is rotten with nostalgia about Ireland. I said I'd come and see into it once and for all. And it *was* easier to come here. If I said I was going to wicked Paris, there'd be an uproar, but old Dublin is nice, clean. So here I am.'

'And you look quite lovely,' I said sincerely.

'Why don't we split this? This place isn't cheap,' she said when the bill came.

'This is mine. Another time you can take me if you wish,' and when we were outside I said, 'It's only a few streets. I'll walk you home.'

Below the granite steps that led to the Georgian doorway where she had rooms I leaned to kiss her. She did not withdraw, but made it clear that it was no more than a courtesy at the end of the evening.

'Would you like to come out some other evening?' I asked awkwardly in the rebuff that was not quite a rebuff.

'Sure,' she said. 'The next time I must take you. When?'

'Next Saturday?'

She thought for a moment and said, 'Next Saturday's fine,' and waved as she took the key out of her purse.

Aimlessly, like old people grateful for mere human presence, we went out together that winter. Only once did I challenge the sexual restraint.

'Is there someone that you're involved with?' I asked one evening.

'Yes.'

'Is it someone in Dublin?'

She named a man I knew, in public relations, whom she had met at Nora Moran's.

'He has this dream of an Irish Ireland, free of outside influences, and he's fiercely anti-American. I get abused all the time,' she explained.

'Do you want to marry him?'

'No,' she laughed. 'I'm not quite that crazy.'

'But you sleep with him?' I felt deprived and jealous.

'Yes, but it's a bad business. He always leaves before morning. Whenever we meet he does all the talking and we only meet whenever he wants. Yet I keep missing him.'

'I'm sorry,' I said in the face of an openness I was unused to.

'I'm sorry too but it's a relief to talk about these things sometimes.'

After that evening she must have suspected my desire or jealousy. Whenever I would ask about her life outside our meetings she would avoid a direct answer and then try to make her life sound humdrum and dull. She always wore her plainest clothes when we met.

IV

I could not help but feel irony when I noticed the light of competition in Nora Moran's eyes when next we met.

'We hardly ever see you now,' she said. 'I hear you and Kate see a great deal of one another. She's a very attractive girl.'

'We see each other very little. People exaggerate. I was going to call you but I always think you're busy.'

'Why don't we drop everything today? I've been intending to go down to the farm. We'll drive down.'

'I'm free all day.'

There was a mist that promised to break into a fine day as we drove out of the city. Nora had a large heavy car, with warm mahogany panelling, and she drove very fast and badly, continually taking her eyes off the road to search my face for responses.

'Do you see that beech tree over there, Nora?' I resorted to saying when we got out into the country. 'There's something about its trunk that reminds me of some of the recurring shapes in your work,' leaning cravenly towards the windscreen to narrow her angle when she would look back. It was a relief when the car lurched into the long gravelled avenue that led to the house.

'I lose money on it all the time,' she said as we looked over the rich acres, 'but it's the last thing I'd ever sell. My father built up this place from nothing. I like to think he'd approve of everything I've done if he were to come back.'

'Still, it's a solid investment.'

'He was fond of saying that. "Never be fool enough to keep your money in cash." You'd have loved my father,' she said. 'He was that sort of a man if he were to take a fork to his soup at a dinner table all the others would take up their forks. "You have us all brainwashed, Mr Moran," old Michael, the gardener, used to say to him. He was the only one who dared say it, he was with us so long.'

After meeting the herdsmen, and the two farmhands, we opened the big white house and went through it room by room. Nora's paintings hung on the walls alongside paintings her father had purchased, many of them valuable. When pressed by Nora I said that I had no faith in my judgement, not having been brought up with pictures, but that I liked everything in the house. Late in the evening I made a log fire in the dining-room while Nora made cheese and tomato sandwiches. We had sandwiches with a half-bottle of red wine Nora brought from the cellar.

'Do you miss not being married, Nora?' I asked so as not to appear too passive.

'No. My life is too full for me to be married, but sometimes I wish I had someone, a young man making his way in the world, an academic, or young artist. I'd set him up close to me. We'd make no demands on one another. All I'd ask is that between certain hours I could come to him if I was tired.' She looked at me so steadily that I began to feel uneasy, and changed the subject to her paintings.

Afterwards, I took nothing in of the long river of words. I took care to make only the barest responses. By the time we left even they were not necessary. I was glad of the darkness as we drove back to the city, both of us keeping our eyes fixed on the empty floodlit roads. The black hands of an orange clockface on a steeple were fixed at twelve-ten as we reached the outskirts of the city.

'Do you mind if I drop round to Mother before leaving you off?' she said. 'I never feel easy without saying goodnight to Mother.'

'I don't mind at all.'

We crossed a cattle grid into the courtyard of a luxury block of flats and Nora drove round to the side.

Suddenly, without switching the engine off, she started to blow the horn. She blew until a fragile woman in a nightdress appeared in the groundfloor window. 'Goodnight, Mother.' Nora rolled down the window and waved and blew the horn again. The old mother waved feebly back.

'It costs a fortune to keep Mother in that place but she's never satisfied. She's never without some complaint. My father was too proud to admit it but his marriage was the one real failure in his life. She was never in his style.'

'It'll be all right if you let me out here, Nora. I'd be glad of the few minutes' walk,' I said as she drove me to the Green.

We grimaced and waved goodnight to one another like any special pair of monkeys. I was numbed by the day. I was probably numbed anyhow. I hadn't even resentment of my own passivity. Barnaby and Bartleby were far closer to my style than any of this day had been.

As soon as I thought of them in their doorways, the sound of my own footsteps in the empty silence of a sleeping city seemed to take on a kind of healing.

V

If anything, I now took an even keener interest in Barnaby and Bartleby. Barnaby's sallow face behind the steel rims did not change as the winter gave way to a hot early summer, but Bartleby positively bloomed in the doorways and even in his rigidly belted overcoat he looked as tanned as if he had just come from the seaside.

Later, Barnaby began to sport a plastic yellow cap, such as girl bicyclists wear in rain, and to make sudden gestures. I put it down to the irritation of the heat. It was enough to suggest that I go on holiday. Instead of going abroad I had a sudden desire to go to the sea that I had gone to as a child. I wrote to Jimmy McDermott in Sligo. We had grown up together, gone to our first dances there, taken girls we had met at the dances in harmless summers to Dollymount and Howth; and before the time came for us to drift naturally apart he was transferred to Sligo. I wrote to him to ask if he could find me a cheap room in Sligo for the summer. He wrote back that there was room in his own place and that he would be glad if I came. About the same time Kate O'Mara told me that her affair had ended.

'What happened?'

'He got married. There were even pictures in the papers, confetti and buttonhole carnations,' she said with self-mocking bitterness. 'He'd the gall to come round and tell me about it, saying sanctimoniously how things would never have worked out between us anyhow. Practically asked my blessing.'

'And what did you do?'

'I told him to go to hell.'

'Good,' I said. 'How do you feel now?'

'My vanity took a hammering. I guess I'm not used to rejection.'

'You should have gone out with me instead. We might be married now.'

'Thanks,' she laughed, 'but that could never be.'

I told her I was going on holiday for the summer, to Sligo. 'Maybe you might like to come down later,' I said.

'I doubt it. I have to work. I've done hardly any work.'

'I'll write you. You may change your mind.'

Her face was very pale and strained as she waved goodbye to me.

Doorways

VI

Jimmy met me at Sligo Station. He had put on weight and I could see the light through his thinning hair, but the way the porters and the drivers playing cards at the taxi rank hailed him he was as popular here as he had been everywhere. Soon, walking with him and remembering the part of our lives that had been passed together, it was like walking in a continuance of days that had suffered no interruption.

'I hope getting the digs didn't put you to a great deal of trouble,' I said.

'No. The old birds were pleased as punch. Ordinarily it's full, but this time they've always rooms because of people gone on holidays.'

The 'old birds' were two sisters in their fifties who owned the big stone house down by the harbour where Jimmy had digs and where I had come on holiday. A brother who was a Monsignor in California had bought it for them. I had never seen before walls so completely laden with cribs and religious pictures. There was the usual smell of digs, of cooking and feet and sweat, the sharp scent of HP sauce, the brown bottle on every lino-covered table.

'They're religious mad but they're good sorts and they won't bother you. They have to cook for more than thirty,' Jimmy said after he had introduced me and showed me to my room, mockingly sprinkling holy water from a font between the feet of a large statue of the Virgin as he left. There were at least thirty men at tea that evening. Out of the aggressive bantering and horseplay as they ate, fear and insecurity and hatred of one another showed like a familiar face.

'It's the usual,' Jimmy said when I mentioned it to him afterwards as we walked to the pub to talk. He was excited and greedy for news of the city. He even asked about Barnaby and Bartleby. 'The gents of Abbey Street'.

'Why do you remember them?'

'I don't know. I never paid them any attention when I was there. It's only since I came here that I started to think about them.'

'But why?'

'I suppose,' he said slowly, 'they highlight what we're all at.'

'Do you miss the city, then?'

'I don't know. I suppose. In a way my life ended when I left it.'

165

When I was there it still seemed to have possibilities, but now I know it's all fixed.'

'And that girl – was it Mary Jo?' I named a dark, swarthy girl, extraordinarily attractive rather than goodlooking.

'The Crystal, National, Metropole, Clerys.' He repeated the names of the ballrooms they had gone to together. 'She went to England.'

'Why didn't you keep her?'

'Maybe it wasn't on. There seemed to be so much time then that there was no hurry. I went to London to try to see her but she was working at Littlewoods and had shacked up with a married Englishman.'

I could tell that he had suffered and changed. 'Do you have anyone here?'

'Yes. There was so much choice in Dublin. But here, if you get anything you have to hold on to it. There are so few women here.' He sounded as if he was already apologizing. She was a dark pretty girl but she never spoke a word when we met. I noticed that only when alone with Jimmy did she grow animated.

'And you, have you anybody?' he asked.

'No. There's an American girl, but there's nothing sexual. We're just friends,' and when I saw that he didn't believe me I added, 'There's a slight chance she may still come down.'

The Blue Anchor was filling. All of the men nodded to Jimmy and many of them joined us with their pints. When an old fisherman came, Jack Kelly, place was made for him in the centre of the party beside Jimmy. It turned out that they were all members of the newly formed Pint Drinkers' Association. Jack Kelly was the President and Jimmy was both Secretary and Treasurer. The publicans of the town had got together and fixed a minimum price for the pint, a few pence higher than what had been charged previously. The Pint Drinkers' Association had been formed to fight this rise. They canvassed bars and pledged that the Pint Drinkers would drink only at those bars that kept to the old price. There cannot have been great solidarity among the publicans, for already six, including the Blue Anchor, which had become the Association's headquarters, had agreed to return to the old price. When I paid the fee Jimmy wrote my name down in a child's blue exercise book and Jack Kelly silently witnessed it. Soon afterwards we left the Blue Anchor and began a round of the bars that had gone back to the old price.

Doorways

Time went by without being noticed in the days that followed: watching the boats in the harbour, leaning on the bridge of Sligo, the white foam churning under the weir, a weed or fish swaying lazily to the current; reading the morning paper on a windowsill or bar stool; the sea at Rosses and Strandhill. Often in the evenings we played handball at the harbour alley, and though our hands were swollen and all our muscles ached, again it was as if the years had fallen away and we were striking the small rubber inside the netting-wire of our old school, the cabbage stumps in the black clay of the garden between the alley and orchard. Afterwards we would meet in the Blue Anchor, from where we could set out on our nightly round of the bars that had agreed to keep the pint at its old price. As their number was growing steadily, it made for thirsty work.

'It's catching on like wildfire,' I said to Jimmy as we lurched away from the last bar one evening, voluble with six or seven pints.

'I'll wait and see,' Jimmy said. 'It'll probably be like everything else here. It'll catch on for a while, then fall away.'

At this time Jimmy began to miss three evenings every week now that the Association, as he put it, was on a firm footing. He took his girl to the cinema or went dancing, and this disturbed Jack Kelly.

'Jimmy's beginning to show the white flag,' he complained. 'He's missing again this evening. Watch my word. The leg-irons will be coming up soon.'

VII

These days might have stretched into weeks but for a card I sent to Kate O'Mara. I wrote that I was happy at the sea and that if she changed her mind and wished to join me to just write. Instead, she telegrammed that she was coming on the early train the next day. I booked two single rooms in a small hotel at Strandhill and Jimmy and I met her off the train. She was wearing sandals, and had on a sleeveless dress of blue denim, and dark glasses.

'Jimmy's an old friend. I thought we'd all have a glass and some sandwiches,' I said when she seemed puzzled by Jimmy's presence.

'I had lunch on the train.'

'That doesn't matter. You can have a drink,' Jimmy said as we took her bags.

'I'm afraid I'm not a big drinker,' she laughed nervously.

167

'What'll you have?' I asked her in a bar down from the station, quiet with three porters discussing the racing page as they finished their lunch hour.

'I'll take a chance,' she grew more easy. 'Can I have an Irish coffee?'

All our attempts at speech were awkward and soon Jimmy made a show of examining his watch and rose. 'Some of the population has to work,' he grinned ruefully.

'I'll come in tomorrow or the next day,' I said.

'I'll keep any letters for you, then,' he said.

'How do you feel?' I asked when we were alone.

She took up the story of her broken affair. She hadn't been able to work or read and she began to go to the Green, sitting behind dark glasses in one of the canvas deck-chairs placed in a half-circle round the fountain in hot weather; and she just sat there watching the people pass or remembering her life in New York, and gradually was growing calm when one day Nora Moran found her and took her down the country. The day seemed to have been an exact replica of the day I had spent there.

'The workmen were so servile with her,' Kate complained.

'They don't mind that. It's their way,' I said.

'But American workmen would never be like that.'

'Listen, won't we miss the bus?' An edge had crept into the talk.

'You don't want to hear about Nora?'

'I do, but you should know that Nora needs a fresh person every day, the way some people need a bottle of whiskey.'

'If she wasn't around she was on the phone. A few nights ago, as she was going on about herself, I put the phone down. When I picked it up again, there was Nora still talking. She hadn't noticed that I hadn't been listening.'

'You don't have to worry now,' I gripped her shoulders. 'You're here now.'

'I can't tell you how happy I am to be here,' she said as we went to the bus. The bus dropped us at the church across from the hotel. A large taciturn man, Costello, had us sign our names in the register and then showed us to our rooms on separate floors.

VIII

The eight o'clock bells woke me the next morning. It was a Sunday and we came downstairs almost together. She had on a black lace scarf and leather gloves and a missal with a simple gold cross.

'Are you going to Mass before having breakfast?' I asked.

'Yes.' She laughed a light girlish laugh.

'I'll come too,' I said, and since she was looking at me in surprise I added, 'It makes a good impression round here,' as we walked across and joined other worshippers on the white gravel between the rows of escallonia that led to the church door. I remembered her saying once, 'I'm a bad Catholic but I am one because if I wasn't I couldn't bear all the thinking I'd have to do'; and for me, as I knelt by her side in the church or stood or sat, it was more like wandering in endless corridors of lost mornings than being present in this actual church and day, the church I'd grown up in, with wings to the left and right of the altar and the cypress and evergreen still in the windows.

'We'll have you reconverted soon,' she said playfully as she sprinkled holy water in my direction as we left by the porch door.

'Once you've lost it you can't go back. I think the whole point is not being able to imagine being anything else. Once you can, you're gone.'

'In that sense I'm not one either.'

'I think we should have breakfast.' We hurried quickly past the people shaking hands at the gate.

In spite of what I said, Sunday was suddenly new again for me. The first bell for Second Mass was more than an hour away and we had already done our duty. As children we would have changed out of our stiff Sunday suits and shoes, and the day was still before us, for football or pitch-and-toss or the river, the whole day stretching before us in such a long, amazing prospect of pleasure that we were almost loath to begin it.

In the same recovery of amazement, I watched Kate's beauty against the power of the ocean as we walked afterwards on the shore, traced the fading initials on the wood of the cannon pointed out to sea, watched the early morning golfers move over the fairways, and saw the children come out with their buckets and beach balls, watched by their parents from the edge of the rocks.

'We can have all this and more,' the waves whispered.

IX

As it was a hot Sunday, I knew that relatives or people I had known would come to the sea and if I hung about the hotels or front I was certain to meet them.

'I think I'll steer clear of the ocean for the next five or six hours,' I said to her at lunch, and explained why.

'What do you care? Are you too shy?' she asked sharply.

'It'd be stupid to be shy at my age. It's just too hard to make talk, for them and me.'

When she was silent I said, 'You don't have to come if you don't want to.'

'Where'll you go?'

'I'll take a book or something over to that old roofless church you can barely see in the far distance.'

'I guess I'll come – that's if you have no objection,' she said.

'I'll only be glad.'

As we walked I pointed to the stream of cars going slowly down to the sea. The roofless church was two miles from the hotel. At first, close to the hotel, we had come across some half-circles of tents in the hollows, then odd single tents, and soon there was nothing but the rough sea grass and sand and rabbit warrens. Some small birds flew out of the ivy rooted in the old walls of the church, and we sat among the faceless stones, close to a big clump of sea thistle. Far away the beach was crowded with small dark figures within the coastguard flags.

'In America,' she said, looking at the lighthouse, 'they have a bell to warn ships. On a wet misty evening it's eerie to hear it toll, like lost is the wanderer.'

'It must be,' I repeated. I felt I should say something more about it but there was nothing I could say.

We began to read but the tension between us increased rather than lessened. I saw the white tinsel of the sea thistle, the old church, the slopes of Knocknarea, the endless pounding of the ocean mingled with bird and distant child cries, the sun hot on the old stones, the very day in its suspension, and thought if there was not this tension between us, if only we could touch or kiss we could have all this and more, the whole day and sea and sky and far beyond.

'This country depresses me so much it makes me mad,' she said suddenly.

'Why?' I looked up slowly.

'Everybody comes to the beach and just sits around. In America they'd be doing handstands, playing volleyball, riding the surf. Forgive me, but I had to say something.'

'I don't mind at all.'

'That's part of the trouble. You should mind.'

'I don't mind.' I thought that if we were Barnaby and Bartleby we could hardly be further apart.

'Kate,' I said suddenly, 'why can't we be lovers?'

'No.' She shook her head and smiled.

'You're free now. We could have so much more together and if nothing came of it we'd have very little to lose.'

'No, I don't think of you that way. I couldn't.'

'Why not?'

'No. I'm sorry.' She shook her head. 'I couldn't think of us that way.'

I thought bitterly of what she said – like Nora Moran's workmen I had been brought up a different way, that was all – but asked, 'You mean you can't think of us as ever being together?'

'I'm very fond of you but I could never think of us in that way. I think we're far too alike.'

'I had to ask.' I conceded I had lost. She did not want me the way some people cannot eat shellfish or certain meats. There was once a robin who sang against the church bells striking midnight thinking that the yellow street lamps in the road below were tokens of the day.

Hours later, in the tiredness of the evening, spaces now on the hill between the cars leaving the beach for the day, she said gently, 'I hope it'll make no difference between us.'

'It won't.'

'I think we can have far more as we are. What's between us is only a beginning.'

'I don't think so but it seems it's the way it must be.'

X

The next day was wet, a mist that closed in from the sea so that the church was barely visible from the hotel, but though the rain was soft as a caress on the face it wet one through. I played billiards all that morning in a bar down on the front and then rang Jimmy. I arranged to meet him in Sligo.

'I'm going to Sligo. Would you like to come?' I asked her over lunch.

'Why?'

'Jimmy and his girl are going to the cinema and he asked if we'd like to go with them and have a drink afterwards.'

'Like two happy couples?'

'Well, you don't have to come,' I said, and we began to talk about Nora Moran. The more we talked the more I felt how much more honest was Nora's brutal egotism set against our pale lives here by the sea.

'If Nora has ears to hear they must be burning now,' she laughed when we had ended.

We went to our rooms to read. Outside the window the road shone black with rain. Through the mist it was as if fine threads of rain were being teased slowly down. We did not meet till the flat gong that hung in the hallway rang for tea.

'You haven't changed your mind?' I asked cautiously.

'Listen,' she said. 'I want you to do something for me. I want you not to go to Sligo.'

'But I can't not go. I promised Jimmy.'

'You can call him up.'

'There's no phone in the digs and he's left work by now.'

She was eating so slowly that I began to fear I would miss the bus if I waited for her.

'I'm sorry. I have to go,' I said as I rose.

'Do you have to go so soon?'

'The bus'll be outside in five minutes or so.'

To my puzzlement she laid her knife and fork side by side on the plate, rose, took her raincoat from the bentwood stand in the hall, and came out with me into the rain. In uncomfortable silence we watched the bus pass down, waited for it to turn at the cannon and come back, the waves crashing incessantly on the shore beyond the soft, endlessly drifting veils of rain.

'Are you sure you won't change your mind and come?' I asked as I heard the bus.

'No.' She shook her head. As the veiled yellow sidelights showed in the rain she suddenly tugged my sleeve and said earnestly, 'I want you to do this for me. I want you not to get on the bus.'

'Is there any good reason?' I demanded. Only a beloved could ask so much, so capriciously. Did she want all this as well as the voices, without any of the burden of love or work?

'Just that I want you not to.'

'I can't not go,' I said, 'but what I'll do is get the next bus back. I'll be back within an hour. Maybe we'll go out for a drink then,' and pressing her arm climbed into the bus. As soon as I paid the conductor I looked back. Already the bus had changed gear to climb the hill and I could not see through the rain and misted windows whether she was still standing there or had gone back into the hotel. I stirred uneasily, feeling that I had left some hurt behind. Yet what she had demanded had been unreasonable; but far more insistently than reason, or the grinding of the bus, came, 'If you had loved her you would have stayed.' But all of life turns away from its own eventual hopelessness, leaving insomnia and night to lovers and the dying.

I had come far in time since first I travelled on this bus. Surprised as a boy by the conductor's outstretched hand, I had reached up and shaken it. The whole bus had rocked with laughter and one man cheered. 'It's the fare now I'd be looking for,' and though he had smiled the conductor had been as embarrassed and confused as I had been.

As much through the light of years as through this wet evening the bus seemed to move. It was an August evening. We were going home at the end of another summer holiday. When the bus stopped at the Central, Michael Henry got on. His clothes hung about him and the only sign of his old jauntiness was the green teal's feather in the felt hat. After years in America he had come home, bought a shop and farm, married, had children. We kept an account in his shop and every Christmas he gave us a bottle of Redbreast and a tin of Jacob's figrolls.

'How is it, Michael, that you seem to be going home and we've never met in all this time at the sea?' my father asked.

'I guess it's because I just came down yesterday,' Michael Henry said as he put his small leather case in the overhead rack.

'How is it you're going home so soon?'

'I guess I thought the sea might do me some good but I only felt worse last night. I don't believe in shelling out good money to a hotel when you can be just as badly off at home. America teaches you those things.'

He sat the whole way home with my father. They talked of America and the war in Europe. Not many weeks later, in scarlet and white, I was to follow the priest round Michael Henry's coffin as he blessed it with holy water from the brass jar in my hands.

And suddenly the dead man climbing on the bus, the living girl asking me not to go to Sligo in the rain outside the hotel, I on the bus to Sligo to collect some letters, Barnaby and Bartleby, even now in their Dublin doorways patiently watching the day fade, all seemed to be equally awash in time and indistinguishable, the same mute human presence beneath the unchanging sky, and for one moment I could not see how anyone could wish another pain. We were all waiting in the doorways.

XI

I went straight from the bus station to the Blue Anchor. I got letters that had come for me from Jimmy, saw some of the Pint Drinkers. They were planning to take two barrels of stout out to Strandhill in a van one of these evenings, dig for clams and have a party on the shore. Already it was a world I could no longer join. As we made our excuses for leaving, I to get the next bus back to Strandhill, Jimmy to meet his girl outside the cinema, Jack clapped us affectionately on the shoulders and said, 'Soon the pint days will be over. They'll have the leg-irons on yous in no time now.'

'Some other time we must make an evening of it,' Jimmy and his girl said as I left them at the cinema.

'Some other time,' I echoed but already my anxiety was returning. The rain was heavier now and the drops fell like small yellow stones into the headlights of the bus. I hurried across the wet sand outside the hotel, and when I did not find her downstairs climbed to her room. I saw Costello's eyes follow me with open suspicion. When I knocked on her door there was no answer.

'Are you in, Kate?' I called softly. Then I heard her low sobbing.

'I've just come back on the bus. I wondered if you'd like to come out for a drink?'

'No, thanks.'

'I came back in the hope you'd come out. Are you sure you won't come?'

'No, thanks. I want to be alone.'

Slowly I retraced my steps down the narrow creaking corridor. There was nothing I could do but wait for morning.

XII

With a reluctance to face what the morning might bring in the light of the evening before, I was late in coming down. The first thing that met my eyes was her luggage in the hallway. She was leaving.

'I see Miss O'Mara decided to leave today after all,' I tried to say as casually as possible to Costello, who seemed to be as much on guard over the bags as in his usual place in the office.

'She told me to tell you that she's settled her account and is leaving,' he said in a tone which seemed to convey that I must have given her some good reason to leave with such suddenness.

She had had breakfast, and as I ate mine it grew clear that even outside the discomfort of remaining in Costello's hostility I had no longer any reason to stay, not indeed that there seemed any reason ever to have come. A kind of anger against her for giving me no warning hardened my decision to leave at once. There was only one way she could leave, on the eleven o'clock bus, and I would leave with her on the same bus.

'I'd like to have the bill. I'm leaving,' I said to Costello, and as I was now meeting his aggression with aggression he did not trouble to answer. After pretending to consult some records, he presented me with the bill for the whole week. Hostile as I felt, I was forced to smile. 'But I've been here only four days.'

'You booked for a week.'

'Well, in that case, keep the room open for me.' I counted out what he had demanded. 'I'll probably come back tomorrow,' at which he exploded: 'No. Your type is not wanted again here,' and he slid the difference towards me.

The tide must be far out I thought as I sat and listened to the pounding of the sea while waiting for the bus to turn at the cannon. It was a clear, fresh morning after the rain, only a few tattered shreds of white cloud in the blue sky. She did not come out until the bus was almost due. She was tense and looked as if she hadn't slept and was

175

afraid when she saw me. Costello carried her bags, and as they prepared to wait together at a separate distance I decided to join them.

'I decided to leave too,' I said, and she then turned to Costello: 'You needn't wait any longer, Mr Costello. I'll be fine now. And are you sure you won't take something?' And when he refused for what was obviously the second time he shook her hand warmly and went in. Even then she might not have spoken if I had not said, 'You should have let me know. It gave me no chance at all.'

'Does it matter so much?'

'No, not that much. But why make it more difficult than it has to be?'

'I'm sorry,' she said. 'I had to do it this way. I couldn't do it any other way. I didn't mean for you to leave at all.'

The bus was coming. As it was empty the conductor told us to take our bags on the bus, and we dumped them on the front seat. The waves seemed to pound louder than ever behind us above the creaky running of the bus.

'Did he charge you for the whole week?' I asked.

'I offered but he wouldn't take it.'

'The brute.' I smiled. 'He tried to charge me.'

I wanted to ask her about the evening before, about all that had gone before since we had first met at Nora Moran's, but I knew it was all hopeless, and I was blinded by no passion; I had not even that grace: at most it had been a seed, thrown on poor ground, half wishing it might come to something, in the wrong time of year. As if my silence was itself a question, she said as the bus came into Sligo, 'I can't explain anything that happened. I'll tell you some day but I can't now.'

'It's all right. Don't worry about it.' We were back in the safety of the phrases that mean nothing. 'Anything worth explaining generally can't be explained anyhow.'

'We'll say goodbye here,' she said when we got off the bus. 'I'm sorry but I want to be alone.'

'Where'll you go?'

'To the hotel.' She motioned with her head. 'I'll get the two o'clock train. I hope you'll ring me when you get to Dublin. I won't be this way then.'

I turned away but saw her climb the steps, the glass door open and the doorman take her bags, a flash of light as the door closed. She would have a salad and a glass of wine and coffee, feel the expensive linen and smile at the waiter's smiles. She would be almost back in her own world before her train left, as I was almost back in mine.

How empty the doorways were, empty coffins stood on end.

Already Barnaby and Bartleby would be in their doorway in Abbey Street firmly fitting them till night, when they would silently leave.

All the people I had met at Nora Moran's, bowing and scraping and smiling in their doorways. Nora rushing from doorway to doorway, trying to bring all the doorways with her. 'I never feel easy without saying goodnight to Mother'; Michael Henry climbing on the bus, 'I don't believe in shelling out good money to a hotel when you can be just as badly off at home. America teaches you those things,' the vivid green of the teal's feather in his hat as he disappeared into the years.

Kate O'Mara sitting in the big dining-room of the hotel. The Pint Drinkers' Association, Jimmy McDermott, the last weeks in Sligo, the Kincora, the sea . . . everything seemed to be without shape. I understood nothing. Perhaps we had come to expect too much. Neither Barnaby nor Bartleby would tell. They didn't know. They just lived it.

I opened both my hands. They were quite empty. A clear morning came to me. It was on the edge of a town, close to the asylum, and a crowd of presumably harmless patients were hedging whitethorns along the main road, watched over by their male nurses. One patient seemed to be having a wonderful time. He lifted every branch he cut, and after a careful examination of each sprig he began to laugh uproariously. I felt my empty hands were worthy of such uproarious mirth. Wasn't my present calm an equal, more courteous madness?

I was free in the Sligo morning. I could do as I pleased. There were all sorts of wonderful impossibilities in sight. The real difficulty was that the day was fast falling into its own night.

The Wine Breath

If I were to die, I'd miss most the mornings and the evenings, he thought as he walked the narrow dirt-track by the lake in the late evening, and then wondered if his mind was failing, for how could anybody think anything so stupid: being a man he had no choice, he was doomed to die; and being dead he'd miss nothing, being nothing. It went against everything in his life as a priest.

The solid world, though, was everywhere around him. There was the lake, the road, the evening, and he was going to call on Gillespie. Gillespie was sawing. Gillespie was always sawing. The roaring rise-and-fall of the two-stroke stayed like a rent in the evening. When he got to the black gate there was Gillespie, his overalled bulk framed in the short avenue of alders, and he was sawing not alders but beech, four or five tractor-loads dumped in the front of the house. The priest put a hand to the black gate, bolted to the first of the alders, and was at once arrested by showery sunlight falling down the avenue. It lit up one boot holding the length of beech in place, it lit the arms moving the blade slowly up and down as it tore through the beech, white chips milling out on the chain.

Suddenly, as he was about to rattle the gate loudly to see if this would penetrate the sawing, he felt himself (bathed as in a dream) in an incredible sweetness of light. It was the evening light on snow. The gate on which he had his hand vanished, the alders, Gillespie's formidable bulk, the roaring of the saw. He was in another day, the lost day of Michael Bruen's funeral nearly thirty years before. All was silent and still there. Slow feet crunched on the snow. Ahead, at the foot of the hill, the coffin rode slowly forward on shoulders, its brown varnish and metal trappings dull in the glittering snow, riding just below the long waste of snow eight or ten feet deep over the whole countryside. The long dark line of mourners following the coffin stretched away towards Oakport Wood in the pathway cut through the snow. High on Killeelan

178

Hill the graveyard evergreens rose out of the snow. The graveyard wall was covered, the narrow path cut up the side of the hill stopping at the little gate deep in the snow. The coffin climbed with painful slowness, as if it might never reach the gate, often pausing for the bearers to be changed; and someone started to pray, the prayer travelling down the whole mile-long line of the mourners as they shuffled behind the coffin in the narrow tunnel cut in the snow.

It was the day in February 1947 that they buried Michael Bruen. Never before or since had he experienced the Mystery in such awesomeness. Now, as he stood at the gate, there was no awe or terror, only the coffin moving slowly towards the dark trees on the hill, the long line of the mourners, and everywhere the blinding white light, among the half-buried thorn bushes and beyond Killeelan, on the covered waste of Gloria Bog, on the sides of Slieve an Iarainn.

He did not know how long he had stood in that lost day, in that white light, probably for no more than a moment. He could not have stood the intensity for any longer. When he woke out of it the grey light of the alders had reasserted itself. His hand was still on the bar of the gate. Gillespie was still sawing, bent over the sawhorse, his boot on the length of beechwood, completely enclosed in the roaring rise-and-fall of the saw. The priest felt as vulnerable as if he had suddenly woken out of sleep, shaken and somewhat ashamed to have been caught asleep in the actual day and life, without any protection of walls.

He was about to rattle the gate again, feeling a washed-out parody of a child or old man on what was after all nothing more than a poor errand: to tell the Gillespies that a bed had at long last been made available in the Regional Hospital for the operation on Mrs Gillespie's piles, when his eyes were caught again by the quality of the light. It was one of those late October days, small white clouds drifting about the sun, and the watery light was shining down the alder rows to fall on the white chips of the beechwood strewn all about Gillespie, some inches deep. It was the same white light as the light on snow. As he watched, the light went out on the beech chips, and it was the grey day again around Gillespie's sawing. It had been as simple as that. The suggestion of snow had been enough to plunge him into the lost day of Michael

Bruen's funeral. Everything in that remembered day was so pure and perfect that he felt purged of all tiredness, was, for a moment, eager to begin life again.

Making sure that Gillespie hadn't noticed him at the gate, he turned back. The bed wouldn't be ready for another week. The news could wait a day or more. Before leaving he stole a last look at the dull white ground about the saw-horse. The most difficult things always seem to lie closest to us, to lie around our feet.

Ever since his mother's death he found himself stumbling into these dead days. Once, crushed mint in the garden had given him back a day he'd spent with her at the sea in such reality that he had been frightened, as if he'd suddenly fallen through time; it was as if the world of the dead was as available to him as the world of the living. It was also humiliating for him to realize that she must have been the mainspring of his days. Now that the mainspring was broken, the hands were weakly falling here and falling there. Today there had been the sudden light on the bits of white beech. He'd not have noticed it if he hadn't been alone, if Gillespie had not been so absorbed in his sawing. Before, there must have been some such simple trigger that he'd been too ashamed or bewildered to notice.

Stealthily and quickly he went down the dirt-track by the lake till he got to the main road. To the left was the church in a rookery of old trees, and behind it the house where he lived. Safe on the wide main road he let his mind go back to the beech chips. They rested there around Gillespie's large bulk, and paler still was the line of mourners following the coffin through the snow, a picture you could believe or disbelieve but not be in. In idle exasperation he began to count the trees in the hedge along the road as he walked: ash, green oak, whitehorn, ash; the last leaves a vivid yellow on the wild cherry, empty October fields in dull wet light behind the hedges. This, then, was the actual day, the only day that mattered, the day from which our salvation had to be won or lost: it stood solidly and impenetrably there, denying the weak life of the person, with nothing of the eternal other than it would dully endure, while the day set alight in his mind by the light of the white beech, though it had been nothing more than a funeral he had attended during a dramatic snowfall when a boy, seemed bathed in the eternal, seemed everything we had been taught and told of the world of God.

Dissatisfied, and feeling as tired again as he'd been on his way to Gillespie's, he did not go through the church gate with its circle and cross, nor did he call to the sexton locking up under the bellrope. In order to be certain of being left alone he went by the circular path at the side. A high laurel hedge hid the path from the graveyard and church. There he made coffee without turning on the light. Always when about to give birth or die cattle sought out a clean place in some corner of the field.

Michael Bruen had been a big kindly agreeable man, what was called a lovely man. His hair was a coarse grey. He wore loose-fitting tweeds with red cattleman's boots. When young he had been a policeman in Dublin. It was said he had either won or inherited money, and had come home to where he'd come from to buy the big Crossna farm, to marry and grow rich.

He had a large family. Men were employed on the farm. The yard and its big outhouses with the red roofs rang with work: cans, machinery, raillery, the sliding of hooves, someone whistling. Within the house, away from the yard, was the enormous cave of a kitchen, the long table down its centre, the fireplace at its end, the plates and pots and presses along the walls, sides of bacon wrapped in gauze hanging from hooks in the ceiling, the whole room full of the excitement and bustle of women.

Often as a boy the priest had gone to Michael Bruen's on some errand for his father. Once the beast was housed or the load emptied Michael would take him into the kitchen. The huge fire of wood blazed all the brighter because of the frost.

'Give this man something.' Michael had led him. 'Something solid that'll warm the life back into him.'

'A cup of tea will do fine,' he had protested in the custom.

'Nonsense. Don't pay him the slightest attention. Empty bags can't stand.'

Eileen, the prettiest of Michael's daughters, laughed as she took down the pan. Her arms were white to the elbows with a fine dusting of flour.

'He'll remember this was a good place to come to when he has to start thinking about a wife.' Michael's words gave licence to general hilarity.

It was hard to concentrate on Michael's questions about his father, so delicious was the smell of frying. The mug of steaming tea was put by his side. The butter melted on the fresh bread on the plate. There were sausages, liver, bacon, a slice of black-pudding and sweetest grisceens.

'Now set to,' Michael laughed. 'We don't want any empty bags leaving Bruen's.'

Michael came with him to the gate when he left. 'Tell your father it's ages since we had a drink in the Royal. And that if he doesn't search me out in the Royal the next Fair Day I'll have to go over and bate the lugs off him.' As he shook his hand in the half-light of the yard lamp it was the last time he was to see him alive. Before the last flakes had stopped falling, when old people were searching back to 'the great snows when Count Plunkett was elected' to find another such fall, Michael Bruen had died, and his life was already another such watermark of memory.

The snow lay eight feet deep on the roads, and dead cattle and sheep were found in drifts of fifteen feet in the fields. All of the people who hadn't lost sheep or cattle were in extraordinary good humour, their own ills buried for a time as deep as their envy of any other's good fortune in the general difficulty of the snow. It took days to cut a way out to the main road, the snow having to be cut in blocks breast-high out of a face of frozen snow. A wild cheer went up as the men at last cut through to the gang digging in from the main road. Another cheer greeted the first van to come in, Doherty's bread van, and it had hardly died when the hearse came with the coffin for Michael Bruen. That night they cut the path up the side of Killeelan Hill and found the family headstone beside the big yew just inside the gate and opened the grave. They hadn't finished digging when the first funeral bell came clearly over the snow the next day to tell them that the coffin had started on its way.

The priest hadn't thought of the day for years or of Michael Bruen till he had stumbled into it without warning by way of the sudden light on the beech chips. It did not augur well. There were days, especially of late, when he seemed to be lost in dead days, to see time present as a flimsy accumulating tissue over all the time that was lost. Sometimes he saw himself as an old man children were helping down to the shore, restraining the tension of their need to laugh as they pointed out a rock in the path he seemed about to stumble over, and then they had to lift their eyes and smile apologetically to the passersby while he stood staring out to sea, having forgotten all about the rock in his path. 'It's this way we're going.' He felt the imaginary tug on his sleeve, and he was drawn again into the tortuous existence of the everyday, away from the eternal of the sea or the lost light on frozen snow across Killeelan Hill.

Never before though had he noticed anything like the beech chips. There was the joy of holding what had eluded him for so long, in its amazing simplicity: but mastered knowledge was no longer knowledge unless it opened, became part of a greater knowledge, and what did the beech chips do but turn back to his own death?

Like the sudden snowfall and Michael Bruen's burial his life had been like any other, except to himself, and then only in odd visions of it, as a lost life. When it had been agreeable and equitable he had no vision of it at all.

The country childhood. His mother and father. The arrival at the shocking knowledge of birth and death. His attraction to the priesthood as a way of vanquishing death and avoiding birth. O hurry it, he thought. There is not much to a life. Many have it. There is not enough room. His father and mother were old when they married; he was 'the fruit of old things', he heard derisively. His mother had been a seamstress. He could still see the needle flashing in her strong hands, that single needle-flash composed of thousands of hours.

'His mother had the vocation for him.' Perhaps she had, perhaps all the mothers of the country had, it had so passed into the speech of the country, in all the forms of both beatification and derision; but it was out of fear of death he became a priest, which became in time the fear of life. Wasn't it natural to turn back to the mother in this fear? She was older than fear, having given him his life, and who would give a life if they knew its end? There was, then, his father's death, his acceptance of it, as he had accepted all poor fortune all his life long as his due, refusing to credit the good.

And afterwards his mother sold the land to 'Horse' McLaughlin and came to live with him and was happy. She attended all the Masses and Devotions, took messages, and she sewed, though she had no longer any need, linen for the altar, soutanes and surplices, his shirts and all her own clothes. Sometimes her concern for him irritated him to exasperation but he hardly ever let it show. He was busy with the many duties of a priest. The fences on the past and future were secure. He must have been what is called happy, and there was a whole part of his life that, without his knowing, had come to turn to her for its own expression.

He discovered it when she began her death. He came home one summer evening to find all the lights on in the house. She was in the living-room, in the usual chair. The table was piled high with dresses. Round the chair was a pile of rags. She did not look up when he entered, her still strong hands tearing apart a herring-bone skirt she had made only the year before.

'What on earth are you doing, Mother?' He caught her by the hands when she didn't answer.

'It's time you were up for Mass,' she said.

'What are you doing with your dresses?'

'What dresses?'

'All the dresses you've just been tearing up.'

'I don't know anything about dresses,' and then he saw there was something wrong. She made no resistance when he led her up the stairs.

For some days she seemed absent and confused but, though he watched her carefully, she was otherwise very little different from her old self, and she did not appear ill. Then he came home one evening to find her standing like a child in the middle of the room, surrounded by an enormous pile of rags. She had taken up from where she'd been interrupted at the herring-bone skirt and torn up every dress or article of clothing she had ever made. After his initial shock he sent for the doctor.

'I'm afraid it's just the onset of senility,' the doctor said.

'It's irreversible?'

The doctor nodded, 'It very seldom takes such a violent form, but that's what it is. She'll have to be looked after.' With a sadness that part of his life was over, he took her to the Home and saw her settled there.

She recognized him when he visited her there the first year, but without excitement, as if he was already far away; and then the day came when he had to admit that she no longer knew who he was, had become like a dog kennelled out too long. He was with her when she died. She'd turned her face towards him. There came a light of recognition in the eyes like a last glow of a match before it goes out, and then she died.

There was nothing left but his own life. There had been nothing but that all along, but it had been obscured, comfortably obscured.

He turned on the radio.

A man had lost both legs in an explosion. There was violence on the night-shift at Ford's. The pound had steadied towards the close but was still down on the day.

Letting his fingers linger on the knob he turned it off. The disembodied voice on the air was not unlike the lost day he'd stumbled into through the light on the beech chips, except it had nothing of its radiance – the funeral during the years he carried it around with him lost the sheltered burden of the everyday, had become light as the air in all the clarity of light. It was all timeless, and seemed at least a promise of the eternal.

He went to draw the curtain. She had made the red curtain too with its pale lining but hadn't torn it. How often must she have watched the moonlight on the still headstones beyond the laurel as it lay evenly on them this night. She had been afraid of ghosts: old priests who had lived in this house, who through whiskey or some other ill had neglected to say some Mass for the dead and because of the neglect the soul for whom the Mass should have been offered was forced to linger beyond its time in Purgatory, and the priest guilty of the omission could himself not be released until the living priest had said the Mass, and was forced to come at midnight to the house in all his bondage until the Mass was said.

'They must have been all good priests, Mother. Good steady old fellows like myself. They never come back,' he used to assure her. He remembered his own idle words as he drew the curtain, lingering as much over the drawing of the curtain as he had lingered over the turning off of the radio. He would be glad of a ghost tonight, be glad of any visitation from beyond the walls of sense.

He took up the battered and friendly missal, which had been with him all his adult life, to read the office of the day. On bad days he kept it till late, the familiar words that changed with the changing year, that he had grown to love, and were as well his daily duty. It must be surely the greatest grace of life, the greatest freedom, to have to do what we love because it is also our duty. He wasn't able to read on this evening among the old familiar words for long. An annoyance came between him and the page, the Mass he had to repeat every day, the Mass in English. He wasn't sure whether he hated it or the guitar-playing priests more. It was humiliating to think that these had never been such a scourge when his mother had been alive. Was his life the calm vessel it had seemed, dully setting out and returning from the fishing grounds? Or had he been always what he seemed now? 'Oh yes. There you go again,' he heard the familiar voice in the empty room. 'Complaining about the Mass in the vernacular. When you prefer the common names of flowers to their proper names,' and the sharp, energetic, almost brutal laugh. It was Peter Joyce, he was not dead. Peter Joyce had risen to become a bishop at the other end of the country, an old friend he no longer saw.

'But they are more beautiful. Dog rose, wild woodbine, buttercup, daisy . . .'

He heard his own protest. It was in a hotel that they used to go to every summer on the Atlantic, a small hotel where you could read after dinner without fear of a rising roar from the bar beginning to outrival the Atlantic by ten o'clock.

'And, no doubt, the little rose of Scotland, sharp and sweet and breaks the heart,' he heard his friend quote maliciously. 'And it's not the point. The reason that names of flowers must be in Latin is that when flower lovers meet they know what they are talking about, no matter whether they're French or Greeks or Arabs. They have a universal language.'

'I prefer the humble names, no matter what you say.'

'Of course you do. And it's parochial sentimentalists like yourself who prefer the *smooth sowthistle* to *Sonchus oleraceus* that's the whole cause of your late lamented Mass in Latin disappearing. I have no sympathy with you. You people tire me.'

The memory of that truculent argument dispelled his annoyance, as its simple logic had once taken his breath away, but he was curiously tired after the vividness of the recall. It was only by a sheer act of will, sometimes having to count the words, that he was able to finish his office. 'I know one thing, Peter Joyce. I know that I know nothing,' he murmured when he finished. But when he looked at the room about him he could hardly believe it was so empty and dead and dry, the empty chair where she should be sewing, the oaken table with the scattered books, the clock on the mantel. Wildly and aridly he wanted to curse, but his desire to curse was as unfair as life. He had not wanted it.

Then, quietly, he saw that he had a ghost all right, one that he had been walking around with for a long time, a ghost he had not wanted to recognize – his own death. He might as well get to know him well. It would never leave now and had no mortal shape. Absence does not cast a shadow.

All that was there was the white light of the lamp on the open book, on the white marble; the brief sun of God on beechwood, and the sudden light of that glistening snow, and the timeless mourners moving towards the yews on Killeelan Hill almost thirty years ago. It was as good a day as any, if there ever was a good day to go.

Somewhere, outside this room that was an end, he knew that a young man, not unlike he had once been, stood on a granite step and listened to the doorbell ring, smiled as he heard a woman's footsteps come down the hallway, ran his fingers through his hair, and turned the bottle of white wine he held in his hands completely around as he prepared to enter a pleasant and uncomplicated evening, feeling himself immersed in time without end.

Along the Edges

EVENING

'I must go now.' She tried to rise from the bed.

'Stay.' His arms about her pale shoulders held her back as she pressed upwards with her hands. 'Let me kiss you there once more.'

'Don't be silly,' she laughed and fell back into his arms. 'I have to go.' Her body trembled with low laughter as he went beneath the sheet to kiss her; and then they stretched full length against one another, kissing over and back on the mouth, in a last grasping embrace.

'I wish I could eat and drink you.'

'Then I'd be gone.' She pushed him loose with her palms. They both rose and dressed quickly.

'I'll leave you home. It's too late for you to go alone.' Lately she had seemed to want to assert their separateness after each lovemaking.

'All right. I don't mind,' she said, a seeming challenge in her eyes.

'Besides I want to.' He leaned to kiss her on the side of the throat as she drew on her jacket. They stole down the stairs, and outside he held the door firmly until the catch clicked quietly behind them. The fading moonlight was weak on the leaves of the single laurel in the front garden, and he grew uneasy at the apparent reluctance with which she seemed to give him her gloved hand on the pavement, with the way she hurried, their separate footsteps loud in the silence of the sleeping suburbs.

They'd met just after broken love affairs, and had drifted casually into going out together two or three evenings every week. They went to cinemas or dancehalls or restaurants, to the races at Leopardstown or the Park, making no demands on one another, sharing only one another's pleasures, making love together as on this night in his student's room.

Sensing her hard separateness in their separate footsteps as they walked towards her home in the sleeping suburbs, he began to feel that by now there should be more between them than this sensual ease. Till now, for him, the luxury of this ease had been perfect. This uncomplicated pleasure seemed the very fullness of life, seemed all that life could yearn towards. Yet it could not go on for ever. There comes a point in all living things when they must change or die, and maybe they had passed that point already without noticing. He had already lost her while longing to draw closer.

'When will we meet again?' he asked her as usual at the gate before she went in.

'When do you want?'

'Saturday, at eight, outside the Metropole.'

'Saturday – at eight, then,' she agreed.

There was no need to seek for more. His anxiety had been groundless. Wednesdays and Saturdays were always given. No matter how hard the week was he had always Saturdays and Wednesdays to look forward to: he could lean upon their sensual ease and luxury as reliably as upon a drug. Now that Saturday was once more promised his life was perfectly arranged. With all the casualness of the self-satisfied male, he kissed her goodnight and it caused her to look sharply at him before she went in, but he noticed nothing. He waited until he heard the latch click and then went whistling home through the empty silent streets just beginning to grow light.

That next Saturday he stayed alone in the room, studying by the light of a bulb fixed on a Chianti bottle, the texts and diagrams spread out on newspaper that shielded his arms from the cold of the marble top that had once been a washstand, the faded velvet curtain drawn on the garden and hot day outside, on cries of the ice-cream wagons, on the long queues within the city for buses to the sea, the sea of Dollymount, the swimmers going in off the rocks, pleasures sharpened a hundredfold by the drawn curtain. Finally, late in the afternoon, when he discovered that he had just reached the bottom of a page without taking in a single sentence, he left the room and went down to the front. At the corner shop he bought an orange and sat on a bench. The sea lay dazzling in the heat out past the Bull and Howth Head. An old couple and a terrier with a newspaper in his mouth went past him as he peeled the orange. Music came from a transistor somewhere. Exams should be held in winter, he thought tiredly, for he seemed to be looking at the people walking past him, sitting on benches or on the grass as if through plate glass.

Still, at eight o'clock she would come to him, out of the milling crowds about the Metropole, her long limbs burning nakedly beneath the swinging folds of the brown dress, the face that came towards him and then drew back as she laughed, and he would begin to live again. He had all that forgetting to go towards, the losing of the day in all the sweetness of her night. He rose, threw the orange peel into a wire basket, and walked back to the room. He imagined he must have been working for about an hour when he heard the heavy knocker of the front door. When he looked at his watch he found that he had been working already for more than two hours.

He listened as the front door opened, and heard voices – the landlord's, probably the vegetable man or the coal man – but went quite still as steps came up the stairs towards the door of the room, the landlord's step because of the heavy breathing. A knock came on the door, and the fat, little old landlord put his head in, stains of egg yolk on his lapels. 'A visitor for you,' he whispered and winked.

She stood below in the hallway beside the dark bentwood coat-rack, her legs crossed as if for a casual photo, arms folded, a tense smile fixed on her face, her hair brushed high. She had never come to the house on her own before.

'Thanks,' she said to the landlord when he came down.

'Won't you come up?' he called from the head of the stairs.

The landlord made a face and winked again as she climbed.

'I'm sorry coming like this,' she said.

'That doesn't matter,' he said as he closed the door. 'I was just about to get ready to go to meet you. This way we can have even more time together.'

'It's not that,' she said quickly. 'I came round to see if you'd mind putting the evening off.'

'Is there something wrong?'

'No. It's just that Margaret has come up of a sudden from the country.'

'Your friend from school days?'

'Yes. She hardly ever comes up. And I thought you wouldn't mind giving the evening up so that we could go out together.'

'Did she not tell you she was coming up?' The whole long-looked-forward-to balm of the evening was threatened by this whim.

'No. She came on a chance. Someone was coming up and offered her a lift.'

'And she expects you to drop everything?'

'She doesn't expect anything.' She met his annoyance with her own.

'All I can say is that you must care very little about the evening if you can change it that quickly.'

'Well, if you're that huffed about it we can go through with the evening. I didn't think you'd mind.'

'Where is this Margaret?'

'She's outside. Why do you want to know?'

'I suppose I should pay my respects and let the pair of you away.'

'Don't put yourself out.'

'It'll be a pleasure,' but then his anger broke before he opened the door. 'If that's all our going out means to you we might as well forget the whole thing.'

'What do you mean?' she asked.

'We might as well break the whole thing off,' he said less certainly.

'That can be easily arranged.'

The door was open and they both came downstairs in silent anger.

Outside, Margaret was leaning against the railing by the bus stop. She was a large country girl, with a mane of black hair and broad athlete's shoulders. The three made polite, awkward conversation that did not cover over the tenseness till the bus came.

'I hope you have a nice evening,' he said as they boarded the bus.

'That's what we intend.' Her lovely face was unflinching, but Margaret waved. He watched them take a seat together on the lower deck and waited to see if they would look back, but they did not.

Rattling coins, he went towards the telephone box at the end of the road to ring round to see if any of his friends were free for the evening.

They did not meet again till two Saturdays later, at the Metropole, as usual at eight. She had a floppy blue hat and dark glasses. Her summer dress was sleeveless, and she had a race card in her long gloved hands.

'You must have just come from the races.'

'I was at the Park. I even won some money.' She smiled her old roguish smile.

'You must be hungry, then. Why don't we go somewhere nice to eat?'

'That's fine with me,' she said with all her mocking brightness. 'I can take you – this evening – with the winnings.'

'If that suits you. I have money too.'

'You took long enough in calling,' she said with a flash of real resentment.

'It didn't seem to make much difference to you. It'd be nice if I was wrong. That's how it seemed.'

'Where are we going?' She stopped; that they were adversaries now was in the open.

'To Bernardo's. We always had good times there. Even coming from the races you look very beautiful,' he said by way of appeasement.

The restaurant was just beginning to fill. The blindman was playing the piano at its end, his white stick leaning against the dark varnish. They ate in tenseness and mostly silence, the piano thumping away. Now that he was about to lose her she had never looked so beautiful.

'You're not eating much,' she said when she saw him struggle with the veal.

'It must be the damned exam,' he said. 'It's starting next week. And, after all, I wasn't at the races.'

'That's true,' she laughed.

'I'm sorry about the ridiculous fuss I made a few weeks back,' he said openly.

'It's all right. It's all over now.'

'Do you think you'll be able to come back with me this evening?'

For a wild sensual moment he hoped everything would suddenly be as it had been before.

'Is it for – the usual?' she asked slowly.

'I suppose.'

'No.' She shook her head.

'Why?'

'I don't see any point. Do you?'

'We've often . . . many times before.'

'We've gone on that way for too long,' she said.

'But I love you. And I thought – when things are more settled – we might be married.'

'No.' She was looking at him with affection and trying to speak softly and slowly. 'You must know that the only time things are settled, if they are ever settled, is *now*. And I've had some hard thinking to do since that last evening. You were quite right to be angry. If I was seriously interested in you I'd not have broken the date for someone coming casually to town. There was a time I thought I was getting involved with you, but then you didn't seem interested, and women are practical. I'm very fond of you, and we've had good times, and maybe the good times just went on for too long, when we just should have had a romp, and let it go.' She spoke as if their life together already belonged to a life that was over.

'Is there no hope, no hope at all, that it might change?' he asked with nothing more than an echo of desperation.

Through the sensual caresses, laughter, evenings of pleasure, the instinct had been beginning to assemble a dream, a hope; soon, little by little, without knowing, he would have woken to find that he had fallen in love. We assemble a love as we assemble our life and grow so absorbed in the assembling that we wake in terror at the knowledge that all that we have built is terminal, that, in our pain, we must undo it again.

There had been that moment too that might have been grasped, and had not, and love had died – she had admitted as much. It would have led on to what? To happiness, for a while, or the absence of this present sense of loss, or to some other sense of loss . . .

He thought he saw that moment, as well that moment now as any other: an evening in O'Connell Street, a Saturday evening like any other, full of the excitement of the herding. She had taken his arm.

'My young sister is to be engaged tomorrow. Why don't we drive up? There's to be a party. And afterwards we could have the weekend on our own,' and when he answered, 'It's the one weekend I can't,' and started to explain, he saw the sudden glow go from her face; an impoverishment of calculation replaced it that had made him momentarily afraid. Anyhow, it was all evening now. That crossroad at which they had actually separated had been passed long before in the day.

'No,' she said gently. 'And you'd not be so reckless if I'd said yes. We were both more in love with the idea of falling in love.'

'Still it's no fun walking round the world on your own.'

'It's not so bad as being with someone you can't stand after the pleasure has worn off,' she said as if she were looking past the evening.

'I give up,' he said and called for the bill.

'Ring me sometime,' she said as she got on the bus outside.

'Right, then.' He waved and knew neither of them would. They had played at a game of life, and had not fallen, and were now as indifferent to one another, outside the memory of pleasure, as if they were both already dead to one another. If they were not together in the evening how could they ever have been so in the morning . . .

And if she had come to him instead of leaving him, those limbs would never reach whomever they were going to . . .

And why should we wish the darkness harm, it is our element; or curse the darkness because we are doomed to love in it, and die . . .

And those that move along the edges can see it so until they fall.

MORNING

'What does your friend do for a living?' the man asked the blonde woman in front of him after Marion, an enormous ungainly girl, had gone to the Ladies in Bernardo's.

'She's not a friend. In fact, she's more than a friend. She's a client. A star. A pop star.' The woman smiled as she drew slowly on her cigarette. 'You're behind the times. You see, I'm here to bring you up to date.'

'But how can she be a pop star?'

'You mean because she's ugly? That doesn't matter. That helps. The public's tired of long, pale, beautiful slenders. Ugliness and energy – that's what's wanted now, and she has a good voice. She can belt them out.'

'Does she have men friends and all that?'

'As many as she wants. Proposals. Everything a woman's supposed to want.'

'She's certainly not what you'd call beautiful.'

'Publicity makes her beautiful. It moves her closer to the sun. In fact, it is the sun and still has its worshippers.'

'It doesn't make her so to me,' the man said doggedly, 'though I think you are beautiful.'

'What *is* it anyhow? A good clothes rack or flesh rack? I don't know.'

'Whatever it is, you have it.' He changed. 'It doesn't look as if Peter will come back now.'

'No,' she said. 'Peter isn't trustworthy. I wish they'd let the blindman go home,' she said as he struck up another number on the piano.

'I suppose, for them, it's the hopeful hours.' The man referred to the large noisy table in the centre of the restaurant. They had come from a party and bribed the blindman to play on after he had risen at midnight to catch his usual garage bus to Inchicore.

'Do you have anything to do with Peter?'

'How?' she asked sharply.

'Sleep with him?'

She laughed. 'I've never even thought of Peter that way. He's a contact. In the trade,' and without warning she leaned across the table and placed the burning tip of the cigarette against the back of the man's hand.

'What did you do that for?' he asked angrily.

'I felt like it. I suppose I should be sorry.'

'No,' he changed. 'Not if you come home with me.'

'To sleep with you?' she parodied.

'That would be best of all but it's not important. We can spend the morning together,' he said eagerly.

'All right.' She nodded.

They were both uneasy after the agreement. They had left one level and had not entered any other.

'Do you think I should go to see if anything's the matter with Marion?'

'Maybe. Wait a little,' he said.

Marion was pale when she came back. 'I'm afraid I'm not used to the wine,' she apologized.

'I'm sorry, but we can go now. Do you think you'll be all right?'

'I'll be fine,' she said.

'Anyhow, you'll both see Peter tomorrow. He said he'd definitely be at the reception.'

The last thing their eyes rested on before they went through the door the Italian manager was holding open was the blindman's cane leaning against the side of the piano.

'Do you think they'll make the poor man play all night?' she asked.

'He seems satisfied. I even heard them arranging for a taxi to take him home. I suppose we too should be thinking of a taxi.'

'I'd rather walk, if that's all right.'

They walked slowly towards the hotel. The night was fine but without moon or stars. Just before they got to the hotel, the man shook hands with Marion, and the two women walked together to the hotel door. They stood a while in conversation there before the star went in and the blonde woman turned back towards the man.

'It always makes me uncomfortable. Being part of the couple, leaving the single person alone,' he said.

'The single person is usually glad to be left alone.'

'I know that but it doesn't stop the feeling.' He had the same feeling passing hospitals late at night.

'Anyhow, you've had your wish. We're together,' the woman said, and they kissed for the first time. They crossed to the taxi rank facing the railings of the Green, and they did not speak in the taxi. What hung between them might be brutal and powerful, but it was as frail as the flesh out of which it grew, for any endurance. They had chosen one another because of the empty night, and the wrong words might betray them early, making one hateful to the other; but even the right words, if there were right words, had not the power to force it. It had to grow or wither like a plant or flower. What they needed most was patience, luck, and that twice-difficult thing, to be lucky in one another, and at the same time, and to be able to wait for that time.

'Will I switch on the light?' he asked her as he let her into the flat.

'Whatever you like.'

'Then I'd rather not.'

After they had kissed he said, 'There's my room and the spare room. I don't mind if you think it too soon and use the spare room.'

'Wait,' she said softly, and her arms leaned heavily round his shoulders, as if she had forgotten him, and was going over her life to see if she could gather it into this one place. Suddenly she felt him trembling. She pulled him towards her.

'Do you bring many people back like this?' she asked close to morning, almost proprietorially.

'No. Not for ages.'

'Why?'

'First you have to find a person who'll consent,' he half joked. 'And there's not much use after a while unless there seems a chance of something more.'

'Of what?'

'Of it going on, I suppose.'

There was a silence in which a moth blundering about the half-darkness overhead was too audible.

'And you, have you men?' he asked awkwardly.

'No. Until recently I had one man.'

'What happened?'

'Nothing. He was married. The man in question had a quite awful dilemma, and he suffered, how he suffered, especially with me. You see, he was torn between his wife and me, and he could not make up his mind. Women are, I think, more primal than men. They don't bother too much about who pays the bill as long as they get what they want. So I gave him an ultimatum. And when he still couldn't make up his mind I left him. That must sound pretty poor stuff.'

'No. It sounds true.'

That hard as porcelain singleness of women, seeming sometimes to take pleasure in cruelty, was a part of the beauty.

'Would you like to be married?'

'Yes. And you?'

'I suppose I would.'

197

'You know that speech about those who are married or kind to their friends. They become olives, pomegranate, mulberry, flowers, precious stones, eminent stars.'

'I'd rather stay as I am,' she laughed.

'I suppose it is all in life.' He drew her towards him.

'We didn't choose it any more than those before us or those who may come after us.'

When they rose and washed in the flat in all its daylight, it seemed as if it was not only a new day but the beginning of a new life. The pictures, the plates, the table in its stolidity seemed to have been set askew by the accidental night, to want new shapes, to look comical in their old places. The books on the wall seemed to belong to an old relative to whom one did not even owe a responsibility of affection. Gaily one could pick or discard among them, choosing only those useful to the new. For, like a plant, the old outer leaves would have to lie withered for new green shoots to push upwards at the heart.

'What are you thinking?'

'Nothing much. Of another morning. A Paris morning, opening shutters, a water truck was going past, and behind came four Algerians with long-handled brooms.'

'Were you alone or with someone?' He was ashamed of the first pang of irrational jealousy.

'Actually, I was alone. I suppose one usually is those mornings.' Her gravity, much like a small child's, took all the light to itself.

They had come from four separate people, two men and two women, lying together in two separate nights; and those two nights were joined in the night they had left, had grown into the morning.

She was not garlanded by farms or orchards, by any house by the sea, by neither judges nor philosophers. She stood as she was, belonging to the morning, as they both hoped to belong to the evening. They could not possess the morning, no more than they could disagree with it or go against its joy.

She was wearing what she wore at the dinner while the blindman played, a dress of blue denim, buttoned down the front, and on her stockingless feet were thonged sandals.

'What are you going to do today?'

'I have to go to the hotel and then to the reception. I suppose we'll see the busy Peter there. After that I'm free. And you?'

'I'm free all day.'

'Maybe we'll begin to learn a little more about one another then.'

'As long as we know it'll be more of nothing. We know hardly anything now and we may never be as well off.'

They would have to know that they could know nothing to go through the low door of love, the door that was the same doorway between the self and the other everywhere.

'Well, anyhow we have to face the day,' she said, dispelling it in one movement; and they took one another's hands as they went to meet the day, the day already following them, and all about them.

Swallows

The wind blew the stinging rain from the Gut, where earlier in the bright weather of the summer the Sergeant had sat in the tarred boat, anchored by a rope to an old Ford radiator that clung to the weeds outside the rushes, and watched taut line after taut line cut like cheesewire through the water as hooked roach after hooked roach made a last surge towards the freedom of the open lake before landing slapping on the floorboards. The wind blew the rain from the Gut against the black limestone of the Quarry, where on the wet tar, its pools ruffling in the wet wind, the Sergeant and the young State Surveyor measured the scene of the road accident, both with their collars up and hatted against the rain, the black plastic chinstrap a shining strip on the Sergeant's jaw. 'What age was he?' the Surveyor asked, as he noted the last measurement in his official notebook and put the tapewheel in his pocket.

'Eighteen. Wheeling his bicycle up the hill on his way to Carrick, apparently for a haircut, when bang – into the next world via the bonnet, without as much as by your leave.'

'Will you be able to get manslaughter? From the measurements she wouldn't appear to have a leg to stand on.'

'Not a snowballs's chance in hell. The family's too well in. You see the wooden cross on the wall there his parents put up, two sticks no more, and they're already complaining: the poor woman has to pass it twice a day on the way to her school and back, and the cross disturbs her, brings back memories, when bygones should be let to be bygones. Her defence is that the sun blinded her as she came round the Quarry. She'll lose her licence for six months and there'll be an order from the bench for the bend to be properly signposted.'

The Surveyor whistled as he turned towards his car in the forecourt of the Quarry, his back to the rain sweeping from the mouth of the Gut.

'They're poor, his parents, then?'

'As mountain snipe.'

'Fortunately, Sergeant, you and I don't have to concern ourselves with the justice or injustice. Only with the accurate presentation of the evidence. And I have to thank you for those drawings. They are as near professional as makes no difference. I wish all my jobs could be made as easy.'

'I was good at figures at school,' the Sergeant said awkwardly.

'Why don't you let me drive you back in the rain?'

'There's the bike.'

'That's no problem. I can dump it on the back.'

An evening suit hung in the back of the car, a scarf of white silk draped round the shoulders. On the seat lay an old violin-case.

'You play the fiddle?' the Sergeant noticed, glad to be in out of the rain beating on the windscreen.

'Indeed I do. The violin travels with me everywhere. Do you have much taste for music?'

'When I was young. At the dances. "Rakes of Mallow". "Devil Among the Tailors", jigs and reels.'

'I had to choose once, when I was at university, between surveying and a career in music. I'm afraid I chose security.'

'We all have to eat.'

'Anyhow, I've never regretted it, except in the usual sentimental moments. In fact, I think if I had to depend on it for my daily bread it might lose half its magic.'

'Is it old, the fiddle? The case looks old.'

'Very old, but I have had it only four years. It has its story. I'm afraid it's a longish story.'

'I'd like to hear it.'

'I was in Avignon in France an evening an old Italian musician was playing between the café tables, and the moment I heard its tone I knew I'd have to have it. I followed him from café to café until he'd finished for the evening, and then invited him to join me over a glass of wine. Over the wine I asked him if he'd sell. First he refused. Then I asked him to name some price he couldn't afford not to take. I'm afraid to tell you the price, it was so high. I tried to haggle but it was no use. The last thing he wanted was to sell, but because of his family he couldn't afford to refuse that price if I was prepared to pay it. With the money he could get proper medical treatment – I couldn't completely follow his French – for his daughter, who was consumptive or something, and he'd do the best he could about the cafés with an ordinary violin. I'm afraid I paid up on the spot, but the experts who have examined it since say it was dead cheap at the price, that it might even be a genuine Stradivarius.'

Streets of Avignon, white walls of the royal popes in the sun, glasses of red wine and the old Italian musician playing between the café tables in the evening, a girl dying of consumption, and the sweeping rain hammering on the windscreen.

'It was in Avignon, wasn't it, if I have the old church history right,' the Sergeant said slowly, 'that those royal popes had their palaces in the schism? Some of them, by all accounts, were capable of a fandango or two besides their Hail Marys.'

'The papal palaces are still there. Avignon is wonderful. You must go there. Some of those wonderful Joe Walsh Specials put it within all our reaches. The very sound of the name makes me long for summer.'

'I'd love to hear you play on that fiddle.'

'I'm sure that's easily arranged. After all, there's only a few more petty things to check, and then our work is done for the day.'

'We can play in the barracks, then. There's no one there. Biddy can get us something to eat, and then you can play.'

'That doesn't matter at all.'

'Still, the inner man has to be seen to too. Biddy's my housekeeper. She's a good soul, but I must warn you she's deaf as a post and shouts.'

'Let that be the least of our worries.' The young Surveyor smiled indulgently as the car ground to a stop on the barracks' gravel. 'Do you find time hard to kill in this place?' he asked as he got out of the car.

'It's no fun in this weather but in the summer it's fine,' the Sergeant answered while they unroped the bicycle. 'I take out the old boat you see upside down there under the sycamore. Row it up into the mouth of the Gut and drop the radiator over the side. Time runs like lightning then, feeling the boat sway in the current, a few sandwiches and stout or a little whiskey, and unless there's a bad east wind you're always sure of fish. It's great to feel the first chuck and see the line cut for the lake.'

'You grill these fish, then?'

'Sometimes Biddy cooks them but mostly I give them away. I don't care about the eating. It's the day in the good weather, and the fishing. I've often noticed that the people mad about fishing hardly ever care about the eating.'

Biddy was turning the handle of the metal sock-machine clamped to the corner of the table when they came into the big kitchen. Its needles clacked. The half-knit sock, weighted with small pieces of lead, hung close to the cement. She didn't turn around. When the Sergeant placed a hand on her shoulder she did not start. She began to shout something to him. Then she saw the Surveyor with the violin-case in his hand at the door, and drew back.

'This is Biddy. She knits socks for half the countryside. More to pass the time than for the few pence it brings her. She's proud as punch of her machine. Pay no attention to her for she'll not hear a word you say.'

The Surveyor changed the violin from his right hand to his left before taking Biddy's hand. 'It's nice to meet you.' As she released his hand she shouted, 'You're very welcome.' The Sergeant went and took a bottle of whiskey and two tumblers from a black press in the corner, its glass covered with a faded curtain, joking uncomfortably, 'I call it the medicine-press,' as the Surveyor opened the violin-case on the table. Biddy stood vacantly by the machine, not sure whether to return to her knitting or not; and as the Sergeant was asking the Surveyor if he would like some water in his whiskey she eventually shouted, 'Would yous be wanting anything to ate now, would yous?' 'Yes. In a minute,' the Sergeant mouthed silently. As soon as he poured the water in the whiskey and placed it beside the Surveyor, who had taken the violin from its case and was lovingly removing its frayed black silk, he apologized, 'I won't be a minute,' and beckoned Biddy to follow him into the scullery. The door was opened on to a small yard, where elder and ash saplings grew out of a crumbling wall. Three hens were perched on the rim of a sawn barrel, gobbling mashed potatoes. As soon as Biddy saw the hens she seized a broom.

'Nobody can take eyes off yous, for one minute.'

She struck with the broom so that one hen in panic flew straight to the window, rocking the shaving mirror.

'Oh Jesus.' The Sergeant seized the broom from Biddy, who

stood stock-still in superstitious horror before the rocking shaving mirror, and then he quietly shooed the frightened hen from the window and out the door. He banged the door shut and bolted it with its wooden bolt.

'We'd have had seven years without a day's luck,' she shouted, as she fixed the mirror in the window.

'Never mind the mirror.' He turned her around by the shoulders.

'Never mind the mirror,' she shouted, frightened, to show him that she had read his lips.

'Keep your voice down.'

'Keep your voice down,' she shouted back.

'We want something to eat.'

'We want something to eat,' she shouted back, but she was calming. 'There's eggs and bacon.'

'Get something decent from the shop. Cheddar and ham. There's salad still in the garden.'

'Cheddar and ham,' she shouted. 'What if his ham is crawling and the price he charges? Not the first time for him to try to pass off crawling ham on me.'

'Go,' the Sergeant said and forced her into a coat he took from the scullery wall.

'Will I pay cash or get it put on the Book?' she shouted.

'The Book.' He handed her a small notebook covered with old policeman's cloth from where it hung from a nail in the wall and rushed her out the door. After he bolted it he whispered, 'Jesus, this night,' and drew his sleeve slowly across his forehead, feeling the braided coarseness of the three silver stripes of his rank, before facing back into the kitchen.

'If you live like pigs you can't expect sweet airs and musics all the time,' the Sergeant said in shame and exasperation as he swallowed his glass of whiskey. The Surveyor hadn't touched his whiskey. He was tuning the strings.

'It'd never do if we were all on the side of the angels,' the Surveyor answered absently.

The Sergeant filled his glass again. He drew up his chair to the fire and threw on a length of ash. The whiskey began to thaw away his unease. He raised his glass to the Surveyor and smiled. He was waiting.

Swallows

'The Italian street-musician was playing Paganini that first evening in Avignon.'

The bow flowed on the strings, the dark honey of the wood glowing in the early evening. Wind gently rustled the leaves of a Genoan olive grove. Metallic moonlight shone on their glistening silver as a man and a woman walked in the moonlight in a vague sweet ecstasy of feeling.

'Wonderful. I've never heard better, not even on the radio.' The Sergeant downed another glass of whiskey as the playing ended.

'Isn't the tone something?'

'It's priceless, that fiddle. You got a bargain.'

'I'm sure the experts are not far out when they say it most probably is a genuine Stradivarius.'

'The experts know. You go to the priest for religion. You go to the doctor for medicine. Who are we to trust if we can't trust the experts? On the broad of our backs we'd be without the experts.'

A man of extraordinary interest was Paganini, the Surveyor started to explain. He was born in Genoa in 1782, of a poor family, but such was his genius and dedication that he brought the world to his feet. In London, the mob used to try to touch him, in the hope that some of his magic might pass over to them, in the way they once tried to touch the hem of Christ's garments – like pop stars in our own day – but nothing could divert him from his calling. Even the last hours given to him in life were spent in marvellous improvisations on his Guarnerius. The Church proved to be the one fly in the ointment. She had doubts as to his orthodoxy, and refused for five years to have him buried in consecrated grounds. In the end, of course, in her usual politic fashion, she relented, and he was laid to rest in a village graveyard on his own land.

'And the Church bumming herself up all the time as helping musicians and painters out,' the Sergeant declaimed fervently when the Surveyor finished. 'It'd make a jackass bray backwards. But why don't you drink up? You have more than earned it.'

Apologetically, the Surveyor covered his glass with his palm. 'It's the driving, the new laws.'

'Well, I'm the law in these parts, for what it's worth. And there's the CWA party tonight. You could play there. It'd give the ignoramuses there a glimpse past their noses to hear playing the like of the Paganini. You could stay the night here in the barracks, there's tons of room.'

'No. I have to drive to Galway tonight.'

'Well, what's one man's poison. I was never a one for the forcing but that's no reason to stint my own hand,' he said as he filled his own glass again.

'It's your turn now to play, those lovely jigs and reels,' the Surveyor demanded.

'Not since the dances have I played, not for ages.'

'Can't you take the case down anyhow? You never know where the inspiration may come from.' The Surveyor smiled.

The case lay on the long mantel above the fire between a tea-box and a little red lamp that burned before a picture of the Sacred Heart in a crib bordered by fretted shamrocks. Clumsily he got it down. It was thick with dust. His hands left tracks on the case, and the ashes or dust scattered in a cloud when he started to beat it clean with an old towel. The Surveyor coughed in the dust and the Sergeant had to go to the scullery to wash his hands in the iron basin before the mirror. When he came in and finally got the case open, one string of the plain little fiddle was broken. The bow had obviously not been used for years, it was so slack.

'It's no Strad, but it would play after proper repairing. It would be a fine pastime for you on the long nights.'

'Play to old deaf Biddy, is it now. It had a sweet note too in its day though, and I had no need of the old whiskey to hurry the time then, sitting on the planks between the barrels, fiddling away as they danced past while they shouted up to me, "Rise it, Jimmy. More power to your elbow, Jimmy Boy!"'

Going back with the fellows over the fields in the morning as the cold day came up, he remembered; and life was as full of promise as the smile the girl with cloth fuchsia bells in her dark hair threw him as she danced past where he played on the planks. The Surveyor looked from the whiskey bottle to the regret on the sunken face with careless superiority and asked, 'Would you like me to play one of the old tunes?'

'I'd like that very much.'

'Is there anything in particular?'

'"The Kerry Dances."'

'Can you hum the opening part?'

Swallows

The Sergeant hummed it and confidently the Surveyor took up the playing. 'That's it, that's it.' The Sergeant excitedly beat time with his boots till a loud hammering came on the door.

'Oh my God, it's that woman again.' He pushed his hand through his grey hair, having to go to the scullery door to draw back the bolt.

She was in such a state when she came in that she did not seem to notice the Surveyor playing. 'Wet to the skin I got. And I tauld him his ham was crawling, or if it wasn't crawling it was next door to crawling if I have a nose. Eight-and-six he wanted,' she shouted.

The Surveyor broke off his playing. He watched her shake the rain from her coat and scarf.

'Yous will have to do with bacon and eggs, and that's the end all,' she shouted.

'A simple cup of tea would do me very well,' the Surveyor said.

'But you've had nothing for the inner man,' the Sergeant said as he filled his own glass from the whiskey bottle.

'I'll have to have a proper dinner this evening and I'd rather not eat now.'

'You can't be even tempted to have a drop of this stuff itself?' He offered the bottle.

'No thanks, I'll just finish this. Is there anything else you'd like me to play for you?'

'"Danny Boy", play "Danny Boy", then.'

'Is it bacon and eggs, then?' Biddy shouted.

'Tea and brown bread,' the Sergeant groaned as he framed silently the speech on his lips.

'Tea and brown bread,' she repeated, and he nodded as he gulped the whiskey.

The Surveyor quietly moved into 'Danny Boy', but as the rattle of a kettle entered 'When Summer's in the Meadows', his irritated face above the lovely old violin was plainly fighting to hold its concentration as he played.

'Maybe we might be able to persuade you to stay the night yet after all?' the Sergeant pressed with the fading strength of the whiskey while they drank sobering tea at the table with the knitting-machine clamped to its end. 'It'd be a great charity. Never before would they have heard playing the like of what you can play. It might occupy their minds with something other than pigs and hens and bullocks for once. Biddy could make up the spare room for you in no time and you could have a good drink without worry of the driving.'

'There's nothing I'd like better than to stay the night and play.'

'That's great. You can stay, then?'

'No, no. It's unfortunately impossible. I have to be at the Seapoint Hotel in Galway at six.'

'You could use the barrack phone to cancel.'

'No. Every time I get a case in the west I stay at the Seapoint. Eileen O'Neill is manageress there, and she is the best accompanist I know. She could have been a concert pianist. She has already taken the evening off. I'll have a bath when I get to the hotel and change into the evening suit you saw hanging in the car. We'll have dinner together and afterwards we'll play. We've been studying Kreisler and I can hardly wait to see how some of those lovely melodies play. Some day you must meet her. This evening she'll probably wear the long dress of burgundy velvet with the satin bow in her hair as she plays.'

'I'm sorry I tried to force you. If I'd known I wouldn't have tried to get the CWA function between you and that attraction.'

'Otherwise I'd be delighted. I consider it an honour to be invited. But I suppose,' he said, glancing at his watch, 'that if I intend to be there by six I better be making the road shorter.' He wrapped the violin in its frayed black silk and carefully returned it to its case. 'What's nice, though, is it's not really goodbye,' he said as they shook hands. 'We'll meet on the court day. And I can't thank you enough for those drawings you made of the accident.'

'They're for nothing, and a safe journey.'

At the door the Surveyor paused, intending to say goodbye to Biddy, but she was so intent on adjusting the needles of the machine to turn the heel of the sock that he decided not to bring his leaving to her notice.

The lighting of the oil-lamp dispelled the increasing blood-red gloom of the globe before the Sacred Heart after he had gone, as dusk deepened into night and Biddy placed suit and white shirt and tie on the chair before the fire of flickering ash.

'Will you be wanting anything to ate before the Function?' she shouted.

'No, Biddy.' He shook his head.

'Well, your clothes will be aired for you there and then when you want to change out of your uniform.'

'Thanks, Biddy,' he said.

'I'll leave your shoes polished by the table. I'll not wait up for you as no doubt it'll be the small hours. I'll put your hot waterjar in the bed.'

'Thanks, thanks, Biddy.'

Quietly he rose and replaced the cheap fiddle in the case, fingering the broken string before adding the slack bow. He shut the case and replaced it between the tea-box and the red globe of the Sacred Heart lamp on the mantel.

The smell of porter and whiskey, blue swirls of cigarette smoke, pounding of boots on the floorboards as they danced, the sudden yahoos as they swung, and the smile of the girl with the cloth fuchsia bells in her hair as he played, petrified for ever in his memory even as his stumblings home over the cold waking fields.

Tonight in Galway, in a long dress of burgundy velvet, satin in her hair, the delicate white hands of Eileen O'Neill would flicker on the white keyboard as the Surveyor played, while Mrs Kilboy would say to him at the CWA, 'Something will have to be done about Jackson's thieving ass, Sergeant, it'll take the law to bring him to his senses, nothing less, and those thistles of his will be blowing again over the townland this year with him dead drunk in the pub, and is Biddy's hens laying at all this weather, mine have gone on unholy strike, and I hear you were measuring the road today, you and a young whipper-snapper from Dublin, not even the guards can do anything unknownst in this place, and everybody's agog as to how the case will go, the poor woman's nerves I hear are in an awful condition, having to pass that wooden cross twice a day, and what was the use putting it up if it disturbs her so, it won't bring him back to life, poor Michael, God rest him, going to Carrick for his haircut. The living have remindedness enough of their last ends and testaments without putting up wooden crosses on the highways and byways, and did you ever see such a winter, torrents of rain and expectedness of snow, it'll be a long haul indeed to the summer.'

It would be a long haul to summer and the old tarred boat anchored to the Ford radiator in the mouth of the Gut, the line cutting the water as hooked roach after hooked roach made a last surge towards the freedom of the open lake.

When he had knotted his tie in the mirror his eye fell on the last of the whiskey and he filled the glass to the brim. He shivered as it went down but the melancholy passed from his face. He turned the chair round so that he could sit with his arms on its back, facing Biddy. 'Do you know what I'll say to Mrs Kilboy?' he addressed the unheeding Biddy who was intent on the turning of the heel. 'It'll be a long haul indeed until the summer, Mrs Kilboy,' I'll say. 'And now, Mrs Kilboy, let us talk of higher things. Some of the palaces of the royal popes in Avignon are wonderful, wonderful, Mrs Kilboy, in the sun; and wonderful the cafés and wonderful, Mrs Kilboy, the music. Did you ever hear of a gentleman called Paganini, Mrs Kilboy? A man of extraordinary interest is Paganini. Through his genius he climbed out of the filth of his local Genoa to wealth and fame. So that when he came to London, Mrs Kilboy, the crowds there crowded to touch him as they once trampled on one another to get their hands on Christ; but he stuck to his guns to the very end, improvising marvellously, Mrs Kilboy, during his last hours on his Guarnerius. I wonder what Guarnerius myself and yourself, Mrs Kilboy, or Biddy down in the barracks will be improvising on during our last hours before they hearse us across Cootehall bridge to old Ardcarne? Well, at least we'll be buried in consecrated ground – for I doubt if old Father Glynn will have much doubts as to our orthodoxy – which is more than they did for poor old Paganini, for I was informed today, Mrs Kilboy, that they left him in some field for five years, just like an old dead cow, before they relented and allowed him to be buried in a churchyard on his own land.'

The Sergeant tired of the mockery and rose from the chair, but he finished the dregs of the glass with a flourish, and placed it solidly down on the table. He put on his hat and overcoat. 'We better be making a start, Biddy, if we're ever going to put Mrs Kilboy on the straight and narrow.'

Biddy did not look up. She had turned the heel and would not have to adjust the needles again till she had to start narrowing the sock close to the toe. Her body swayed happily on the chair as she turned and turned the handle, for she knew it would be all plain sailing till she got close to the toe.

Gold Watch

It was in Grafton Street we met, aimlessly strolling in one of the lazy lovely Saturday mornings in spring, the week of work over, the weekend still as fresh as the bunch of anemones that seemed the only purchase in her cane shopping basket.

'What a lovely surprise,' I said.

I was about to take her hand when a man with an armload of parcels parted us as she was shifting the basket to her other hand, and we withdrew out of the pushing crowds into the comparative quiet of Harry Street. We had not met since we had graduated in the same law class from University College five years before. I had heard she'd become engaged to the medical student she used to knock around with and had gone into private practice down the country, perhaps waiting for him to graduate.

'Are you up for the weekend or on holiday or what?' I asked.

'No. I work here now.' She named a big firm that specialized in tax law. 'I felt I needed a change.'

She was wearing a beautiful suit, the colour of oatmeal, the narrow skirt slit from the knee. The long gold hair of her student days was drawn tightly into a neat bun at the back.

'You look different but as beautiful as ever,' I said. 'I thought you'd be married by now.'

'And do you still go home every summer?' she countered, perhaps out of confusion.

'It doesn't seem as if I'll ever break that bad habit.'

We had coffee in Bewley's – the scent of the roasting beans blowing through the vents out on to Grafton Street for ever mixed with the memory of that morning – and we went on to spend the whole idle day together until she laughingly and firmly returned my first hesitant kiss; and it was she who silenced my even more fumbled offer of marriage several weeks later. 'No,' she said. 'I don't want to be married. But we can move in together and see how it goes. If it doesn't turn out well we can split and there'll be no bitterness.'

And it was she who found the flat in Hume Street, on the top floor of one of those old Georgian houses in off the Green, within walking distance of both our places of work. There was extraordinary peace and loveliness in those first weeks together that I will always link with those high-ceilinged rooms – the eager rush of excitement I felt as I left the office at the end of the day; the lingering in the streets to buy some offering of flowers or fruit or wine or a bowl and, once, one copper pan; and then rushing up the stairs to call her name, the emptiness of those same rooms when I'd find she hadn't got home yet.

'Why are we so happy?' I would ask.

'Don't worry it,' she always said, and sealed my lips with a touch.

That early summer we drove down one weekend to the small town in Kilkenny where she had grown up, and above her father's bakery we slept in separate rooms. That Sunday a whole stream of relatives – aunts, cousins, two uncles, with trains of children – kept arriving at the house. Word had gone out and they had plainly come to look me over. This brought the tension between herself and her school-teacher mother into open quarrel late that evening after dinner. Her father sat with me in the front room, cautiously kind, sipping whiskey as we measured each careful cliché, listening to the quarrel slow and rise and crack in the far-off kitchen. I found the sense of comfort and space charming for a while, but by the time we left I too was beginning to find the small town claustrophobic.

'Unfortunately the best part of these visits is always the leaving,' she said as we drove away. 'After a while away you're lured into thinking that the next time will somehow be different, but it never is.'

'Wait – wait until you see my place. Then you may well think differently. At least your crowd made an effort. And your father is a nice man.'

'And yet you keep going back to the old place?'

'That's true. I have to face that now. That way I don't feel guilty. I don't feel anything.'

I knew myself too well. There was more caution than any love or charity in my habitual going home. It was unattractive and it had been learned in the bitter school of my father. I would fall into no guilt, and I was already fast outwearing him. For a time, it seemed, I could outstare the one eye of nature.

I had even waited for love, if love this was; for it was happiness such as I had never known.

'You see, I waited long enough for you,' I said as we drove away from her Kilkenny town. 'I hope I can keep you now.'

'If it wasn't me it would be some other. My mother will never understand that. I might as well say I waited long enough for you.'

The visit we made to my father some weeks later quickly turned to a far worse disaster than I could have envisaged. I saw him watch us as I got out of the car to open the iron gate under the yew, but instead of coming out to greet us he withdrew into the shadows of the hallway. It was my stepmother, Rose, who came out to the car when we both got out and were opening the small garden gate. We had to follow her smiles and trills of speech all the way into the kitchen to find my father, who was seated in the car chair, and he did not rise to take our hands.

After a lunch that was silent, in spite of several shuttlecocks of speech Rose tried to keep in the air, he said as he took his hat from the sill, 'I want to ask you about these walnuts,' and I followed him out into the fields. The mock orange was in blossom, and it was where the mock orange stood out from the clump of egg bushes that he turned suddenly and said, 'What age is your intended? She looks well on her way to forty.'

'She's the same age as I am,' I said blankly. I could hardly think, caught between the shock and pure amazement.

'I don't believe it,' he said.

'You don't have to, but we were in the same class at university.' I turned away.

Walking with her in the same field close to the mock orange tree late that evening, I said, 'Do you know what my father said to me?'

'No,' she said happily. 'But from what I've seen I don't think anything will surprise me.'

'We were walking just here,' I began, and repeated what he'd said. When I saw her go still and pale I knew I should not have spoken.

'He said I look close to forty,' she repeated. 'I have to get out of this place.'

'Stay this one night,' I begged. 'It's late now. We'd have to stay in a hotel. It'd be making it into too big a production. You don't ever have to come back again, if you don't want to, but stay the night. It'll be easier.'

'I'll not want to come back,' she said as she agreed to see out this one night.

'But why do you think he said it?' I asked her later when we were both quiet, sitting on a wall at the end of the Big Meadow, watching the shadows of the evening deepen between the beeches, putting off the time when we'd have to go into the house, not unlike two grown children.

'Is there any doubt? Out of simple hatred. There's no living with that kind of hatred.'

'We'll leave first thing in the morning,' I promised.

'And why did you,' she asked, tickling my throat with a blade of ryegrass, 'say I was, if anything, too beautiful?'

'Because it's true. It makes you public and it's harder to live naturally. You live in too many eyes – in envy or confusion or even simple admiration, it's all the same. I think it makes it harder to live luckily.'

'But it gives you many advantages.'

'If you make use of those advantages, you're drawn even deeper in. And of course I'm afraid it'll attract people who'll try to steal you from me.'

'That won't happen.' She laughed. She'd recovered all her natural good spirits. 'And now I suppose we better go in and face the ogre. We have to do it sooner or later and it's getting chilly.'

My father tried to be charming when we went in, but there was a false heartiness in the voice that made clear that it grew out of no well-meaning. He felt he'd lost ground, and was now trying to recover it far too quickly. Using silence and politeness like a single weapon, we refused to be drawn in; and when pressed to stay the next morning, we said unequivocally that we had to get back. Except for one summer when I went to work in England, the summer my father married Rose, I had always gone home to help at the hay; and after I entered the civil service I was able to arrange holidays so that they fell around haytime. They had come to depend on me and I liked the work. My father had never forgiven me for taking my chance to go to university. He had wanted me to stay at home to work the land. I had always fought his need to turn my refusal into betrayal, and by going home each summer I felt I was affirming that the great betrayal was not mine but nature's own.

I had arranged the holidays to fall at haytime that year as I had all the years before I met her, but since he'd turned to me at the mock orange tree I was no longer sure I had to go. I was no longer free, since in everything but name our life together seemed to be growing into marriage. It might even make him happy for a time if he could call it my betrayal.

'I don't know what to do,' I confessed to her a week before I was due to take holidays. 'They've come to depend on me for the hay. Everything else they can manage themselves. I know they'll expect me.'

'What do you want to do?'

'I suppose I'd prefer to go home – that's if you don't mind.'

'Why do you prefer?'

'I like working at the hay. You come back to the city feeling fit and well.'

'Is that the real reason?'

'No. It's something that might even be called sinister. I've gone home for so long that I'd like to see it through. I don't want to be blamed for finishing it, though it'll finish soon, with or without me. But this way I don't have to think about it.'

'Maybe it would be kinder, then, to do just that, and take the blame.'

'It probably would be kinder, but kindness died between us so long ago that it doesn't enter into it.'

'So there was some kindness?'

'When I was younger.' I had to smile. 'He looked on it as weakness. I suspect he couldn't deal with it. Anyhow it always redoubled his fury. He was kind, too, in fits, when he was feeling good about things. That was even more unacceptable. And that phrase from the Bible is true that after enough suffering a kind of iron enters the soul. It's very far from commendable, but now I do want to see it through.'

'Well, then go,' she said. 'I don't understand it but I can see you want to go. Being new, the earliest I can get holidays will be September.'

We had pasta and two bottles of red wine in the flat the evening before I was to leave for the hay, and with all the talking we were almost late for our walk in the Green. We liked to walk there every good evening before turning home for the night.

The bells were fairly clamouring from all corners, rooting vagrants and lovers from the shrubbery, as we passed through the half-closed gates. Two women at the pond's edge were hurriedly feeding the ducks bread from a plastic bag. We crossed the bridge where the Japanese cherry leaned, down among the empty benches round the paths and flowerbeds within their low railings. The deck-chairs had been gathered in, the sprinklers turned off. There was about the Green always at this hour some of the melancholy of the beach at the close of holiday. The gate we had entered was already locked. The attendant was rattling an enormous bunch of keys at the one through which we had to leave.

'You know,' she said, 'I'd like to be married before long. I hadn't thought it would make much difference to me, but, oddly, now I want to be married.'

'I hope it's to me,' I said.

'You haven't asked me.'

I could feel her laughter as she held my arm close.

'I'm asking now.'

I made a flourish of removing a non-existent hat. 'Will you marry me?'

'I will.'

'When?'

'Before the year is out.'

'Would you like to go for a drink to celebrate, then?'

'I always like any excuse to celebrate.' She was biting her lip. 'Where will you take me?'

'The Shelbourne. Our local. It'll be quiet.'

I thought of the aggressive boot thrown after the bridal car, the marbles suddenly rattling in the hubs of the honeymoon car, the metal smeared with oil so that the thrown boxes of confetti would stick, the legs of the comic pyjamas hilariously sewn up. We would avoid all that. We had promised one another the simplest wedding.

'We live in a lucky time,' she said and raised her glass, her calm, grey, intelligent eyes shining. 'We wouldn't have been allowed to do it this way even a decade ago. Will you tell your father that we're to be married?'

'I don't know. Probably not unless it comes up. And you?'

'I'd better. As it is, Mother will probably be furious that it is not going to be a big splash.'

'I'm so grateful for these months together, that we were able to drift into marriage without the drowning plunge. What will you do while I'm away?'

'I'll pine,' she teased. 'I might even try to decorate the flat out of simple desperation. There's a play at the Abbey that I want to see. There are some good restaurants in the city if I get too depressed. And in the meantime, have a wonderful time with your father and poor Rose in the nineteenth century at the bloody hay.'

'Oh, for the Lord's sake,' I said, and rose to leave. Outside she was still laughing so provocatively that I drew her towards me.

The next morning on the train home I heard a transistor far down the carriage promise a prolonged spell of good weather. Meadows were being mowed all along the line, and I saw men testing handfuls of hay in the breeze as they waited for the sun to burn the dew off the fallen swards. It was weather people prayed for at this time.

I walked the three miles from the station. Meadows were down all along the road, some already saved, in stacked bales. The scent of cut grass was everywhere. As I drew close to the stone house in its trees I could hardly wait to see if the Big Meadow was down beyond the row of beech trees. When I lived here I'd felt this same excitement as the train rattled across the bridges into the city or when I approached the first sight of the ocean. Now that I lived in a city on the sea the excitement had been gradually transferred home.

Before I reached the gate I could tell by the emptiness beyond the beeches that the Big Meadow had been cut. Rose and my father were in the house. They were waiting in high excitement.

'Everything's ready for you,' Rose said as she shook my hand, and through the window I saw my old clothes outside in the sun draped across the back of a chair.

'As soon as you get a bite you can jump into your old duds,' my father said. 'I knocked the Big Meadow yesterday. All's ready for go.'

Rose had washed my old clothes before hanging them outside to air. When I changed into them they were still warm from the sun, and they had that lovely clean feel that worn clothes have after washing. Within an hour we were working the machines.

The machines had taken much of the uncertainty and slavery from haymaking, but there was still the anxiety of rain. Each cloud that drifted into the blue above us we watched as apprehensively across the sky as if it were an enemy ship, and we seemed as tired at the end of every day as we were before we had the machines, eating late in silence, waking from listless watching of the television only when the weather forecast showed; and afterwards it was an effort to drag feet to our rooms where the bed lit with moonlight showed like heaven, and sleep was as instant as it was dreamless.

And it was into the stupor of such an evening that the gold watch fell. We were slumped in front of the television set. Rose had been working outside in the front garden, came in and put the tea kettle on the ring, and started to take folded sheets from the linen closet. Without warning, the gold watch spilled out on to the floor. She'd pulled it from the closet with one of the sheets. The pale face was upwards in the poor light. I bent to pick it up. The glass had not broken. 'It's lucky it no longer goes,' Rose breathed.

'Well, if it did you'd soon take good care of that.' My father rose angrily from the rocking chair.

'It just pulled out with the sheets,' Rose said. 'I was running into it everywhere round the house. I put it in with the sheets so that it'd be out of the way.'

'I'm sure you had it well planned. Give us this day our daily crash. Tell me this: would you sleep at night if you didn't manage to smash or break something during the day?' He'd been frightened out of light sleep in the chair. He was intent on avenging his fright.

'Why did the watch stop?' I asked.

I turned the cold gold in my hand. *Elgin* was the one word on the white face. The delicate hands were of blue steel. All through my childhood it had shone.

'Can there be two reasons why it stopped?' His anger veered towards me now. 'It stopped because it got broke.'

'Why can't it be fixed?' I ignored the anger.

'Poor Taylor in the town doesn't take in watches any more,' Rose answered. 'And the last time it stopped we sent it to Sligo. Sligo even sent it to Dublin but it was sent back. A part that holds the balance wheel is broke. What they told us is that they've stopped making parts for those watches. They have to be specially handmade. They said that the quality of the gold wasn't high enough to justify that expense. That it was only gold plated. I don't suppose it'll ever go again. I put it in with the sheets to have it out of the way. I was running into it everywhere.'

'Well, if it wasn't fixed before, you must certainly have fixed it for good and for ever this time.' My father would not let go.

His hand trembled on the arm of the rocking chair, the same hand that drew out the gold watch long ago as the first strokes of the Angelus came to us over the heather and pale wheaten sedge of Gloria Bog: 'Twenty minutes late, no more than usual . . . One of these years Jimmy Lynch will startle himself and the whole country-side by ringing the Angelus at exactly twelve . . . Only in Ireland is there right time and wrong time. In other countries there is just time.' We'd stand and stretch our backs, aching from scattering the turf, and wait for him to lift his straw hat.

Waiting with him under the yew, suitcases round our feet, for the bus that took us each year to the sea at Strandhill after the hay was in and the turf home; and to quiet us he'd take the watch out and let it lie in his open palm, where we'd follow the small second hand low down on the face endlessly circling until the bus came into sight at the top of Doherty's Hill. How clearly everything sang now set free by the distance of the years, with what heaviness the actual scenes and days had weighed.

'If the watch isn't going to be fixed, then, I might as well have it.' I was amazed at the calm sound of my own words. The watch had come to him from his father. Through all the long years of childhood I had assumed that one day he would pass it on to me. Then all weakness would be gone. I would possess its power. Once in a generous fit he even promised it to me, but he did not keep that promise. Unfairly, perhaps, I expected him to give it to me when I graduated, when I passed into the civil service, when I won my first promotion, but he did not. I had forgotten about it until it had spilled out of the folded sheets on to the floor.

I saw a look pass between my father and stepmother before he said, 'What good would it be to you?'

'No good. Just a keepsake. I'll get you a good new watch in its place. I often see watches in the duty-free airports.' My work often took me outside the country.

'I don't need a watch,' he said, and pulled himself up from his chair.

Rose cast me a furtive look, much the same look that had passed a few moments before between her and my father. 'Maybe your father wants to keep the watch,' it pleaded, but I ignored it.

'Didn't the watch once belong to your father?' I asked as he shuffled towards his room, but the only answer he made was to turn and yawn back before continuing the slow, exaggerated shuffle towards his room.

When the train pulled into Amiens Street Station, to my delight I saw her outside the ticket barrier, in the same tweed suit she'd worn the Saturday morning we met in Grafton Street. I could tell that she'd been to the hairdresser, but there were specks of white paint on her hands.

'Did you tell them that we're to be married?' she asked as we left the station.

'No.'

'Why not?'

'It never came up. And you, did you write home?'

'No. In fact, I drove down last weekend and told them.'

'How did they take it?'

'They seemed glad. You seemed to have made a good impression.' She smiled. 'As I guessed, Mother is quite annoyed that it's not going to be a big do.'

'You won't change our plans because of that.'

'Of course not. She's not much given to change herself, except to changing other people so that they fit in with her ideas.'

'This fell my way at last,' I said and showed her the silent watch. 'I've always wanted it. If we believed in signs it would seem life is falling into our hands at last.'

'And not before our time, I think I can risk adding.'

We were married that October by a Franciscan in their church on the quay, with two vergers as witnesses, and we drank far too much wine at lunch afterwards in a new restaurant that had opened in Lincoln Court. Staggering home in the late afternoon, I saw some people in the street smile at my attempt to lift her across the step. We did not even hear the bells closing the Green.

It was dark when we woke, and she said, 'I have something for you,' taking a small, wrapped package from the bedside table.

'You know we promised not to give presents,' I said.

'I know but this is different. Open it. Anyhow, you said you didn't believe in signs.'

It was the gold watch. I held it to my ear. It was running perfectly. The small second hand was circling endlessly low down on the face. The blue hands pointed to past midnight.

'Did it cost much?'

'No. Very little, but that's not your business.'

'I thought the parts had to be specially made.'

'That wasn't true. They probably never even asked.'

'You shouldn't have bothered.'

'Now I'm hoping to see you wear it,' she laughed.

I did not wear it. I left it on the mantel. The gold and white face and delicate blue hands looked very beautiful to me on the white marble. It gave me a curious pleasure mixed with guilt to wind it and watch it run; and the following spring, coming from a conference in Ottawa, I bought an expensive modern watch in the duty-free shop of Montreal Airport. It was guaranteed for five years, and was shockproof, dustproof, waterproof.

'What do you think of it?' I asked her when I returned to Dublin. 'I bought it for my father.'

'Well, it's no beauty, but my mother would certainly approve of it. It's what she'd describe as *serviceable*.'

'It was expensive enough.'

'It looks expensive. You'll bring it when you go down for the hay?'

'It'll probably be my last summer with them at the hay,' I said apologetically. 'Won't you change your mind and come down with me?'

She shook her head. 'He'd probably say I look fifty now.' She was as strong-willed as the schoolteacher mother she disliked, and I did not press. She was with child and looked calm and lovely.

'What'll they do about the hay when they no longer have you to help them?' she said.

'What does anybody do? Do without me. Stop. Get it done by contract. They have plenty of money. It'll just be the end of something that has gone on for a very long time.'

'That it certainly has.'

I came by train at the same time in July as I'd come every summer, the excitement tainted with melancholy that it'd probably be the last summer I would come. I had not even a wish to see it to its natural end any more. I had come because it seemed less violent to come than to stay away, and I had the good new modern watch to hand over in place of the old gold. The night before, at dinner, we had talked about buying a house with a garden out near the strand in Sandymount. Any melancholy I was feeling lasted only until I came in sight of the house.

All the meadows had been cut and saved, the bales stacked in groups of five or six and roofed with green grass. The Big Meadow beyond the beeches was completely clean, the bales having been taken in. Though I had come intending to make it my last summer at the hay, I now felt a keen outrage that it had been ended without me. Rose and my father were nowhere to be seen.

'What happened?' I asked when I found them at last, weeding the potato ridge one side of the orchard.

'The winter feeding got too much for us,' my father said. 'We decided to let the meadows. Gillespie took them. He cut early – two weeks ago.'

'Why didn't you tell me?'

My father and Rose exchanged looks, and my father spoke as if he was delivering a prepared statement.

'We didn't like to. And anyhow we thought you'd want to come, hay or no hay. It's more normal to come for a rest instead of just to kill yourself at the old hay. And indeed there's plenty else for you to do if you have a mind to do it. I've taken up the garden again myself.'

'Anyhow, I've brought these.' I handed Rose the box of chocolates and bottle of scent, and gave my father the watch.

'What's this for?'

'It's the watch I told you I'd get in place of the old watch.'

'I don't need a watch.'

'I got it anyhow. What do you think of it?'

'It's ugly,' he said, turning it over.

'It was expensive enough.' I named the price. 'And that was duty free.'

'They must have seen you coming, then.'

'No. It's guaranteed for five years. It's dustproof, shockproof, waterproof.'

'The old gold watch – do you still have that?' He changed after silence.

'Of course.'

'Did you ever get it working?'

'No,' I lied. 'But it's sort of nice to have.'

'That doesn't make much sense to me.'

'Well, you'll find that the new watch is working well anyway.'

'What use have I for time here any more?' he said, but I saw him start to wind and examine the new watch, and he was wearing it at breakfast the next morning. He seemed to want it to be seen as he buttered toast and reached across for milk and sugar.

'What did you want to get up so early for?' he said to me. 'You should have lain in and taken a good rest when you had the chance.'

'What will you be doing today?' I asked.

'Not much. A bit of fooling around. I might get spray ready for the potatoes.'

'It'd be an ideal day for hay,' I said, looking out the window on the fields. The morning was as blue and cool as the plums still touched with dew down by the hayshed. There was a white spider webbing over the grass. I took a book and headed towards the shelter of the beeches in the Big Meadow, for, when the sun would eventually beat through, the day would be uncomfortably hot.

It was a poor attempt at reading. Halfway down each page I'd find I had lost every thread and was staring blankly at the words. I thought at first that the trees and green and those few wisps of cloud, hazy and calm in the emerging blue, brought the tension of past exams and summers too close to the book I held in my hand, but then I found myself stirring uncomfortably in my suit – missing my old loose clothes, the smell of diesel in the meadow, the blades of grass shivering as they fell, the long teeth of the raker kicking the hay into rows, all the jangle and bustle and busyness of the meadows.

I heard the clear blows of a hammer on stone. My father was sledging stones that had fallen from the archway where once the workmen's bell had hung. Some of the stones had been part of the arch and were quite beautiful. There seemed no point in breaking them up. I moved closer, taking care to stay hidden in the shade of the beeches.

As the sledge rose, the watch glittered on my father's wrist. I followed it down, saw the shudder that ran through his arms as the metal met the stone. A watch was always removed from the wrist before such violent work. I waited. In this heat he could not keep up such work for long. He brought the sledge down again and again, the watch glittering, the shock shuddering through his arms. When he stopped, before he wiped the sweat away, he put the watch to his ear and listened intently. What I'd guessed was certain now. From the irritable way he threw the sledge aside, it was clear that the watch was still running.

That afternoon I helped him fill the tar barrel with water for spraying the potatoes, though he made it clear he didn't want help. When he put the bag of blue stone into the barrel to steep, he thrust the watch deep into the water before my eyes.

'I'm going back to Dublin tomorrow,' I said.

'I thought you were coming for two weeks. You always stayed two weeks before.'

'There's no need for me now.'

'It's your holiday. You're as well off here as by the sea. It's as much of a change and far cheaper.'

'I meant to tell you before, and should have but didn't. I am married now.'

'Tell me more news,' he said with an attempt at cool surprise, but I saw by his eyes that he already knew. 'We heard but we didn't like to believe it. It's a bit late in the day for formal engagements, never mind invitations. I suppose we weren't important enough to be invited.'

'There was no one at the wedding but ourselves. We invited no one, neither her people nor mine.'

'Well, I suppose it was cheaper that way,' he agreed.

'When will you spray?'

'I'll spray tomorrow,' he said, and we left the blue stone to steep in the barrel of water.

With relief, I noticed he was no longer wearing the watch, but the feeling of unease was so great in the house that after dinner I went outside. It was a perfect moonlit night, the empty fields and beech trees and walls in clear yellow outline. The night seemed so full of serenity that it brought the very ache of longing for all of life to reflect its moonlit calm, but I knew too well it neither was nor could be. It was a dream of death.

I went idly towards the orchard, and as I passed the tar barrel I saw a thin fishing line hanging from a part of the low yew branch down into the barrel. I heard the ticking even before the wrist watch came up tied to the end of the line. What shocked me was that I felt neither surprise nor shock.

I felt the bag that we'd left to steep earlier in the water. The blue stone had all melted down. It was a barrel of pure poison, ready for spraying.

I listened to the ticking of the watch on the end of the line in silence before letting it drop back into the barrel. The poison had already eaten into the casing of the watch. The shining rim and back were no longer smooth. It could hardly run much past morning.

The night was so still that the shadows of the beeches did not waver on the moonlit grass, seemed fixed like a leaf in rock. On the white marble the gold watch must now be lying face upwards in this same light, silent or running. The ticking of the watch down in the barrel was so completely muffled by the spray that only by imagination could it be heard. A bird moved in some high branch, but afterwards the silence was so deep it began to hurt, and the longing grew for the bird or anything to stir again.

I stood in that moonlit silence as if waiting for some word or truth, but none came, none ever came; and I grew amused at that part of myself that still expected something, standing like a fool out there in all the moonlit silence, when only what *was* increased or diminished as it changed, became only what is, becoming again what *was* even faster than the small second hand endlessly circling in the poison.

Suddenly, the lights in the house went out. Rose had gone to join my father in bed. Before going into the house this last night to my room, I drew the watch up again out of the barrel by the line and listened to it tick, now purely amused by the expectation it renewed – that if I continued to listen to the ticking some word or truth might come. And when I finally lowered the watch back down into the poison, I did it so carefully that no ripple or splash disturbed the quiet, and time, hardly surprisingly, was still running; time that did not have to run to any conclusion.

Parachutes

'I want to ask you one very small last favour.'

'What is it?'

'Will you stay behind for just five minutes after I leave?'

It was the offer of the blindfold, to accept the darkness for a few moments before it finally fell.

'If we leave together we'll just start to argue again and it's no use. You know it's over. It's been over for a long time now. Will you please stay five minutes?' She put her gloved hand on my arm as she rose. 'Just this last time.'

She turned and walked away. I was powerless to follow. She did not once look back. The door swung in the emptiness after she had gone. I saw the barman looking at me strangely but I did not care. The long hand of the clock stood at two minutes to eight. It did not seem to move at all. She was gone, slipping further out of reach with every leaden second, and I was powerless to follow.

'A small Jameson. With water,' I said to the barman. As I sipped the whiskey, the whole absurdity of my situation came with a rush of anger. It was over. She was gone. Nothing said or done would matter any more, and yet I was sitting like a fool because she'd simply asked me to. Without glancing at the clock, I rose and headed towards the door. Outside she was nowhere in sight.

I could see down on the city, its maze of roads already lighted in the still, white evening, each single road leading in hundreds of directions. I started to run, but then had to stop, realizing I didn't know where to run. If there were an instrument like radar . . . but that might show her half-stripped in some car . . . her pale shoulders gleaming as she slipped out of her clothes in a room in Rathmines . . .

I stared at the street. Cars ran. Buses stopped. Lights changed. Shop windows stayed where they were. People answered to their names. All the days from now on would have to begin without her. The one thing I couldn't bear was to face back to the room, the room that had seen such a tenuous happiness.

I went into the Stag's Head and then O'Neills. Both bars were crowded. There was no one there that I knew. I passed slowly through without trying to order anything. The barmen were too busy to call out. I moved to the bars off Grafton Street, and at the third bar I saw the Mulveys before I heard my name called. It was Claire Mulvey who had called my name. Paddy Mulvey was reading a book, his eyes constantly flickering from the page to the door, but as soon as he heard my name called his eyes returned fixedly to the page. They were sitting between the pillars at the back. Eamonn Kelly appeared to be sitting with them.

'We thought you were avoiding us,' Claire Mulvey said as we shook hands. Her strained, nervous features still showed frayed remnants of beauty. 'We haven't seen you for months.'

'For God's sake, isn't it a free country?' Paddy Mulvey said brightly. 'Hasn't the man a right to do his own things in his own way?'

'Blackguard,' Eamonn Kelly said gravely, his beautiful, pale face relaxing in a wintry smile.

'Why are you not drinking?' Empty half-glasses stood in front of them on the table.

'I'm afraid we're suffering from that old perplexity,' Mulvey said. 'And we've been waiting for Halloran. He was supposed to be here more than an hour ago. He owes us a cheque. He even left us a hostage for reassurance.' He pointed to a brown leather suitcase upright against the pillar.

'I'll get the drinks,' I offered.

'Halloran went off with a boy. I've been telling them he'll not be back,' Eamonn Kelly volunteered.

I got four pints and four whiskeys from the bar.

'I should thank you for this,' Eamonn Kelly said as he lifted his whiskey. 'But after careful consideration have come down against it.'

'Why?'

'Because I've decided you're a blackguard.'

'Why me?'

'Because one must have some fixed principles. I've decided you are a blackguard. That's an end of it. There is no appeal.'

'Oh, for God's sake,' Mulvey said. 'You're not drunk enough for that yet. Here's health.'

'Good luck,' Claire Mulvey said.

'What are you reading?'

'Another slim volume. I'm writing it up for Halloran,' and he started to speak of the book in a tone of spirited mockery.

I tried to listen but found the arid, mocking words unbearable. Nothing lived. Then I found myself turning towards a worse torture, to all I wanted not to think about.

She had asked me to a dinner in her sister's house a few days before Christmas. We'd met inside a crowded GPO. She was wearing a pale raincoat with the detachable fur collar she wore with so many coats. Outside in O'Connell Street the wind was cold, spitting rain, and we'd stood in a doorway as we waited for a bus to take us to the house in the suburbs.

The house her sister lived in was a small semi-detached in a new estate: a double gate, a garage, a piece of lawn hemmed in with concrete, a light above the door. The rooms were small, carpeted. A coal fire burned in the tiled fireplace of the front room.

Her sister was as tall as she, black-haired, and beautiful, pregnant with her first child. Her husband was small, energetic, and taught maths in a nearby school.

The bottles of wine we'd brought were handed over. Glasses of whiskey were poured. We touched the glasses in front of the coal fire. They'd gone to a great deal of trouble with the meal. There were small roast potatoes, peas, breadcrumb stuffing with the roast turkey. Brandy was poured over the plum pudding and lit. Some vague unease curdled the food and cheer in that small front room, was sharpened by the determined gaiety. It was as if we were looking down a long institutional corridor; the child in the feeding chair could be seen already, the next child, and the next, the postman, the milkman, the van with fresh eggs and vegetables from the country, the tired clasp over the back of the hand to show tenderness as real as the lump in the throat, the lawnmowers in summer, the thickening waists. It hardly seemed necessary to live it.

'What did you think of them?' she'd asked as she took my arm in the road outside.

'I thought they were very nice. They went to a great deal of trouble.'

'What did you think of the house?'

'It's not my kind of house. It's the sort of house that would drive me crackers.'

'What sort of house would you like?'

'Something bigger than that. Something with a bit more space. An older house. Nearer the city.'

'Excuse me,' she said with pointed sarcasm as she withdrew her arm.

I should have said, 'It's a lovely house. Any house with you would be a lovely house,' and caught and kissed her in the wind and rain. And it was true. Any house with her would have been a lovely house. I had been the fool to think that I could stand outside life. I would agree to anything now. I would not even ask for love. If she stayed, love might come in its own time, I reasoned blindly.

'Do you realize how rich the English language is, that it should have two words, for instance, such as "comprehension" and "apprehension", so subtly different in shading and yet so subtly alike? Has anything like that ever occurred to you?' This was Mulvey now.

'No. I hadn't realized.'

'Of course you wouldn't. And I'd rather comprehend another drink.'

'Comprehension. Apprehension,' Eamonn Kelly started to say as I went to get the drinks. 'I'll apprehend you for a story. An extraordinarily obscene story.'

'Jesus,' Mulvey groaned.

'I hope it's not long,' Claire Mulvey said. 'Where have you been all this time?' she asked as he began. 'We don't have to listen to that. Those stories are all the same.'

'I got mixed up with a girl.'

'Why didn't you bring her here? You should at least have given us the chance to look her over.'

'She wouldn't like it here. Anyhow it's over now.'

'I'm glad you're here,' she said.

'Is he?' Eamonn Kelly shouted, annoyed that we hadn't listened to the story he'd been telling.

'Is he what?' Mulvey asked.

'Is he here? Am I here?'

'Unfortunately you're here,' Mulvey replied.

'Hypocrites. Liars.'

'Lies are the oil of the social machinery.'

'Don't mind him,' Mulvey said.

'Lies,' he ignored. 'She ate green plums. She was pregnant. That's why she's not here. Blackguard.'

'This is terrible,' Mulvey said.

The anxiety as to where she was at this moment struck without warning. 'Did you ever wish for some device like radar that could track a person down at any given moment, light up where they were, like on a screen?' I turned to Mulvey.

'That would be a nightmare.' Mulvey surprisingly rallied to the question, his interest caught. 'I was never very worried about what other people were up to. My concern has always been that they might discover what *I* was up to.'

'Then you've never loved,' Eamonn Kelly said grandly. 'I know what he's talking about. There were times I too wished for radar.'

'I wouldn't mind putting radar on Halloran just now. To get him to give me that cheque, to give him back his damned suitcase. We've ferried the thing around for two whole days now.' Mulvey turned aside to complain.

'You must have wanted to know sometimes what I was doing,' Claire Mulvey said.

'Never.'

'Even if that is true, I don't think you should say it.'

'That's precisely why it should be said. Because it is true. Why else should anything be said?'

They started to quarrel. I bought a last round. It was getting close to closing time. Eamonn Kelly had begun an energetic conversation with himself, accompanied by equally vigorous gestures, a dumbshow of removing hat and gloves, handshakes, movements forward and back, a great muttering of some complicated sentence, replacing of hat and gloves. The Mulveys had retreated into stewing silences. I was bewildered as to what I was doing here but was even blinder still about possible alternatives. A whole world had been cut from under me.

'Do you have enough for a sugar bag?' Mulvey suddenly asked. 'We could go back to my place.'

'I have plenty.'

'I'll make it up to you as soon as I see Halloran.'

The sugar bags were strong grey paper bags used to carry out bottles of stout. They usually held a dozen. I bought three. Eamonn Kelly assumed he was going back to Mulvey's with us, for he offered to carry one of the bags. Claire Mulvey carried Halloran's suitcase. There were many drunks on the street. One made a playful pass at the sugar bag Mulvey carried, and got berated, the abuse too elevated and fluent to get us into trouble. We could not have looked too sober ourselves, for I noticed a pair of guards stand to watch our progress with the case and sugar bags. Mulvey's house was in a terrace along the canal. A young moon lay in a little water between the weeds and cans and bottles.

'*The wan moon is setting on the still wave,*' Eamonn Kelly took up from the reflection as he swayed along with a sugar bag.

'Burns,' Mulvey said savagely. 'And there's not a wave in sight. What do you think of old Burns?' he said as he put the key in the door.

A red-eyed child in a nightdress met us. She was hungry. Claire Mulvey soothed her, started to get her some food from the cold press, and we took the sugar bags upstairs. There was no furniture of any kind in the room other than empty orange crates. There were plenty of books on the floor along the walls. The room was chilly, and Mulvey stamped on some of the orange crates until they were broken enough to fit into the grate. He lit them with newspaper and they quickly caught.

Eamonn Kelly was busy opening the bottles with a silver penknife. When Claire Mulvey joined us he had opened all the bottles in one of the sugar bags. The orange boxes had all burned down, taking the chill from the room, leaving delicate traceries of blackened wire in the grate.

'She's gone to sleep again. There was some milk and cereal,' Claire Mulvey said.

We drank steadily. Eamonn Kelly opened more bottles. Mulvey lectured Kelly. Then he lectured me. The toilet in the corridor didn't work. I fought sleep.

The room was full of early light when I awoke. I'd been placed on a mattress and given a pillow and rug. There was nobody else in the room. The books were scattered all along the walls. Empty bottles were everywhere, the room filled with the sour-sweet odour of decaying stout. The shapes of blackened wire stood in the empty grate.

It was the first morning without her, and I could hardly believe I'd slept. I got up, picked my way between the bottles to the outside toilet that didn't work, ran the water in the sink, picked my way back to the mattress. The palest of crescent moons still lay on the dirty water of the canal.

Church bells started to beat the air. It was Sunday – seven o'clock. I got up and let myself out of the house. Everywhere people were going to Mass. I drifted with them as far as the church door, turning back into the empty streets once Mass had started, walking fast until I came to a quiet side street where I sat on the steps of one of the houses. There were five steps up to each house. The stone was granite. Many of the iron railings were painted blue. Across the street was a dishevelled lilac bush. They'd taught us to notice such things when young. They said it was the world. A lilac bush, railings, three milk bottles with silver caps, granite steps . . . I had to rise and walk to beat back a rush of anger. I'd have to learn the world all over again.

The Mulveys were sitting round the table in the kitchen when I got back. The child was eating cereal, the parents drinking tea from mugs.

'I'm sorry I passed out, last night.'

'It's all right. You were tired.' Mulvey smiled – often he could be charming in the morning.

'Did Kelly go home?'

'He always goes home no matter how drunk he is.'

I handed round newspapers I'd bought on the way back and was given tea. The child inspected me gravely from behind her spoon.

'Can you lend me a fiver?' Mulvey asked me about midday. 'I'll give it back to you as soon as I find Halloran.'

'You don't have to worry about that.' It was a sort of freedom to be rid of the money.

'There's no reason I should be spending all your money. I'll give it back to you this evening. We're bound to unearth Halloran this evening,' and the rest of the day was more or less arranged. We had drinks at a tiny local along the canal. The child had lemonade and crisps.

Stew was heated when we got back to the house. Then Mulvey shut himself upstairs to write a review. Claire Mulvey watched an old movie with Cary Grant on the black-and-white television. I played draughts with the child. It was four when Mulvey came down.

'How did it go?' I asked without looking up from the pieces on the board.

'It didn't go at all. I couldn't get started with thinking of that damned Halloran. He's ruined the day as well.' He was plainly in foul humour.

We left the child to play with neighbours and set out towards Grafton Street to look for Halloran, Mulvey carrying the suitcase. He had been at his most affable and bluff-charming while handing over the child to the neighbours, but as soon as we were alone he started to seethe with resentment.

'It's an affront to expect someone to lug this thing round for two whole days.'

'What harm is it?' his wife made the mistake of saying. 'He's not a very happy person.'

'What do you know about his happiness or unhappiness?'

'He sweats a kind of unhappiness. He's bald and huge and not much more than thirty.'

'I never heard such rubbish. He's probably in some good hotel down in Wicklow at this very moment, relaxing with a gin and tonic, watching the sun set from a deck-chair, regaling this boy with poetry or love or some other obscenity. I'm not carrying the fat ponce's suitcase a yard farther,' and he flung it from him, the suitcase sliding to a violent stop against the ledge of the area railing without breaking open.

'I'll carry it.' His wife went and picked up the case, but Mulvey was already striding ahead.

'When we were first together I used to hate these rows. I used to be ill afterwards, but Paddy taught me that there was nothing bad about them. He taught me that fights shouldn't be taken too seriously. They often clear the air. They're just another form of expression,' she confided.

'I hate rowing.'

'I used to feel that way!'

This, I thought, was a true waste. If she was with me now we could be by the sea.

But we'd gone to the sea four Sundays before, to Dollymount.

She'd been silent and withdrawn all that day. I was afraid to challenge her mood, too anxious just to have her near. She said we'd go over to the sandhills on the edge of the links, away from the wall and the crowded beach. She seemed to be searching for a particular place among the sandhills, and when she found it smiled that familiar roguish smile I hadn't seen for months and took a photo from her handbag.

'Willie Moran took the photo on this very spot,' she said. 'Do you recognize it at all?'

Willie Moran was a young solicitor she'd gone out with. She'd wanted to marry him. It had ended a few months before we met. After it ended she hadn't been able to live alone and had gone back to an older sister's house.

I used to be jealous of Willie Moran but by now even that had been burned away. I just thought him a fool for not marrying her, wished that I'd been he. I handed her back the photo. 'You look beautiful in it.'

'You see, it was afterwards it was taken. I'm well tousled.' She laughed and drew me down. She wanted to make love there. There seemed to be no one passing. We covered ourselves with a white raincoat.

Her mood changed as quickly again as soon as we rose. She wanted to end the day, to separate.

'We could go to one of the cinemas in O'Connell Street or to eat somewhere.' I would offer anything.

'No. Not this evening. I just want to have an early night. I've a kind of headache.'

It was then she pointed out that she'd lost an earring in the sandhills, one of a pair of silver pendants I'd given her for her birthday.

As soon as she left me I retracked my way back into the sandhills. Our shapes were still where we had lain in the loose sand. With a pocket comb I came on the pendant where the sand and long white grass met. I was happy, only too anxious to believe that it augured well, that it was a sign that the whole course of the affair had turned towards an impossible happiness. 'We will be happy. We'll be happy. It will turn out all right now.' It was a dream of paradise.

But all the finding of the pendant did was to hold off this hell for four whole weeks. It was strange to think that but for coming on the simple earring in the sand, this day, this unendurable day, would have fallen four weeks ago. She had said so.

The Harcourt Street lights brought Mulvey's enraged stride to a stop. He turned and came back towards us. 'If I can't carry it, it's an even worse form of humiliation to have to watch my wife carry it. Throw it there,' and when she protested he took it from her and threw it down.

'I'll carry it,' I said. It was so light it could be empty, but when I swung it I felt things move within the leather.

'What business is it of yours?' he demanded.

'None. But I don't want to leave it behind on the street.'

'You take it too seriously.' He brightened. 'It wouldn't be left behind.'

'I don't mind carrying it at all,' I said.

'Do you know what colour of sky that is?' He pointed above the roofs of Harcourt Street.

'It's blue,' I said. 'A blue sky.'

'It's not a blue sky, but it goes without saying that blue is what it would be called by everybody in this sloppy country. *Agate* is the exact word. There are many blues. That is an agate sky.'

'How do you know it's agate?'

'A painter I used to knock around with taught me the different colours.'

'It's a beautiful word,' I said.

'It's the *right* word,' he replied.

'I've just noticed what a lovely evening it is,' Claire Mulvey said wistfully. 'There's just the faintest hint of autumn.'

'The last time we met I seem to remember you saying that Halloran was all right,' I said. 'You said he was a sensitive person.'

'Oh, I was just making him up,' Mulvey laughed, breaking as quickly into jocular good humour as he had into anger. 'You don't have to take what I say about people so solemnly. People need a great deal of making up. I don't see how they'd be tolerable otherwise. Everybody does it. You'll learn that soon enough.'

The light seemed to glow in a gentle fullness on the bullet-scarred stone of the College of Surgeons. Stephen's Green looked full of peace within its green railings. There was a smoky blue in the air that warned of autumn. Claire Mulvey had been silent for several minutes.

Her face was beautiful in its tiredness, her thoughts plainly elsewhere.

'We have to be thankful for this good weather while it lasts,' she said when we reached the bar. 'It's lovely to see the doors of the bars open so late in the summer.'

Halloran was not in the bar. We counted out the money and found we'd enough for one round but not for a second. Mulvey bought the drinks and took them to a table near the door. We could see the whole way across the street to the closed shoeshop.

'Where's that case?' Mulvey said in an exasperation of waiting. 'We've been lugging it around for so long we might as well see what we've been lugging around.'

'What does it matter? He left it with us,' Claire Mulvey pleaded. 'And he may come at any minute.'

The opposition seemed to drive Mulvey on. When the lock held, he lifted the suitcase to his knees and, holding it just below the level of the table, took a nail file from his pocket.

'Don't open it,' his wife pleaded. 'He left it locked. It's like opening someone's letters.'

Suddenly the lock sprung beneath the probing of the small file, and he opened it slowly, keeping one eye on the door. An assortment of women's underclothes lay in the bottom of the case, all black: a slip, a brassière, panties, long nylon stockings, a pair of red shoes; and beneath, a small Roman missal, its ribbons of white and green and yellow and red hanging from the edges. *In Latin and English for every day in the year*.

I thought he'd make a joke of it, call to have a bucket of water in readiness when Halloran appeared with the boy. 'This is just too much,' he said, and closed the suitcase, probing again with the nail file till the catch locked.

'It wasn't right to open it,' Claire Mulvey said.

'Of course it was right. Now we know what we're really dealing with. Plain, dull, unimaginative perversity. Imagine the ponce dressing himself up in that gear. It's too much.'

'It mightn't be his,' she protested.

'Of course it's his. Whose else could it be!'

Eamonn Kelly came in. He'd met Halloran and the boy in Baggot Street that morning after Mass. He said that he'd be here at six and had given him money to buy us drinks till he came. We all asked for pints. I went to help Eamonn Kelly bring the drinks from the counter.

'Did you get home all right last night?' I asked as we waited on the pulling of the pints.

'Would I be here if I hadn't?' he retorted. I didn't answer. I brought the drinks back to the table.

'Well, at least this is a move in the right direction,' Mulvey said as he raised his glass to his lips. I felt leaden with tiredness, the actual bar close to the enamelled memories of the morning. Everything around me looked like that dishevelled lilac bush, those milk bottles, granite steps . . .

The state was so close to dreaming that I stared in disbelief when I saw the first thistledown, its thin, pale parachute drifting so slowly across the open doorway that it seemed to move more in water than in air. A second came soon after the first had crossed out of sight, moving in the same unhurried way. A third. A fourth. There were three of the delicate parachutes moving together, at the same dream-like pace across the doorway.

'Do you see the thistles?' I said. 'It's strange to see them in the middle of Grafton Street.'

'There are backyards and dumps around Grafton Street too. You only see the fronts,' Mulvey said. 'Yes. There's plenty of dumps.'

Several more arrived and passed on in the same slow dream. There was always one or several in the doorway. When at last there were none it seemed strange, but then one would appear when they seemed quite stopped, move slowly across, but the intervals were lengthening.

'They seem to be coming from the direction of Duke Street,' Claire Mulvey said. 'There are no gardens or dumps that I can think of there.'

'You think that because you can't see any. There are dumps and yards and gardens, and everything bloody people do, but they're at the back.'

'They may have come from even farther away,' I said. 'I wonder how far they can travel.'

'It'd be easy to look it up,' Mulvey said. 'That's what books are for.'

'They can't come on many easy seed-beds in the environs of Grafton Street.'

'There's a dump near Mercer's. And there's another in Castle Street.' Mulvey started to laugh at some private joke. 'And nature will have provided her usual hundredfold overkill. For the hundred that fall on stone or pavement one will find its dump and grow up into a proud thistle and produce thousands of fresh new thistledowns.'

'Hazlitt,' Eamonn Kelly ventured.

'Hazlitt's far too refined,' Mulvey said. 'Just old boring rural Ireland strikes again. Even its principal city has one foot in a manure heap.' The discussion had put Mulvey in extraordinary good humour.

Halloran and the boy appeared. Halloran was larger than I remembered, bald, wearing a dishevelled pinstripe suit, sweating profusely. He started to explain something in a very agitated manner even before he got to our table. The boy followed behind like a small dog, his black hair cropped very close to his skull, quiet and looking around, seemingly unafraid. As he came towards the table, a single thistledown appeared, and seemed to hang for a still moment beyond his shoulder in the doorway. A hand reached out, the small fresh hand of a girl or boy, but before it had time to close, the last pale parachute moved on out of sight as if breathed on by the hand's own movement.

Lightly as they, we must have drifted to the dancehall a summer ago. The late daylight had shone through the glass dome above the dancefloor, strong as the light of the ballroom, the red and blue lights that started to sweep the floor as soon as the waltz began.

She'd been standing with a large blonde girl on the edge of the dancefloor. I could not take my eyes from her black hair, the pale curve of her throat. A man crossed to the pair of girls: it was the blonde girl he asked to dance.

I followed him across the ballroom and, as soon as I touched her elbow, she turned and came with me on to the floor.

'Do you like waltzes?' were the first words she spoke as we began to dance.

She did not speak again. As we kept turning to the music, we moved through the circle where the glass dome was still letting in daylight, and kept on after we'd passed the last of the pillars hung with the wire baskets of flowers, out beyond the draped curtains, until we seemed to be turning in nothing but air beneath the sky, a sky that was neither agate nor blue, just the anonymous sky of any and every day above our lives as we set out.

A Ballad

'Do you think it will be late when Cronin tumbles in?' Ryan asked sleepily.

'It won't be early. He went to a dance with O'Reilly and the two women.'

Pale light from the street lamp just outside the window shone on the varnished ceiling boards of the room. Cronin would have to cross the room to get to his bed by the window.

'I don't mind if he comes in near morning. What I hate is just to have got to sleep and then get woke up,' Ryan said.

'You can be sure he'll wake us up. He's bound to have some story to get off his chest.'

Ryan was large and gentle and worked as an inseminator at the A.I. station in the town, as did Cronin. The three of us shared this small room in the roof of the Bridge Restaurant. O'Reilly was the only other lodger Mrs McKinney kept, but he had a room of his own downstairs. He was the site engineer on the construction of the new bridge.

'What do you think will happen between O'Reilly and Rachael when the bridge is finished?'

I was startled when Ryan spoke. The intervals of silence before we fell asleep seemed always deeper than sleep. 'I don't know. They've been going out a good while together. Maybe they'll be married . . . What do you think?'

'I don't know. He's had a good few other women here and there in the last few months. I doubt if he wants to get hitched.'

'She'd have no trouble finding someone else.'

She had been the queen of one beauty competition the summer before and runner-up in another. She was fair-haired and tall.

'She mightn't want that,' Ryan said. 'The Bachelors' Ball will be interesting on Friday night. Why don't you change your mind and come? The dress suits are arriving on the bus Friday evening. All we'd have to do is ring in your measurements.'

'No. I'll not go. You know I'd go but I want to have the money for Christmas.'

An old bicycle went rattling down the hill and across the bridge, a voice shouting out, '*Fàg à bealach.*'

'That's Paddy Mick on his way home. He has no bell. It means the last of the after-hour houses are shut.'

'It's time to try to get to sleep – Cronin or no Cronin.'

It was very late when Cronin woke us, but daylight hadn't yet started to thin the yellow light from the street lamp. We would have pretended to have gone on sleeping but he repeated, 'Are yous awake?'

'We are now.'

'That O'Reilly should be run out of town,' he said.

'What's wrong now?' I had suspected for a while that his lean, intense good looks concealed a deep stupidity.

'What he made that girl do tonight no poor girl should have to do, and in front of people too.'

'What was it?' Ryan raised himself on an elbow in the bed while Cronin slipped out of his clothes.

'It was horrible.'

'You can't just wake us up like this and not tell us.'

'It was too foul to put in words.'

'What's so suddenly sacred about words! Why didn't you stop it if you felt so badly about it?'

'What could you say once it was done? Once he made her do it. My woman was so upset that she didn't talk for the rest of the night.'

Cronin had been going out casually with a hairdresser some years older than he was, who owned her own business in the town. He was taking her to the ball on Friday.

'Are you going to tell us what happened? Or are you going to let us get back to sleep?'

'I wouldn't disgrace myself by telling it.' He turned his back to us in the bed.

'I hope you have nightmares.' Ryan swore before pulling the clothes and pillow violently over his head.

The four of us had breakfast together the next morning. There was no one else in the big dining-room except some night-shift workers from the mill across the road in their white caps and overalls and the pale dusting of flour still on their arms and faces. I'd always envied their high spirits in the morning. Breakfast was for them a celebration. Cronin was gloomily taciturn until near the end of the meal when he said, 'You're an awful effin' so and so, O'Reilly, to do what you did last night.'

'I haven't even a notion what you're talking about.' O'Reilly bloomed. He was a small barrel of a man with a fine handsome head. He had played cornerback for Cavan in two All-Irelands.

'No girl should have to do what you made that girl do last night.'

'You know nothing about women, Cronin,' O'Reilly said loudly, hoping to get the ear of the mill workers, but they were having too good a time of their own. 'Women like to do that. Only they have to pretend that they don't. Let me tell you that all women take a poor view of a man who accepts everything at its face value.'

'It was a disgrace,' Cronin said doggedly.

'You're a one to talk.' O'Reilly rose from the table in high good humour. 'Whatever yourself and the hairdresser were up to in the back of the car, I thought it was about to turn over.'

'It was a pure disgrace,' Cronin said to his plate.

Ryan and myself stayed cautiously neutral. I had clashed with O'Reilly from the beginning when I'd refused to become involved with the town football team, which he ran with a fierce fanaticism, and we were all the more cautious because Cronin usually hero-worshipped O'Reilly. In the long evenings they could be seen kicking a ball round for hours in the park after training sessions. Lately, they'd taken to throwing shoes and pieces of cutlery at the ceiling if they thought I was upstairs with a book or correcting school exercises. I was looking forward to the opening of the new bridge.

Ryan's unwashed Beetle was waiting outside the gate when I finished school at three that evening.

'I've calls in the Gaeltacht. Maybe you'll come in case there's need of a bit of translating.'

It was a polite excuse. There was never need of translation. The tied cow could be always pointed out. The breed of the bulls – Shorthorn, Charolais, Friesian – were the same in Gaelic as in English. The different colours of the straws of semen in the stainless steel container on the floor of the Beetle needed no translation. Ryan just didn't like driving on the empty roads between these silent, alien houses on his own.

'I got the whole business out of Cronin in the office this morning.' A wide grin showed on his face as the VW rocked over the narrow roads between the bare whitethorns.

'What was it, then? I won't be shocked.'

'It shocked Cronin.'

'What was it, for Christ's sake?'

'O'Reilly got Rachael to take his lad in her mouth,' Ryan said. 'Then he wouldn't let her spit it out.'

'Spit what out?'

'What's in the bucket?' He gestured towards the bright steel container on the floor of the VW where the straws were kept in liquid nitrogen.

'They say it's fattening,' I said to hide my own shock.

'Not half as fattening as in the other place.' I was unprepared for the huge roar of laughter my words induced.

'What do you mean?'

'O'Reilly's in a white fright. He's got Rachael up the pole.'

'Then he'll marry her.'

'Not unless he has to. Cronin told me that he spent all last week applying for engineering jobs in South Africa. It seems they're building lots of bridges in South Africa.'

'But he has a permanent job to go to in Galway as soon as the bridge finishes. He's been boasting about it long enough.'

'He could go if he married Rachael, but it mightn't be so easy if he refused to do the decent. News travels.'

We'd come to the first of the plain ugly cottages the government had built on these twenty-acre farms. They were all alike. A woman met us, showed us to the cow, gave Ryan a basin of hot water, soap, a towel to wash and dry his rubbered arm afterwards. She responded to my few questions with deep suspicion, fearful that I was some government official sent out to check on grants or the speaking of Irish.

These people had been transplanted here from the seaboard as part of de Valera's dream; lighthouses put down on the plain from which Gaelic would spread from tongue to tongue throughout the land like pentecostal flame. Used to a little fishing, a potato patch, grass for a cow between the rocks, they were lost in the rich green acres of Meath. A few cattle were kept knee-deep in grass, or the land was put out on conacre to the grain contractors who supplied the mill – and the men went to work in England. It was dark by the time we'd finished. The last call had to be done by the light of a paraffin lantern.

'What will Rachael do if O'Reilly ditches her?' I asked as we drove back.

'What does any girl do? She has to nail her man. If she doesn't . . . ' He spread his hands upwards underneath a half-circle of the steering wheel. 'You might as well come to the Ball. It'll be twice as much fun now that we know what's afoot.'

'I'll not go. For me it's just another reason to stay away.'

The dress suits came in flat cardboard boxes on the evening bus the Friday of the Ball. Tulips came in similar boxes for the altar. O'Reilly changed into his suit as soon as he came home from work and went to the hotel to have drinks with subcontractors on the bridge. There had plainly been a falling out between him and Cronin. Ryan and Cronin waited till after tea to change. They'd never worn dress suits before and were restless with excitement, twisting themselves in mirrors, laughing nervously as they paraded in front of the McKinneys. They found time slow to pass while waiting to pick up their girls. Ryan was bringing the girl who took the calls in their office.

I went with them to the Midland Bar, where we had three rounds of hot whiskeys. Still it wasn't late enough to leave when we got back, and they went alone to some other bar, this time taking their cars. O'Reilly had taken his car to the hotel. I'd meant to read, but when left alone I found that I wasn't able to because of the excitement and the whiskey. I was half tempted to go back up to the Midland's with old Paddy McKinney when he went for his nightly jar, and glad when Mrs McKinney came in soon afterwards to join me at the fire.

'You didn't go to the Ball after all?'

'No. I didn't go.'

'You may be as well off. Old Paddy was a great one for dances and balls in his day, would never miss one. And he got me. And I got him. That's all it ever seems to have amounted to,' she said with vigorous incomprehension. Later, I tried to ask her if she'd let me have O'Reilly's room when he left, but she'd give no firm answer, knowing it'd be easier to let the room than to fill the bed in the upstairs room, and, as if to make up for her evasion, she made delicious turkey sandwiches and a big pot of tea instead of the usual glass of milk and biscuits.

The screeching of a car to a violent stop beneath the window woke me some time in the early hours. A door banged but I could hear no voices. A key turned in the front door. I sat up as footsteps started to come up the stairs. O'Reilly opened the door. His oiled hair was dishevelled as was the suit and bow.

'I want you to convey a message for me when they return.' He had to concentrate fiercely to frame the words.

'Where are the others?'

'They're still at the Ball. I abandoned them there.'

'Is Rachael there, too?' I asked cautiously.

'The last I saw of her she was dancing with Cronin. Cronin made a speech. He got up on the stage for a special request and took the microphone. It was most embarrassing. One should never associate with uncultivated people. I decided that the gentlemanly thing to do was to leave at once on my own. So I'm here.' He stood solid as a stone on the floor, but it was obvious from the effort of concentration and small hiccups that he was extraordinarily drunk.

'Tell them that I'm not to be disturbed. Tell them not to go banging on the door. The door will be locked.'

'I'll tell them.'

'I'm most obliged. I'll recompense you in due course.'

I heard him move about for a little while downstairs. Then his door closed.

The others were so long in coming that I was beginning to think they must have met with some accident. They made much noise. I heard them try O'Reilly's door several times, calling out before they came upstairs. Cronin was wild with drink, Ryan just merry and foolish.

'Bloody O'Reilly got home. He's locked the door.' Cronin staggered violently as he spoke.

'He was up here,' I said. 'He asked not to be disturbed when you came home.'

'Not to be disturbed.' Cronin glared.

'I'm just giving the message.'

'That's the notice he has hung on the doorknob,' Ryan giggled.

'I made a speech,' Cronin said. 'A most impressive speech.'

'What sort of speech?' I asked as gently as possible in the hope of diverting the drilling stare.

'That it was the bounden duty of every single man to get married. Of course I was referring to O'Reilly in particular, but it had universal significance as well. To show that I was serious I proposed that I myself be married immediately. This week if possible.'

Any temptation to laugh was out. It would be far too dangerous.

'Of course *you* make no effort to get married. You just lie here in bed,' he continued. The stare would not be diverted, and then suddenly he jumped on me in the bed, but his movements were so slow and drunken that all I had to do was draw my knees upwards and to the side for him to roll across the bed out on the floor the far side. This was repeated three times. 'Make no effort. Just lie there,' he kept saying, and each time the breathing grew heavier. I was afraid the farce could go on for some time, until, rising, he caught sight of himself in the wardrobe mirror.

'I've never seen myself in a dress suit before. I am most impressed. Instead of giving it back, I think I'll buy it. I'll wear it in my professional capacity. The farmers will be most impressed.' Dress suits seemed to be having a formalizing effect on speech.

I used the diversion to rise and dress. Then another car drew up outside. Looking out the window, Ryan, who all this time had stood there grinning and smiling, said, 'Rachael's back. She's looking to get O'Reilly to drive her home.'

'How did she get this far?'

'With Johnny from the mill and his girl. She wouldn't come with us. They had to leave Johnny's girl home first. We'd better go down. They have no key.'

'It is our duty to go down,' Cronin said.

I sat for a long time on the bed's edge before following them down.

A piece of cardboard hung from the doorknob of O'Reilly's room. I lifted it and read PLEASE DO NOT DISTURB.

Rachael was sitting at the corner of the small table in the kitchen, and with her was Johnny Byrne, the foreman of the mill. She was smoking, plainly upset, but it made her the more beautiful. She'd pulled a jacket over her bare shoulders, and silver shoes showed beneath the long yellow dress. Ryan and Cronin had taken Mrs

McKinney's cooked turkey from the fridge and placed it on the high wooden table. Cronin was waving a turkey leg about as he inspected himself in Paddy McKinney's shaving mirror.

'It's no trouble now for me to run you the rest of the way home,' Johnny was saying to Rachael.

'No thanks, Johnny.'

'We'll get him up now. It is our duty,' Cronin suddenly said.

We heard him rattling the doorknob in the hallway. 'Get up, O'Reilly. Rachael's here. You have to run her home.'

After a lot of rattling and a threat to break down the door, a hollow voice sounded within the room as if spoken through a sheet by a man whose life was fast ebbing. 'Please inspect notice and go away,' at which point Rachael went out and ushered Cronin back into the kitchen. He was amazingly docile in her hands. Ryan was peeling the turkey breastbone clean with his fingers.

'You must leave him alone. It's between us.' Rachael moved him gently back towards the turkey on the table.

'Even if you got him up now he'd hardly be fit to drive you home,' Johnny Byrne said.

'We could give him coffee,' and after a time she added, 'I'll try just once more.' She called him, asking him to let her into the room. All that came in the silence were loud, simulated snores.

'It'd only take a minute to run you home,' Johnny said when she came back into the kitchen.

'No, Johnny. I'll wait. You should go home now. You won't find till you have to go to work,' and reluctantly, pausing a number of times, he rose and left. Having stripped the turkey clean, Cronin and Ryan fell asleep in chairs. In the garishly lit kitchen, I sat in Byrne's place at the table. A foolish, sentimental, idle longing grew: to leave her home, to marry her, to bring up O'Reilly's child with her in some vague, long vista of happiness; and after an hour I said, 'I could get one of their car keys,' indicating the sleeping inseminators, 'and drive you home.'

'No,' she said firmly. 'I'll wait now till morning.'

She was there when Mrs McKinney came down to get the breakfasts in the morning, there to face her bustling annoyance at the disturbances of the rowdy night turn to outrage at the sight of the pillaged turkey on the table.

'I'm sorry to be here. I'm waiting for Peter to get up. He was drunk and locked the door. He took me to the dance and he has to take me home,' she explained with a quiet firmness.

'Was it him did for the turkey too?' The old woman made no effort to conceal her anger.

'No. I don't think so.'

'It must be those other bowsies, then.'

In her long yellow dress and silver shoes Rachael helped tidy the kitchen and prepare for the breakfasts until the old woman was completely pacified, and the two sat down like ancient allies to scalding tea and thickly buttered toast. Through the thin wall they heard O'Reilly's alarm clock go off.

'They're not worth half the trouble they put us to,' the old woman grumbled.

They heard him rise, unlock the door, go upstairs to the bathroom, and as he came down Rachael went out to meet him in the hallway. It was several minutes before she returned to the kitchen, and then it was to borrow a kettle of boiling water. Outside on the street it was a white world. The windscreen of O'Reilly's car was frosted over, the doorhandles stuck.

'You were right to make him leave you home. They should be all learned a bit of manners,' Mrs McKinney said approvingly as she took the empty kettle back, the noise of the car warming up coming from outside.

O'Reilly was a long time leaving Rachael home, and when he came back he checked that no one had been looking for him on the site, reported sick, and went to bed. He did not get up till the following morning.

When Mrs McKinney saw the state of Cronin and Ryan later that morning, she decided to postpone the business of the turkey for a day or two. They tried to drink a glass of Bols eggnog in the Midland's as a cure before work, but it made them violently ill, and they had to go back to bed.

The town had not had such a piece of scandal since some members of the Pioneer excursion to Knock had to be taken from the bus in Longford for disorderly conduct three years before. Circling the Virgin's Shrine in a solid downpour while responding with Hail Marys to the electronic Our Fathers had proved too severe a trial for three recent recruits.

I was stopped on my way to school, was stopped again on my

way back, to see if I could add anything to the news of the night, but everything, down to the devastated turkey, seemed to be already known.

Rachael and O'Reilly were married in early January. Only Cronin was invited to the wedding from the Bridge Restaurant, he and O'Reilly having become great pals again. He told us that it was quiet and very pleasant, just a few people, the way weddings should be. We made a collection in the restaurant, and with the money Mrs McKinney bought a mantel clock in a mahogany frame and had all our names inscribed on a bright metal scroll. After a honeymoon in London, the new couple went to Galway, where he took up his position with the County Council.

It was some years before Rachael and O'Reilly were seen again. A crowd up for the Christmas shopping saw them in Henry Street a Saturday morning before Christmas. They were both wearing sheepskin coats. Rachael's coat fell to her ankles and a beautiful fair-haired child held her hand as they walked. She had lost her lean beauty but was still a handsome woman. A small boy rode on O'Reilly's shoulders. The boy was pointing excitedly at the jumping monkeys on the pavement and the toy trumpets the sellers blew. Sometimes when they paused at the shops the mother would turn away from the glitter of the silver snow to smile on them both. They disappeared into Arnott's before anybody had gathered enough courage to greet them.

Within a decade O'Reilly had risen to be a county engineer, and a few years afterwards became the county manager. Everywhere local officials gather it is heard whispered along the grapevine, as if to ease the rebuke of his rise over older and less forceful, less lucky men, that O'Reilly would not be half the man he is if he had not married Rachael.

Oldfashioned

The Protestants had so dwindled that there was no longer a living in Ardcarne: the old Georgian parsonage had been closed, its avenue of great beech trees, the walled orchard, the paddock and lawn and garden, all let run wild. The church with its Purser windows was opened once every year for harvest thanksgiving to keep certain conditional endowments. There was always a turnout on that one Sunday, from the big farms and houses, gamekeepers and stewards of the Rockingham estate, and some years Sir Cecil and Lady Stafford King-Harmon came from the Nash house above Lough Key, in which there were so many windows it was said there was one for every day of the year.

The Catholic church, hiding its stark ugliness amid the graveyard evergreens in the centre of the village, was so crowded for both Masses on Sundays that often children and old people would faint in the bad air and have to be carried outside. Each day saw continual traffic to the blue-and-white presbytery, blue doors and windows, white walls, at the end of the young avenue of limes. They came for references, for birth certificates, to arrange for calls to the sick and dying, for baptism, marriages, churchings, to report their neighbours: they brought offerings and payments of dues. No one came in the late evening except on the gravest matters, for by then Canon Glynn and Danny, who had retired early from the civil service to come and live with his brother, could be extremely irritable, and often smelled of whiskey. 'You could get run,' was the word that was out.

A green mail car crossed the bridge to the post office each morning and evening at nine o'clock and six. Stephen Maughan crossed the same bridge on his heavy carrier bicycle every Thursday evening with fresh herrings off the Sligo train, setting up the bicycle on its legs outside the post office to shout, 'If you don't buy you can't fry,' to the annoyance of the Miss Applebees within, Annie and Lizzie, with their spectacles and neat white hair and their glittering brass scales. There were two pubs, Charlie's and Henry's, and they both had grocery stores as well. There was a three-teacher school, a dancehall, a barracks with three guards and a sergeant.

There was much traffic on the roads, carts, bicycles, people on foot who always climbed on the walls or grass margins when the occasional motor was heard. People could be seen walking the whole seven miles to Boyle before the big matches, and after the digging of the potatoes, when the dreaded long nights had to be faced, holding wet batteries stiffly. Every summer Sunday the cattle were driven from the football field at the back of Charlie's and the fouled lines marked white again with lime. To the slow sog of the football in the distance, handball of sorts was played against the back of Jimmy Shivnan's forge, the bounce uncertain because of the unswept stones, and there, too, the coins were tossed from the backs of rulers and greasy pocket combs, each copper row arranged so that all the harps faced upwards before being thrown. Everywhere there was the craving for news. News, any news, passing like flame from mouth to eager mouth, slowly savoured in the eyes. 'Bruen's cow rolled over into a drain, was found dead on her back, the feet in the air . . .' 'Where? When? Who came on the cow? Was she long on her back? That'll put them back a step. It's no joke no matter who it happens to. Terror what life puts people through.' 'A sewing machine was the only thing left standing four floors up in a bombed factory in Coventry.' 'Imagine . . . four floors up . . . a sewing machine standing on a girder out there on its own . . . a terror . . . a sight.'

Suddenly the war was over. Britain had to be rebuilt. The countryside emptied towards London and Luton. The boat trains were full and talk was of never-ending overtime. After weeks in England, once-easy gentle manners, set free from the narrow rule of church and custom, grew loud, uncertain, coarse.

At home a vaguely worried church joined a dying language to declare that learning Irish would help to keep much foreign corrupting influence out. Red Algier tractors with long steering columns and the sound of low-flying airplanes – they were said to have the original Messerschmitt engine – started to replace the horse and cart. A secondary school was opened by the Brothers in the town. The word *Salamanca*, having endured for most of a century as a mighty ball booted on the wind out of defence in Charlie's field, grew sails again on an open sea, became distant spires within a walled city in the sun. Race memories of hedge schools and the poor scholar were stirred, as boys, like uncertain flocks of birds on bicycles, came long distances from the villages and outlying farms to grapple with calculus and George Gordon and the delta of the River Plate.

Against this tide the Sinclairs came from London to the empty parsonage in Ardcarne, where Colonel Sinclair had grown up, where Mrs Sinclair, as a young army wife and mother, had spent happy summers with her gentle parents-in-law, the old canon and his second wife. After the war, the Colonel had settled uneasily into the life of a commuter between their house in Wimbledon and the ministry. Their son had been killed in the war and their daughter was married to a lecturer in sociology at Durham University, with two children of her own. They both wanted to live in the country, and when they discovered that the church commissioners would be only too glad to give the decaying parsonage for a nominal sum to a son of the manse, they sold the house in Wimbledon, and the Colonel took early retirement.

They stayed in the Royal Hotel while the parsonage was being restored, and as they employed local tradesmen, it was not resented. Once they moved in, the grounds, the garden and orchard, even the white paddock railings, they brought back with their own hands. They loved the house. Each year just after Christmas they went to England for two months, and every summer their daughter and her children came from Durham. Each Thursday they did a big shopping in the town, and when it was done went to the Royal Hotel for a drink. It was the one time in the week they drank at the Royal, but every evening except on Sunday, at exactly nine o'clock, their black Jaguar would cross the bridge and roll to a stop outside Charlie's Bar. It was so punctual that people began to check their watches as it passed, the way they did with the mail van and the church bells and the distant rattle of the diesel trains across the Plains. Mrs Sinclair never left the Jaguar, but each night had three gin and tonics sitting in the car, the radio tuned to the BBC World Service, the engine running in the cold weather. It was the Colonel who brought out the drinks, handing them through the car window, but his own three large Black Bushmills he drank at the big oval table in Charlie's front room or parlour. 'Wouldn't Mrs Sinclair be more comfortable in at the fire on a night the like of that?' Charlie himself had suggested one bad night of rain and a rocking wind not long after they had started to come regularly. 'No, Charlie. She'd not like that. Women of her generation were brought up never to set foot in bars,' and the matter ended there; and though it caused a veritable hedgerow of talk for a few weeks, it provoked no laughter.

'They're strange. They're different. They're not brought up the like of us. Those hot climates they get sent to does things to people.'

At first, the late night drinkers entering Charlie's used to hurry past the car and woman, but later some could be seen to pause a moment before pushing open the door as if in reflection on the mystery of the woman sitting alone drinking gin in the darkness, the car radio on and the engine running wastefully, the way they might pause coming on the otter's feeding place along the riverbank, its little private lawn and scattering of blue crayfish shells.

When they left for England after Christmas, the car was missed like any familiar absence, and when suddenly it reappeared in March, 'They're back,' would be announced with relief as well as genuine gladness.

'How long have we been here now? How long is it since we've left Wimbledon?' the Sinclairs would sometimes ask one another as the years gathered above them. Now they found they had to count; it must be three, no four, five my God, using birthdays and the deaths of friends like tracks across the sky.

'They're flying now.'

'Still, it must mean we've been happy.'

Company they seemed not to need. Occasionally, they ran into their own class, on Thursday in the Royal, after their shopping was done, the town full of the excitement of the market, bundles of cabbage plants knotted with straw on offer all along the Shambles; but as they never had more than the one drink, and evaded exploratory invitations to tea or bridge, they became in time just a matter of hostile curiosity. 'How did you get through the winter?' 'Dreadful. Up to our hocks in mud, my dear.' 'But the Bishop is coming for Easter.' Mostly, the Colonel was as alone in Charlie's parlour as Mrs Sinclair was outside in the closed car, though sometimes Charlie joined him with a glass of whiskey if the bar wasn't busy and Mrs Charlie wasn't on the prowl. They'd sit at the table and talk of fruit trees and vegetables and whiskey until the bell rang or Mrs Charlie was heard surfacing. Sometimes the Colonel had the doubtful benefit of a local priest or doctor or vet or solicitor out on the razzle, but if they were very drunken he just finished his drink and left politely. 'I never discuss religion because its base is faith – not reason.' What brought them most into contact with people was the giving away of fruit and vegetables. They grew more than they could use. To some they gave in return for small favours, more usually by proximity and chance.

It was because of help the Sergeant had given with the renewal of a gun licence that they came with the large basket of apples to the barracks. The day had been eventful at the barracks, but only in the sense that anything at all had happened. An old donkey found abandoned on the roads had been brought in that morning. Every rib showed, the hooves hadn't been pared in years, the knees were broken and twisted and cut, clusters of blue-black flies about the sores. He was too weak even to pluck at the clover on the lawn, and just lay between the two circles of flowerbeds while they waited for the Burnhouse lorry, an old shaky green lorry with a heavy metal box like the lorries that draw stones, too wide to get through the barrack gates.

'It'd be better if we could get him alive on the lorry. That way it'd save having to winch him up,' the driver said.

They had to lift the donkey from the lawn and push, shove, and carry the unresisting animal over the gravel and up a makeshift ramp on to the lorry.

'Whatever you do keep a good hault of his tail.'

'I have his head. He can't fall.'

'Christ rode into Jerusalem on an ass.'

'He'd not ride far on this one.'

They expected the donkey to fall once they let go of him on the lorry, but he stayed on his feet without stirring while the driver got the humane killer out of the cab. When the back of the metal horn was tapped with the small hammer close to the skull, he crumpled more silently after the shot rang than a page thrust into flame. The tailboard was lifted up, the bar dropped in place. A docket had to be signed.

The Sergeant and two of the policemen signed themselves out on delayed patrol after the lorry had rattled across the bridge with its load. Guard Casey remained behind as barrack orderly and with him the Sergeant's sixteen-year-old son, Johnny. As soon as the policemen had split out in different directions on their bicycles at the bridge, Casey turned to the boy. 'What about a game?'

They were friends, and often played together on the gravel, dribbling the ball around one another, using the open gates as goal. The old policeman was the more skilled of the two. Before he'd joined the Force he'd been given a trial by Glasgow Celtic, but he would leave off the game at once if any stranger came to the barracks. What annoyed the boy most during the games was that he'd always try to detain people past the call of their business. He had an insatiable hunger for news.

'I don't feel like playing this evening,' the boy said.

'What's biting you?'

'What'd you do if you caught the owner of that donkey?'

'Not to give you a short answer, we'd do nothing.'

'Why?'

'We've trouble enough without going looking for it. If we applied the law strictly in every case, we'd have half the people of the country in court, and you know how popular that would make us.'

'It's lousy. An old donkey who's spent his whole life pulling and drawing for someone, and then when he's no use any more is turned out on the road to starve. How can that be justified?'

'That's life,' Casey replied cheerfully. He went in and took one of the yellow dayroom chairs and the *Independent* out on the gravel and started the crossword. Sometimes he lifted his head to ask about the words, and though the boy answered quickly and readily the answers did not lead to further conversation.

It was getting cold enough for both of them to think about going in when they heard the noise of a car approaching from the other side of the river. As soon as Casey looked at his watch he said, 'I bet you it's the Colonel and the wife on their way to Charlie's. I told you,' he said as soon as the black Jaguar appeared, but suddenly stiffened. Instead of continuing straight on for Charlie's, the Jaguar turned down the hill and up the short avenue of sycamores to stop at the barrack gate. Casey left the newspaper on the chair to go forward to the gate. Mrs Sinclair was in the car, but it was the Colonel who got out, taking a large basket of apples from the back seat.

'Good evening, Colonel.' Casey saluted.

'Good evening, Guard.' The effortless sharp return of the salute made Casey's effort seem more florid than it probably was. 'Is the Sergeant about?'

'He's out on patrol, but his son is here.'

'That will do just as well. Will you give these few apples to your father with our compliments and tell him the licence arrived?'

Big yellow apples in a bed of green leaves and twigs ringed the rim of the basket, and in the centre red Honeycombs and Beauty of Bath were arranged in a striking pattern.

'Thank you, sir. They're very beautiful.'

'What is?' The Colonel was taken by the remark.

'The way the apples are arranged.' He coloured.

'Mrs Sinclair did the arranging but I doubt if she ever expected it to be noticed.'

'Do you want your basket back, sir?'

'No. Your father can drop it in some time he's our way. Or it can be left in Charlie's. But come. You must meet Mrs Sinclair,' and the boy suddenly found himself before the open window.

'This young man has been admiring your arrangement of the apples.' The Colonel was smiling.

'How very kind. Thank you,' she said.

In his confusion he hardly knew how the Colonel took leave of them, and he was still standing stock-still with the basket in his hand as the car turned for Charlie's.

Guard Casey reached down for an apple. 'One thing sure is that you seem to have struck on the right note there,' but he was too kind to tease the boy, and after he'd bitten into the apple said, 'No matter what way they're arranged they'll be all the same by the time they get to your belly. Those people spent a lot of their life in India.'

The boy showed his father the basket of apples as soon as he came in off patrol. 'It's to thank you for getting them the gun licence. There's no hurry with the basket. They said we could bring it to the house some time or leave it in Charlie's.'

'Of course I'll leave it to the house. It'd not be polite to dump it in Charlie's,' and he was in great good humour after he'd left the basket back with the Sinclairs the very next day.

'Colonel and Mrs Sinclair have been singing your praises. They said they never expected to come on such manners in this part of the country. Of course it doesn't say much for the part of the country.'

'I only thanked them.'

'They said you remarked on how the apples were arranged. You certainly seemed to have got above yourself. I kept wondering if we were talking about the same person. They want to know if you'd help them in the garden for a few hours after they come back from England.'

'What kind of help?'

'Light work about the garden. And they'd pay you. All that work they do isn't work at all. They imagine it is. It's just fooling about. What do you say?'

'Whatever you think is best.' He was quite anxious to go to the Sinclairs, drawn to them and, consequently, he was careful not to dampen his father's enthusiasm by showing any of his own.

'Anyhow, we have plenty of time to think about it. I'd say to go. You never know what might come of it if the Sinclairs started to take an interest in you. More people got their start in life that way than by burning the midnight oil.' He could not resist a hit at the late hours the boy studied; 'a woeful waste of fire and light'.

The Sinclairs left for England three days after Christmas, and the Jaguar was absent from Charlie's in the evenings until the first week in March. The night they returned, as the bell above Charlie's door rang out, there was gladness in each, 'They're back!' They had become 'old regulars'. That Saturday Johnny went to the parsonage for the first time.

The jobs were light. He dug, cleared ground, made ridges, wheeled or carried. He had never worked in a garden with anybody before but his father, and by comparison it was a dream working for the Sinclairs. They explained each thing they wanted done clearly, would go over it a second or third time with good humour if he hadn't got it right the first time, always pleased with what had been done well. Though he was uncomfortable at first over the formal lunch, the good hour they spent over a meal, they were so attentive and cheerful that they put him at ease. The hours of the Saturday seemed to fly, were far too short, and often he found himself dreaming of such a life for himself with a woman like Mrs Sinclair in the faraway future when he would grow old.

The wheel of the summer turned pleasantly. The seeds pushed above ground, were thinned. The roses and the other flowers bloomed. The soft fruit ripened and Mrs Sinclair started to make jams in the big brass pot. Each Saturday the boy went home laden with so much fruit and vegetables that he was able to supply Casey's house as well as their own.

Beyond the order and luxury, what he liked best about the house was the silence. There was no idle speech. What words were spoken were direct and towards some definite point. At the barracks, the movement of a fly across the windowpane, Jimmy Farry pushing towards the bridge with his head down, and the cattle cane strapped to the bar of the bicycle, were enough to start an endless flow of conjecture and criticism, especially if Casey was around. 'If you could get close enough to the "huar" you'd hear him counting, counting his cattle and money, counting, counting, counting . . .'

On one of the more idle Saturdays of the autumn, when they were burning leaves and old stakes and broken branches, the boy felt easy enough with the Colonel to ask him about war and the army.

'The best wars are the wars that are never fought, but for that you need a professional army, so sharp that any possible aggressor would think twice before taking it on. Actual war is a sordid business, but once it begins the army has to do the job as efficiently as possible. It means blowing people's heads off. That's never a pretty business.'

'Did you fight in the front lines?'

'Yes. An officer has to be prepared to go anywhere he sends his men. It is a bad business no matter what civilian nonsense is talked about heroism.' It was plain he had no intention of giving lurid detail and after a silence asked, 'What do you think you'll do when you enter the big bad world, Johnny?'

'I don't know.'

'You must have some idea of what you'd like to do when you finish school?'

'It depends on what comes up.'

'What do you mean by *what comes up*?'

'Whatever jobs are on offer.'

'Have you ever thought of becoming a soldier – looking for a commission?'

'I'd have no chance of that.' The boy laughed lightly.

'Why not? I thought you were rather good at school, especially at maths.'

'It's not that. I'd have to be a star athlete to stand a chance of a cadetship.'

'For the Irish army?' the Colonel laughed heartily. 'The mile in four minutes.'

'Of course, what other . . . ?'

'There are other armies.' The Colonel was greatly amused. 'What would you say to the British army?'

'That must be even harder still to get into,' the boy answered lightly again, certain that it could never be of any real concern.

'I was trained at Sandhurst. There are some who think it the best military academy in the world. If you were offered a place there, would it interest you?'

'Of course I would be interested.' His own assent seemed far off, so unreal it hardly touched him.

'Would you be interested in a military career?'

'No, not more than any other.' The boy smiled. 'But it'd be more interesting than anything I'd have a chance of here.'

'You know that you could be killed or badly wounded early in life.'

'I know that, but it would be better than working in an office.'

'There's much office work in the military too – but I take it you are interested.'

'Yes, Colonel, but you'd have to ask my father. It all depends on what he'd think,' and it occurred to the boy that the father mightn't take to the idea at all. The unreality was sure to end there. The years his father was most proud of were the years of the War of Independence when he was the commander of a small company of men on the run.

The leaves they were burning were catching light, and he went to get the baskets of leaves Mrs Sinclair had left waiting. It was one of the tasks he liked best. When he piled on the leaves he stood back to watch the thick white smoke lift slowly above the beech trees and, as there was no wind, hang like clouds in the dead air.

Oldfashioned

That evening the Colonel talked with Mrs Sinclair about the idea
of getting a commission for Johnny. It was decided that the Colonel
should go to the headmaster of the school secretly to find out
exactly how fitted the boy might be.

The school and monastery had been once a British military barracks, though now it had a rounded ecclesiastical door in the high
wall, and what had been the drilling square was now a lawn with a
few evergreens, one lilac tree, white lawn blocks, and a concrete
path that ran straight from the gate to the monastery door.

As soon as Brother Benedict appeared, they shook hands,
introducing themslves; and, when the Colonel explained what had
brought him, the Brother showed him into a large dining-room full
of mahogany and leather, an array of polished silver on the heavy
sideboard.

'He does some work for us on Saturdays. Mrs Sinclair and I are
quite impressed with him and would like to help him, if that's
possible. We just wondered how able is he. He is the type that
doesn't give much away.'

'He's the best student we've had for some years.' Brother Benedict smiled. He was from the south, with a clever, handsome face.
He wore rimless steel spectacles which he had the habit of polishing
from time to time with a pocket handkerchief kept up his sleeve for
that purpose alone, holding the spectacles at full length after
polishing, while weighing up a situation or person. When not
wearing spectacles he seemed to be always smiling, but there was
calculation behind the smile. He had heard about the Colonel's
visits to Charlie's and was curious to meet him. He was very fond of
good whiskey himself and thought it a proper occasion to produce
his own. From a large bunch hanging from his belt he selected a
small key, unlocked the sideboard, took out a bottle of Redbreast,
and poured two large measures. 'So, naturally, we are interested in
him too. The old Sergeant is our problem. He's forever trying to
push Johnny into what he calls "gainful" employment. But for all
his quiet, he shouldn't be underestimated. He's a survivor and far
from being without guile. Like the rest of the country he has a great
store of negative capability. He'd much prefer not to.'

'He certainly seemed positive enough about the army.'

After a second Redbreast, the Colonel left well satisfied and
drove directly to the parsonage.

259

'The boy is as bright as we suspected,' he told Mrs Sinclair. 'His headmaster turned out to be quite a remarkable man.'

'In what way?'

'Oh, clever, civilized, decent, very clever, in fact. Sort of man you'd expect to find high up in the army. He keeps an excellent whiskey. We mustn't forget to leave him a bottle of Black Bush for Christmas. They don't seem to live badly at all in there.'

That evening the Sinclairs left for Charlie's a half-hour early. They did not have to go all the way to the barrack gate. The Sergeant was digging potatoes inside the line of sycamores. When he saw the Jaguar stop in the avenue, at once he came up to the wall, bringing the spade to lean on, a glow of pleasure on his face at the unexpected break in the evening's work.

'Just digging out the few potatoes,' he said to the Colonel, who got out of the car. 'A real sign that the old year is almost done.'

'Very good ones they seem to be too,' the Colonel responded, and at once began his proposition.

At first, the Sergeant listened smiling. Obscurely, he had always felt that some benefit would flow from the association with the Sinclairs. Soon it grew clear that what was being proposed was no benefit at all. He was not a man to look for any abstraction in the sparrow's fall. If that small disturbance of the air was to earn a moment's attention, he would want to know at once what effect it would have on him or that larger version of himself that he was fond of referring to as 'my family'. By the time the Colonel had finished he was speechless with rage.

'It'd mean he'd come out of all that as a British army officer?'

'Precisely. That is, of course, if he is accepted, and proves satisfactory.'

'He couldn't.' He was so choked with emotion that he was barely able to get out the words.

'He seemed to have no objection to the idea.'

'He can't. That's the end and the be-all.'

'Very well, then. I'm sorry to have disturbed you. Goodbye, Sergeant.'

The Sergeant didn't know what to do with his rage as he watched the black car back out the avenue, turn and snake round by the bridge to Charlie's. He did not move till the post office shut the car from sight, and then, mouthing curses, started to beat the sides of ridges with the spade, only stopping when he felt the handle crack, realizing that he could be seen by someone passing the road. There was no one passing, but even if there were he could always pretend that it was a rat he had been pursuing among the furrows.

The Sergeant waited until the barrack orderly came back on duty and the dayroom door shut again before he went in search of the boy.

'I hear we're about to have a young Sassenach on our hands, an officer and gentleman to boot, not just the usual fool of an Irishman who rushes to the railway station at the first news of a war,' he opened.

'It was Colonel Sinclair who brought it up. I told him he'd have to ask you.'

'And I'm told you're favourably inclined to the idea.'

'I said you'd have to be asked first.'

'Well, then. I have news for you. You're going to no Sandhurst whether they'd have you or not, and I even doubt if the Empire is that hard up. And you're not going to the Sinclairs' this Saturday or any other Saturday, for that matter. I was a fool to countenance the idea in the first place. Well, what do you have to say for yourself?'

'I say that I'm not going,' the boy said, barely able to speak with disappointment and anger.

'And you can say it again if you want,' and the father left him, well satisfied with the damaging restraint of his performance, his self-esteem completely restored.

The following Saturday the Sinclairs lingered a long time over breakfast but at ten-thirty the Colonel rose. 'He's not coming. He was always punctual. He's been stopped.'

'There's a chance he may be ill,' Mrs Sinclair said.

'That would be too much of a coincidence.'

They prepared as usual for the garden, but neither had heart for their separate tasks. They found themselves straying into one another's company, until Mrs Sinclair smiled sadly and said what they had been avoiding. 'It's a hurt.'

'Yes. It is.'

'That's the trouble. We can't help but get attached,' she added quietly. It was the end of no world, they had been through too much for that, but these small hurts seemed to gather with the hurts that had gone before to form a weight that was dispiriting;

and, with the perfect tact that is a kind of mind-reading, she said, 'Why don't we forget the garden? I know we have a rule against drinking during the day, but I think we can make an exception today. I promise to try to make an especially nice lunch.'

'What kind of wine?' he asked.

'Red wine,' she said at once.

'I suppose the lesson is that we should have let well enough alone,' he said.

'I had my doubts all along but, I suppose, I was hoping they weren't true. I don't really think we'd have managed to get him into Sandhurst in the first place; but if we had, his trouble would have just begun – his whole background, his accent most of all. It's hopeless to even contemplate. Let's make lunch.'

The boy hung about the gravel outside the barracks that morning. Casey was the barrack orderly again. All the others were out on patrol. After he had finished the *Independent*, Casey came out to join the boy on the gravel.

'This must be the first Saturday in a long time you aren't away helping the Colonel,' Guard Casey probed gently.

'I was stopped,' he replied with open bitterness.

'I suppose it'll be the end of the free fruit and vegetables. I hear they were threatening to make a British officer out of you.'

'I wouldn't have minded. Many go from here to England to work.'

'Your father would never have been able to live with that. You really have to be born into that class of people. You don't ever find robins feeding with the sparrows.'

'Will the Sergeant be out on evening patrol?'

'I'll have a look.'

Johnny followed Casey over the hollow, scrubbed boards of the dayroom, where the policeman looked in the big ledger.

'He is. From six to nine. In the Crossna direction.'

It was in the opposite direction to the Colonel's. During those hours he would go to the parsonage to explain why he had not come to them, how it had ended.

Just after six, as soon as the Sergeant was out of sight, the boy crossed the bridge with a hazel fishing rod. Though it was too late for the small fish, perch or roach, he could say he was throwing a line out as a sort of experiment, for fun; but as soon as he was across the bridge he hid it behind a wall and took to the fields. Running, walking, running, scrambling across the stone walls, keeping well away from the farmhouses, he was soon close to the parsonage, which he circled, coming up through the orchard at the back. He was so mindless with the fear of not getting to the house in secret that he could hardly remember why he had set out, when he found himself at the kitchen window looking in at the Colonel and Mrs Sinclair seated at the big table with wine glasses in their hands. They were so absorbed in their conversation that he had to tap the window before they noticed. They both rose to let him in.

'It wasn't my fault, I would have come today as usual if he'd let me.' Hard as he tried, he wasn't able to beat down a sudden attack of sobbing. They allowed him to quiet and Mrs Sinclair got him a large glass of raspberry cordial.

'Of course it wasn't your fault. That's the very last thing anybody could imagine.' Mrs Sinclair put the glass in his hand, gently touching his hair.

'In fact, it was all our fault. Our proposal upset everything,' Colonel Sinclair said. 'We didn't think it through.' He didn't know what to give the boy, knew he wouldn't accept money and, in a fit of weary inspiration, he went upstairs to fetch a book on natural history that had been their son's favourite book when young. He first checked with his wife, and when she nodded he gave it to the boy. 'It's something we want you to have. We intended to give it to you for Christmas.'

In spite of the gift, he knew that it was all closing down. With kindness but with firmness, the Sinclairs were now more separate than the evening the Colonel had come to the barracks with the basket of apples. A world had opened that evening; it was closing now like curtains being silently drawn, and all the more finally because there was not even a shadow of violence.

It had not been easy to face the Sinclairs. He had made clear his own position, and he felt freed. When he got to the bridge, he took the hazel rod from beneath the wall and held it in full view, hiding the book under his coat. He met no one. There were no bicycles against the barrack wall. The policemen hadn't come in off patrol. He was about to drop in on Casey when he noticed that there was already someone there, a tall young man who was standing in his bare feet against the wall beneath the measuring bar, which Casey was adjusting.

'You're the height, all right. A good five-eleven and a half. Now lift your arms till we find out if you have the chest measurements as well.'

'I've them, all right, Guard Casey,' the young man laughed nervously. 'But what I'm most afraid of is the Irish.'

'You needn't be a bit afeard. I'm one of the few guards fluent in two languages, the best *Rosses Blas* from the cradle, and I haven't a quarter use for even one language, so don't you worry about the Irish.'

The weak sun was going down beyond Oakport Wood. Only the muscling river moved. In another hour the Sinclairs' car would be crossing the bridge to Charlie's. An hour after that the Sergeant would come in off patrol. That seemed the whole endless world then.

The burning of Rockingham House stood out from all else in the still-emptying countryside in the next few years. In that amazing night all was lit up, the whole lake and its islands all the way across to the Rockadoon and first slopes of the Curlews, the great beech walk going towards Boyle, the woods behind the house, and over them the High Plains, the light leaping even to Great Meadow. The glass of the three hundred and sixty-five windows shattered. The roof came down. Among the priceless things said to have been lost was a rocking chair that could be drawn as a sleigh, beautifully carved leopards asleep on the armrests, one of three made by the great German craftsmen of St Petersburg for Catherine the Great. All that remained of the front of the house overlooking the lake and islands was the magnificent shell and portals, now full of sky and dangerous in high winds. Only rooms in the servants' quarters in the part of the basement next to the sunken tennis courts had escaped the fire. Sir Cecil and Lady King-Harmon, who had been much photographed during the week at the Newmarket Yearling Sales, came home at once, and took over a floor of the Royal Hotel.

Talk ran riot. All small suspicious burnings usual to the area were forgotten about: ramshackle farmhouses soaked in paraffin, a candle lit in a tin container above saturated rags and wood, doors and windows secured, the owners off to town for the day. During the six hours it would take the candle to burn down, they'd make sure to be seen in every shop and pub in town, and come home in darkness to find the house blazing in a bright promise of insurance money.

No house had been insured more handsomely than the great house built by Nash above Lough Key. Suspicion and old caste hostility scenting power in the turning of the wheel was enough to rouse the Sergeant to covert but vigorous investigation. There had been carelessness. A house steward under suspicion in a number of cases of arson in Canada had been hired just six weeks before. A wild drunken party had been held in the servants' quarters the night before the fire, champagne and rare brandies drunk. There had been loose talk. The Sergeant filed all this as preliminary evidence and asked permission to begin formal inquiries. He was warned off at once. Sir Cecil was one of the Councillors of State. When the Sergeant obstinately persisted, he was given notice of transfer to Donegal. This he countered by resigning. He had reached the age when he was entitled to retire on reduced pension. A twelve-acre farm that had once been the nursery farm for the gardens of Rockingham, with a stone house, the traditional residence of the head gardener of Rockingham, came on the market. He bought it and left the barracks. It stood just outside the Demesne Wall, a small iron gate in the wall, and a bridle path led from it to Rockingham House. It was said to have been used by the different ladies of Rockingham when they came to choose plants for the house gardens. The surprisingly exotic plants from as far away as China and India that grew wild here and there on the farm meant nothing to the Sergeant. He bought cows and a tractor, began to send milk to the creamery, put down a potato patch, fought a losing battle each harvest with the pigeons from the estate woods over his rood of oats. It was an exact replica of the life he'd lived as a boy.

A small ceremony in the rose garden of the parsonage at Ardcarne that year would have passed unnoticed even if there had been no great fire. Mrs Sinclair had died in a London clinic after a long illness. She had asked for her ashes to be scattered in the rose garden of 'the dear house'. The Colonel, his daughter, son-in-law, and two grandchildren brought the ashes from London. On a wet, windy afternoon the daughter released the ashes from the urn. She did it nervously and some of the dust blew back in her face, sticking to her hair and clothes. They all stayed in the Royal that night, and the next day the young family left for Durham.

The Colonel opened the house as soon as they'd gone. But he did not go to Charlie's that evening. Instead, he went to the Royal, and this he continued to do as regularly as once Mrs Sinclair and he had set out for Charlie's. The Rockingham woods were sold. Sawmills were set up, and to everybody's surprise the Colonel became manager of McAinish's Mill. To begin with, he was unpopular with the workmen, insisting on strict timekeeping, which was in opposition to the casual local sense of coming and going, fining each man an hour's pay for every fifteen minutes late; but he was fair, and it was said that he came to know as much about the saws and machinery as any mechanic in the woods, and it became the best and happiest of the mills. Though he always remained aloof, there grew an unspoken loyalty between him and his men.

Colonel Sinclair bought a small turkey in Boyle that Christmas Eve. It was all he needed for the holiday. There was fruit in the house, wine, a few heads of lettuce still in the greenhouse. Then he went for a stroll in the streets. Mrs Sinclair had been very fond of this town. It was a bright, clear night, brighter still with the strings of Christmas lights climbing towards the star above the clock on the Crescent. *Gerald Dodd, Town Commissioner* had gone to join the Rockinghams on the clock's memorial stone. The Colonel approved but it also made him smile. Surrounded on the stone by the formidable roll call of Staffords and King-Harmons the name Gerald Dodd had the effect of a charming and innocent affrontery. The King-Harmons would certainly not have approved. The Staffords would have been outraged. On the other side of the river the broken roof of the old British military barracks was white with frost. From one chimneypiece an elder grew. Amid it all the shallow river raced beneath the gentle curve of the bridge, rushed past the white walls of the Royal on its way out towards Key. About him people clapped one another on backs and shoulders. The air was thickly warm with Happy Christmases. The Colonel walked very slowly, enjoying the crowd but feeling outside the excitement. He shook hands affably with a few neighbours, touched his cap to the women, wishing them a Merry Christmas. He shook hands with men who worked for him in the mill, but he neither offered drinks nor was he asked.

In the Royal, he caught the page boy in the mirror making faces behind his back as he took off his old Burberry, but he did not mind. He was old and the page boy could do without his tip. He sat alone at one of the river windows and ordered smoked salmon with brown bread and a half-bottle of white wine.

When he did not appear at the mill the first morning after the holiday, the foreman and one of the men went to the parsonage. The key was in the front door, but there was no answer to their knocking. They found him just inside the door, at the foot of the stairs. In the kitchen two places were laid at the head of the big table. There was a pair of napkins in silver rings and two wine glasses beside the usual cutlery. A small turkey lay in an ovenware dish beside the stove, larded and stuffed, ready for roasting. An unwashed wilting head of lettuce stood on the running board of the sink.

As an announcement of a wedding or pregnancy after a lull seems to provoke a sudden increase in such activities, so it happened with the Sergeant's early retirement from the Force. The first to follow was Guard Casey. He had no interest in land and used his gratuity to pay the deposit on a house in Sligo. There he got a job as the yardman in a small bakery, and years of intense happiness began. His alertness, natural kindness, interest in everything that went on around him, made him instantly loved. What wasn't noticed at first was his insatiable thirst for news. Some of the bread vans went as far as the barracks, and it seemed natural enough that he should be interested in places and people he had served most of his life. In fact, these van men took his interest as a form of flattery, lifting for a few moments the daily dullness of their round; but then it was noticed that he was almost equally interested in people he had never met, places he had never been to. In a comparatively short time he had acquired a detailed knowledge of all the van routes and the characters of the more colourful shopkeepers, even of some who had little colour.

'A pure child. No wit. Mad for news,' was the way the passion was affectionately indulged. 'He should be fed lots. Tell him plenty of lies.' But he seemed to have an unerring sense of what was fact and what malicious invention.

'Sunday is so long. It's so hard to put in.'

Guard Casey kept the walk and air of a young man well into his seventies and went on working at the bakery. It was a simple fall crossing the yard to open the gates one wet morning that heralded an end, a broken hip that would not heal. He and his family had grown unused to one another over the years. They now found each other's company burdensome, and it was to his relief as well as theirs when it was agreed that he would get better care in the regional hospital when it was clear that he wasn't going to get well, as everything but his spirit was sinking. Then his family, through their religious connections, found a bed for him in St Joseph's Hospice of the Dying in Dublin. It was there he was visited by the Sergeant's son, who had heard that he missed company.

'They're nearly all gone now anyhow, God have mercy on them. *Is me Oisín i ndiadh na feinne,*' he laughed.

'Wouldn't you think when they're so full of religion that they'd have shifted themselves this far to see you?' It was open criticism of his family.

'No, not at all. It's too far.' He lifted his hand as if to clear the harshness which seemed to take on an unpleasant moral note in the face of this largeness of spirit. 'No one in their right mind travels so far to follow losing teams. And this is a losing team.' He started to laugh again but was forced to stop because of coughing. 'Still, I've known the whole world,' he said when he recovered.

Johnny justified Brother Benedict's account of his ability to Colonel Sinclair by winning a scholarship to university the following year.

'You'll be like the rest of the country – educated away beyond your intelligence,' was the father's unenthusiastic response, and they saw very little of one another over the next few years. Johnny spent vacations in England working on building sites and in canning factories around London. A good primary degree allowed him to baffle his father even further by continuing postgraduate study in psychology, and he was given a lectureship in the university when he completed his doctorate. Then he obtained work with the new television station, first in an advisory role, but later he made a series of documentary films about the darker aspects of Irish life. As they were controversial, they won him a sort of fame: some thought they were serious, well made, and compulsive viewing, bringing things to light that were in bad need of light; but others maintained that they were humourless, morbid, and restricted to a narrow view that was more revealing of private obsessions than any truths about life or Irish life in general. During this time he made a few attempts to get on with his father, but it was more useless than ever. 'There must be rules if there's to be any fairness or freedom,' he argued the last time they met.

The tide that emptied the countryside more than any other since the famine has turned. Hardly anybody now goes to England. Some who went came home to claim inheritances, and stayed, old men waiting at the ends of lanes on Sunday evenings for the minibus to take them to church bingo. Most houses have a car and colour television. The bicycles and horses, carts and traps and sidecars, have gone from the roads. A big yellow bus brings the budding scholars to school in the town, and it is no longer uncommon to go on to university. The mail car is orange. Just one policeman with a squad car lives in the barracks.

The tide that had gone out to America and every part of Britain now reaches only as far as a bursting Dublin, and every Friday night crammed buses take the aliens home. For a few free days in country light they feel important until the same buses take them back on Sunday night to shared flats and bed-sits.

Storage heaters were installed in the church in the village because of the dampness but the damp did not leave the limestone. The dark evergreens shutting out the light were blamed and cut down, revealing the church in all its huge, astonishing ugliness amid the headstones of former priests of the parish inside the low wall that marked off a corner of Henry's field. The damp still did not leave the limestone, but in spite of it the church is full to overflowing every Sunday.

As in other churches, the priest now faces the people, acknowledging that they are the mystery. He is a young priest and tells them that God is on their side and wants them to want children, bungalow bliss, a car, and colour television. Heaven is all about us, hell is in ourselves and in one moment can be exorcized. Many of the congregation chat with one another and read newspapers all through the Sacrifice. The words are in English and understandable. The congregation gives out the responses. The altar boys kneeling in scarlet and white at the foot of the altar steps ring the bell and attend the priest, but they no longer have to learn Latin.

No one beats a path to the presbytery. The young priest is seldom there and has no housekeeper. Nights, when he's not supervising church bingo, he plays the guitar and sings at local hotels where he is a hit with tourists. He seldom wears black or the Roman collar. To show how little it means to him, one convivial evening in a hotel at Lough Arrow he pulled the collar from his neck and dropped it into the soup. When the piece of white plastic was fished out amid the laughter, it was found to have been made in Japan.

A politician lives outside the village, and the crowd that once flocked to the presbytery now go to him instead. Certain nights he holds 'clinics'. They are advertised. On clinic nights a line of cars can be seen standing for several hundred yards along the road past his house, the car radios playing. On cold nights the engines run. No one thinks it wasteful any more. They come to look for grants, to try to get drunken driving convictions squashed, to get free medical cards, sickness benefit, to have planning application decisions that have gone against them reversed, to get children into jobs. As they all have votes they are never 'run'.

The Protestants have all gone, but the church in Ardcarne is still opened once a year. No one attends it now. There was a move to have the famous Purser windows taken out and installed in a new church being built in the North of Ireland. This was prevented by the conditions of the endowment. They have not been vandalized.

Sir Cecil and Lady King-Harmon bought a stud farm outside Dublin. The Land Commission took over the estate and split it into farms, preserving the gardens and woods and walks immediately around the house as a forest park. The roofless shell of the Chapel-of-Ease stands by the boathouse. Within, lovers scratch their names on the stone. Pleasure craft ply the lake and its islands with day trippers all through the summer. The tall Nash shell stood for a few years above the lake until it was condemned as dangerous, and dynamited. A grey concrete lookout tower, looking cold and wet even in the sun, was built in its place.

In every house across the countryside there glows at night the strange living light of television sets, more widespread than the little red lamps before the pictures of the Sacred Heart years before.

The Sergeant's son came with a television crew to make a film for a series called *My Own Place*. He was older than when his father first came to the barracks. The crew put up in the Royal, and the priest was invited to dinner the first night to counter any hostility they might run into while filming. It showed how out of touch the producer was with the place. He should have invited the politician.

The light was good the next morning, and they decided to begin filming at the old Georgian parsonage in Ardcarne. They hoped to go from there to the Protestant church and the burial place of the King-Harmons, and then to the village if the light held. They would be doing well if they got through all that in one day. They set up the cameras and microphones under the beech trees on the avenue where once he had happily burned leaves for the Sinclairs. It would be a dull film. There would be no people in it. The people that interested him were all dead.

'Take two, cut one.' The clapboard was brought down and the continuity girl lifted her stopwatch. The Sergeant's son started walking slowly down the grass-grown avenue into the camera.

'After the war, Colonel Sinclair and his wife came home from London to this parsonage. His father had been the parson here. It must have looked much as it looks now when they first came. They restored it, house and garden and orchard and paddocks and lawn. I think they were very happy here, but now all is wilderness again.'

The camera panned slowly away from the narrator to the house, and continued along the railings that had long lost their second whiteness, whirring steadily in the silence as it took in only what was in front of it, despite the cunning hand of the cameraman: lingering on the bright rain of cherries on the tramped grass beneath the trees, the flaked white paint of the paddock railing, the Iron Mountains smoky and blue as they stretched into the North against the rim of the sky.

Like All Other Men

He watched her for a long time among the women across the dancefloor in the half-light of the afternoon. She wasn't tall or beautiful, but he couldn't take his eyes away. Some of the women winced palpably and fell back as they were passed over. Others stood their ground and stared defiantly back. She seemed quietly indifferent, taking a few steps back into the thinning crowd each time she found herself isolated on the floor. When she was asked to dance, she behaved exactly the same. She flashed no smile, gave no giddy shrug of triumph to betray the tension of the wait, the redeemed vanity.

Nurses, students, actors and actresses, musicians, some prostitutes, people who worked in restaurants and newspapers, nightwatchmen, a medley of the old and very young, came to these afternoon dances. Michael Duggan came every Saturday and Sunday. He was a teacher of Latin and history in a midlands town forty miles from Dublin, and each Friday he came in on the evening bus to spend the whole weekend round the cinemas and restaurants and dancehalls of O'Connell Street. A year before he had been within a couple of months of ordination.

When he did cross to ask her to dance, she followed him with the same unconcern on to the floor as she had showed just standing there. She danced beautifully, with a strong, easy freedom. She was a nurse in the Blanchardstown Chest Hospital. She came from Kerry. Her father was a National Teacher near Killarney. She had been to these afternoon dances before, but not for a couple of years. Her name was Susan Spillane.

'I suppose everybody asks you these questions,' he said.

'The last one did anyhow.' She smiled. 'You'd better tell me about yourself as well.' She had close curly black hair, an intelligent face, and there was something strange about her eyes.

'Are your eyes two different colours?'

'One eye is brown, the other grey. I may have got the grey eye by mistake. All the others in the house have brown eyes.'

'They are lovely.' The dance had ended. He had let her go. It was not easy to thread a way through these inanities of speech.

A girl could often stand unnoticed a long time, and then it was enough for one man to show an interest to start a rush. When the next two dances were called, though he moved quickly each time, he was beaten to her side. The third dance was a ladies' choice, and he withdrew back into the crowd of men. She followed him into the crowd, and this time he did not let her slip away when the dance ended. It was a polite convention for women to make a show of surprise when invited for a drink, of having difficulty making up their minds, but she said at once she'd love a drink, and asked for whiskey.

'I hardly drink at all, but I like the burnt taste,' and she sipped the small measure neat for the two hours that were left of the dance. 'My father loves a glass of whiskey late at night. I've often sat and had a sip with him.'

They danced again and afterwards came back to the table, sipped the drinks, sat and talked, and danced again. Time raced.

'Do you have to go on night duty tonight?' he asked as it moved near the time when the band would stand and play the anthem. He was afraid he would lose her then.

'No. I'm on tomorrow night.'

'Maybe you'd eat something with me this evening?'

'I'd like that.'

There was still some daylight left when they came from the dancehall, and they turned away from it into a bar. They both had coffee. An hour later, when he knew it was dark outside, he asked awkwardly, 'I suppose it's a bit outrageous to suggest a walk before we look for a place to eat,' his guilty smile apologizing for such a poor and plain admission of the sexual.

'I don't see why not.' She smiled. 'I'd like a walk.'

'What if it's raining?' He gave them both the excuse to draw back.

'There's only one way to find out,' she said.

It was raining very lightly, the street black and shining under the lamps, but she didn't seem to mind the rain, nor that the walk led towards the dark shabby streets west of O'Connell Street. There they found a dark doorway and embraced. She returned his kisses with the same directness and freedom with which she had danced, but people kept continually passing in the early evening dark, until they seemed to break off together to say, 'This is useless,' and arm in arm to head back towards the light.

'It's a pity we haven't some room or place of our own,' he said.

'Where did you spend last night?' she asked.

'Where I stay every weekend, a rooming house in North Earl Street, four beds to the room.'

It was no place to go. A dumb man in the next bed to his had been very nearly beaten up the night before. The men who took the last two beds had been drinking. They woke the dumb man while they fumbled for the light, and he sat up in his bed and gestured towards the partly open window as soon as the light came on. Twice he made the same upward movement with his thumb: he wanted them to try to close the window because of the cold wind blowing in. The smaller of the two men misinterpreted the gesture and with a shout fell on the man. They realized that he was dumb when he started to squeal. She didn't laugh at the story.

'It's not hard to give the wrong signals in this world.'

'We could go to a hotel,' she said. He was stopped dead in his tracks. 'That's if you want to, and only – only – if I can pay half.'

'Which hotel?'

'Are you certain you'd want that? It doesn't matter to me.' She was looking into his face.

'There's nothing I want more in the world, but where?' He stood between desire and fear.

'The Clarence across the river is comfortable and fairly inexpensive.'

'Will we see if we can get a room before we eat or afterwards?' He was clumsy with diffidence in the face of what she had proposed.

'We might as well look now, but are you certain?'

'I'm certain. And you?'

'As long as you agree that I can pay half,' she said.

'I agree.'

They sealed one another's lips and crossed the river by the Halfpenny Bridge.

'Do you think we will have any trouble?' he asked as they drew close to the hotel.

'We'll soon find out. I think we both look respectable enough,' and for the first time he thought he felt some nervousness in her handclasp, and it made him feel a little easier.

There was no trouble. They were given a room with a bath on the second floor.

'I liked very much that you gave your real name,' she said when they were alone.

'Why?'

'It seemed more honest . . .'

'It was the only name I could think of at the time,' and their nervousness found release in laughter.

The bathroom was just inside the door. The bed and bedside lamp and table were by the window, a chair and writing table in the opposite corner, two armchairs in the middle of the room. The window looked down on the night city and the river. He drew the curtains and took her in his arms.

'Wait,' she said. 'We've plenty of time before going out to eat.'

While she was in the bathroom he turned off the light, slipped from his clothes, and got into the bed to wait for her.

'Why did you turn out the light?' she asked sharply when she came from the bathroom.

'I thought you'd want it out.'

'I want to see.'

It was not clear whether she wanted the light for the practical acts of undressing or if she wanted these preliminaries to what is called the act of darkness to be free of all furtiveness, that they should be noted with care like the names of places passed on an important journey.

'I'm sorry,' he said, and turned on the bedside lamp. He watched her slow, sure movements as she stepped from her clothes, how strong and confident and beautiful she was. 'Do you still want the light on?' he asked as she came towards him.

'No.'

'You are beautiful.' He wanted to say that her naked beauty took his breath away, was almost hurtful.

What he had wanted so much that it had become frightening she made easy, but it was almost impossible to believe that he now rested in the still centre of what had long been a dream. After long deprivation the plain pleasures of bed and table grow sadly mystical.

'Have you slept with anyone before?' he asked.

'Yes, with one person.'

'Were you in love with him?'

'Yes.'

'Are you still in love with him?'

'No. Not at all.'

'I never have.'

'I know.'

They came again into one another's arms. There was such peace afterwards that the harsh shrieking of the gulls outside, the even swish of the traffic along the quays, was more part of that peace.

Is this all? Common greed and restlessness rose easily to despise what was so hard come by as soon as it was gained, so luckily, so openly given. Before it had any time to grow there was the grace of dressing, of going out to eat together in the surety that they were coming back to this closed room. He felt like a young husband as he waited for her to finish dressing.

The light drizzle of the early evening had turned into a downpour by the time they came down, the hotel lobby crowded with people in raincoats, many carrying umbrellas.

'We're guaranteed a drowning if we head out in that.'

'We don't need to. We can eat here. The grill is open.'

It was a large, very pleasant room with light wood panelling and an open fire at its end. She picked the lamb cutlets, he the charcoaled steak, and they each had a glass of red wine.

'This has to be split evenly as well,' she said.

'I don't see why. I'd like to take you.'

'That was the bargain. It must be kept.' She smiled. 'How long have you been teaching?'

'Less than a year. I was in Maynooth for a long time.'

'Were you studying for the priesthood?'

'That's what people mostly do there,' he said drily. 'I left with only a couple of months to go. It must sound quite bad.'

'It's better than leaving afterwards. Why did you leave?' she asked with formidable seriousness. It could not be turned aside with sarcasm or irony.

'Because I no longer believed. I could hardly lead others to a life that I didn't believe in myself. When I entered Maynooth at eighteen I thought the whole course of my life was settled. It wasn't.'

'There must be something,' she insisted.

'There may well be, but I don't know what it is.'

'Was it because you needed . . . to be married?'

'No, not sex,' he said. 'Though that's what many people think. If anything, the giving up of sex – renunciation was the word we used – gave the vocation far more force. We weren't doing anything easy. That has its own pride. We were giving up an idea of pleasure for a far greater good. That is . . . until belief started to go . . . and then all went.'

'You don't believe in anything at all, then?' she said with a gravity that both charmed and nettled.

'I have no talent for profundity.' He had spoken more than he had intended and was beginning to be irritated by the turn of the conversation.

'You must believe in something?' she insisted.

'"Tis most certain. Have not the schoolmen said it?' he quoted to tease gently, but saw she disliked the tone. 'I believe in honour, decency, affection, in pleasure. This, for instance, is a very good steak.'

'You don't seem bitter.' This faint praise was harder to take than blame.

'That would be stupid. That would be worst of all. How is the lamb?'

'It's good, but I don't like to be fobbed off like that.'

'I wouldn't do that. I still find it painful, that's all. I'm far too grateful to you. I think you were very brave to come here.' He started to fumble again, gently, diffidently.

'I wasn't brave. It was what I wanted.'

'Not many women would have the courage to propose an hotel.'

'They might be the wise ones.'

It was her turn to want to change the direction of the conversation. A silence fell that wasn't silence. They were unsure, their minds working furiously behind the silence to find some safe way to turn.

'That man you were in love with,' he suggested.

'He was married. He had a son. He travelled in pharmaceuticals.'

'That doesn't sound too good for you.'

'It wasn't. It was a mess.'

They had taken another wrong turning.

It was still raining heavily when they came from the grill. They had one very slow drink in the hotel bar, watching the people drink and come and go before the room and night drew them.

In the morning he asked, 'What are you doing today?'

'I'll go back to the hospital, probably try to get some sleep. I'm on night duty at eight.'

'We didn't get much sleep last night.'

'No, we didn't,' she answered gently enough, but making it plain that she had no interest in the reference. 'What are you doing?' she changed the subject.

'There are three buses back. I'll have to get one of them.'

'Which one?'

'Probably the twelve o'clock, since you're going back to the hospital. When will we meet again?' he asked in a tone that already took the meeting for granted.

She was half dressed. The vague shape of her thighs shone through the pale slip as she turned towards him. 'We can't meet again.'

'Why not?' The casualness changed. 'Is there something wrong?'

'Nothing. Nothing at all. The very opposite.'

'What's the matter, then? Why can't we meet?'

'I was going to tell you last night and didn't. I thought it might spoil everything. After all, you were in Maynooth once. I'm joining an Order.'

'You must be joking.'

'I was never more serious in my life. I'm joining next Thursday ... the Medical Missionaries.' She had about her that presence that had attracted him in the dancehall; she stood free of everything around her, secure in her own light.

'I can't believe you.'

'It's true,' she said.

'But the whole thing is a lie, a waste, a fabrication.'

'It's not for me and it wasn't once for you.'

'But I believed then.'

'Don't you think I do?' she said sharply.

'To mouth Hail Marys and Our Fathers all of your life.'

'You know that's cheap. It'll be mostly work. I'll nurse as I nurse now. In two years' time I'll probably be sent to medical school. The Order has a great need of its own doctors.'

'Wasn't last night a strange preparation for your new life?'

'I don't see much wrong with it.'

'From your point of view, wasn't it a sin?' He was angry now.

'Not much of a one, if it was. I've known women who spent the night before their marriage with another man. It was an end to their free or single life.'

'And I was the goodbye, the shake-hands?'

'I didn't plan it. I was attracted to you. We were free. That's the way it fell. If I did it after joining, it would be different. It would be a very great sin.'

'Perhaps we could be married?' he pressed blindly.

'No. You wouldn't ask so lightly if we could.'

'We wouldn't have much at first but we would have one another and we could work,' he pursued.

'No. I'm sorry. I like you very much, but it cannot be. My mind has been made up for a long time.'

'Well, one last time, then,' he cut her short.

'Hadn't we the whole night?'

'One last time.' His hands insisted: and as soon as it was over he was sorry, left with less than if it had never taken place.

'I'm sorry,' he said.

'It doesn't matter.'

After they had paid downstairs, they did not want to eat in the hotel, though the grill room was serving breakfast. They went to one of the big plastic and chrome places on O'Connell Street. They ate slowly in uneasy silence.

'I hope you'll forgive me, if there's anything to forgive,' she said after a long time.

'I was going to ask the same thing. There's nothing to forgive. I wanted to see you again, to go on seeing you. I never thought I'd have the luck to meet someone so open . . . so unafraid.' He was entangled in his own words before he'd finished.

'I'm not like that at all.' She laughed as she hadn't for a long time.

'I'm a coward. I'm frightened of next week. I'm frightened by most things.'

'Why don't you take an address that'll always find me in case you change your mind?'

'I'll not change.'

'I thought that once too.'

'No. I'll not. I can't,' she said, but he still wrote the address and slipped it in her pocket.

'You can throw it away as soon as I'm out of sight.'

As they rose he saw that her eyes were filled with tears.

They now leaned completely on those small acts of ceremony that help us better out of life than any drug. He paid at the cash desk and waited afterwards while she fixed her scarf, smiled ruefully as he stood aside to allow her the inside of the stairs, opened the large swing-door at the bottom of the steps. They walked slowly to the bus stop. At the stop they tried to foretell the evening's weather by the dark cloudy appearance of the sky towards the west. The only thing that seemed certain was that there'd be more rain. They shook hands as the bus came in. He waited until all the passengers had got on and it had moved away.

The river out beyond the Custom House, the straight quays, seemed to stretch out in the emptiness after she had gone. In my end is my beginning, he recalled. In my beginning is my end, his and hers, mine and thine. It seemed to stretch out, complete as the emptiness, endless as a wedding ring. He knew it like his own breathing. There might well be nothing, but she was still prepared to live by that one thing, to will it true.

Thinking of her, he found himself walking eagerly towards the Busarus . . . but almost as quickly his walking slowed. His steps grew hesitant, as if he was thinking of turning back. He knew that no matter how eagerly he found himself walking in any direction it could only take him to the next day and the next.

Eddie Mac

The summer Annie May Moran came to work for Mrs Kirkwood was the great year of St Michael's football. The team had reached the Final of the Senior Cup for the second year running. Eddie Mac was their star, their finest forward. He worked for the Kirkwoods and lived in the three-roomed herdsman's cottage at the end of the yard, its galvanized roof sprayed the same shade of green as the stables. The two Kirkwoods, father and son, old William and young Master William, went to Roscommon to watch the Final. They barely understood the game and were not touched by the wild fever that emptied the countryside on that late August Sunday: 'We went because Eddie was playing. His father would have enjoyed this day, had he stayed.'

Annie May helped Mrs Kirkwood set the dinner table in the front room that afternoon while the game was being played. Mrs Kirkwood went to particular care with the linen and silver, and the best set of bone china was on display. The Nutleys of Oakport, the oldest and last of her local friends, were coming to dinner that evening. When she was satisfied with the arrangement of the room and had checked the food, she took her book and sat in the rocking chair in the library, where, looking out on the lawn and white paling and the winding avenue of copper and green beech, she rocked herself to sleep as she did every day at this hour.

Exploding cans of carbide, random shouts and cheers and whistles as fires were lit on the hills and on every cross on the roadways woke her early. St Michael's had won the Senior Cup for the first time since its founding. She rose and came down to Annie May in the kitchen. 'It's an unmitigated disaster,' she confided to the servant girl. 'It was bad enough last year, and they lost. What'll it be like now that they have won?'

'Eddie was the hero,' William Kirkwood announced when they returned from Roscommon. 'The two goals he scored in the second half won the game – it broke the other team's heart. They carried

281

him on their shoulders all around the field with the cup at the end.' Annie May coloured as he spoke. She was already in love with the young herdsman who had yet to acknowledge her presence in the house.

A week later, the big silver cup arrived in Kirkwood's yard on its round of the parish, the red and green ribbons streaming from the handles. Again Eddie Mac was hoisted on shoulders and carried aloft with the cup to his own door. Inside the small house the cup was filled to the brim with whiskey. Cheers rang out as each person drank from the cup. A large bonfire was set ablaze in the middle of the yard. A melodeon started to play.

'It's so childish,' Mrs Kirkwood complained in the big house. 'We can abandon any hope of sleep tonight.'

'They're entitled to the night,' her husband argued. 'It's a pity Eddie's father isn't around. He would have greatly enjoyed the night. They've had a famous victory.'

'And they use it to get drunk! Is that a way to celebrate decently? Listen to that din down in the yard.'

'I think you are too hard on them, Elisabeth,' William Kirkwood countered gently.

At that time, Annie May was too young to go to the dances and Eddie Mac had not yet the reputation of a womanizer. He went with the one girl, Kathleen Duignan. She was tall and dark and they looked like brother and sister. As the Duignans owned land, they were a class above the Macs, and when Kathleen Duignan went to England at Christmas it was thought she had thrown Eddie over. He was never to go with another girl for so long.

A few months later, a torn knee in spring training was to end his football glory. Without him the team struggled through the early rounds of the championship, and when he returned for the semi-final he played poorly. The injury did not affect his walk but showed as soon as he tried to sprint or leap. His whole game was based on speed and anticipation. He had neither taste nor appetite for the rough and tumble. Now that his deadly grace was gone, his style of hanging back till the last moment looked like cowardice. As soon as it was plain that the cup was about to be lost, Eddie was taunted and jeered every time he went near the ball by the same people that had chaired him shoulder high from the field the year before. On the surface he showed no feeling, and walked stone-faced from the field; but on the following Wednesday, the evening every week he walked to the village to collect his copy of the *Herald* and to buy in a few groceries, he put his studded boots, football socks, togs, bandages in his green and red jersey, and by drawing the sleeves round and knotting them tightly made it a secure bundle, which he dropped in the deepest arch as he crossed the bridge into the village, only waiting long enough after the splash to be certain it had sunk.

A gentle and even more final end came that September to Mrs Kirkwood. She had gone with her book to sit in the rocking chair in front of the library window 'in the one hour of the day selfishly my own'. When she did not come down to the kitchen at her usual time, Annie May waited for half an hour before going up to the front room. The chair was still imperceptibly rocking before the window, but the book had fallen, and when she called there was no answer. An intense stillness was in the room. Even the spaces between the beech trees down the rich avenue seemed to gaze back in their emptiness, and she ran shouting for help to the yard.

The formal heart of the house, perhaps the heart of the house itself, stopped with Mrs Kirkwood. William Kirkwood and his son seemed only too glad not to have to go out to dinner any more, and they no longer received people at the house. They took all their meals in the big kitchen and did not dress up even on Sunday. Old William's sole interest for years had been his bees. Now he was able to devote himself to them exclusively; and his son, who had lost money introducing a new strain of Cheviots to the farm and running it according to the tenets of his agricultural college, let it fall back into the hands of Eddie Mac, who ran it on the traditional lines of his father before him, not making money but losing none. All Master William's time now turned back to a boyhood fascination with astronomy, and he pursued the stars with much the same gentle, singular dedication as his father accorded the bees, ordering books and instruments, entering into correspondence with other amateur astronomers. He spent most clear nights out in the fields examining the stars through a long telescope fixed on a tripod.

Freed from Mrs Kirkwood's disapproval of all that went on in the village, Annie May was now able to go to the dances. She was large and plain but had her admirers, young men off farms – and some young no longer but without any sense of their ageing, who judged cattle from the rear and preferred a good armful to any lustre of eye or line of cheekbone or throat. Her eyes were still only for Eddie Mac, but he did not even smile or nod to her in the hall. She would see him standing among the other men at the back of the hall, smoking lazily as his eyes went over the girls that danced past. Sometimes he just stood there for the whole night, not taking any girl out to dance, but when he did almost always that girl went with him. If the girl turned him down, unlike the other men, he never went in pursuit of another but quietly retraced his steps to the back of the hall, and soon afterwards he would leave alone. In those years, 'Who will Eddie Mac try tonight?' was one of the excitements of the dancehall. He seldom went with the same girl twice.

There was a later time, after it was clear that Annie May was likely to be running the big Georgian house for a very long time, when he would ask her to dance because it was politic. 'As an oul neighbour with another oul neighbour,' he would joke; but she was cooking him his midday meal now, which he took with the Kirkwoods in the kitchen. He knew that he could have her whenever he wanted, but her ample, wholesome looks were too plain and they lived and worked too close to one another.

Then came another time when the nights Eddie Mac could dance with one girl and expect her to go with him disappeared. Nights came that saw him take girl after girl out, and none would have him. It was not so much that his dark good looks had coarsened but that he had become too well known over the years in this small place. And a night eventually found him dancing with Annie May, no longer 'as an oul neighbour with another oul neighbour' but as man and woman. The air was thick with dust that had been carried in on shoes and beaten into a fine powder; the yellow light gentle from the tin reflectors behind the row of paraffin lamps around the walls. The coins had been already counted into a neat stack of blue paper bags on the card table at the door.

'I suppose I can hardly ask to leave you home since we are going to the same old place anyhow,' he proposed almost ruefully, and she found herself blushing all over. It was what she had never dared to hope in all the years.

They passed together through the village, the music from the dancehall still following them; but then the national anthem beat stridently in the night air, and suddenly all was silent. Here and there cautious whispers of lovers drifted from the shelter of walls. The village was mostly sleeping. One thin line of yellow along the blind told that there was after-hour drinking in Charlie's. A man keeping a lookout for the law cast an exploratory cough in their direction at Shivnan's forge, but they went by in silence. As they crossed the stone bridge from the dancehall, they saw the lights of bicycles slowly scattering. Below them, the quiet river slid out in silence towards the level sedgelands and the wilder Shannon.

'Now that they've stood up like fools for the Soldier's Song they can all go home in peace,' Eddie Mac remarked.

After a mile, they left the road and took the path through the fields to the house. It was a dark, windless night, without moon or star, but they could both walk this path in their sleep.

'One good thing about the night is that we're not likely to trip over Master William and his telescope,' Eddie Mac said derisively.

'He's a very educated man,' Annie ventured.

'He's a fool. They're both fools.'

'Maybe it is that they are too educated for land,' she continued uneasily, but he ignored what she had said. Even though they were in the fields, he walked apart from her still, not admitting the bitter blow to his vanity that he had been forced to come down to a woman as plain as Annie May after all those years.

'It was different once,' he said suddenly. 'That was long before your time. I was only a boy when Mrs Kirkwood first came to the house. She had been a Miss Darby, old Colonel Darby's daughter. It was an arranged match. The Kirkwoods were almost bankrupt at that time, too – they were never any good – and she had money. The house was done up before she came. It was one of the conditions of the match. The railings were painted, new curtains, everything made shining.

'As soon as they were married, the parties began – bridge parties, tea parties on the lawn. There was a big party every year when the strawberries were ripe. Every Sunday night there was either a dinner party in the house or they went out to some other house to dinner. I heard my father say that old William hated nothing more than those dinners and parties. "It'd make one want to go and live in a cave or under some stone," he said to my father.' Eddie Mac started to laugh. 'All he ever wanted to be with was the bees. The Protestants have always been mad about bees, and there were bee

285

societies at the time. He used to give lectures to the societies. They say the lectures were Mrs Kirkwood's idea. She used always to go with him to the meetings. It was a way of getting him out of the house. Old William never liked to be with people, but Mrs Kirkwood believed in people. "The only reason she goes to church is to meet people," he told my father.'

'Anyhow, he still has his bees,' Annie May said gently.

'Always had, always will have, and now the son has gone the same way, except it's the stars in his case. The only thing you could be certain of is that no matter what he turned to it was bound to be something perfectly useless.'

'The parties had stopped by the time I came,' Annie May said. 'Mrs Kirkwood used to go to the Royal Hotel every Thursday to meet her friends.'

'There weren't enough Protestants left by that time for parties. Once the church in Ardcarne had to be closed it was the beginning of the end. The money Mrs Kirkwood brought was running out too. If I owned their fields, I'd be rolling in money in a few years, and they can't even make ends meet. The whole thing would make a cat laugh.'

'They've been very kind to me,' Annie May said.

'What good did it do them? What good?' he said angrily. 'They're there with one arm as long as the other. Useless to themselves or anybody else. They'll be on the road before long, mark my words, and we'll be with them if we are not careful.'

They had come to the big iron gates of the yard. The gates were chained, and they crossed by the stone stile. The back of the huge house stood away to the left at the head of the yard, and in the darkness, all around them in the yard, were the old stone outhouses. The herdsman's house was some distance beyond the hayshed at the far end of the yard, towards the fields. They stood for a split moment apart on the yard's uneven surface. His natural cunning and vanity still held him back: it was too dangerous, she lived too close to his own doorstep, it could change his life – but his need was too strong.

After that night, around nine every evening, when she had finished the chores, and old William was in bed and Master William reading in the library in the front of the house or out in the fields with his telescope, she would go to the herdsman's house. Too timid to knock, she would make a small scraping sound on the loose door, and sometimes she would have to call. They stayed within the house those first weeks, but after a while he seemed not to want her there. On fine nights, he would take her into the fields. 'We have our own telescope!' And when it rained he still preferred to have her out of the house, though she would have loved to sit with him in the darkness listening to the rain beat on the iron. He would take her across to the dry-stone barn where the fruit was stored, the air sticky sweet with the odour of fermenting apples.

'We can listen to the rain far better here. There's less of roof.'

He kept an old, heavy blanket there above the apple shelves, and he could end the evening whenever he wished. He could not get her out of his own house as easily. The old laws of hospitality were too strong even for him. When he wanted to be rid of her from this neutral storehouse, he could walk her to the corner of the yard across from the big house. Sometimes it seemed to her that the evenings were ending now almost before they began, but she was too ill with desire and fear to complain. A hot Sunday in the middle of June she made her one faint plea for openness or decency.

'Wouldn't it be a good day to take the boat and go on the river?' She was amazed by her own effrontery as soon as the words were spoken. The Kirkwoods had a boathouse on the river and a solid rowboat that was kept in repair but seldom used. To go together on the river would bring what had been furtive and hidden into some small light. It would show that he was not ashamed of her. All courting couples went on Sundays to the river in this kind of weather. Even those who couldn't get boats strolled the riverbank towards the Oakport Woods. Some of her early admirers had been proud to take her. There were soft bluebells under the trees, a hidden spring with water so pure it made the teeth chatter even in the heat, and she had drunk it laughing through a stem.

'No. Not today,' he answered slowly, looking down. A yellow dandelion was growing between the yard stones. He kept moving it forwards and back with his boot.

'Wouldn't it make a change?'

'Not today.' He was still searching for the cover of an acceptable lie. 'There's an animal sick. I wouldn't like to be caught that far from the house if it took a turn for the worse. Anyhow, aren't we as well off round the house here? Maybe later we can ramble down by the orchard. It'll be as cool there as on any river.'

At midday she made a meal that was much liked in this weather – smoked haddock in a cream sauce with cauliflower and young peas and small early potatoes. It must have been all of fourteen years since Mrs Kirkwood had taught her how to bring the sauce to a light consistency, to flavour it with chives and parsley. If Mrs Kirkwood was here on this hot Sunday, William and her son would not be dining with Eddie Mac in the kitchen. The linen and silver would be set in the front room, the front door open, the faded canvas deck-chairs stretched under the walnut tree on the front lawn for coffee and newspapers.

The big kitchen, though, was pleasant enough – a fresh coolness from the brown flagstones she had washed in the morning, the door open on the steps down to the yard, a shimmer of heat above the iron roofs, and the dark green of the trees beyond. The house was too big for all of them. The men did not speak as they ate, and she winced as she listened to the thin clink of knife and fork on the bone china.

'I have to say that was a superb meal, Annie,' William volunteered as they rose.

'I can heartily second that,' his son added.

'I'll be around the yard today,' Eddie Mac said to Master William as he lifted his cap. 'I don't like the look of the blue heifer.'

'If you need help, you'll find me in the library.'

She had not eaten, but even after she had cleared the table and washed and put away the dishes she still had little appetite. She drank a mug of coffee with a slice of fruit cake as she stared out on the empty yard. It was already late in the afternoon when she rose, washed the mug, closed the door, and went heavily down the steps into the dull heat of the yard.

She found him at the corner of the stables waiting with an eagerness he hadn't shown for weeks, a blue cloth coat he sometimes wore to the fair on his arm. They went silently into the orchard, picking a place in the high grass away from the beaten path that ran from the gate to the pale row of beehives facing south under the far ivy-covered wall. A clump of wild raspberries that had spread right up to the outer branches of the russet trees gave added cover, though no one in the world would find them there this blessed day.

'You see, it's washed.' He offered her the blue coat to feel with about as much tenderness as it was ever possible for him to show before he spread it on the ground.

'It's as cool here as on any river,' he said as he reached for her. 'As cool as on any river. They can have the fields and anything they want. This is happiness,' he said in a heavy, hoarsely rhythmic tone as he moved above her. 'This is the centre, centre of everything, they can have all else they want.'

'Then I must be part of that centre too,' she said quietly out of the same dull defeat she had felt alone in the big kitchen, not caring about the words she had said.

He stopped in pure amazement. He could not have looked more taken aback if the deep earth itself had stirred and spoken. For a moment, she thought he was about to strike her, but all he did was quickly straighten his clothes and turn his back to her in the long grass. The oppressive silence was at length broken by the sound of the small orchard gate being opened and closed. Old William came slowly down the worn path between the trees. He was going to the hives, dressed all in white, his white beard tucked beneath the suit, the frame of the veil resting on an old straw hat, the long gloves tied with twine below the elbow. He carried a hive tool and smoker, pausing now and then to fan the smoker as he walked slowly along.

From the shelter of the grass and wild canes they watched him go through the hives. His slow care somehow took away some of the oppression. Each time he lifted a roof, a thin stream of bees would move towards the veil. He paid them no attention, working methodically through the hives, sometimes having to use the tool to prise the frames apart, now and again turning his back to the sun to hold up the frames to the light. When he had gone through all the hives, and the bees were quietly working again, he lifted an old wooden chair out of the grass and sat to one side, staring directly into the flight path, the way people lean on bridges to watch water flow below.

'What's he doing?' she asked.

'Nothing. Just watching. He could sit that way for hours. Once I asked him what they were doing. "They're killing off the drones today, Edward," he said. You'd think he was talking about the weather.'

'Still, he sells part of the honey to Sloans,' she said. 'They buy some of his sections every year.'

'For what? For pennies. Mostly he has to feed it back to the bloody bees. Or give it away. The only certain thing about anything the Kirkwoods ever turn their hand to is that it is guaranteed to be perfectly useless.'

They watched old William rise from the chair, remove the hat and veil, freeing a few bees caught in the mesh with his fine, long fingers. He turned the chair upside down again in the grass and came slowly up the orchard. The sun had already gone down behind the walls. They too soon rose, smoothed the stains and bits of grasses from their clothes, and left in opposite directions. Annie May had changed much from the night she had come with Eddie Mac from the dance, but she still held on to a dull hope, and she was beginning to fear that she was with child.

Soon she was certain, and yet she put off telling Eddie. They hired four casual yardmen for the harvest. All her time seemed to go in preparing meals. There was a time when Eddie used to flirt with her in front of the workmen, but now he just ate morosely and silently.

One day she was coming through the yard with a hurriedly gathered bag of green cooking apples for the men's dessert when she heard cheering from the cattle pen. Eddie Mac was in the centre of the pen, his arm round the neck of a young black bull, his free hand gripping its nostrils, the delicate membrane between finger and thumb. The cheering of the men around the pen rose as he slowly forced the struggling animal to its knees, but then suddenly, either through loss of his footing or the terrified animal gathering all its strength into a last surge, he was thrown violently against the steel bars, and the bull broke loose. He wasn't hurt. He rose at once to race after the bull, to rain kicks at its mouth and throat, the cornered animal bellowing for the rest of the herd as it tried to lift its head away from the blows.

She grew so afraid that she found herself shaking. The fear stayed with her all through the day as she cooked and served and washed. Because she could stand the fear no longer she told him in the evening what she had been putting off for weeks.

He did not look at her as she spoke. He had known from that first night he took her that it would end with his being driven out. He had been expecting it from the very beginning. His only surprise was that it had taken so long.

'How much time is there?' he asked.

'Four months. Maybe a little more.' It was such relief to her that he had listened so quietly. Then she found herself pressing for a wild, common happiness. 'We could do up the small house. Families were brought up in it before. It'd need very little change. I could go on working in the big house. They'd probably be only glad of it. It'd mean the two of us were settled.'

'Don't worry. Everything will work itself out,' he said, and she began to cry. 'We'll have to think things out. It'll take time,' he said.

'Time?'

'We have to see the priest if we're to be settled. Banns will have to be read, certificates got, a lot of things. The harvest business will be all over here in a few days. The yardmen will be let go the end of the week. Then we can start to think.'

'Everything will be all right, then.' She could hardly believe her own happiness.

'You don't have to worry about a single thing. Once this week is over everything will be taken care of.'

'I was afraid,' she said. 'Now I can't believe that everything is going to turn out so good.'

He had been through this before. There was only one difference between this time and the other times. All the other times it was the girls that had to stir themselves and make for England. This time he would have to disappear into England.

That night, after she had gone, he lay for a long time fully clothed on the iron bed in the bare three-roomed house, smoking cigarette after cigarette, though he usually smoked little, staring up at the tongued boards of the ceiling. As a boy he had tried to count right across the ceiling, often by the leaping firelight on a winter's night, but he had never managed to complete a single count, always losing the count among the maze of boards at the centre. Tonight he had no need to count so far. Today had been Monday, the second of the month. Tomorrow: Tuesday. Then Wednesday. The fair of Boyle was held on the first Thursday of every month. That was three days away.

The evening before the fair he picked six of the finest black two-year-olds from the fields, the prize cattle of the farm, and penned them by the road, a rough pen he and his father had put together years before with old railway sleepers. After he closed the pen, he threw hay in a corner so that the cattle would stay quiet through the night. He had been given such a free hand running the land for so long that no one questioned him about the cattle. When he came in it was already dark, and rain had started to fall. He found Annie May ahead of him in the house. Though no lamp was lit, she had stirred the fire and a kettle was boiling. The little table that hung on iron trestles from the wall had been lifted down. Cups and plates were set. She had brought food from the big house.

'As there was no answer, I let myself in,' she apologized.

'You were as well,' he responded.

When she said to him that night, 'You might get finer women, but you'll never find another who'll love you as much as I'll love you,' he knew it to be true in some far-off sense of goodness; but it was not his truth. He saw the child at her breast, the faltering years ahead with the Kirkwoods. He shut it out of his mind.

It was still dark and raining heavily when he put the cattle on the road in the morning. All he had with him was a stick and small bundle. The first miles were the worst. Several times he had to cross into the fields and run alongside the cattle where the walls were broken, their hooves sliding on the road as they raced and checked. It was much easier once they tired and it started to get light. The tanglers looking to buy the cattle cheap before they reached the fair tried to halt him on the outskirts of the town, but with a curse he brushed past them towards the Green. People had put tables and ladders out all along the street to the Green to protect doors and windows. He found a corner along the wall at the very top of the Green. All he had to do now was wait, his clothes stuck to his back with perspiration and rain. As the cattle quietened after their long, hard run, their hooves sore and bleeding, they started to reach up and pluck at the ivy on the wall.

He had to hang around till noon to get the true price. Though the attempts at bargaining attracted onlookers and attention, to sell the cattle quickly and cheaply would have been even more dangerous still, and it was not his way.

'Do you have any more where those came from?' the big

Northern dealer in red cattle boots asked finally as he counted out the notes in a bar off the Green.

'No. Those don't come often,' Eddie Mac replied as he peeled a single note from the wad and handed the luck penny back. The whiskey that sealed the bargain he knocked quickly back. The train was due at three.

Afterwards no one remembered seeing him at the station. He had waited outside among the cars until the train pulled in, and then walked straight on. Each time the tickets were being checked he went to the WC, but he would have paid quietly if challenged. He had more money in his inside pocket than he had ever had in his whole life before.

From Westland Row he walked to the B&I terminal on the river and bought a single ticket to Liverpool a few minutes before the boat was due to sail. When the boat was about an hour out to sea, he began to feel cold with the day's tiredness and went to the bar and ordered whiskey. Warmed by the whiskey, he could see as simply back as forward.

The whole place would be ablaze with talk once it got out about the cattle. The Kirkwoods alone would remain quiet. 'His poor father worked here. He was a boy here, grew up here, how could he go and do what he has done?' old William would say. He had nothing against the Kirkwoods, but they were fools. The old lady was the only one with a bit of iron. When Annie May had to tell them the business, they'd no more think of putting her out on the road than they'd be able to put a dog or a cat out. He could even see them start to get fond of the child by the time it started to wander round the big stone house, old William taking it down by the hand to look at the bees.

'Nursing the hard stuff?' a man next to him at the bar inquired.

'That's right.' He didn't want to be drawn into any talk. 'Nursing it well.'

The boat would get into Liverpool in the morning. Though it would take them days yet to figure out what had happened, he would travel on to Manchester before getting a haircut and change of clothes. From Manchester the teeming cities of the North stretched out: Leeds, Newcastle-upon-Tyne, Glasgow. He would get work. He had no need to work for a long time, but he would still get work. Those not in need always got work before the people who needed it most. It was a fool's world.

The Sergeant and Guard Deasy would call to the big stone house. They would write down dates and information in a notebook and they would search through the herdsman's house. They would find nothing. A notice would be circulated for him, with a photo. All the photos they would find would be old, taken in his footballing days. They would never find him. Who was ever found out of England! That circular they would put out would be about as useful as hope in hell.

Manchester, Leeds, Newcastle-upon-Tyne, Glasgow – they were like cards spread out on a green table. His only regret was that he hadn't hit out for one of them years before. He would miss nothing. If he missed anything, it would probably be the tongued boards of the ceiling he had never managed to count. In those cities a man could stay lost for ever and victory could still be found.

Crossing the Line

A few of the last leaves from the almond saplings that stood at intervals along the pavement were being scattered about under the lamps as he met me off the late bus from the city. He was a big man, prematurely bald, and I could feel his powerful tread by my side as we crossed the street to a Victorian cottage, an old vine above its doorway as whimsical there in the very middle of the town as a patch of thyme or lavender.

'The house is tied to the school,' he explained. 'That's why it's not been bulldozed. We don't have any rent to pay.'

His wife looked younger than he, the faded blonde hair and bird face contrasting with her full body. There was something about her of materials faded in the sun. They had two pubescent daughters in convent skirts and blouse, and a son, a few years older than the girls, with the mother's bird-like face and blonde hair, a frail presence beside his father.

'Oliver here will be going back to the uni in a few days. He's doing chemical engineering. He got first-class honours last year, first in his class,' he explained matter-of-factly, to the mother's obvious pleasure and the discomfiture of the son. 'The fees are stiff. They leave things fairly tight just now, but once he's qualified he'll make more in a few years than you and I will ever make in a whole bloody lifetime of teaching. These two great lumps are boarders in The Bower in Athlone. They have a weekend off.' He spoke about his daughters as if he looked upon them already as other men's future gardens.

'We'd give you tea but the Archdeacon is expecting you. He wants you to have supper with him. I hope you like porridge. Whether you do or not, you better bolt it back like a man and say it was great. As long as you take to the stirabout he'll see nothing much wrong with you. But were you to refuse it, all sorts of moral doubts might start to grow in his old head. He's ninety-eight, the second oldest priest in the whole of Ireland, but he'll tell you all this himself. I'd better leave you there now before he starts to worry. The one thing you have to remember is to address yourself like a boy to the stirabout.'

The wind had died a little outside. We walked up the wide street thronged with people in from the country for the late Saturday shopping. There were queues outside the butcher's, the baker's, within the chemist's. Music came from some of the bars. Everywhere there was much greeting and stopping. Pale-faced children seemed to glide about between the shops in the shadow of their mothers. Some of them raised diffident hands or called, 'Master Kennedy,' to the big man by my side, and he seemed to know them all by name.

One rather well-dressed old man alone passed us in open hostility. It was in such marked contrast to the general friendliness that I asked, 'What's wrong with *him*?'

'He's a teacher from out the country. They don't like me. I'm not in their bloody union. Are you in the INTO by any chance?'

'They offered us a special rate before leaving college. Everybody joined.'

'That's your own business, of course. I never found it much use,' he said irritably.

He left me outside the heavy iron gates of the presbytery. 'Call in on your way back to tell us how you got on. Then I'll bring you down to your digs.'

A light above the varnished door shone on white gravel and the thick hedge of laurel and rhododendron that appeared to hide a garden or lawn. A housekeeper led me into the front room where a very old white-haired priest sat over a coal fire.

'You're from the west – a fine dramatic part of the country, but no fit place at all to live, no depth of soil. Have you ever heard of William Bulfin?' he asked as soon as I was seated by his side.

'*Rambles in Eirinn*?' I remembered.

'For my ordination I was given a present of a Pierce bicycle. I rode all around Ireland that summer on the new Pierce with a copy of the *Rambles*. It was a very weary-dreary business pedalling through the midlands, in spite of the rich land. I could feel my heart lift, though, when at last I got to the west. It's still no place to live. Have you met Mr Kennedy?'

'Yes, Father. He showed me here.'

296

'Does he find you all right?'

'I think so, Father.'

'That's good enough for me, then. Do you think you'll be happy here?'

'I think so, Father.'

'I expect you'll see out my time. I thought the last fellow would, but he left. I dislike changes. I'm ninety-eight years old. There's only one priest older in the whole of Ireland, a Father Michael Kelly from the Diocese of Achonry. He's a hundred-and-two. You might have noticed the fuss when he reached the hundred?'

'I must have missed it, Father.'

'I would have imagined that to be difficult. I thought it excessive, but I take a special interest in him. Kelly is the first name I look for every morning on the front of the *Independent*.' He smiled slyly.

The housekeeper came into the room with a steaming saucepan, two bowls, a jug of milk and water, which she set on a low table between our chairs. Then she took a pair of glasses and a bottle of Powers from a press, and withdrew.

'I don't drink, Father,' I said as he raised the bottle.

'You're wise. The heart doesn't need drink at your age. I didn't touch it till I was forty, but after forty I think every man should drink a little. The heart needs a jab or two every day to remind it of its business once it crosses forty. What do you think the business of the heart is?'

'I suppose it has many businesses, Father.'

'You'll never be convicted on that answer, son, but it has only one main business. That's to keep going. If it doesn't do that all its other businesses can be forgotten about.'

He poured himself a very large whiskey, which he drank neat, and then added a smaller measure, filling the glass with water. The Principal had been right. The saucepan was full of steaming porridge when he lifted the lid. He ladled it into the bowls with a wooden spoon, leaving place enough in the bowl for milk and a sprinkling of sugar. It was all I could do to finish what was in the bowl. I noticed how remarkably steady his hand was as he brought the spoon to his lips.

'If a man sticks to the stirabout he's unlikely to go very far wrong,' he concluded. 'I hope you'll be happy here. Mr Kennedy is a good man. He went on our side in that strike. He kept the school open. It was presumably good for the pupils. I think, though, it brought some trouble on himself. It's seldom wise in the long run to go against your own crowd.'

He'd risen, laying his rug aside, but before I could leave he took me by the shoulder up to a large oil painting in a heavy gilt frame above the mantel. 'Look at it carefully. What do you see?'

'A tropical tree. It looks like an island.'

'Look again. It's a trick painting,' he said, and when I could make nothing more of it he traced lines from the tree, which also depicted a melancholy military figure in a cocked hat. 'Napoleon, on Elba,' he laughed.

The Kennedys had invited me to their Sunday lunch the next day. Their kitchen was pleasant and extremely warm, the two girls setting the big table and smells of roasting chicken and apple stew coming from the black-leaded range. There was wine with the meal, a sweet white wine. Afterwards, the girls cleared the table and, asking permission, disappeared into the town. Oliver sat on in the room. Kennedy filled his wife's glass to the brim with the last of the Sauterne, rose, and got himself a whiskey from the press in place of the wine.

'You were just like he was twenty-one years ago. Your first school. Straight from the training college. Starting out,' Mrs Kennedy said, her face pink with the wine and cooking.

'Teachers' jobs were hard come by in those days. Temporary assistant teacher for one year in the Marist Brothers in Sligo was my first job. There was pay but you could hardly call it pay. Not enough to keep a wren alive.'

'It was the first of July. I remember it well. We had a bar and grocery by the harbour and sold newspapers. He came in for the *Independent*. He was tall then, with a thick head of brown hair. I know it was the first of July, but I forget the year.'

'Nineteen thirty-three. It was the year I got out of college. I bought that *Independent* to see if there were any permanent jobs coming up in October.'

'We were both only twenty. They told us to wait till we had saved some money, that we had plenty of time. But we couldn't wait. My father gave us two rooms above the grocery part of the shop. Do you ever regret not waiting?'

'We wouldn't have saved anyhow. There was nothing to save. And we had those years.'

I felt like an intruder. Their son sat there, shamed and fascinated, unable to cry stop, or tear himself away.

'Those two rooms were rotten with damp, and when there were storms you should have heard the damned panes. You could have wallpapered the rooms with the number of letters beginning "The Manager regrets" that came through the letterbox that winter. Oliver here was on the way.'

'Those two rooms were happiness,' she said, lifting the glass of sweet wine to her lips, while her son writhed with unease on the sofa.

'We could get no job, and then I was suddenly offered three at the same time. It's always the same. You either get more than you want or you get nothing. We came here because the house went with the school. It meant a great deal in those days. It still does us no harm.'

I walked with Kennedy to the school on the Monday. He intro-duced me to the classes I was to teach. We walked together on the concrete during the mid-morning break. Eagerly, he started to talk as we walked up and down among the playing children. The regulation ten minutes ran to twenty before he rang the bell.

'They're as well playing in this weather. The inspectors never try to catch me out. They know the work gets done.'

It was the same at the longer lunchtime, the talk veering again to the early days of his marriage.

'I used to go back to those two rooms for lunch. We'd just go straight to bed, grabbing a sandwich on the way out. Sometimes we had it off against the edge of the table. It was a great feeling afterwards, walking about with the Brothers, knowing that they'd never have it in the whole of their lives.'

I walked with him on that concrete in total silence. I must have been close to the perfect listener for this excited, forceful man. No one had ever spoken to me like this before. I didn't know what to say. The children milled about us in the weak sun. Sometimes I shivered at the premonition that days like this might be a great part of the rest of my life: I had dreamed once that through teaching I would help make the world a better place.

'What made you take up teaching?' he asked. 'I know the hours are good enough, and there's the long holidays, but what the hell good is it without money?'

'I don't know why,' I answered. 'Some notion of service . . . of doing good.'

'It's easy to see that you're young. Teaching is a lousy, tiring old job, and it gets worse as you get older. A new bunch comes at you year after year. They stay the same but you start to go down. You'll not get thanked for service in this world. There were no jobs when I was young. It was considered a bloody miracle to have any sort of a job with a salary. If I was in your boots now I'd do something like dentistry or engineering, even if I had to scrape for the money.'

The time had already gone several minutes past the lunchtime. The children were whirling about us on the concrete in loud abandon, for them the minutes of play stolen from the school day were pure sweetness.

'Still, if I had had those chances, I wouldn't have gone to Sligo and I'd never have met her,' he mused.

I was in my room in the digs after tea one evening when a daughter of the house in the blouse and gymfrock of the convent secondary school knocked and said, 'There's a visitor for you in the front room downstairs.'

A frail, grey-haired man rose as soon as I entered. He had an engaging handshake and smile.

'I'm Owen Beirne, branch secretary of the INTO. I just called in to welcome you to the town and to invite you to our meeting on Friday night. I teach in a small school out in the country. Forgive the speech.' He smiled as he sat down.

I explained briefly that I had joined the union already and suggested that we move from the stiff front room.

'We'll cross in a minute to the Bridge Bar. They always have a nice fire, but it's safer to say what I have to say here. I suppose you don't know about your Principal and the union.'

'He told me he wasn't a member.'

'Did he try to stop you joining?' he asked sharply.

'No. I told him I'd joined already.'

'Well, he was a member before the strike but he refused to come out on strike. For several months he crossed that picket line, while the church and de Valera tried to starve us to our knees.'

There was nothing for me to say.

'As far as we are concerned, I mean the rest of the teachers around here, Kennedy doesn't exist. You're in a different position. He's your Principal. You have to work with the man. But if we were to meet the two of you together, you might find yourself black-balled as well.'

'I don't mind.'

'It means nothing as far as you are concerned. You just go your own way and notice nothing. But should he try to pull the heavy on you in school – he did with one of your predecessors – let us know and we'll fall on him like the proverbial load of bricks.' He had risen. 'That's what I wanted to get out of the way.'

The bar was empty, but there was a bright fire of logs at one end. Owen Beirne ordered a hot whiskey with cloves and lemon. The barman seemed to like and respect him. I had a glass of lemonade.

'Don't you take a drink?'

'Seldom.'

'I drink too much. It's expensive and a waste of time. During the times I don't drink I read far more and feel better in every way. Unfortunately, it's very pleasant.'

He told me his father had been a teacher. 'My poor father had to go to the back door of the presbytery every month for his pay. The priest's housekeeper gave it to him. It was four pounds in those days. I'll never forget my mother's face when he came back from the presbytery one night with three pounds instead of four. The housekeeper had held back a pound because the priest had decided to paint the church that month. One of the great early things the INTO got for the teacher was for the salary to be paid directly into his own hands – to get it through the post instead of from the priest or his housekeeper.

'All that was changed by my time. The inspectors, the dear inspectors, were our hairshirts. A recurring nightmare I have is walking up and down in front of a class with an inspector sitting at the back quietly taking notes. Some were the roaring boys. One rode the bucking mule in Duffy's Circus in Ballinasloe, got badly thrown, but was still out before nine the next morning to check if the particular teacher he'd been drinking with was on time. They were like lords or judges. Full-grown men trembled in front of them at these annual inspections. Women were often in tears. The best hams and fruit cakes were brought out at lunchtime. For some there had to be the whiskey bottle and stout in the schoolhouse after school.

'Then, during the war, the Emergency, we had an inspector in Limerick called Deasy, a fairly young man. I was teaching in his area at the time. He was a real rat. In Newcastle West there was an old landed family, a racehorse and gambling crowd, down on their luck. An uncle was the Bishop of Cashel. One of the sons was a failed medical student, and God knows what else, and as part of a rehabilitation scheme didn't the Bishop get him a temporary teaching job. Deasy was his inspector. I'm sure the teaching was choice, and what Deasy didn't say to his man wasn't worth saying. This crowd wasn't used to being talked to like that. He just walked out of the school without saying a word. Deasy sat down to his tea and ham sandwiches and fruit cake with the schoolmistress. They were still having lunch when your man arrived back. He sat down with them, opened his coat nice and quietly, produced the shotgun and gave Deasy both barrels. He wasn't even offered the Act of Contrition. I was in the cathedral in Limerick the night Deasy's body was brought in. It was a sad sight, the widow and seven children behind the coffin. Every inspector in the country was at the funeral. Things were noticeably easier afterwards.'

'What happened to your man?'

'He was up for murder. He'd have swung at the time but for the Bishop, who got him certified. They say that after a few years he was spirited away to Australia. He was as sane as I was.'

'It seems to be a more decent time now,' I said.

'It's by no means great, but it's certainly better than it was.'

A few people had come into the bar by this time. They looked our way but no one joined us at the fire. He'd had four drinks, and his face was flushed and excited. He wanted to know what poets my generation was reading. He seemed unimpressed by the names I mentioned. His own favourite was Horace. 'Sometimes I translate him for fun, as a kind of discipline. I always feel in good spirits afterwards.'

Almost absently he spilled out a number of coloured capsules from a small plastic container on to the table, got a glass of water from the bar. 'It's the old ticker. I'm afraid it's wobbly. But I hope not to embarrass my friends,' he said.

'I'm sorry. That's lousy luck to have.'

'There's no need,' he answered laughing as we took leave of one another. 'I've had a good innings.'

Kennedy didn't call to the digs next morning, and I made my own way to the school. As I came through the gates I saw that he had all the classes lined up on the concrete, and he was looking so demonstratively at his watch that I checked the time on my own watch. I was in time but only just. Before I got any closer he'd marched his own classes in, disappearing behind a closed door. Instead of coming round with the roll books that morning, he sent one of the senior boys, and at the mid-morning break I found myself alone on the concrete for several minutes, but when he did join me his grievance spilled out at once.

'I heard yourself and Mr Beirne had a long session in the Bridge House last night.'

'He called at the digs. It was more comfortable to cross to the Bridge.'

'I suppose plenty of dirt was fired in my direction.'

'None. He said the fact that you're not in the INTO must be no concern of mine. It was the only time you were mentioned.'

'That was very good of him. There are many people around here who would think him not fit company for a young teacher,' he said angrily.

'Why?'

'Every penny he has goes on booze or books and some of the books are far from edifying, by all accounts. He's either out every night in the bars, or else he shuts himself off for weeks on end. They say his wife was dead in the house for most of a day before he noticed. The priests certainly think he's no addition to the place.'

'He seemed an intelligent man.'

'He knows how to put on a good front, all right.'

'He seemed very decent to me.' I refused to give way.

'He's no friend of mine. You can take my word for that. All that crowd would have had my guts for garters if they got the chance. They'll have a long wait, I can tell you. When I came to this town we hadn't two coins to clink together. Every morsel of food we put in our mouths that first month here was on credit. But I worked.

Every hour of private tuition going round the place I took, and that's the lousiest of all teaching jobs, face to face for a whole hour with a well-heeled dunce. Then I got into surveying work with the solicitors. I must have walked half the fields within miles of this town with the chains. I was just about on my feet when that strike was called. The children were in good schools. Why should I put all that at risk? It wasn't my strike. Some of the ones that went on strike will be in hock for the rest of their days. And if it had lasted even another month they'd have had to crawl back like beaten dogs. Do you think that it was easy for me to pass those pickets with their placards and cornerboy jeers every school day for the whole of seven months? Do you think that was easy?'

'I know it wasn't easy.'

There was a Mass that Friday for the teachers and children of the parish, an official blessing on the new year, and we were given the day off to attend the Mass. Kennedy called for me and we walked up the town together to the church. At the top of Main Street we ran straight into Owen Beirne. Rather than cut us openly, he crossed to a fish stall and pretended to be examining the freshness of a tray of plaice as we went by.

'Your friend Beirne hadn't much to say to you today. You were in the wrong company.'

'I don't mind,' I said.

As we came up to the railings of the church, a red-faced hulk of a man, obviously a teacher, the gold *fáinne* and metal tricolour in his lapel, stared at Kennedy in open hostility, cleared his throat, and spat out into our path. Kennedy said nothing as we hurried into the church. After Mass little groups of teachers stood about in the church grounds, shaking hands, joking, but as soon as we approached they fell silent or turned away. Not a single person spoke to us or raised a hat or even bowed. We passed out in total silence. I had never run such a gauntlet. I had the feeling as we walked back through the town that Kennedy was desperately searching for something to say but that he was too disturbed to settle on any one phrase.

'You might as well come into my place for a cup of tea or something,' he said eventually. 'You have a good hour yet to go till your lunch.'

His house was empty and he made the tea himself. 'They can try as hard as they are able but they can't harm me now,' he began slowly as he made the tea. 'In another two years Oliver will be qualified. By that time, the pair of girls will be on their way into the civil service or training college. That summer we'll buy the car. We could buy it now but we decided to wait till we can do it right. It'll be no secondhand. That summer we'll take the first holiday since we were married. We'll drive all round Ireland, staying in the best hotels. We'll not spare or stint on anything. We'll have wine, prawns, smoked salmon, sole or lobster or sirloin or lamb, anything on the menu we feel like, no matter what the price.'

I was beginning to think that people grow less spiritual the older they become, contrary to what is thought. It was as if some desire to plunge their arms up to the elbow into the steaming entrails of the world grew more fierce the closer they got to leaving. It was a very different dream to the young priest's, cycling round Ireland with a copy of the *Rambles* all those years ago.

'Have you noticed Eileen O'Reilly?' he changed as we sat with the cups of tea.

'She's very pretty,' I said.

Eileen O'Reilly worked in one of the solicitor's offices. She was small and blonde with a perfect figure. I thought she'd smiled at me as she passed on a bicycle during a lunch hour. She was standing on the pedals to force the bike across the hill.

'If I was in your place, I'd go for her,' he said wistfully. 'She has no steady boyfriend. I do surveying for her office and we always have a joke or an old flirt. When I brought up your name a few days back she blushed beetroot. I can tell she's interested in you. In two years Oliver will be qualified and I'll have no more need of the surveying. I could hand it over to you. You'd not be rich, but with the fees on top of the teaching you'd be very comfortable for a young man. You could well afford to marry. I'd not leave her hanging around long if I was in your boots. In two years' time if you stayed on at the school here and married Eileen I'd give you the surveying. There's nothing to it once you get the knack of the chains.'

High Ground

I let the boat drift on the river beneath the deep arch of the bridge, the keel scraping the gravel as it crossed the shallows out from Walsh's, past the boathouse at the mouth, and out into the lake. It was only the slow growing distance from the ring of reeds round the shore that told that the boat moved at all on the lake. More slowly still, the light was going from the August evening.

I was feeling leaden with tiredness but did not want to sleep. I had gone on the river in order to be alone, the way one goes to a dark room.

The Brothers' Building Fund Dance had been held the night before. A big marquee had been set up in the grounds behind the monastery. Most of the people I had gone to school with were there, awkward in their new estate, and nearly all the Brothers who had taught us: Joseph, Francis, Benedictus, Martin. They stood in a black line beneath the low canvas near the entrance and waited for their old pupils to go up to them. When they were alone, watching us dance, rapid comment passed up and down the line, and often Joseph and Martin doubled up, unable or unwilling to conceal laughter; but by midnight they had gone, and a night of a sort was ours, the fine dust from the floor rising into the perfume and sweat and hair oil as we danced in the thresh of the music.

There was a full moon as I drove Una to her home in Arigna in the borrowed Prefect, the whole wide water of Allen taking in the wonderful mysteriousness of the light. We sat in the car and kissed and talked, and morning was there before we noticed. After the harshness of growing up, a world of love and beauty, of vague gardens and dresses and laughter, one woman in a gleaming distance seemed to be almost within reach. We would enter this world. We would make it true.

I was home just before the house had risen, and lay on the bed and waited till everybody was up, then changed into old clothes. I was helping my father put up a new roof on the house. Because of the tiredness, I had to concentrate completely on the work, even then nearly losing my footing several times between the stripped beams, sometimes annoying my father by handing him the wrong lath or tool; but when evening came the last thing I wanted was sleep. I wanted to be alone, to go over the night, to try to see clearly, which only meant turning again and again on the wheel of dreaming.

'Hi there! Hi! Do you hear me, young Moran!' The voice came with startling clarity over the water, was taken up by the fields across the lake, echoed back. 'Hi there! Hi! Do you hear me, young Moran!'

I looked all around. The voice came from the road. I couldn't make out the figure at first, leaning in a broken gap of the wall above the lake, but when he called again I knew it was Eddie Reegan, Senator Reegan.

'Hi there, young Moran. Since the mountain can't come to Mahomet, Mahomet will have to come to the mountain. Row over here a minute. I want to have a word with you.'

I rowed slowly, watching each oar-splash slip away from the boat in the mirror of water. I disliked him, having unconsciously, perhaps, picked up my people's dislike. He had come poor to the place, buying Lynch's small farm cheap, and soon afterwards the farmhouse burned down. At once, a bigger house was built with the insurance money, closer to the road, though that in its turn was due to burn down too, to be replaced by the present mansion, the avenue of Lawson cypresses now seven years old. Soon he was buying up other small farms, but no one had ever seen him work with shovel or with spade. He always appeared immaculately dressed. It was as if he understood instinctively that it was only the shortest of short steps from appearance to becoming. 'A man who works never makes any money. He has no time to see how the money is made,' he was fond of boasting. He set up as an auction-eer. He entered politics. He married Kathleen Relihan, the eldest of old Paddy Relihan's daughters, the richest man in the area, Chair-man of the County Council. 'Do you see those two girls? I'm going to marry one of those girls,' he was reported to have remarked to a friend. 'Which one?' 'It doesn't matter. They're both Paddy Relihan's daughters'; and when Paddy retired it was Reegan rather than any of his own sons who succeeded Paddy in the Council.

Now that he had surpassed Paddy Relihan and become a Senator and it seemed only a matter of time before he was elected to the Dáil, he no longer joked about 'the aul effort of a fire', and was gravely concerned about the reluctance of insurance companies to grant cover for fire to dwelling houses in our part of the country. He had bulldozed the hazel and briar from the hills above the lake, and as I turned to see how close the boat had come to the wall I could see behind him the white and black of his Friesians grazing between the electric fences on the far side of the reseeded hill.

I let the boat turn so that I could place my hand on the stone, but the evening was so calm that it would have rested beneath the high wall without any hand. The Senator had seated himself on the wall as I was rowing in, and his shoes hung six or eight feet above the boat.

'It's not the first time I've had to congratulate you, though I'm too high up here to shake your hand. And what I'm certain of is that it won't be the last time either,' he began.

'Thanks. You're very kind,' I answered.

'Have you any idea where you'll go from here?'

'No. I've applied for the grant. It depends on whether I get the grant or not.'

'What'll you do if you get it?'

'Go on, I suppose. Go a bit farther . . .'

'What'll you do then?'

'I don't know. Sooner or later, I suppose, I'll have to look for a job.'

'That's the point I've been coming to. You are qualified to teach, aren't you?'

'Yes. But I've only taught for a few months. Before I got that chance to go to the university.'

'You didn't like teaching?' he asked sharply.

'No.' I was careful. 'I didn't dislike it. It was a job.'

'I like that straightness. And what I'm looking to know is – if you were offered a very good job would you be likely to take it?'

'What job?'

'I won't beat around the bush either. I'm talking of the Principalship of the school here. It's a very fine position for a young man. You'd be among your own people. You'd be doing good where you belong. I hear you're interested in a very attractive young lady not a hundred miles from here. If you decided to marry and settle down I'm in a position to put other advantages your way.'

Master Leddy was the Principal of the school. He had been the Principal as long as I could remember. He had taught me, many before me. I had called to see him just three days before. The very idea of replacing him was shocking. And anyhow, I knew the politicians had nothing to do with the appointment of teachers. It was the priest who ran the school. What he was saying didn't even begin to make sense, but I had been warned about his cunning and was wary. 'You must be codding. Isn't Master Leddy the Principal?'

'He is now but he won't be for long more – not if I have anything to do with it.'

'How?' I asked very quietly in the face of the outburst.

'That need be no concern of yours. If you can give me your word that you'll take the job, I can promise you that the job is as good as yours.'

'I can't do that. I can't follow anything right. Isn't it Canon Gallagher who appoints the teachers?'

'Listen. There are many people who feel the same way as I do. If I go to the Canon in the name of all those people and say that you're willing to take the job, the job is yours. Even if he didn't want to, he'd have no choice but to appoint you . . .'

'Why should you want to do that for me? Say, even if it is possible.' I was more curious now than alarmed.

'It's more than possible. It's bloody necessary. I'll be plain. I have three sons. They go to that school. They have nothing to fall back on but whatever education they get. And with the education they're getting at that school up there, all they'll ever be fit for is to dig ditches. Now, I've never dug ditches, but even at my age I'd take off my coat and go down into a ditch rather than ever have to watch any of my sons dig. The whole school is a shambles. Someone described it lately as one big bear garden.'

'What makes you think I'd be any better?'

'You're young. You're qualified. You're ambitious. It's a very good job for someone of your age. I'd give you all the backing you'd want. You'd have every reason to make a go of it. With you there, I'd feel my children would still be in with a chance. In another year or two even that'll be gone.'

'I don't see why you want my word at this stage,' I said evasively, hoping to slip away from it all. I saw his face return to its natural look of shrewdness in what was left of the late summer light.

'If I go to the Canon now it'll be just another complaint in a long line of complaints. If I can go to him and say that things can't be allowed to go on as they have been going and we have a young man here, from a good family, a local, more than qualified, who's willing to take the job, who has everyone's backing, it's a different proposition entirely. And I can guarantee you here this very evening that you'll be the Principal of that school when it opens in September.'

For the first time it was all coming clear to me.

'What'll happen to the Master? What'll he do?'

'What I'm more concerned about is what'll my children do if he stays,' he burst out again. 'But you don't have to concern yourself about it. It'll be all taken care of.'

I had called on the Master three evenings before, walking beyond the village to the big ramshackle farmhouse. He was just rising, having taken all his meals of the day in bed, and was shaving and dressing upstairs, one time calling down for a towel, and again for a laundered shirt.

'Is that young Moran?' He must have recognized my voice or name. 'Make him a good cup of tea. And he'll be able to be back up the road with myself.'

A very old mongrel greyhound was routed from the leather armchair one side of the fire, and I was given tea and slices of buttered bread. The Master's wife, who was small and frail with pale skin and lovely brown eyes, kept up a cheerful chatter that required no response as she busied herself about the enormous cluttered kitchen which seemed not to possess a square foot of room. There were buckets everywhere, all sorts of chairs, basins, bags of meal and flour, cats, the greyhound, pots and pans. The pattern had faded from the bulging wallpaper, a dark ochre, and some of the several calendars that hung around the walls had faded into the paper. It would have been difficult to find space for an extra cup or saucer on the long wooden table. Plainly there were no set meal times. Two of the Master's sons, now grown men, came singly in from the fields while I waited. Plates of food were served at once, bacon and liver, a mug of tea. They took from the plate of bread already on the table, the butter, the sugar, the salt, the bottle of sauce. They spent no more than a few minutes over the meal, blessing themselves at its end, leaving as suddenly as they'd entered, smiling and nodding in a friendly way in my direction but making little attempt at conversation, though Gerald did ask, before he reached for his hat – a hat I recognized as having belonged to the Master back in my school days, a brown hat with a blue teal's feather and a small hole burned in its side – 'Well, how are things getting along in the big smoke?' The whole effect was of a garden and orchard gone completely wild, but happily.

'You couldn't have come at a better time. We'll be able to be up the road together,' the Master said as he came heavily down the stairs in his stockinged feet. He'd shaved, was dressed in a grey suit, with a collar and tie, the old watch-chain crossing a heavy paunch. He had failed since last I'd seen him, the face red and puffy, the white hair thinned, and there was a bruise on the cheekbone where he must have fallen. The old hound went towards him, licking at his hand.

'Good boy! Good boy,' he said as he came towards me, patting the hound. As soon as we shook hands he slipped his feet into shoes which had stood beside the leather chair. He did not bend or sit, and as he talked I saw the small bird-like woman at his feet, tying up the laces.

'It's a very nice thing to see old pupils coming back. Though not many of them bring me laurels like yourself, it's still a very nice thing. Loyalty is a fine quality. A very fine quality.'

'Now,' his wife stood by his side, 'all you need is your hat and stick,' and she went and brought them.

'Thank you. Thank you indeed. I don't know what I'd do but for my dear wife,' he said.

'Do you hear him now! He was never stuck for the charm. Off with you now before you get the back of me hand,' she bantered, and called as we went slowly towards the gate, 'Do you want me to send any of the boys up for you?'

'No. Not unless they have some business of their own to attend to in the village. No,' he said gravely, turning very slowly.

He spoke the whole way on the slow walk to the village. All the time he seemed to lag behind my snail's pace, sometimes standing because he was out of breath, tapping at the road with the cane. Even when the walk slowed to a virtual standstill it seemed to be still far too energetic for him.

'I always refer to you as my star pupil. When the whole enterprise seems to be going more or less askew, I always point to young Moran: that's one good job I turned out. Let the fools prate.'

I walked, stooping by his side, restraining myself within the slow walk, embarrassed, ashamed, confused. I had once looked to him in pure infatuation, would rush to his defence against every careless whisper. He had shone like a clear star. I was in love with what I hardly dared to hope I might become. It seemed horrible now that I might come to this.

'None of my own family were clever,' he confided. 'It was a great disappointment. And yet they may well be happier for it. Life is an extraordinary thing. A very great mystery. Wonderful . . . shocking . . . thing.'

Each halting speech seemed to lead in some haphazard way into the next.

'Now that you're coming out into the world you'll have to be constantly on your guard. You'll have to be on your guard first of all against intellectual pride. That's the worst sin, the sin of Satan. And always be kind to women. Help them. Women are weak. They'll be attracted to you.' I had to smile ruefully, never having noticed much of a stampede in my direction. 'There was this girl I left home from a dance once,' he continued. 'And as we were getting closer to her house I noticed her growing steadily more amorous until I had to say, "None of that now, girl. It is not the proper time!" Later, when we were both old and married, she thanked me. She said I was a true gentleman.'

The short walk seemed to take a deep age, but once outside Ryan's door he took quick leave of me. 'I won't invite you inside. Though I set poor enough of an example, I want to bring no one with me. I say to all my pupils: *Beware* of the high stool. The downward slope from the high stool is longer and steeper than from the top of Everest. God bless and guard you, young Moran. Come and see me again before you head back to the city.' And with that he left me. I stood facing the opaque glass of the door, the small print of the notice above it: *Seven Days Licence to Sell Wine, Beer, Spirits.* How can he know what he knows and still do what he does, I say to the sudden silence before turning away.

'Do you mean the Master'll be out on the road, then?' I asked
Senator Reegan from the boat, disturbed by the turn the conversation had taken.

'You need have no fear of that. There's a whole union behind
him. In our enlightened day alcoholism is looked upon as just
another illness. And they wonder how the country can be so badly
off,' he laughed sarcastically. 'No. He'll probably be offered a rest
cure on full pay. I doubt if he'd take it. If he did, it'd delay official
recognition of your appointment by a few months, that'd be all, a
matter of paperwork. The very worst that could happen to him is
that he'd be forced to take early retirement, which would probably
add years to his life. He'd just have that bit less of a pension with
which to drink himself into an early grave. You need have no
worries on that score. You'd be doing everybody a favour, including him most of all, if you'd take the job. Well, what do you say? I
could still go to the Canon tonight. It's late but not too late. He'd
just be addressing himself to his hot toddy. It could be as good a
time as any to attack him. Well, what do you say?'

'I'll have to think about it.'

'It's a very fine position for a young man like yourself starting out
in life.'

'I know it is. I'm very grateful.'

'To hell with gratitude. Gratitude doesn't matter a damn. It's one
of those moves that benefits everybody involved. You'll come to
learn that there aren't many moves like that in life.'

'I'll have to think about it.' I was anxious to turn away from any
direct confrontation.

'I can't wait for very long. Something has to be done and done
soon.'

'I know that but I still have to think about it.'

'Listen. Let's not close on anything this evening. Naturally you
have to consider everything. Why don't you drop over to my place
tomorrow night? You'll have a chance to meet my lads. And herself
has been saying for a long time now that she'd like to meet you.
Come about nine. Everything will be out of the way by then.'

I rowed very slowly away, just stroking the boat forward in the
deadly silence of the half-darkness. I watched Reegan cross the
road, climb the hill, pausing now and then among the white blobs
of his Friesians. His figure stood for a while at the top of the hill

where he seemed to be looking back towards the boat and water before he disappeared.

When I got back to the house everyone was asleep except a younger sister who had waited up for me. She was reading by the fire, the small black cat on her knee.

'They've all gone to bed,' she explained. 'Since you were on the river, they let me wait up for you. Only there's no tea. I've just found out that there's not a drop of spring water in the house.'

'I'll go to the well, then. Otherwise someone will have to go first thing in the morning. You don't have to wait up for me.' I was too agitated to go straight to bed and glad of the distraction of any activity.

'I'll wait,' she said. 'I'll wait and make the tea when you get back.'

'I'll be less than ten minutes.' The late hour held for her the attractiveness of the stolen.

I walked quickly, swinging the bucket. The whole village seemed dead under a benign moon, but as I passed along the church wall I heard voices. They came from Ryan's Bar. It was shut, the blinds down, but then I noticed cracks of yellow light along the edges of the big blue blind. They were drinking after hours. I paused to see if I could recognize any of the voices, but before I had time Charlie Ryan hissed, 'Will you keep your voices down, will yous? At the rate you're going you'll soon have the Sergeant out of his bed,' and the voices quietened to a whisper. Afraid of being noticed in the silence, I passed on to get the bucket of spring water from the well, but the voices were in full song again by the time I returned. I let the bucket softly down in the dust and stood in the shadow of the church wall to listen. I recognized the Master's slurred voice at once, and then voices of some of the men who worked the sawmill in the wood.

'That sixth class in 1933 was a great class, Master.' It was Johnny Connor's voice, the saw mechanic. 'I was never much good at the Irish, but I was a terror at the maths, especially the Euclid.'

I shivered as I listened under the church wall. Nineteen thirty-three was the year before I was born.

'You were a topper, Johnny. You were a topper at the maths,' I heard the Master's voice. It was full of authority. He seemed to have no sense at all that he was in danger.

'Tommy Morahan that went to England was the best of us all in

314

that class,' another voice took up, a voice I wasn't able to recognize.

'He wasn't half as good as he imagined he was. He suffered from a swelled head,' Johnny Connor said.

'Ye were toppers, now. Ye were all toppers,' the Master said diplomatically.

'One thing sure is that you made a great job of us, Master. You were a powerful teacher. I remember to this day everything you told us about the Orinoco River.'

'It was no trouble. Ye had the brains. There are people in this part of the country digging ditches who could have been engineers or doctors or judges or philosophers had they been given the opportunity. But the opportunity was lacking. That was all that was lacking.' The Master spoke again with great authority.

'The same again all round, Charlie,' a voice ordered. 'And a large brandy for the Master.'

'Still, we kept sailing, didn't we, Master? That's the main thing. We kept sailing.'

'Ye had the brains. The people in this part of the country had powerful brains.'

'If you had to pick one thing, Master, what would you put those brains down to?'

'Will you hush now! The Sergeant wouldn't even have to be passing outside to hear yous. Soon he'll be hearing yous down in the barracks,' Charlie hissed.

There was a lull again in the voices in which a coin fell and seemed to roll across the floor.

'Well, the people with the brains mostly stayed here. They had to. They had no choice. They didn't go to the cities. So the brains was passed on to the next generation. Then there's the trees. There's the water. And we're very high up here. We're practically at the source of the Shannon. If I had to pick on one thing more than another, I'd put it down to that. I'd attribute it to the high ground.'

Sierra Leone

'I suppose it won't be long now till your friend is here,' the barman said as he held the glass to the light after polishing.

'If it's not too wet,' I said.

'It's a bad evening,' he yawned, the rain drifting across the bandstand and small trees of Fairview Park to stream down the long window.

She showed hardly any signs of rain when she came, lifting the scarf from her black hair. 'You seem to have escaped the wet.' The barman was all smiles as he greeted her.

'I'm afraid I was a bit extravagant and took a taxi,' she said in the rapid speech she used when she was nervous or simulating confusion to create an effect.

'What would you like?'

'Would a hot whiskey be too much trouble?'

'No trouble at all.' The barman smiled and lifted the electric kettle. I moved the table to make room for her in the corner of the varnished partition beside the small coal fire in the grate. There was the sound of water boiling, and the scent of cloves and lemon. When I rose to go to the counter for the hot drink, the barman motioned that he would bring it over to the fire.

'The spoon is really to keep the glass from cracking' – I nodded towards the steaming glass in front of her on the table. It was a poor attempt to acknowledge the intimacy of the favour. For several months I had been frustrating all his attempts to get to know us, for we had picked Gaffneys because it was out of the way and we had to meet like thieves. Dublin was too small a city to give even our names away.

'This has just come.' I handed her the telegram as soon as the barman had resumed his polishing of the glasses. It was from my father, saying it was urgent I go home at once. She read it without speaking. 'What are you going to do?'

'I don't know. I suppose I'll have to go home.'

'It doesn't say *why*.'
'Of course not. He never gives room.'
'Is it likely to be serious?'
'No, but if I don't go there's the nagging doubt that it may be.'
'What are you doing to do, then?'
'Go, I suppose.' I looked at her apprehensively.
'Then that's goodbye to our poor weekend,' she said.

We were the same age and had known each other casually for years. I had first met her with Jerry McCredy, a politician in his early fifties, who had a wife and family in the suburbs, and a reputation as a womanizer round the city; but by my time all the other women had disappeared. The black-haired Geraldine was with him everywhere, and he seemed to have fallen in love at last when old, even to the point of endangering his career. I had thought her young and lovely and wasted, but we didn't meet in any serious way till the night of the Cuban Crisis.

There was a general fever in the city that night, so quiet as to be almost unreal, the streets and faces hushed. I had been wandering from window to window in the area round Grafton Street. On every television set in the windows the Russian ships were still on course for Cuba. There was a growing air that we were walking in the last quiet evening of the world before it was all consumed by fire. 'It looks none too good.' I heard her quick laugh at my side as I stood staring at the ships moving silently across the screen.

'None too good.' I turned. 'Are you scared?'
'Of course I'm scared.'
'Do you know it's the first time we've ever met on our own?' I said. 'Where's Jerry?'
'He's in Cork. At a meeting. One that a loose woman like myself can't appear at.' She laughed her quick provocative laugh.
'Why don't you come for a drink, then?'
'I'd love to. With the way things are I was even thinking of going in for one on my own.'

There was a stillness in the bar such as I had never known. People looked up from their drinks as each fresh newsflash came on the set high in the corner, and it was with visible relief that they bent down again to the darkness of their pints.

'It's a real tester for that old chestnut about the Jesuit when he

317

was asked what he'd do if he was playing cards at five minutes to midnight and was suddenly told that the world was going to end at midnight,' I said as I took our drinks to the table in one of the far corners of the bar, out of sight of the screen.

'And what would *he* do?'

'He'd continue playing cards, of course, to show that all things are equal. It's only love that matters.'

'That's a fine old farce.' She lifted her glass.

'It's strange, how I've always wanted to ask you out, and that it should happen this way. I always thought you very beautiful.'

'Why didn't you tell me?'

'You were with Jerry.'

'You should still have told me. I don't think Jerry ever minded the niceties very much when *he* was after a woman,' she laughed, and then added softly, 'Actually, I thought you disliked me.'

'Anyhow, we're here this night.'

'I know, but it's somehow hard to believe it.'

It was the stillness that was unreal, the comfortable sitting in chairs with drinks in our hands, the ships leaving a white wake behind them on the screen. We were in the condemned cell waiting for reprieve or execution, except that this time the whole world was the cell. There was nothing we could do. The withering would happen as simply as the turning on or off of a light bulb.

Her hair shone dark blue in the light. Her skin had the bloom of ripe fruit. The white teeth glittered when she smiled. We had struggled towards the best years; now they waited for us, and all was to be laid waste as we were about to enter into them. In the freedom of the fear I moved my face close to hers. Our lips met. I put my hand on hers.

'Is Jerry coming back tonight?'

'No.'

'Can I stay with you tonight?'

'If you want that.' Her lips touched my face again.

'It's all I could wish for – except, maybe, a better time.'

'Why don't we go, then?' she said softly.

We walked by the Green, closed and hushed within its railings, not talking much. When she said, 'I wonder what they're doing in the Pentagon as we walk these steps by the Green?' it seemed more part of the silence than any speech.

'It's probably just as well we can't know.'

'I hope they do something. It'd be such a waste. All this to go, and us too.'

'We'd be enough.'

There was a bicycle against the wall of the hallway when she turned the key, and it somehow made the stairs and lino-covered hallway more bare.

'It's the man's upstairs.' She nodded towards the bicycle. 'He works on the buses.'

The flat was small and untidy.

'I had always imagined Jerry kept you in more style,' I said idly.

'He doesn't keep me. I pay for this place. He always wanted me to move, but I would never give up my own place,' she said sharply, but she could not be harsh for long, and began to laugh. 'Anyhow he always leaves before morning. He has his breakfast in the other house'; and she switched off the light on the disordered bed and chairs and came into my arms. The night had been so tense and sudden that we had no desire except to lie in one another's arms, and as we kissed a last time before turning to seek our sleep she whispered, 'If you want me during the night, don't be afraid to wake me up.'

The Russian ships had stopped and were lying off Cuba, the radio told us as she made coffee on the small gas stove beside the sink in the corner of the room the next morning. The danger seemed about to pass. Again the world breathed, and it looked foolish to have believed it had ever been threatened.

Jerry was coming back from Cork that evening, and we agreed as we kissed to let this day go by without meeting but to meet at five the next day in Gaffneys of Fairview.

The bicycle had gone from the hallway by the time I left. The morning met me as other damp cold Dublin mornings, the world almost restored already to the everyday. The rich uses we dreamed last night when it was threatened that we would put it to if spared were now forgotten, when again it lay all about us in such tedious abundance.

'Did Jerry notice or suspect anything?' I asked over the coal fire in Gaffneys when we met, both of us shy in our first meeting as separate persons after the intimacy of flesh.

'No. All he talked about was the Cuban business. Apparently, they were just as scared. They stayed up drinking all night in the hotel. He just had a terrible hangover.'

That evening we went to my room, and she was, in a calm and quiet way, completely free with her body, offering it as a gift, completely open. With the firelight leaping on the walls of the locked room, I said, 'There is no Cuba now. It is the first time, you and I,' but in my desire was too quick; 'I should have been able to wait,' but she took my face between her hands and drew it down. 'Don't worry. There will come a time soon enough when you won't have that trouble.'

'How did you first meet Jerry?' I asked to cover the silence.

'My father was mixed up in politics in a small way and he was friendly with Jerry; and then my father died while I was at the convent in Eccles Street. Jerry seemed to do most of the arranging at the funeral, and it seemed natural for him to take me out on those halfdays and Sundays that we were given free.'

'Did you know of his reputation?'

'Everybody did. It made him dangerous and attractive. And one Saturday halfday we went to this flat in an attic off Baggot Street. He must have borrowed it for the occasion for I've never been in it since. I was foolish. I knew so little. I just thought you lay in bed with a man and that was all that happened. I remember it was raining. The flat was right in the roof and there was the loud drumming of rain all the time. That's how it began. And it's gone on from there ever since.'

She drew me towards her, in the full openness of desire, but she quickly rose. 'I have to hurry. I have to meet Jerry at nine'; and the pattern of her thieving had been set.

Often when I saw her dress to leave, combing her hair in the big cane armchair, drawing lipstick across her rich curving lips in the looking glass, I felt that she had come with stolen silver to the room. We had dined with the silver, and now that the meal was ended she was wiping and shining the silver anew, replacing it in the black jewel case to be taken out and used again in Jerry's bed or at his table, doubly soiled; and when I complained she said angrily, 'What about it? He doesn't know.'

'At least you and Jerry aren't fouling up anybody.'

'What about his wife? You seem very moral all of a sudden.'

'I'm sorry. I didn't mean to,' I apologized, but already the bloom had gone from the first careless fruits, and we felt the responsibility enter softly, but definitely, as any burden.

'Why can't you stay another hour?'

'I know what'd happen in one of those hours,' she said spiritedly, but the tone was affectionate and dreamy, perhaps with the desire for children. 'I'd get pregnant as hell.'

'What should we do?'

'Maybe we should tell Jerry,' she said. It was my turn to be alarmed.

'What would we tell him?'

The days of Jerry's profligacy were over. Not only had he grown jealous but violent. Not long before, hearing that she had been seen in a bar with a man and not being able to find her, he had taken a razor and slashed the dresses in her wardrobe to ribbons.

'We could tell him everything,' she said without conviction. 'That we want to be together.'

'He'd go berserk. You know that.'

'He's often said that the one thing he feels guilty about is having taken my young life. That we should have met when both of us were young.'

'That doesn't mean he'll think me the ideal man for the job,' I said. 'They say the world would be a better place if we looked at ourselves objectively and subjectively at others, but that's never the way the ball bounces.'

'Well, what are we to do?'

'By telling Jerry about us, you're just using one relationship to break up another. I think you should leave Jerry. Tell him that you just want to start up a life of your own.'

'But he'll know that there's someone.'

'That's his problem. You don't have to tell him. We can stay apart for a while. And then take up without any fear, like two free people.'

'I don't know,' she said as she put on her coat. 'And then, after all that, if I found that you didn't want me, I'd be in a nice fix.'

'There'd be no fear of that. Where are you going tonight?'

'There's a dinner that a younger branch of the Party is giving. It's all right for me to go. They think it rather dashing of Jerry to appear with a young woman.'

'I'm not so sure. Young people don't like to see themselves caricatured either.'

'Anyhow I'm going,' she said.

'Will it be five in Gaffneys tomorrow?'

'At five, then,' I heard as the door opened and softly closed.

'Does Jerry suspect at all?' I asked her again another evening over Gaffneys' small coal fire.

'No. Not at all. Odd that he often was suspicious when nothing at all was going on and now that there is he suspects nothing. Only the other day he was asking about you. He was wondering what had become of you. It seemed so long since we had seen you last.'

Our easy thieving that was hardly loving, anxiety curbed by caution, appetite so luxuriously satisfied that it could not give way to the dreaming that draws us close to danger, was wearing itself naturally away when a different relationship was made alarmingly possible. Jerry was suddenly offered a lucrative contract to found a new radio/television network in Sierra Leone, and he was thinking of accepting. Ireland as a small nation with a history of oppression was suddenly becoming useful in the Third World.

'He goes to London the weekend after next for the interview and he'll almost certainly take it.'

'That means the end of his political career here.'

'There's not much further he can get here. It gives him prestige, a different platform, and a lot of cash.'

'How do you fit into this?'

'I don't know.'

'Does he want to take you with him?'

'He'll go out on his own first, but he says that as soon as he's settled there and sees the state of play that he wants me to follow him.'

'What'll you do?'

'I don't know,' she said in a voice that implied that I was now part of these considerations.

Slane was a lovely old village in the English style close to Dublin. One Sunday we had lunch at the one hotel, more like a village inn than a hotel, plain wooden tables and chairs, the walls and fireplaces simple black and white, iron scrapers on the steps outside the entrance. She had suggested that we go there the weekend Jerry was on interview in London. The country weekend, the walks along the wooded banks of the river, coming back to the hotel with sharp appetites to have one drink in the bar and then to linger over lunch, in the knowledge that we had the whole long curtained afternoon spread before us, was dream enough. But was it to be that simple? Did we know one another outside the carnal pleasures we shared, and were we prepared to spend our lives together in the good or nightmare they might bring? It was growing clearer that she wasn't sure of me and that I wasn't sure. So when the telegram came from the country I was almost glad of the usual drama and mysteriousness.

'Then that's goodbye to our poor weekend.' She handed me back the telegram in Gaffneys.

'It's only one weekend,' I protested. 'We'll have as many as we want once Jerry goes.'

'You remember when I wanted to tell Jerry that we were in love and you wouldn't have it? You said we didn't know one another well enough, and then when we can have two whole days together you get this telegram. How are we ever going to get to know one another except by being together?'

'Maybe we can still go?'

'No. Not if you are doubtful. I think you should go home.'

'Will you come back with me this evening?'

'I have to have dinner with Jerry.'

'When?'

'At eight.'

'We'll have time. We can take a taxi.'

'No, love.' She was quite definite.

'Will you meet me when I come back, then?' I asked uncertainly.

'Jerry comes back from London on Sunday.'

'On Monday, then?'

'All right, on Monday.' There was no need to say where or when. She even said, 'See you Monday,' to the barman's silent inquiry as we left, and he waved 'Have a nice weekend,' as he gathered in our glasses.

I was returning home: a last look at the telegram before throwing it away – an overnight bag, the ticket, the train – the old wheel turned

323

and turned anew, wearing my life away; but if it wasn't this wheel it would be another.

Rose, my stepmother, seemed glad to see me, smiling hard, speaking rapidly. 'We even thought you might come on the late train last night. We said he might be very well on that train when we heard it pass. We kept the kettle on till after the news, and then we said you'll hardly come now, but even then we didn't go to bed till we were certain you'd not come.'

'Is there something wrong?'

'No. There's nothing wrong.'

'What does he want me for?'

'I suppose he wants to see you. I didn't know there was anything special, but he's been worrying or brooding lately. I'm sure he'll tell you himself. And now you'll be wanting something to eat. He's not been himself lately,' she added conspiratorially. 'If you can, go with him, do your best to humour him.'

We shook hands when he came, but did not speak, and Rose and myself carried the burden of the conversation during the meal. Suddenly, as we rose at the end of the meal, he said, 'I want you to walk over with me and look at the walnuts.'

'Why the walnuts?'

'He's thinking of selling the walnut trees,' Rose said. 'They've offered a great price. It's for the veneer, but I said you wouldn't want us to sell.'

'A lot you'd know about that,' he said to her in a half-snarl, but she covertly winked at me, and we left it that way.

'Was the telegram about the selling of the walnut trees, then?' I asked as we walked together towards the plantation. 'Sell anything you want as far as I'm concerned.'

'No. I have no intention of selling the walnuts. I threaten to sell them from time to time, just to stir things up. She's fond of those damned walnuts. I just mentioned it as an excuse to get out. We can talk in peace here,' he said, and I waited.

'You know about this Act they're bringing in?' he began ponderously.

'No.'

'They're giving it a first reading, but it's not the law yet.'

'What is this Act?'

'It's an Act that makes sure that the widow gets so much of a man's property as makes no difference after he's dead – whether *he* likes it or not.'

'What's this got to do with us?'

'You can't be that thick. I'll not live for ever. After this Act who'll get this place? Now do you get my drift? Rose will. And who'll Rose give it to? Those damned relatives will be swarming all over this place before I'm even cold.'

'How do you know that?' I was asking questions now simply to gain time to think.

'How do I know?' he said with manic grievance. 'Already the place is disappearing fast beneath our feet. Only a few weeks back the tractor was missing. Her damned nephew had it. Without as much as by my leave. They forgot to inform me. And she never goes near them that there's not something missing from the house.'

'That's hardly fair. It's usual to share things round in the country. She always brought more back than she took.'

I remembered the baskets of raspberries and plums she used to bring back from their mountain farm.

'That's right. Don't take my word for it,' he shouted. 'Soon you'll know.'

'But what's this got to do with the telegram?' I asked, and he quietened.

'I was in to see Callan the solicitor. That's why I sent the telegram. If I transfer the place to you before that Act becomes law, then the Act can't touch us. Do you get me now?'

I did – too well. He would disinherit Rose by signing the place over to me. I would inherit both Rose and the place if he died.

'You won't have it signed over to you, then?'

'No, I won't. Have you said any of this to Rose?'

'Of course I haven't. Do you take me for a fool or something? Are you saying to me for the last time that you won't take it?' And when I wouldn't answer he said with great bitterness, 'I should have known. You don't even have respect for your own blood,' and muttering, walked away towards the cattle gathered between the stone wall and the first of the walnut trees. Once or twice he moved as if he might turn back, but he did not. We did not speak any common language.

We avoided each other that evening, the tension making us

The Collected Stories

prisoners of every small movement, and the next day I tried to slip quietly away.

'Is it going you are?' Rose said sharply when she saw me about to leave.

'That's right, Rose.'

'You shouldn't pass any heed on your father. You should let it go with him. He won't change his ways now. You're worse than he is, not to let it go with him.'

For a moment I wanted to ask her, 'Do you know that he wanted to leave you at my sweet mercy after his death?' but I knew she would answer, 'What does that matter? You know he gets these ideas. You should let it go with him'; and when I said, 'Goodbye, Rose,' she did not answer.

As the train trundled across the bridges into Dublin and by the grey back of Croke Park, all I could do was stare. The weekend was over like a life. If it had happened differently it would still be over. Differently, we would have had our walks and drinks, made love in the curtained rooms, experimented in the ways of love, pretending we were taming instinct, imagining we were getting more out of it than had been intended, and afterwards . . . Where were we to go from there, our pleasure now its grinning head? And it would be over and not over. I had gone home instead, a grotesquerie of other homegoings, and it too was over now.

She would have met him at the airport, they would have had dinner, and if their evenings remained the same as when I used to meet them together they would now be having drinks in some bar. As the train came slowly into Amiens Street, I suddenly wanted to find them, to see us all together. They were not in any of the Grafton Street bars, and I was on the point of giving up the impulse – with gratitude that I hadn't been able to satisfy it – when I found them in a hotel lounge by the river. They were sitting at the counter, picking at a bowl of salted peanuts between their drinks. He seemed glad to see me, getting off his stool, 'I was just saying here how long it is since we last saw you,' in his remorseless slow voice, as if my coming might lighten an already heavy-hanging evening. He was so friendly that I could easily have asked him how his interview had gone, amid the profusion of my lies, forgetting that I wasn't supposed to know.

326

'I've just come from London. We've had dinner at the airport.' He began to tell me all that I already knew.

'And will you take this job?' I asked after he had told me at length about the weekend, without any attempt to select between details, other than to put the whole lot in.

'It's all arranged. It'll be in the papers tomorrow. I leave in three weeks' time,' he said.

'Congratulations,' I proffered uneasily. 'But do you have any regrets about leaving?'

'No. None whatever. I've done my marching stint and speeching stint. Let the young do that now. It's my time to sit back. There comes a time of life when your grapefruit in the morning is important.'

'And will her ladyship go with you?'

'I'll see how the land lies first, and then she'll follow. And by the way,' he began to shake with laughter and gripped my arm so that it hurt, 'don't you think to get up to anything with her while I'm gone.'

'Now that you've put it into my head I might try my hand.' I looked for danger but he was only enjoying his own joke, shaking with laughter as he rose from the bar stool. 'I better spend a penny on the strength of that.'

'That – was – mean,' she said without looking up.

'I suppose it was. I couldn't help it.'

'You knew we'd be around.'

'Will you see me tomorrow?'

'What do you think?'

'Anyhow, I'll be there.'

'How did your weekend in the country go?' she asked sarcastically.

'It went as usual, nothing but the usual,' I echoed her own sarcasm.

McCredy was still laughing when he came back. 'I've just been thinking that you two should be the young couple and me the uncle, and if you do decide to get up to something you must ask Uncle's dispensation first,' and he clapped me on the back.

'Well, I better start by asking now,' I said quickly in case my dismay would show, and he let out a bellow of helpless laughter. He must have been drinking, for he put his arms round both of us,

'I just love you two young people,' and tears of laughter slipped from his eyes. 'Hi, barman, give us another round before I die.'

I sat inside the partition in Gaffneys the next evening as on all other evenings, the barman as usual polishing glasses, nobody but the two of us in the bar.

'Your friend seems a bit later than usual this evening,' he said.

'I don't think she'll come this evening,' I said, and he looked at me inquiringly. 'She went down the country for the weekend. She was doubtful if she'd get back.'

'I hope there's nothing wrong . . .'

'No. Her mother is old. You know the way.' I was making for the safety of the roomy clichés.

'That's the sadness. You don't know whether to look after them or your own life.'

Before any pain of her absence could begin to hang about the opening and closing doors as the early evening drinkers bustled in, I got up and left; and yet her absence was certainly less painful than the responsibility of a life together. But what then of love? Love flies out the window, I had heard them say.

'She'll not come now,' I said.

'No. It doesn't seem,' he said as he took my glass with a glance in which suspicion equalled exasperation.

We did not meet till several weeks later. We met in Grafton Street, close to where we had met the first night. A little nervously she agreed to come for a drink with me. She looked quite beautiful, a collar of dark fur pinned to her raincoat.

'Jerry's in Sierra Leone now,' she said when I brought the drinks.

'I know. I read it in the papers.'

'He rang me last night,' she said. 'He was in the house of a friend – a judge. I could hear music in the background. I think they were a bit tight. The judge insisted he speak to me too. He had an Oxford accent. Very posh but apparently he's as black as the ace of spades,' she laughed. I could see that she treasured the wasteful call more than if it had been a gift of brilliant stones.

She began to tell me about Sierra Leone, its swamps and markets, the avocado and pineapple and cacao and banana trees, its crocodile-infested rivers. Jerry lived in a white-columned house with pillars on a hillside above the sea, and he had been given a chauffeur-driven Mercedes. She laughed when she told me that a native bride had to spend the first nine months of her marriage indoors so that she grew light-skinned.

'Will you be joining Jerry soon?' I asked.

'Soon. He knows enough people high up now to arrange it. They're getting the papers in order.'

'I don't suppose you'll come home with me tonight, then?'

'No.' There wasn't a hint of hesitation in the answer; difficulty and distance were obviously great restorers of the moral order. 'You must let me take you to dinner, then, before you leave. As old friends. No strings attached,' I smoothed. 'That'll be nice,' she said.

Out in Grafton Street we parted as easily as two leaves sent spinning apart by any sudden gust. All things begin in dreams, and it must be wonderful to have your mind full of a whole country like Sierra Leone before you go there and risk discovering that it might be your life.

Nothing seems ever to end except ourselves. On the eve of her departure for Sierra Leone, another telegram came from the country. There was nothing mysterious about it this time. Rose had died.

The overnight bag, the ticket, the train . . .

The iron gate under the yew was open and the blinds of the stone house at the end of the gravel were drawn. Her flower garden, inside the wooden gate in the low whitethorn hedge just before the house, had been freshly weeded and the coarse grass had been cut with shears. Who would tend the flowers now? I shook hands with everybody in the still house, including my father, who did not rise from the converted car chair.

I heard them go over and over what happened, as if by going over and over it they would return it to the everyday. 'Rose got up, put on the fire, left the breakfast ready, and went to let out the chickens. She had her hand on the latch coming in, when he heard this thump, and there she was lying, the door half-open.' And they were succeeding. They had to. She had too much of the day.

I went into the room to look on her face. The face was over too. If she had been happy or unhappy it did not show now. Would she have been happier with another? Who knows the person another will find their happiness or unhappiness with? Enough to say that weighed in this scale it makes little difference or every difference.

'Why don't you let it go with him?' I heard her voice. 'You know what he's like.' She had lived rooted in this one place and life, with this one man, like the black sally in the one hedge, as pliant as it is knobbed and gnarled, keeping close to the ground as it invades the darker corners of the meadows.

The coffin was taken in. The house was closed. I saw some of the mourners trample on the flowers as they waited in the front garden for her to be taken out. She was light on our shoulders.

Her people did not return to the house after the funeral. They had relinquished any hopes they had to the land.

'We seem to have it all to ourselves,' I said to my father in the empty house. He gave me a venomous look but did not reply for long.

'Yes,' he said. 'Yes. We seem to have it all to ourselves. But where do we go from here?'

Not, anyhow, to Sierra Leone. For a moment I saw the tall colonial building on a hill above the sea, its white pillars, the cool of the veranda in the evening . . . Maybe they were facing one another across a dinner table at this very moment, a servant removing the dishes.

Where now is Rose?

I see her come on a bicycle, a cane basket on the handlebars. The brakes mustn't be working for she has to jump off and run alongside the bicycle. Her face glows with happiness as she pulls away the newspaper that covers the basket. It is full of dark plums, and eggs wrapped in pieces of newspaper are packed here and there among the plums. Behind her there shivers an enormous breath of pure sky.

'Yes,' my father shouted. 'Where do we go from here?'

'I suppose we might as well try and stay put for a time,' I answered, and when he looked at me sharply I added, for the sake of my own peace, 'that is, until things settle a bit, and we can find our feet again, and think.'

The Conversion of William Kirkwood

There might well have been no other room in the big stone house but the kitchen, as the rain beat on the slates and windows, swirled about the yard outside. Dampened coats were laid against the foot of the back door, and the panelled oak door that led to the rest of the house was locked because of the faulty handle, the heavy key in the lock. A wood fire flickered in the open door of the huge old range which was freshly black-leaded, its brass fittings gleaming; and beside it Annie May Moran, servant to the Kirkwoods since she was fourteen, sat knitting a brown jersey for her daughter, occasionally bending down to feed logs to the range from a cane basket by her side. At the corner of the long deal table closest to the fire, William Kirkwood sat with her daughter Lucy, helping the child with school exercises. They were struggling more with one another than with algebra, the girl resisting every enticement to understand the use of symbols, but the man was endlessly patient. He spread coins out on the table, then an array of fresh walnuts, and finally took green cooking apples from a bucket. Each time he moved the coins, the nuts, the apples into separate piles she watched him with the utmost suspicion, but each time was forced into giving the correct answer to the simple subtraction by being made to count; but once he substituted x and y for the coins and fruit no number of demonstrations could elicit an answer, and when pressed she avoided understanding with wild guesses.

'You are just being stubborn, Lucy. Sticking your heels in, as usual,' he was forced at length to concede to her.

'It's all right for you, but I'm no good at maths,' she responded angrily.

'It's not that you're no good. It's that you don't want to understand. I don't know what's wrong with you. It seems almost a perversity.'

'I can't understand.'

'Now Lucy. You can't talk to Master William like that,' Annie

May said. She still called him Master William though he was now forty-five and last of the Kirkwoods.

'It's all right, Annie May. It'd be worth it all if we could get her to understand. She refuses to understand.'

'It's all right for you to say that, Master William.' Lucy laughed.

'Now, what's next?' he hurried her. 'English and church history?'

'English and catechism notes for tomorrow,' she corrected.

English she loved, and they raced through the exercises. She was tall and strong for her thirteen years and had boyish good looks. When they came to the doctrinal notes, it was plain that he was taking more interest in the exercises than the pupil. Through helping Lucy with these exercises in the evenings, he had first become interested in the Catholic Church. In a way, it had been the first step to his impending conversion. He smiled with pure affection on the girl as she tidied all her books into her leather satchel, and after the three had tea and buttered bread together she came into his arms to kiss him goodnight with the same naturalness as on every night since she had been a small child and he had read her stories. When Annie May unlocked the panelled door, a rush of cold met them from the rest of the house, and she hurried to take the hot water jar and the lighted candle in its blue tin holder to show the child to her upstairs room.

After Eddie Mac, herdsman to the Kirkwoods, as his father had been herdsman before that, had sold the pick of the Kirkwood cattle on the Green in Boyle and disappeared into England with the money, leaving Annie May pregnant, it was old William, William Kirkwood's father, who persuaded Annie May to stay and have the child in the house.

'Why should you have to go to England where you'll know nobody? You did no wrong. Stay and have the child here. We don't have to care what people think. We'll be glad of the child.'

Annie May never once thought of calling the girl by her own name, and she was named Lucy after a favourite aunt of the Kirkwoods. The girl grew strong and healthy, with her father's dark hair. She loved to shout in the big empty rooms of the stone house and to laugh with hands on hips as her voice was echoed back, the laugh then echoing hollowly again, voice and laugh closer to the clipped commanding accents of the Kirkwoods than to her mother's soft obscured speech, vowel melting into vowel. The old man and child were inseparable. Every good day they could be seen together going down to the orchard to look at the bees, she, clattering away like an alarmed bird, trying to hold his hand and hop on one foot at the same time, he, slow by her side, inscrutable behind the beekeeper's veil. And it was Lucy he sent to find William that final day when he wasn't able to lift the tops of the hives, imagining that they had all been stuck down by the bees. It was a sunny spring day. The bees were making cleansing flights from the hives.

'I can't understand it, William,' the beekeeper explained to his son when Lucy brought him to the hives.

'If the bees have stuck the roofs down, Father, we may need a hive tool. I'll try to twist them and ease them up slowly,' William said, but to his consternation found that the roof was loose in his hands and lifted easily. 'They're not stuck at all. They're quite free.' He began to laugh, only to fall into amazed silence when he saw that his father had grown too weak to lift the few boards of painted pine. Gently he led the old man and puzzled child back to the house.

'You must have caught something, Father. A few days in bed and you'll be fine.'

During that same windless spring night in which a light rain fell around the big house and its trees like a veil, the old beekeeper sank steadily, and near morning slipped as gently out of life as he had passed through.

Annie May wept bitterly for the old man, but Lucy was too young for grief and turned naturally to William. She started to go with him everywhere, about the sheds and out into the fields. She was as good as any boy at driving sheep and cattle. Annie May tried to put some curb on these travels, but Lucy was headstrong and hated housework. Besides, not only did William seem to like the girl's company in the fields but he often found her extremely useful. It was as a gesture of some recompense to Annie May for stealing the child's hours in the fields – as well as that of a naturally pedagogic nature – that led him to help Lucy from her early years with her school exercises in the winter evenings.

Except for his isolation with Annie May and Lucy in the stone house, the war found William Kirkwood little better off than his Catholic neighbours, poorer than some Catholics already on the rise. He had a drawing-room and library and lawn and orchard and spreading fields within stone walls, but the lawn was like a meadow and many of the books on the high shelves of the library had been damaged by the damp. The orchard was wild, his father's beehives rotting away unseen in the high grass at its foot. The many acres had been understocked and half farmed for too long, and there were broken gaps in the stone walls. Nearly all the other Protestant landowners, friends of his parents, presences in his youth, seeing the erosion of their old ascendancy, had emigrated to Canada, Australia, or moved to the North. William Kirkwood stayed, blessedly unaware that he had become a mild figure of fun, out watching the stars at night as a young man when he should have been partying with the Protestant blades or parading their confident women among the prize floral arrangements and cattle and horses and sheaves of barley of the shows; now struggling on miles of good land to support himself, an old servant woman and her illegitimate child. But this laughter was based on no knowledge of the man. It came from casual observation, complacent ignorance, simple prejudice, that lazy judgement that comes more easily than any sympathy, and it was to receive a severe jolt because of the war away in Europe. A neutral Ireland declared it *The Emergency*. Local defence forces were formed. William Kirkwood saw no division of loyalty and was among the first to join. He was given a commission, and the whole local view of him – humorous, derisory, patronizing – changed. He proved to be a crack marksman. He could read field maps at a glance.

His mother's father had been old Colonel Darby, half deaf, with a stiff leg and a devotion to gin, who was not much mentioned around the stone house because he had never let slip a single opportunity to pour sarcasm and insult on his gentle sober son-in-law, William's father. The Darbys had been British officers far back, and once William Kirkwood put on uniform it was as if they gathered to claim him. Men who had joined for the free army boots and uniform, for the three weeks in Finner Camp by the sea on full pay every summer, got an immediate shock. The clipped commands demanded instant compliance. A cold eye searched out every small disorder of dress or stance or movement. There were mutterings, 'Put one of them back on a horse and it's as if they never left the saddle. They'd ride you down like a dog,' but they had to admit that he was fair, and when he led the rifle team to overall victory in the first Western Shield, and was promoted Captain, Commanding Officer for the north of the county, a predictable pride stirred and slow praise, 'He's not as bad as he appears at first,' began to grow about his name.

Out of uniform he was as withdrawn as before and as useless on land. Lucy was with him everywhere still. Though school and church had softened her accent, it still held more than a hint of the unmistakable Protestant bark, and she took great pride in William's new uniform and rank. She had caused a disturbance at school by taking a stick and driving some boys from the ball alley who had sneered at William's Protestantism: 'He doesn't even go to his own church.'

'He has no church to go to. It was closed,' she responded and took up her stick.

Annie May had lost all control of her, and often William found himself ruling in favour of the mother, caught uncomfortably between them, but mostly Lucy did William's bidding. To be confined with her mother in the house was the one unacceptable punishment. To be with William in the fields was joy. She helped him all that poor wet summer at the hay. She could drive the horse-raker and was more agile than he. Beyond what work she did, and it was considerable, her presence by his side in the field was a deep sustenance. He shuddered to think of facing the long empty fields stretching ahead like heartache, the broken sky above, without her cheerful chatter by his side, her fierce energy.

And it seemed only right that she was by his side on the morning that the long isolation of the Kirkwoods ended.

The hay had been turned in the big rock meadow but rain was promised by evening. What lay ahead of them, even with the help of the horse-raker, was disheartening. They would have to try to save as much as they were able. What still lay on the ground by evening would have to take its chance of better weather. They could do no more.

Suddenly, there was a shout in the meadow, and Francie Harte came swaggering towards them. Francie had given William much trouble in the early days of the Force. He had been forever indulging in practical jokes.

'Is there anything wrong with me dress today, Captain?' he

335

shouted out as he came close. His walk was awkward because of the hayfork hidden behind his back.

'No, Francie. We are not in uniform today,' William Kirkwood replied mildly, not knowing what to make of the apparition. Then a cheer went up from behind the roadside hedge and the whole company of men swarmed into the field. Another man was opening the gate to let in an extra horse and raker. Haycocks started to spring up the field before the shouting, joking, cursing, jostling tide of men. Lucy was sent racing to the house to tell Annie May to start making sandwiches. William himself went to Charlie's for a half-barrel of porter. Long before night the whole field was swept clean. After the men had gone William Kirkwood walked the field, saw all the haycocks raked and tied down.

'That would take you and me most of a week, Lucy, and we'd probably lose half of it,' he said in his reflective way, almost humbly.

The promised rain arrived by evening. Its rhythmic beating on the slates brought him no anxiety. He heard it fall like heartsease and slept.

The same help arrived to bring the hay in from the fields, and they came for the compulsory wheat and root crops as well. Not even in the best years, when they could afford to take on plenty of labour, had the whole work of summer and harvest gone so easily. To return the favours, since none of the men would accept money, William Kirkwood had to go in turn to the other farms. Each time that she wasn't allowed to go with him Lucy was furious and sulked for days. He was no use at heavy labouring work on the farms, and he was never subjected to the cruelty of competition with other men, but he had an understanding of machinery that sometimes made him more useful than stronger men. As well as by his new military rank, he was protected by the position that the Kirkwoods had held for generations and had never appeared to abuse. He was a novelty in the fields, a source of talk and gossip against the relentless monotony of the work and days. His strangeness and gentle manners made him exceedingly popular with the girls and women, and the distance he always kept, like the unavailability of a young priest, only increased his attractiveness. After the years of isolation, he seemed very happy amid all the new bustle and, for the first time in years, he found that the land was actually making money. At Christmas he offered Annie May a substantial sum as a sort of reparation for the meagre pay she had been receiving unchanged for years. This she indignantly refused.

'It was pay enough for me to be let stay on here all these years without a word. I wouldn't ever want to insult you, but I'll throw that sort of money on the floor if you force it on me.'

'Well then, we'll take Lucy to the town. She's no longer a child. She needs a whole new outfit like the other girls.'

'Isn't she all right the way she is? All it'll do is give her notions. What'll notions do in her place but bring in trouble!'

She would take nothing for herself, but on Lucy she yielded. They went together to Boles. Annie May had never set foot in Boles before and she was awed into silence, starting with fright each time the pulleys sent the brass cups hurtling along the wires to the cashier in her glass case above in the shop, starting again each time the cups came crashing back with receipts and change. With much help from Mrs Boles, and the confused choices of Lucy, it was William himself who decided the outfit, old Boles all the time hovering around at the sight of the last of the Kirkwoods.

'I was only that height when I used see your dear mother come into the shop. Oh, she was a lady,' rubbing his hands, the eternal red rose in his buttonhole seemingly never affected by winter or summer.

'You look beautiful, Lucy, but I hate to see you growing up,' Wiliam complimented the girl simply. Lucy blushed and went to kiss him on the lips, but he found that he was hardly able to lift her into his arms.

The first Sunday she went to Mass and the rails in this outfit she created an even greater sensation than did William when he first stood as just another workman in one of his neighbour's fields.

The war ground on with little effect. The activities of the local Force were now routine: the three weeks in Finner Camp, rifle competitions, drill on Thursday evenings, rifle practice on Sunday afternoons – firing from the Oakport shore at targets set in the back of McCabe's Hill. On certain Sunday mornings the Force assembled in full dress at the Hall, marched through the village to the church, where they stood on guard in front of the altar during the sung Mass, presenting arms before and after the consecration. Captain Kirkwood marched his men through the village on these Sundays, but at the church door turned over his command to the school-teacher, Lieutenant McLoughlin, and remained outside until Mass had ended. Now that he had become such a part of the people it was felt that such a pointed difference was a little sad. This was brought up in bumbling fashion to William's face by Garda Sergeant Moran in Charlie's front room or parlour one Sunday after rifle practice. It was usual for the whole company to go to Charlie's for a drink after these Sunday practices. The men drank standing up behind the wooden partition that separated the bar from the grocery, but the two officers, Captain Kirkwood and Lieutenant McLoughlin, sat with the Garda Sergeant around the big oval table in the front room. The Sergeant attended these rifle practices to make sure that certain safety precautions were observed. He had been drinking after Mass, and had made a nuisance of himself at the practice, wandering around during firing looking for someone to talk to, but as he did not come under his command there was very little Captain Kirkwood could do. As soon as Charlie brought the whiskeys to the front room, the Sergeant began: 'Before the war, William, you were there on your own in that big house, helping nobody, getting no help. Now you're in with everybody. Only for your being a Protestant, there'd not be the slightest difference now between you and the rest of us. I fear it takes war to bring people to their senses.'

Lieutenant McLoughlin was searching furiously for some phrase to stifle the embarrassing speech, a verbal continuation of the nuisance they had been subjected to all day when William Kirkwood drily remarked, 'Actually, Sergeant, I'm seriously considering becoming a Catholic, but not, I'm afraid, in the interests of conformity,' which brought a stunned silence to the room even more embarrassing than the Sergeant's speech.

To remark that it was a little sad that such a pointed difference still stood out was polite weak sentiment; for William Kirkwood to turn Catholic was alarming. It broke the law that everybody stayed within the crowd they were born into, like the sparrows or blackbirds. They changed for a few reasons, and for those reasons only, money or position, mostly inseparable anyway, and *love*, if it can be called love when the instinct fastens on one person and will commit any madness to obtain its desire. Catholics had turned Protestant for money or position, it was an old sore and taunt; but the only reason a Protestant was ever known to turn was in order to marry. They had even a living effigy of it within the parish, the Englishman Sinclair, who had married one of the Conways, his poor wife telling the people in Boyle he had gone to Mass in Cootehall, then fibbing to the Cootehall people that he went to Mass in Boyle, when the whole world knew that he was at home toasting his shins and criticizing everything and everybody within sight: 'It was no rush of faith that led to my conversion. I was dragged into your Apostolic Roman Catholic Church by my male member,' he would shout and chuckle.

'How did it come about that *you* got interested . . . ?' McLoughlin asked William tentatively.

'Helping Lucy with her school exercises,' William answered readily. 'I became interested in some of the catechism answers, then church history. It's true it is the older church. I found books by Newman and the Oxford Movement in the library. My mother must have been interested once.'

'Still, it must be no joke turning your back on your own crowd, more or less saying that they were wrong all those centuries,' the Sergeant said.

'No. Not if one is convinced of the truth.' William pushed his glass away and rose. 'They lived according to their light. It is our day now.'

'Well, whatever you do, we hope it'll be for the best,' both men echoed as he left. William never took more than one drink and this had always been put down to Protestant abstemiousness.

'That's a lemoner for you. I'll need a good slow pint to get the better of that,' the Sergeant breathed when he had gone, and pressed the bell. They both had pints.

'What's behind it?' the Sergeant demanded.

'I'd not give you many guesses.'

'How?'

'It's fairly plain. I'd give you no more than one guess.'

'You have me beaten.'

'How did he get interested in Catholicism?'

'With Lucy and the catechism,' the Sergeant said in amazement. 'I should have seen it sooner. He took her to Boles before Christmas and dressed her like the Queen of Sheba, and she hardly fourteen!'

'In some ways Kirkwood is a very clever masterful man, but in other ways he is half a child. Lucy is not good at school but she's far from stupid and in many ways she's older than her years. She's more a Kirkwood to the bone than the daughter of poor old Annie May. Isn't she with him everywhere?'

'He couldn't marry her though.'

'Three or four years isn't that far away. Wouldn't it leave Annie May sitting pretty!'

'God, I'd never have thought of that in a hundred years.'

The news of the impending conversion was so strange that they kept it to themselves. On reflection they didn't quite believe it and wanted not to appear fools, but when William was seen walking the avenue of young lime trees to the presbytery every Tuesday and Thursday evening for mandatory instruction it became widespread. Miracles would never cease among the stars of heaven. William Kirkwood, last of the Kirkwoods, was about to renounce the error of their ways and become a Catholic.

Canon Glynn, the old priest, was perfectly suited to his place. He had grown up on a farm, was fond of cards and whiskey, but his real passion in life was for the purebred shorthorns he grazed on the church grounds. In public he was given to emphasizing the mercy rather than the wrath of God and in private believed that the affairs of the earth ran more happily the less God was brought into them. At first he found the visits of this odd catechumen a welcome break in his all too predictable evenings, but soon began to be worn out by his pupil's seemingly insatiable appetite for theological speculation. William was now pursuing Catholicism with the same zeal he had given for years to astronomy, reading every book on theology and church history he could lay hands on. Rather than be faced with this strenuous analysis of the Council of Trent, the old priest would have much preferred to have poured this over-intellectual childlike man a large glass of whiskey and to have talked about the five purebred shorthorns he was keeping over the winter and which he foddered himself in all weathers before saying daily Mass.

'Look, William. You already know far more about doctrine than any of my parishioners, and I've never seen much good come from all this probing,' he was driven to state one late evening. 'We are human. We cannot know God or Truth. It is shut away from our eyes. We can only accept and believe. It may be no more than the mother's instinct for the child, and as blind, but it is all we have. In two weeks' time, when I'll ask you "Do you believe?" all I want from you is the loud and clear response, "I do." There our part will end. Yours will begin. In my experience anything too much discussed and worried about always leads to staleness.'

William Kirkwood was far from blind. He understood at once that he had tired the old priest whom he had grown to like and respect. For the next two weeks, like the too obedient son he had always been, he was content to sit and follow wherever the priest's conversation led, which, after the second whiskey, was invariably to the five purebred shorthorns now grazing on the short sweet grass that grew above the ruins of the once famous eighth-century monastery.

'You can still see the monks' tracks everywhere in the fields, their main road or street, the cells, what must have been their stables, all like a plan on paper. Of course the walls of the main buildings still stand, but they are much later, twelfth century. Great minds thundered at one another there once. Now my shorthorns take their place. It is all good, William,' he would laugh.

At the end of the period of instruction, when the priest, a mischievous twinkle in his old eyes, asked, 'Do you accept and believe all those revealed truths and mysteries?' William Kirkwood smiled, bowed his head and said, 'I do, Father.'

The next morning, beside the stone font at the back of the Cootehall church, water was poured over the fine greying head of William Kirkwood. As it trickled down on to the brown flagstones, it must have seemed a final pale bloodletting to any ghosts of the Kirkwoods hovering in the air around.

Annie May and Lieutenant McLoughlin stood as his godparents. Afterwards there were smiles, handshakes, congratulatory armclasps, and after Mass a big festive breakfast in the presbytery, attended by all the local priests and teachers and prominent parishioners. Annie May and Lucy were there as well. The only flaw in the perfect morning was that Lucy looked pale and tense throughout and on the very verge of tears when having to respond to a few polite questions during the breakfast. She had been strange with William ever since he began instruction, as if she somehow sensed that this change threatened the whole secure world of her girlhood.

As soon as they got home from the breakfast, she burst into an uncontrollable fit of weeping and ran to her room. By evening she was better but would not explain her weeping, and that night was the first night in years that she did not come to him to be kissed on her way to bed. The following Sunday every eye was on the recent convert as he marched his men through the village and all the way up the church to the foot of the high altar. Lucy felt light-headed with pride as she saw him ascend the church at the head of his men. But the old ease between them had disappeared. She no longer wanted his help in the evenings with her exercises, preferring to go to school unprepared if necessary, and he did not try to force his help, waiting until this mood would pass.

'Now that you have come this far, and everything has gone so well, you might as well go the whole distance,' the Sergeant suggested with amiable vagueness one Sunday soon afterwards in Charlie's. Rifle practice had been abandoned early. A ricochet had somehow come off the hill, had struck a red bullock of Murphy's in the eye in a nearby field. The bullock, lowing wildly, began to stagger in circles round the field. A vet had to put it down. A report would have to be written. The accident had been the first in his command and William Kirkwood was inordinately annoyed. There must have been carelessness or wilful folly somewhere among the riflemen.

'What do you mean?' he asked very sharply.

'It was nothing about today,' McLoughlin interjected. 'I think the Sergeant was only trying to say what we all feel. Everything has gone wonderfully well and it would complete the picture if we were to see you married,' and both men saw William Kirkwood suddenly colour to the roots of his hair.

'I'm too old,' he said.

'You left it late but it's certainly far from too late.'

The conversation had brought on so much confusion that it was let drop. William left as usual after the one whiskey.

'I'm afraid you struck the mark there,' McLoughlin said as soon as they were alone.

'How?'

'You said what was plainly on his mind.'

'It's hardly Lucy.'

'Lucy's not in it at this stage, though she's upset enough at school about something or other,' the teacher said.

'What are we to do, then? We can't just go out and find any old bird for the last of the Kirkwoods. She'll have to be able to flap at least one good wing.'

'I suppose you'll be changing to pints now.' Charlie appeared at the doorway, and, without waiting for an answer, went and cleared the whiskey glasses from the table.

'A pair of pints, Charlie,' the Sergeant said exuberantly. 'Nothing decent ever stands alone. How long is it since we bundled you into the car that Sunday and found your good woman for you?'

'It must be the best part of five years, Sergeant,' Charlie laughed defensively, and when he laughed the tip of his small red nose wrinkled upwards in a curl.

'It was a drastic solution to a drastic problem. You had the place nearly drunk out after your mother died. The first six women we called on that Sunday turned us down flat.'

'I doubt they did right. I was no great catch.'

'We were about to give up for that Sunday when we called on Baby. She said before we finished, "I'll take him. I know the bar and the farm," and we brought you in out of the car.'

'Maybe that's when she made her big mistake,' Charlie tried to joke.

'She made no mistake,' the teacher put in gently, afraid that Charlie was being hurt by the Sergeant's egotism, oblivious of everything but his own part in that Sunday. 'She made the best move of her life. Look where you both are today – children, money. Who could want more?'

'Maybe it's as good as the other thing anyhow.' Charlie laughed with unchanged defensiveness.

'It's far better. This love business we hear so much about nowadays is a pure washout,' the teacher said definitively.

'One thing is sure,' the Sergeant said after Charlie had brought them the pints. 'We can't bundle William Kirkwood into the back of a car and drive *him* around for a whole Sunday until we find him a wife,' and at the very absurdity of the picture both men began to laugh until tears ran from their eyes, and they had to pound their glasses on the table. When they were quiet, the Sergeant said, 'There are more ways of choking a dog than with butter,' which renewed the laughter.

What they didn't know was that Charlie had been standing in the hallway all the time, rigid with anger as he listened. 'The pair of bitches,' he said quietly, his anger calming as he moved to face the men who were growing rowdy behind the wooden partition.

'What will we do about the Captain? He didn't seem averse to the idea,' the Sergeant was saying in the parlour.

'We can't, as you put it, bring in any old bird. We'll have to look hard and carefully. It'd be a very nice thing to see the Captain married.' The teacher was serious.

The first to be approached was Eileen Casey, the junior mistress in the school in Keadue. She was twenty-eight, small, with very blonde straight hair, fond of reading, pretty in a withdrawn way. Her headmaster, a friend of McLoughlin's, brought it up over the tea and sandwiches of the school lunch hour. When it was clear that she was not interested and was going out with a boy from her own place near Killala and was looking for a school closer to home so that they could marry, he pretended it had been nothing but a joke on his part. 'We like to see how these rich converts look in our girls' eyes.'

After this, the Sergeant and McLoughlin sat for a whole evening and compiled a list of girls. They were true to their word that they couldn't bring in just any old bird. All the girls they picked were local flowers, and they knew they faced the probability of many rebuffs, but they studied how to go about it as circuitously and discreetly as possible.

Before this got under way, William Kirkwood came to McLoughlin's bungalow to dinner for the first time. He felt ill at ease in the low rooms, the general cosiness, the sweet wine in cut glasses, and Mrs McLoughlin's attempts at polite conversation. Not in all the years of his Protestantism had he ever felt his difference so keenly. What struck him most was the absence of books in a schoolmaster's house. He disliked spirits after dinner, but this evening he was glad of the glass of whiskey in his hand as he faced McLoughlin in his front room while Mrs McLoughlin did the washing up. Around him, among the religious pictures and small statues, were all the heirlooms and photos of a married life that seemed to advance with resolute cheerfulness towards some sought-after stereotype. He was on edge, and when McLoughlin said, 'We've started looking,' he practically barked, 'For what?'

'For a good woman for you.' McLoughlin didn't notice the edge and smiled sweetly.

'Dear Peter . . . I had no idea . . . This is too ridiculous.' William Kirkwood was on his feet at once. 'It is positively antediluvian.' He had started to laugh dangerously. 'Fortunately, no one will have me. Imagine the embarrassment of some poor woman who was fool enough to have me when she found I couldn't abide her! I'd have to marry her. You couldn't do otherwise to any unfortunate two-legged.'

McLoughlin sat the outburst through in open-mouthed dismay. 'We thought you'd like to be married.'

'That's true. I would.'

He was even further taken aback by the positiveness of the ready response. 'Is there any person you had in mind yourself?' McLoughlin was glad to find any words on his lips.

'Yes. There is,' came even more readily still. 'But what's the use? She'd never have me.'

'May I ask who she is?'

'Of course you can. I was thinking of Miss Kennedy. Mary Kennedy.'

'Well then. I don't see why you had to get in such a state.' It was McLoughlin's turn to attack. 'She was the first girl we were thinking of approaching.'

McLoughlin was not so much surprised by the preference as by the fact that the solitary isolated 'odd' Kirkwood should have a preference at all.

The Kennedys were a large local family, had good rock land and part of the woods, owned a sawmill and a small adjoining factory making crates and huge wooden drums on which electric cable was rolled. They had been rich enough to send Mary and her sisters to the Ursulines in Sligo. There she was nicknamed 'big hips', more for her laughing vitality than measurements. From the Ursulines she went to train as a nurse in the Mater Hospital in Dublin. She was black-haired and tall, too sharp featured to be beautiful, but there was about her an excitement and vitality that was more than beauty. Even the way she had of scratching her head as she laughed, her wide stance, intrigued men. At the Mater, she fell in love with a pale young doctor, conscientious and dull, who was flattered at first, but gradually he backed away from her high

345

spirits. When he broke with her, she came home and hung listlessly about the house for six months, sometimes going for long solitary walks.

It was on one of those walks that William Kirkwood met her in his own fields. She had been surprised by a play of the late October light all the way across the top of the hill, and there being no purpose to her walk she had crossed the stone wall to follow the streak of evening along the hill. To William's polite inquiry, 'May I help you in any way, Miss Kennedy?' she had responded with a certain mischievousness – 'No, thank you, Mr Kirkwood. I'm just out for a walk' – because it was unheard of for a local person to be just out for a walk. Mary Kennedy was surprised to find the 'young Mr Kirkwood' that they used to laugh about when she was a child – the same Mr Kirkwood who spent all fine nights out in the fields studying the stars through a telescope and his days reading or in bed – a middle-aged man, tall and beautifully mannered certainly, but middle-aged. They chatted for a while before separating. She didn't think much about the meeting but, apart from the good manners, what she remembered most was his openness and lack of furtiveness. Furtiveness was what she found in most Irish men when faced with a young woman.

She returned to the Mater, but her confidence was broken and she had to school herself to meet the young doctor on the wards or along corridors, to smile and be polite when she felt like hiding or running. She saw with dull clarity that most women's social position in Ireland was decided for the rest of their lives by one single unfair throw of the dice, and she had too much of the Kennedys' sense of themselves to be interested in the young civil servants, policemen, and prison officers that were available to the other nurses. William Kirkwood felt that *he* should approach Mary Kennedy himself, but he knew too well that if left to his own devices he would think a great deal about it and do nothing.

'How did you propose to approach Miss Kennedy?' he asked McLoughlin.

'We didn't intend to put you into the back of a car and drive you round some fine Sunday anyhow.' McLoughlin was now in the ascendant. 'I know one of her brothers. If she has someone else or wasn't interested, that would be the end of it. The Kennedys do not talk. If on the other hand . . .' McLoughlin spread his hands in a gesture that meant that all things were possible.

Mary Kennedy listened carefully to the proposal her brother brought. She had suffered and was close to the age of reconcilement. The tide was not lingering.

She recalled the meeting in the fields. The few times they had met since then he had smiled and saluted in passing. There was the big stone house in its trees, the walled orchard, the avenue, the lawn, the spreading fields . . . no mean setting.

A boast she had made carelessly once among girls came back to her. Love was not important, she had declared. She would love whichever man she married, whether she loved him or not before they married. This could be tested at last. She told her brother that she would meet William Kirkwood but could promise nothing.

They met in the Wicklow Hotel and had dinner there. She wore a suit of black corduroy with a plain silver necklace and was more at ease than he with the formalities of dinner.

'I was surprised you knew my name the time we met in the fields,' she said.

'That's quite simple. I admired you and asked your name. But you knew my name?'

'There was only one Mr Kirkwood. There are many Kennedys.' She smiled back.

When she saw him waiting for her later in the hotel foyer, the worn but well-cut blue pinstripe, the thick, lank grey hair, the jutting Anglo-Irish jaw, the military appearance of alertness, she knew that he was superior to most men she was likely to come on in the city, and she noticed how soft and long his hands were from years of gentle living. The hands of her own brothers were already large and coarse by comparison. They had two other meetings in the city before she agreed to come down and look over the big stone house and its grounds, but she had already made up her mind that she would marry William Kirkwood.

The first sight Annie May had of her the Sunday she came to the house was standing beneath the copper beech on the front avenue. A handbag hung from her shoulder. William Kirkwood was smiling on her. The flurry of the past weeks, the visits to Dublin, the need for ironed shirts and polished shoes fell into place. The pain that filled her chest climbed into a tight band about her forehead. That there was no one to blame, that it was in the natural order of things only made it more painful. She couldn't even be angry.

They came to the big kitchen by way of the front door, looking in on the library and drawing-room, and Annie May heard her admiring the stairs.

'What is this room with all the marble?' she heard her ask as they drew closer.

'It's just a pantry now. In the old days it was the flower-cutting room . . . where the roses were cut.'

When they came through the door, there was nothing but smiles and handshakes, but it was extremely tense. If William Kirkwood knew more of human nature, he would have seen that the two women were territorial enemies.

'Where's Lucy?' he asked.

'I don't know. She was here up to a minute ago,' Annie May said and offered to make tea.

'I'd love a cup of tea,' Mary Kennedy said. 'But first I'd like to see the upstairs rooms.'

While they were taking tea, after having spent a long time walking through the upstairs rooms, darkness fell but still there was no sight of Lucy.

'She must have gone outside,' Annie May said worriedly, her own anxiety already transferred to the child.

William Kirkwood walked Mary Kennedy over the fields to the road that led to her house. When they got to the house, it was full of the Kennedys and their families, most of whom William was meeting for the first time. It was a pleasant evening, and by its end it was clear to Mary that both William Kirkwood and the match were approved of. For his part, he liked the big old ramshackle farmhouse, the crowd of people, the lashings of food and whiskey, the natural cheerfulness of people enjoying themselves, the absence of formality and selfconsciousness, reminding him more of political celebration than a family evening. When he left, Mary walked with him to the avenue. On the walk she kissed him for the first time. She was planning the wedding for June. The house would have to be painted, new curtains bought, some new furniture chosen. 'The whole house will have to be opened up again. As it stands, the kitchen is the only room that looks lived in.'

As he walked with her, he felt that the night was bathed in a dream of happiness, and would start in disbelief that this tall elegant high-spirited woman was about to become his wife. For her part, she felt that her girlish boast was coming true. She knew that she was going to love this strange man who spoke terms of endearment as if they were commands. 'Venus, Mars, Saturn, Jupiter to the east over there.' He was barking out the names in the clear sky, and she had to bite back laughter. She knew of men less knowledgeable about the stars who would be able to turn them to better advantage, but she would take care of that in her own time.

'There's one thing more,' she said before they parted. 'Annie May will have to be given notice.'

'That I could never do,' he said with such vehemence that it took her back. 'She came as a very young girl to work for my mother. Lucy was born here, grew up here. I could never tell them to leave.'

When she saw how disturbed he was, she put her hand on his arm. 'Don't worry, love. You'll not have to do anything. I doubt very much if Annie May will want to stay once she hears I am moving into the house in June.'

They were both standing still at the gate, and she turned and raised her lips to his, and he, feeling her body stir against his, took her into his arms.

His own house was in darkness when he got home. He knew the back door was unlocked, but rather than go through the empty kitchen he let himself in by the front door with his key. There he sat for a long time in the cold of the library. He had many things to think about, and not least among them was this: whether there was any way his marriage could take place without bringing suffering on two people who had been a great part of his life, who had done nothing themselves to deserve being driven out into a world they were hardly prepared for.

Bank Holiday

It had been unusual weather, hot for weeks, and the white morning
mist above the river, making ghostly the figures crossing the metal
bridge, seemed a certain promise that the good weather was going
to last beyond the holiday. All week in the Department he had
heard the girls talking of going down the country, of the ocean, and
the dances in the carnival marquees. Already, across the river,
queues were forming for the buses that went to the sea – Howth,
Dollymount, Malahide. He, Patrick McDonough, had no plans for
the holiday, other than to walk about the city, or maybe to go out
into the mountains later. He felt a certain elation of being loose in
the morning, as if in space. The solid sound of his walking shoes on
the pavement seemed to belong to someone else, to be going
elsewhere.

A year ago he had spent this holiday in the country, among the
rooms and fields and stone walls he had grown up with, as he had
spent it every year going back many years. His mother was still
living, his father had died the previous February. The cruellest
thing about that last holiday was to watch her come into the house
speaking to his father of something she had noticed in the yard – a
big bullfinch feeding on the wild strawberries of the bank, rust
spreading in the iron of one of the sheds – and then to see her
realize in the midst of speech that her old partner of the guaranteed
responses was no longer there. They had been close. His father had
continued to indulge her once great good looks long after they had
disappeared.

That last holiday he had asked his mother to come and live with
him in the city, but she had refused without giving it serious
thought. 'I'd be only in the way up there. I could never fit in with
their ways now.' He had gone down to see her as often as he was
able to after that, which was most weekends, and had paid a local
woman to look in on her every day. Soon he saw that his visits no
longer excited her. She had even lost interest in most of the things

around her, and whenever that interest briefly gleamed she turned not to him but to his dead father. When pneumonia took her in a couple of days just before Christmas, and her body was put down beside her husband's in Aughawillian churchyard, he was almost glad. The natural wind now blew directly on him.

He sold the house and lands. The land had been rich enough to send him away to college, not rich enough to bring him back other than on holiday, and now this holiday was the first such in years that he had nowhere in particular to go, no one special to see, nothing much to do. As well as the dangerous elation this sense of freedom gave, he looked on it with some of the cold apprehension of an experiment.

Instead of continuing on down the quays, he crossed to the low granite wall above the river and stayed a long time staring down through the vaporous mist at the frenzy and filth of the low tide. He could have stood mindlessly there for most of the morning but he pulled himself away and continued on down the quays until he turned into Webb's Bookshop.

The floor in Webb's had been freshly sprinkled and swept, but it was dark within after the river light. He went from stack to stack among the secondhands until he came on a book that caught his interest, and he began to read. He stood there a long time until he was disturbed by the brown-overalled manager speaking by his side.

'Would you be interested in buying the book, sir? We could do something perhaps about the price. The books in this stack have been here a long time.' He held a duster in his hand, some feathers tied round the tip of a cane.

'I was just looking.'

The manager moved away, flicking the feathers along a row of spines in a gesture of annoyance. The spell was ended, but it was fair enough; the shop had to sell books, and he knew that if he bought the book it was unlikely that he would ever give it the same attention again. He moved to the next stack, not wanting to appear driven from the shop. He pretended to inspect other volumes. He lifted and put down *The Wooing of Elisabeth McCrum*, examining other books cursorily, all the time moving towards the door. It was no longer pleasant to remain. He tried to ignore the manager's stare as he went out, to find himself in blinding sunshine on the pavement. The mist had completely lifted. The day was uncomfortably hot. His early excitement and sense of freedom had disappeared.

Afterwards he was to go over the little incident in the bookshop. If it had not happened would he have just ventured again out into the day, found the city too hot for walking, taken a train to Bray as he thought he might and walked all day in the mountains until he was dog-tired and hungry? Or was this sort of let-down the inescapable end of the kind of elation he had felt walking to the river in the early morning? He would never know. What he did know was that once outside the bookshop he no longer felt like going anywhere, and he started to retrace his steps back to where he lived, buying a newspaper on the way. When he opened the door a telegram was lying on the floor of the hallway.

It was signed 'Mary Kelleher', a name he didn't know. It seemed that a very old friend, James White, who worked for the Tourist Board in New York, had given her his name. There was a number to call.

He put it aside to sit and read through the newspaper, but he knew by the continuing awareness of the telegram on the table that he would call. He was now too restless to want to remain alone.

James White and he had met when they were both young civil servants, White slightly the older – though they both seemed the same age now – the better read, the more forthright, the more sociable. They met at eight-thirty on the Friday night of every week for several years, the evening interrupted only by holidays and illnesses, proof against girlfriends, and later wives, ended only by White's transfer abroad. They met in bars, changing only when they became known to the barmen or regulars and in danger of losing their anonymity. They talked about ideas, books, 'the human situation', and 'reality and consciousness' often surfaced with the second or third pint. Now he could hardly remember a sentence from those hundreds of evenings. What he did remember was a barman's face, white hair drawn over baldness, an avid follower of Christy Ring; a clock, a spiral iron staircase to the Gents, the cold of marble on the wristbone, footsteps passing outside in summer, the sound of heavy rain falling before closing time. The few times they had met in recent years they had both spoken of nothing but people and happenings, as if those early meetings were some deep embarrassment: they had leaned on them too heavily once and were now like lost strength.

He rang. The number was that of a small hotel on the quays. Mary Kelleher answered. He invited her to lunch and they arranged to meet in the hotel foyer. He walked to the hotel, and as he walked he felt again the heady, unreal feeling of moving in an umblemished morning, though it was now past midday.

When she rose to meet him in the foyer, he saw that she was as tall as he. A red kerchief with polka dots bound her blonde hair. She was too strong-boned to be beautiful but her face and skin glowed. They talked about James White. She had met him at a party in New York. 'He said that I must meet you if I was going to Dublin. I was about to check out of the hotel when you rang.' She had relations in Dundalk she intended to look up. Trinity College had manuscripts she wanted to see. They walked up Dame Street and round by the Trinity Railings to the restaurant he had picked in Lincoln Place. She was from Mount Vernon, New York, but had been living in Chicago, finishing her doctorate in medieval poetry at the University of Chicago. There were very pale hairs on the brown skin of her legs and her leather sandals slapped as she walked. When she turned her face to his, he could see a silver locket below the line of the cotton dress.

Bernardo's door was open on to the street, and all but two of the tables were empty.

'Everybody's out of town for the holiday. We have the place to ourselves.' They were given a table for four just inside the door. They ordered the same things, melon with Parma ham, veal Milanese, a carafe of chilled white wine. He urged her to have more, to try the raspberries in season, the cream cake, but she ate carefully and would not be persuaded.

'Do you come here often?' she asked.

'Often enough. I work near here, round the corner, in Kildare Street. An old civil servant.'

'You don't look the part at all, but James White did say you worked in the civil service. He said you were quite high up.' She smiled teasingly. 'What do you do?'

'Nothing as exciting as medieval poetry. I deal in law, industrial law in particular.'

'I can imagine that to be quite exciting.'

'Interesting maybe, but mostly it's a job – like any other.'

'Do you live in the city, or outside?'

'Very near here. I can walk most places, even walk to work.' And when he saw her hesitate, as if she wanted to ask something and did not think it right, he added, 'I have a flat. I live by myself there, though I was married once.'

'Are you divorced? Or am I allowed to ask that?'

'Of course you are. Divorce isn't allowed in this country. We are separated. For something like twenty years now we haven't laid eyes on one another. And you? Do you have a husband or friend?' he changed the subject.

'Yes. Someone I met at college, but we have agreed to separate for a time.'

There was no silence or unease. Their interest in one another already far outran their knowledge. She offered to split the bill but he refused.

'Thanks for the lunch, the company,' she said as they faced one another outside the restaurant.

'It was a pleasure,' and then he hesitated and asked, 'What are you doing for the afternoon?' not wanting to see this flow that was between them checked, though he knew to follow it was hardly wise.

'I was going to check tomorrow's trains to Dundalk.'

'We could do that at Westland Row around the corner. I was wondering if you'd be interested in going out to the sea where the world and its mother is in this weather?'

'I'd love to,' she said simply.

It was with a certain relief that he paid the taxi at the Bull Wall. Lately the luxury and convenience of a taxi had become for him the privilege of being no longer young, of being cut off from the people he had come from, and this was exasperated by the glowing young woman by his side, her eager responses to each view he pointed out, including the wired-down palms along the front.

'They look so funny. Why is it done?'

'It's simple. So that they will not be blown away in storms. They are not natural to this climate.'

He took off his tie and jacket as they crossed the planks of the wooden bridge, its legs long and stork-like in the retreated tide. The rocks that sloped down to the sea from the Wall were crowded with

354

people, most of them in bathing costumes, reading, listening to transistors, playing cards, staring out to sea, where three tankers appeared to be nailed down in the milky distance. The caps of the stronger swimmers bobbed far out. Others floated on their backs close to the rocks, crawled in sharp bursts, breast-stroked heavily up and down a parallel line, blowing like walruses as they trod water.

'I used to swim off these rocks once. I liked going in off the rocks because I've always hated getting sand between my toes. Those lower rocks get covered at full tide. You can see the tidal line by the colour.'

'Don't you swim any more?'

'I haven't in years.'

'If I had a costume I wouldn't mind going in.'

'I think you'd find it cold.'

She told him of how she used to go out to the ocean at the Hamptons with her father, her four brothers, their black sheep Uncle John who had made a fortune in scrap metal and was extremely lecherous. She laughed as she recounted one of Uncle John's adventures with an English lady.

When they reached the end of the Wall, they went down to the Strand, but it was so crowded that they had to pick their way through. They moved out to where there were fewer people along the tide's edge. It was there that she decided to wade in the water, and he offered to hold her sandals. As he walked with her sandals, a phrase came without warning from the book he had been reading in Webb's: 'What is he doing with his life, we say: and our judgement makes up for the failure to realize sympathetically the natural process of living.' He must indeed be atrophied if a casual phrase could have more presence for him than this beautiful young woman, and the sea, and the day. The dark blue mass of Howth faced the motionless ships on the horizon, seemed to be even pushing them back.

'Oh, it's cold.' She shivered as she came out of the water, and reached for her sandals.

'Even in heatwaves the sea is cold in Ireland. That's Howth ahead – where Maud Gonne waited at the station as Pallas Athena.' He reached for his role as tourist guide.

'I know that line,' she said and quoted the verse. 'Has all that gone from Dublin?'

'In what way?'

'Are there . . . poets . . . still?'

'Are there poets?' he laughed out loud. 'They say the standing army of poets never falls below ten thousand in this unfortunate country.'

'Why unfortunate?' she said quickly.

'They create no wealth. They are greedy and demanding. They hold themselves in very high opinion. Ten centuries ago there was a national convocation, an attempt to limit their powers and numbers.'

'Wasn't it called *Drum* something?'

'*Drum Ceat*,' he added, made uneasy by his own attack.

'But don't you feel that they have a function – beyond wealth?' she pursued.

'What function?'

'That they sing the tired rowers to the hidden shore?'

'Not in the numbers we possess here, one singing down the other. But maybe I'm unkind. There are a few.'

'Are these poets to be seen?'

'They can't even be hidden. Tomorrow evening I could show you some of the pubs they frequent. Would you like that?'

'I'd like that very much,' she said, and took his hand. A whole day was secured. The crowds hadn't started to head home yet, and they travelled back to the city on a nearly empty bus.

'What will you do for the rest of the evening?'

'There's some work I may look at. And you? What will you do?'

'I think I'll rest. Unpack, read a bit.' She smiled as she raised her hand.

He walked slowly back, everything changed by the petty confrontation in Webb's, the return to the flat, the telegram in the hallway. If he had not come back, she would be in Dundalk by now, and he would be thinking about finding a hotel for the night somewhere round Rathdrum. In the flat, he went through notes that he had made in preparation for a meeting he had with the Minister the coming week. They concerned an obscure section of the Industries Act. Though they were notes he had made himself he found them extremely tedious, and there came on him a restlessness like that which sometimes heralds illness. He felt like going out to a cinema or bar, but knew that what he really wanted to do was to ring Mary Kelleher. If he had learned anything over the years it was the habit of discipline. Tomorrow would bring itself. He would wait for it if necessary with his mind resolutely fixed on its own blankness, as a person prays after fervour has died.

'Section 13, paragraph 4, states clearly that in the event of confrontation or disagreement . . .' he began to write.

The dress of forest green she was wearing when she came down to the lobby the next evening caught his breath; it was shirtwaisted, belling out. A blue ribbon hung casually from her fair hair behind.

'You look marvellous.'

The Sunday streets were empty, and the stones gave out a dull heat. They walked slowly, loitering at some shop windows. The doors of all the bars were open, O'Neills and the International and the Olde Stand, but they were mostly empty within. There was a sense of a cool dark waiting in Mooney's, a barman arranging ashtrays on the marble. They ordered an assortment of sandwiches. It was pleasant to sit in the comparative darkness, and eat and sip and watch the street, and to hear in the silence footsteps going up and down Grafton Street.

It was into this quiet flow of the evening that the poet came, a large man, agitated, without jacket, the shirt open, his thumbs hooked in braces that held up a pair of sagging trousers, a brown hat pushed far back on his head. Coughing harshly and pushing the chair around, he sat at the next table.

'Don't look around,' McDonough leaned forward to say.

'Why?'

'He'll join us if we catch his eye.'

'Who is he?'

'A poet.'

'He doesn't look like one.'

'That should be in his favour. All the younger clerks that work in my place nowadays look like poets. He is the best we have. He's the star of the place across the road. He's practically resident there. He must have been thrown out.'

The potboy in his short white coat came over to the poet's table and waited impassively for the order.

'A Powers,' the order came in a hoarse, rhythmical voice. 'A large Powers and a pint of Bass.'

There was more sharp coughing, a scraping of feet, a sigh, muttering, a word that could have been a prayer or a curse. His agitated presence had more the sound of a crowd than the single person sitting in a chair. After the potboy brought the drinks and was paid, the poet swung one leg vigorously over the other, and with folded arms faced away towards the empty doorway. Then, as suddenly, he was standing in front of them. He had his hand out. There were coins in the hand.

'McDonough,' he called hoarsely, thrusting his palm forward. 'Will you get me a packet of Ci-tanes from across the road?' He mispronounced the brand of French cigarettes so violently that his meaning was far from clear.

'You mean the cigarettes?'

'Ci-tanes,' he called hoarsely again. 'French fags. Twenty. I'm giving you the money.'

'Why don't you get them here?'

'They don't have them here.'

'Why don't you hop across yourself?'

'I'm barred,' he said dramatically. 'They're a crowd of ignorant, bloody apes over there.'

'All right. I'll get them for you.' He took the coins but instead of rising and crossing the road he called the potboy.

'Would you cross the road for twenty Gitanes for me, Jimmy? I'd cross myself but I'm with company,' and he added a large tip of his own to the coins the poet had handed over.

'It's against the rules, sir.'

'I know, but I'd consider it a favour,' and they both looked towards the barman behind the counter who had been following every word and move of the confrontation. The barman nodded that it was all right, and immediately bent his head down to whatever he was doing beneath the level of the counter, as if to disown his acquiescence.

Jimmy crossed, was back in a moment with the blue packet.

'You're a cute hoar, McDonough. You're a mediocrity. It's no wonder you get on so well in the world,' the poet burst out in a wild fury as he was handed the packet, and he finished his drinks in a few violent gulps, and stalked out, muttering and coughing.

'That's just incredible,' she said.

'Why?'

'You buy the man his cigarettes, and then get blown out of it. I don't understand it.'

'It wasn't the cigarettes he wanted.'

'Well, what did he want?'

'Reassurance, maybe, that he still had power, was loved and wanted after having been turfed out across the way. I slithered round it by getting Jimmy here to go over. That's why I was lambasted. He must have done something outrageous to have been barred. He's a tin god there. Maybe I should have gone over after all.'

'Why didn't you?'

'Vanity. I didn't want to be his messenger boy. He could go and inflate his great mouse of an ego somewhere else. To hell with him. He's always trouble.' She listened in silence as he ended. 'Wouldn't it be pleasant to be able to throw people their bones and forget it?'

'You might have to spend an awful lot of time throwing bones if the word got around.' She smiled as she sipped her glass of cider.

'Now that you've seen the star, do you still wish to cross the road and look in on the other pub?'

'I'm not sure. What else could we do?'

'We could go back to my place.'

'I'd like that. I'd much prefer to see how you live.'

'Why don't we look in across the road, have one drink if it's not too crowded,' and he added some coins to the change still on the table. 'It was very nice of them to cross for the Gitanes. They're not supposed to leave their own premises.'

The door of the bar across the way was not open, and when he pushed it a roar met them like heat. The bar was small and jammed. A red-and-blue tint from a stained glass window at the back mixed weirdly with the white lights of the bar, the light of evening from the high windows. A small fan circled helplessly overhead, its original white or yellow long turned to ochre by cigarette smoke. Hands proffered coins and notes across shoulders to the barmen behind the horseshoe counter. Pints and spirit glasses were somehow eased from hand to hand across the three-deep line of shoulders at the counter the way children that get weak are taken out of a crowd. The three barmen were so busy that they seemed to dance.

'What do you think?' he asked.

359

'I think we'll forget it.'

'I always feel a bit apprehensive going in there,' he admitted once they were out on the street again.

'I know. Those places are the same everywhere. For a moment I thought I was in New York at the Cedar Bar.'

'What makes them the same?'

'I don't know. Mania, egotism, vanity, aggression . . . people searching madly in a crowd for something that's never to be found in crowds.'

She was so lovely in the evening that he felt himself leaning towards her. He did not like the weakness. 'I find myself falling increasingly into an unattractive puzzlement,' he said, 'mulling over that old, useless chestnut, What *is* life?'

'It's the fact of being alive, I suppose, a duration of time, as the scholars would say,' and she smiled teasingly. 'Puzzling out what it is must be part of it as well.'

'You're too young and beautiful to be so wise.'

'That sounds a bit patronizing.'

'That's the last thing I meant it to be.'

He showed her the rooms, the large living-room with the oak table and worn red carpet, the brass fender, the white marble of the fireplace, the kitchen, the two bedrooms. He watched her go over the place, lift the sea shell off the mantelpiece, replace it differently.

'It's a lovely flat,' she said, 'though Spartan to my taste '

'I bought the place three years ago. I disliked the idea of owning anything at first, but now I'm glad to have it. Now, would you like a drink, or perhaps some tea?'

'I'd love some tea.'

When he returned he found her thumbing through books in the weakening light.

'Do you have any of the poet's work?'

'You can have a present of this, if you like.' He reached and took a brown volume from the shelf.

'I see it's even signed,' she said as she leafed through the volume. 'For Patrick McDonough, With love,' and she began to laugh.

'I helped him with something once. I doubt if he'd sign it with much love this evening.'

'Thanks,' she said as she closed the volume and placed it in her handbag. 'I'll return it. It wouldn't be right to keep it.' After several minutes of silence, she asked, 'When do you have to go back to your office?'

'Not till Tuesday. Tomorrow is a Bank Holiday.'

'And on Tuesday what do you do?'

'Routine. The Department really runs itself, though many of us think of ourselves as indispensable. In the afternoon I have to brief the Minister.'

'On what, may I ask?'

'A section of the Industries Act.'

'What is the Minister like?'

'He's all right. An opportunist, I suppose. He has energy, certainly, and the terrible Irish gift of familiarity. He first came to the fore by putting parallel bars on the back of a lorry. He did handstands and somersaults before and after speeches, to the delight of the small towns and villages. Miss Democracy thought he was wonderful and voted him in top of the poll. He's more statesmanlike now of course.'

'You don't sound as if you like him very much.'

'We're stuck with one another.'

'Were you upset when your marriage failed?' she changed.

'Naturally. In the end, there was no choice. We couldn't be in the same room together for more than a couple of minutes without fighting. I could never figure out how the fights started, but they always did.'

'Did you meet anyone else?'

'Nothing that lasted. I worked. I visited my parents until they died. Those sort of pieties are sometimes substitutes for life in this country – or life itself. We're back to the old subject and I'm talking too much.'

'No. I'm asking too many questions.'

'What'll you do now that you have your doctorate?'

'Teach. Write. Wait on tables. I don't know.'

'And your husband or friend?'

'Husband,' she said. 'We were married but it's finished. We were too young.'

'Would you like more tea, or for me to walk you back to the Clarence? . . . Or would you like to spend the night here?'

She paused for what seemed an age, and yet it could not have been more than a couple of moments.

'I'd like to spend the night here.'

He did not know how tense his waiting had been until he felt the release her words gave. It was as if blank doors had slid back and he was being allowed again into the mystery of a perpetual morning, a morning without blemish. He knew it by now to be an old con trick of nature, and that it never failed, only deepened the irony and the mystery. 'I'll be able to show you the city tomorrow. You can check out of your hotel then if you wish. And there are the two rooms,' he was beginning to say when she came into his arms.

As he waited for her, the poet's sudden angry accusation came back. Such accusations usually came to rankle and remain long after praise had failed, but not this evening. He turned it over as he might a problem that there seemed no way round, and let it drop. If it was true, there was very little that could be done about it now. It was in turn replaced by the phrase that had come to him earlier by the sea's edge; and had he not seen love in the person of his old mother reduced to noticing things about a farmyard?

'I hope you're not puzzling over something like "life" again,' a teasing call came from the bedroom.

'No. Not this time.' He rose to join her.

In the morning they had coffee and toast in the sunlit kitchen with the expectation of the whole day waiting on them. Then they walked in the empty streets of the city, looked through the Green before going to the hotel to bring her things back to the flat.

The following days were so easy that the only anxiety could be its total absence. The days were heightened by the luxury and pleasure of private evenings, the meals she cooked that were perfection, the good wine he bought, the flowers; desire that was never turned aside or exasperated by difficulty.

At the end of the holiday, he had to go back to the office, and she put off the Dundalk visit and began to go to the Trinity Library. Many people were not back in the office, and he was able to work without interruption for the whole of the first morning. What he had to do was to isolate the relevant parts of the section and reduce them to a few simple sentences.

At the afternoon meeting the Minister was the more nervous. He was tall and muscular, small blue eyes and thick red hair, fifteen years the younger man, with a habit of continually touching any-body close to him that told of the large family he grew up in. They went over and over the few sentences he had prepared until the Minister had them by rote. He was appearing on television that night and was extremely apprehensive.

'Good man.' He grasped McDonough's shoulder with relief when they finished. 'One of these evenings before long you must come out and have a bite with us and meet the hen and chickens.'

'I'll be glad to. And good luck on the TV. I'll be watching.'

'I'll need all the luck I can get. That bitch of an interviewer hates my guts.'

They watched the television debate together in the flat that evening. The Minister had reason to be apprehensive. He was under attack from the beginning, but bludgeoning his way. As he watched, McDonough wondered if his work had been necessary at all. He could hardly discern his few sentences beneath the weight of the Minister's phrases. 'I emphatically state . . . I categorically deny . . . I say without any equivocation whatsoever . . . Having consulted the best available opinions in the matter' (which were presumably McDonough's own).

'What did you think?' he asked when he switched off the set.

'He was almost touching,' she said carefully. 'Amateurish maybe. His counterpart in the States might be no better, but he certainly would have to be more polished.'

'He was good at handstands and somersaults once,' he said, surprised at his own sense of disappointment. 'I've become almost fond of him. Sometimes I wish we had better people. They'll all tell him he did powerfully. What'll we do? Would you like to go for a quick walk?'

'Why don't we?' She reached for her cardigan.

Two days later she went to Dundalk, and it wasn't certain how long she intended to remain there. 'I guess I've come so far that they'll expect me to stay over the weekend.'

'You must please yourself. You have a key. I'll not be going anywhere.'

They had come together so easily that the days together seemed like a marriage without any of the drama of a ceremony.

When he was young he had desired too much, and so spread his own fear. Now that he was close to losing everything – was in the direct path of the wind – it was little short of amazing that he should come on this extraordinary breathing space.

Almost in disbelief he went back in reflection to the one love of his life, a love that was pure suffering. In a hotel bedroom in another city, unable to sleep by her side, he had risen and dressed. He had paused before leaving the room to gaze on the even breathing of her sleep. All that breath had to do was frame one word, and a whole world of happiness would be given, but it was for ever withheld. He had walked the morning streets until circling back to the hotel he came on a market that was just opening and bought a large bunch of grapes. The grapes were very small and turning yellow and still damp, and were of incredible sweetness. She was just waking and had not missed him when he came back into the room. They ate the grapes on the coverlid and each time she lifted the small bunches to her mouth he remembered the dark of her armpits. He ached to touch her but everything seemed to be so fragile between them that he was afraid to even stir. It seemed that any small movement now could bring calamity. Then, laughing, she blew grape seeds in his face and, reaching out her arms, drew him down. She had wanted their last day together to be pleasant. She was marrying another man. Later he remembered running between airport gates looking for flights that had all departed.

It was eerie to set down those days beside the days that had just gone by, call them by the same name. How slowly those days had moved, as if waiting for something to begin: now all the days were speeding, slipping silently by like air.

Two evenings later, when he let himself into the flat and found Mary Kelleher there, it was as if she had never been away.

'You didn't expect me back so soon?'

'I thought you'd still be in Dundalk, but I'm glad, I'm delighted.' He took her in his arms.

'I had as much of Dundalk as I wanted, and I missed you.'

'How did it go?'

'It was all right. The cousins were nice. They had a small house, crammed with things – religious pictures, furniture, photos. There was hardly place to move. Everything they did was so careful, so measured out. After a while I felt I could hardly breathe. They did everything they possibly could to make me welcome. I read the poems at last.' She put the book with the brown cover on the table. 'I

Bank Holiday

read them again on the train coming back. I loved them.'

'I've long suspected that those very pure love sonnets are all addressed to himself,' McDonough said. 'That was how the "ignorant bloody apes and mediocrities" could be all short-circuited.'

'Some are very funny.'

'I'm so glad you liked them. I've lived with some of them for years. Would you like to go out to eat? Say, to Bernardo's?' he asked.

'I'd much prefer to stay home. I've already looked in the fridge. We can rustle something up.'

That weekend they went together for the long walk in the mountains that he had intended to take the day they met. They stopped for a drink and sandwiches in a pub near Blessington just before two o'clock, and there they decided to press on to Rathdrum and stay the night in the hotel rather than turn back into the city.

It was over dinner in the near empty hotel dining-room that he asked if she would consider marrying him. 'There's much against it. I am fifty. You would have to try to settle here, where you'll be a stranger,' and he went on to say that what he had already was more than he ever expected, that he was content to let it be, but if she wanted more then it was there.

'I thought that you couldn't be married here.' Her tone was affectionate.

'I meant it in everything but name, and even that can be arranged if you want it enough.'

'How?'

'With money. An outside divorce. The marriage in some other country. The States, for instance.'

'Can't you see that I already love you? That it doesn't matter? I was half teasing. You looked so serious.'

'I am serious. I want to be clear.'

'It is clear and I am glad – and very grateful.'

They agreed that she would spend one week longer here in Dublin than she had planned. At Christmas he would go to New York for a week. She would have obtained her doctorate by then. James White would be surprised. There were no serious complications in sight. They were so tired and happy that it was as if they were already in possession of endless quantities of time and money.

The Creamery Manager

The books and files had been taken out but no one yet had stopped him from entering his office. Tired of sitting alone listening to the rain beat on the iron, he came out on the platform where he could look down on the long queue of tractors towing in the steel tanks, the wipers making furious, relentless arcs across the windscreens as they waited. He knew all the men sitting behind the glass of the cabs by name; that he had made his first business when he came to manage the creamery years before. Often on a wet summer's day, when there could be no rush at hay, many of them would pull in below the platform to sit and talk. The rough, childish faces would look up in a glow of pleasure at the recognition when he shouted out their names. Some would flash their lights.

Today no one looked up, but he could see them observing him in their mirrors after they had passed. They probably already knew more precisely than he what awaited him. Even with that knowledge he would have preferred it if they looked up. All his life he had the weakness of wanting to please and give pleasure.

When the Angelus bell rang from Cootehall, he began to think that they might have put off coming for him for another day, but soon after the last stroke he heard heavy boots crossing the cement. A low knock came on the door. Guard Casey was in the doorway but there was no sign of the Sergeant. Guard Guider was the other guard.

'You know why we're here, Jim,' Guard Casey said.

'I know, Ned.' Quickly the Guard read out the statement of arrest.

'You'll come with us, then?'

'Sure I'll come.'

'I'm sorry to have to do this but they're the rules.' He brought out a pair of bright handcuffs with a small green ribbon on the linking bar. Guider quickly handcuffed him to Casey and withdrew the key. The bar with the green ribbon kept the wrists apart but the

366

hands and elbows touched. This caused them to walk stiffly and hesitantly and in step. The cement had been hosed clean but the people who worked for him were out of sight. The electric hum of the separators drowned their footsteps as they crossed to the squad car.

In the barracks the Sergeant was waiting for him with a peace commissioner, a teacher from the other end of the parish, and they began committal proceedings at once. The Sergeant was grim-faced and inscrutable.

'I'm sorry for that Sunday in Clones,' the creamery manager blurted out in nervousness. 'I only meant it as a day out together.'

The grimness of the Sergeant's face did not relent; it was as if he had never spoken. He was asked if he had a solicitor. He had none. Did he want to be represented? Did he need to be? he responded. It was not necessary at this stage, he was told. In that case, they could begin. Anything he said, he was warned, could be used against him. He would say nothing. Though it directly concerned him, it seemed to be hardly about him at all, and it did not take long. Tonight he'd spend in the barracks. The cell was already prepared for him. Tomorrow he'd be transferred to Mountjoy to await his trial. The proceedings for the present were at an end. There was a mild air of relief. He felt like a railway carriage that had been pushed by handdown rails into some siding. It suited him well enough. He had never been assertive and he had no hope of being acquitted.

Less than a month before, he had bought stand tickets for the Ulster Final and had taken the Sergeant and Guard Casey to Clones. He already knew then that the end couldn't be far off. It must have been cowardice and an old need to ingratiate. Now it was the only part of the whole business that made him cringe.

They had set off in the Sergeant's small Ford, Guard Casey sitting with the Sergeant in the front. They were both big men, Casey running to flesh, but the Sergeant retained some of an athlete's spareness of feature. He had played three or four times for Cavan and had been on the fringe of the team for a few seasons several years before.

'You were a terrible man to go and buy those stand tickets, Jim,' Casey had said for the fifth time as the car travelled over the dusty white roads.

'What's terrible about it? Aren't we all Ulster men even if we are stranded in the west? It's a day out, a day out of all our lives. And the Sergeant here even played for Cavan.'

'Once or twice. Once or twice. Trial runs. You could hardly call it *played*. I just wasn't good enough.'

'You were more than good enough by all accounts. There was a clique.'

'You're blaming the selectors now. The selectors had a job to do. They couldn't pick everybody.'

'More than me has said they were a clique. They had their favourites. You weren't called "the boiler" for nothing.'

A car parked round the corner forced the Sergeant to swerve out into the road. Nothing was coming.

'You'd think the car was specially parked there to deliver an accident.'

'They're all driving around in cars,' Casey said, 'but the mentality is still of the jennet and cart.'

It had been a sort of suffering to keep the talk going, but silence was even worse. There were many small flowers in the grass margins of the roadside.

They took their seats in the stand halfway through the minor game. There was one grace: though he came from close to Clones, there wasn't a single person he knew sitting in any of the nearby seats. The minor game ended. Once the seniors came on the field he started at the sudden power and speed with which the ball was driven about. The game was never close. Cavan drew gradually ahead to win easily. Such was the air of unreality he felt, of three men watching themselves watch a game, that he was glad to buy oranges from a seller moving between seats, to hand the fruit around, to peel the skin away, to taste the bitter juice. Only once did he start and stir uncomfortably, when Guard Casey remarked about the powerful Cavan full-back who was roughing up the Tyrone forwards: 'The Gunner is taking no prisoners today.'

He was not so lucky on leaving the game. In the packed streets of the town a voice called out, 'Is it not Jimmy McCarron?' And at once the whole street seemed to know him. They stood in his path, put arms around him, drew him to the bars. 'An Ulster Final, look at the evening we'll have, and it's only starting.'

'Another time, Mick. Another time, Joe. Great to see you but we

368

The Creamery Manager

have to get back.' He had pushed desperately on, not introducing his two companions.

'You seem to be the most popular man in town,' the Sergeant said sarcastically once they were clear.

'I'm from round here.'

'It's better to be popular anyhow than buried away out of sight,' Casey came to his defence.

'Up to a point. Up to a point,' the Sergeant said. 'Everything has its point.'

They stopped for tea at the Lawn Hotel in Belturbet. By slipping out to the reception desk while they were eating he managed to pay for the meal. Except for the Sergeant's petrol he had paid for the entire day. This was brought up as they parted outside the barracks in the early evening.

'It was a great day. We'll have to make an annual day of the Ulster Final. But next year will be our day. Next year you'll not be allowed spend a penny,' the Sergeant said, but still he could see their satisfaction that the whole outing had cost them nothing.

Now that the committal proceedings were at an end an air of uncertainty crept into the dayroom. Did they feel compromised by the day? He did not look at their faces. The door on the river had to be unlocked in order to allow the peace commissioner to leave and was again locked after he left. He caught the Sergeant and Guard Casey looking at one another.

'You better show him his place,' the Sergeant said.

To the right of the door on the river was a big, heavy red door. It was not locked. Casey opened it slowly to show him his cell for the night.

'It's not great, Jimmy, but it's as good as we could get it.'

The cement floor was still damp from being washed. Above the cement was a mattress on a low platform of boards. There was a pillow and several heavy grey blankets on the mattress. High in the wall a narrow window was cut, a single steel bar in its centre.

'It's fine. It couldn't be better.'

'If you want anything at all, just bang or shout, Jim,' and the heavy door was closed and locked. He heard bolts being drawn.

Casually he felt the pillow, the coarse blankets, moved the mattress, and with his palm tested the solidity of the wooden platform; its boards were of white deal and they too had been

369

freshly scrubbed. There was an old oil can beside a steel bucket in the corner. Carefully he moved it under the window, and by climbing on the can and gripping the iron bar he could see out on either side: a sort of lawn, a circular flowerbed, netting-wire, a bole of the sycamore tree, sallies, a strip of river. He tried to get down as silently as possible, but as soon as he took his weight off the oil can it rattled.

'Are you all right there, Jimmy?' Casey was at once asking anxiously from the other side of the door.

'I'm fine. I was just surveying the surroundings. Soon I'll lie down for a while.'

He heard Casey hesitate for a moment, but then his feet sounded on the hollow boards of the dayroom, going towards the table and chairs. As much as to reassure Casey as from any need, he covered the mattress with one of the grey blankets and lay down, loosening his collar and tie. The bed was hard but not uncomfortable. He lay there, sometimes thinking, most of the time his mind as blank as the white ceiling, and occasionally he drifted in and out of sleep.

There were things he was grateful for . . . that his parents were dead . . . that he did not have to face his mother's uncomprehending distress. He felt little guilt. The shareholders would write him off as a loss against other profits. The old creamery would not cry out with the hurt. People he had always been afraid of hurting, and even when he disliked them he felt that he partly understood them, could put himself in their place, and that was almost the end of dislike. Sure, he had seen evil and around it a stupid, heartless laughing that echoed darkness; and yet, he had wanted love. He felt that more than ever now, even looking at where he was, to what he had come.

That other darkness, all that surrounded life, used to trouble him once, but he had long given up making anything out of it, like a poor talent, and he no longer cared. Coming into the world was, he was sure now, not unlike getting into this poor cell. There was constant daylight above his head, split by the single bar, and beyond the sycamore leaves a radio aerial disappeared into a high branch. He could make jokes about it, but to make jokes alone was madness. He'd need a crowd for that, a blazing fire, rounds of drinks, and the whole long night awaiting.

There was another fact that struck him now like coldness. In the long juggling act he'd engaged in for years that eventually got him to this cell – four years before only the sudden windfall of a legacy had lifted him clear – whenever he was known to be flush all the monies he had loaned out to others would flow back as soon as he called, but whenever he was seen to be in desperate need, nothing worthwhile was ever given back. It was not a pretty picture, but in this cell he was too far out to care much about it now.

He'd had escapes too, enough of them to want no more. The first had been the Roman collar, to hand the pain and the joy of his own life into the keeping of an idea, and to will the idea true. It had been a near thing, especially because his mother had the vocation for him as well; but the pull of sex had been too strong, a dream of one girl in a silken dress among gardens disguising healthy animality. All his life he had moved among disguises, was moving among them still. He had even escaped marriage. The girl he'd loved, with the black head of hair thrown back and the sideways laugh, had been too wise to marry him: no framework could have withstood that second passion for immolation. There was the woman he didn't love that he was resigned to marry when she told him she was pregnant. The weekend she discovered she wasn't they'd gone to the Metropole and danced and drank the whole night away, he celebrating his escape out to where there were lungfuls of air, she celebrating that they were now free to choose to marry and have many children: 'It will be no Protestant family.' 'It will be no family at all.' Among so many disguises there was no lack of ironies.

The monies he had given out, the sums that were given back, the larger sums that would never be returned, the rounds of drinks he'd paid for, the names he'd called out, the glow of recognition, his own name shouted to the sky, the day Moon Dancer had won at Phoenix Park, other days and horses that had lost – all dwindling down to the small, ingratiating act of taking the Sergeant and Guard Casey to the Ulster Final.

The bolts were being drawn. Casey was standing in the doorway. 'There's something for you to eat, Jimmy.' He hadn't realized how dark the cell had been until he came out into the dayroom, and he had to shade his eyes against the light. He thought he'd be eating at the dayroom table, but he was brought up a long hallway to the Sergeant's living quarters. At the end of the hallway was a huge kitchen, and one place was set on a big table in its centre. The

Sergeant wasn't there but his wife was and several children. No one spoke. In the big sideboard mirror he could see most of the room and Casey standing directly behind him with his arms folded. A lovely, strong girl of fourteen or fifteen placed a plate of sausages, black pudding, bacon and a small piece of liver between his knife and fork and poured him a steaming mug of tea. There was brown bread on the table, sugar, milk, salt, pepper. At first no one spoke and his knife and fork were loud on the plate as the children watched him covertly but with intense curiosity. Then Casey began to tease the children about their day in school.

'Thanks,' he said after he'd signed a docket at the end of the meal which stated that he had been provided with food.

'For nothing at all,' the Sergeant's wife answered quietly, but it was little above a whisper, and he had to fight back a wave of gratitude. With Casey he went back down the long hallway to the dayroom. He was moving across the hollow boards to the cell door when Casey stopped him.

'There's no need to go in there yet, Jimmy. You can sit here for a while in front of the fire.'

They sat on the yellow chairs in front of the fire. Casey spent a long time arranging turf around the blazing centre of the fire with tongs. There were heavy ledgers on the table at their back. A row of baton cases and the gleaming handcuffs with the green ribbons hung from hooks on the wall. A stripped, narrow bed stood along the wall of the cell, its head beneath the phone on the wall. Only the cell wall stood between Casey's bed and his own plain boards.

'When do you think they'll come?' he asked when the guard seemed to have arranged the sods of turf to his satisfaction.

'They'll come some time in the morning. Do you know I feel badly about all this? It's a pity it had to happen at all,' Casey said out of a long silence.

'It's done now anyhow.'

'Do you know what I think? There were too many spongers around. They took advantage. It's them that should by rights be in your place.'

'I don't know . . . I don't think so . . . It was me that allowed it . . . even abetted it.'

'You don't mind me asking this? How did it start? Don't answer if you don't want.'

'As far as I know it began in small things. "He that contemneth small things . . ."'

'Shall fall little by little into grievous error,' Casey finished the quotation in a low, meditative voice as he started to arrange the fire again. 'No. I wouldn't go as far as that. That's too hard. You'd think it was God Almighty we were offending. What's an old creamery anyhow? It'll still go on taking in milk, turning our butter. No. Only in law is it anything at all.'

'There were a few times I thought I might get out of it,' he said slowly. 'But the fact is that I didn't. I don't think people can change. They like to imagine they can, that is all.'

'Maybe they can if they try hard enough – or they have to,' Casey said without much confidence.

'Then it's nearly always too late,' he said. 'The one thing I feel really badly about is taking the Sergeant and yourself to the Ulster Final those few Sundays back. That was dragging the pair of you into the business. That wasn't right.'

'The Sergeant takes that personally. In my opinion he's wrong. What was personal about it? You gave us a great day out, a day out of all of our lives,' Casey said. 'And everything was normal then.'

That was the trouble, everything was not normal then, he was about to say, but decided not to speak. Everything was normal now. He had been afraid of his own fear and was spreading the taint everywhere. Now that what he had feared most had happened he was no longer afraid. His own life seemed to be happening as satisfactorily as if he were free again among people.

Do you think people can change, Ned? he felt like asking Casey. Do you think people can change or are they given a set star at birth that they have to follow? What part does luck play in the whole shemozzle?

Casey had taken to arranging the fire again and would plainly welcome any conversation, but he found that he did not want to continue. He felt that he knew already as much as he'd ever come to know about these matters. Discussing them further could only be a form of idleness or Clones in some other light. He liked the guard, but he did not want to draw any closer.

Soon he'd have to ask him for leave to go back to his cell.

The Country Funeral

After Fonsie Ryan called his brother he sat in his wheelchair and waited with growing impatience for him to appear on the small stairs and then, as soon as Philly came down and sat at the table, Fonsie moved his wheelchair to the far wall to wait for him to finish. This silent pressure exasperated Philly as he ate.

'Did Mother get up yet?' he asked abruptly.

'She didn't feel like getting up. She went back to sleep after I brought her tea.'

Philly let his level stare rest on his brother but all Fonsie did was to move his wheelchair a few inches out from the wall and then, in the same leaning rocking movement, let it the same few inches back, his huge hands all the time gripping the wheels. With his large head and trunk, he sometimes looked like a circus dwarf. The legless trousers were sewn up below the hips.

Slowly and deliberately Philly buttered the toast, picked at the rashers and egg and sausages, took slow sips from his cup, but his nature was not hard. As quickly as he had grown angry he softened towards his brother.

'Would you be interested in pushing down to Mulligan's after a while for a pint?'

'I have the shopping to do.'

'Don't let me hold you up, then,' Philly responded sharply to the rebuff. 'I'll be well able to let myself out.'

'There's no hurry. I'll wait and wash up. It's nice to come back to a clean house.'

'I can wash these things up. I do it all the time in Saudi Arabia.'

'You're on your holidays now,' Fonsie said. 'I'm in no rush but it's too early in the day for me to drink.'

Three weeks before, Philly had come home in a fever of excitement from the oil fields. He always came home in that high state of fever and it lasted for a few days in the distribution of the presents he always brought home, especially to his mother; his delight looking at her sparse filigreed hair bent over the rug he had brought her, the bright tassels resting on her fingers; the meetings with old school friends, the meetings with neighbours, the buying of rounds and rounds of drinks; his own fever for company after the months at the oil wells and delight in the rounds of celebration blinding him to the poor fact that it is not generally light but shadow that we cast; and now all that fever had subsided to leave him alone and companion-less in just another morning as he left the house without further word to Fonsie and with nothing better to do than walk to Mulligan's.

Because of the good weather, many of the terrace doors were open and people sat in the doorways, their feet out on the pavement. A young blonde woman was painting her toenails red in the shadow of a pram in a doorway at the end of the terrace, and she did not look up as he passed. Increasingly people had their own lives here and his homecoming broke the monotony for a few days, and then he did not belong.

As soon as the barman in Mulligan's had pulled his pint he offered Philly the newspaper spread out on the counter that he had been reading.

'Don't you want it yourself?' Philly asked out of a sense of politeness.

'I must have been through it at least twice. I've the complete arse read out of it since the morning.'

There were three other drinkers scattered about the bar nursing their pints at tables.

'There's never anything in those newspapers,' one of the drinkers said.

'Still, you always think you'll come on something,' the barman responded hopefully.

'That's how they get your money,' the drinker said.

Feet passed the open doorway. When it was empty the concrete gave back its own grey dull light. Philly turned the pages slowly and sipped at the pint. The waiting silence of the bar became too close an echo of the emptiness he felt all around his life. As he sipped and turned the pages he resolved to drink no more. The day would be too hard to get through if he had more. He'd go back to the house and tell his mother he was returning early to the oil fields. There were other places he could kill time in. London and Naples were on the way to Bahrain.

'He made a great splash when he came home first,' one of the drinkers said to the empty bar as soon as Philly left. 'He bought rings round him. Now the brother in the wheelchair isn't with him any more.'

'Too much. Too much,' a second drinker added forcefully though it wasn't clear at all to what he referred.

'It must be bad when that brother throws in the towel, because he's a tank for drink. You'd think there was no bottom in that wheelchair.'

The barman stared in silent disapproval at his three customers. There were few things he disliked more than this 'behind-backs' criticism of a customer as soon as he left. He opened the newspaper loudly, staring pointedly out at the three drinkers until they were silent, and then bent his head to travel slowly through the pages again.

'I heard a good one the other day,' one of the drinkers cackled rebelliously. 'The only chance of travel that ever comes to the poor is when they get sick. They go from one state to the other state and back again to base if they're lucky.'

The other two thought this hilarious and one pounded the table with his glass in appreciation. Then they looked towards the bar-man for approval but he just raised his eyes to stare absently out on the grey strip of concrete until the little insurrection died and he was able to continue travelling through the newspaper again.

Philly came slowly back up the street. The blonde had finished painting her toenails – a loud vermilion – and she leaned the back of her head against a door jamb, her eyes closing as she gave her face and throat completely to the sun. The hooded pram above her outstretched legs was silent. Away, behind the area railings, old men wearing berets were playing bowls, a miniature French flag flying on the railings.

Philly expected to enter an empty room but as soon as he put his key in the door he heard the raised voices. He held the key still. His mother was downstairs. She and Fonsie were arguing. With a welcome little rush of expectancy, he turned the key. The two were so engaged with one another that they did not notice him enter. His mother was in her blue dressing gown. She stood remarkably erect.

'What's going on?' They were so involved with one another that they looked towards him as if he were a burglar.

'Your Uncle Peter died last night, in Gloria. The Cullens just phoned,' his mother said, and it was Philly's turn to look at his mother and brother as if he couldn't quite grasp why they were in the room.

'You'll all have to go,' his mother said.

'I don't see why we should have to go. We haven't seen the man in twenty years. He never even liked us,' Fonsie said heatedly, turning the wheelchair to face Philly.

'Of course we'll go. We are all he has now. It wouldn't look right if we didn't go down.' Philly would have grasped at any diversion, but the pictures of Gloria Bog that flooded his mind shut out the day and the room with amazing brightness and calm.

'That doesn't mean I have to go,' Fonsie said.

'Of course you have to go. He was your uncle as well as mine,' Philly said.

'If nobody went to poor Peter's funeral, God rest him, we'd be the talk of the countryside for years,' their mother said. 'If I know nothing else in the world I know what they're like down there.'

'Anyhow, there's no way I can go in this.' Fonsie gestured contemptuously to his wheelchair.

'That's no problem. I'll hire a Mercedes. With a jalopy like that you wouldn't think of coming yourself, Mother?' Philly asked suddenly with the humour and malice of deep knowledge, and the silence that met the suggestion was as great as if some gross obscenity had been uttered.

'I'd look a nice speck in Gloria when I haven't been out of my own house in years. There wouldn't be much point in going to poor Peter's funeral, God rest him, and turning up at my own,' she said in a voice in which a sudden frailty only served to point up the different shades of its steel.

'He never even liked us. There were times I felt if he got a chance he'd throw me into a bog hole the way he drowned the black whippet that started eating the eggs,' Philly said.

'He's gone now,' the mother said. 'He stood to us when he was needed. It made no difference whether he liked us or not.'

'How will you manage on your own?' Fonsie asked as if he had accepted he'd have to go.

'Won't Mrs O'Brien next door look in if you ask her and can't I call her myself on the phone? It'll be good for you to get out of the city for a change. None of the rest can be trusted to bring me back a word of anything that goes on,' she flattered.

'Was John told yet?' Philly interrupted, asking about their eldest brother.

'No. There'd be no use ringing him at home now. You'd have to ring him at the school,' their mother said.

The school's number was written in a notebook. Philly had to wait a long time on the phone after he explained the urgency of the call while the school secretary got John from the classroom.

'John won't take time off school to go to any funeral,' Fonsie said confidently as they waited.

To Fonsie's final disgust John agreed to go to the funeral at once. He'd be waiting for them at whatever time they thought they'd be ready to travel.

Philly hired the Mercedes. The wheelchair folded easily into its cavern-like boot. 'You'll all be careful,' their mother counselled as she kissed them goodbye. 'Everything you do down there will be watched and gone over. I'll be following poor Peter in my mind until you rest him with Father and Mother in Killeelan.'

John was waiting for them outside his front door, a brown hat in his hand, a gabardine raincoat folded on his arm, when the Mercedes pulled up at the low double gate. Before Philly had time to touch the horn John raised the hat and hurried down the concrete path. On both sides of the path the postage-stamp lawns showed the silver tracks of a mower, and roses were stacked and tied along the earthen borders.

'The wife doesn't seem to appear at all these days?' Philly asked, the vibrations of the engine shaking the car as they waited while John closed the gate.

'Herself and Mother never pulled,' Fonsie offered.

There was dull peace between the two brothers now. Fonsie knew he was more or less in Philly's hands for the next two days. He did not like it but the stupid death had moved the next two days out of his control.

'What's she like now?'

'I suppose she's much like the rest of us. She was always nippy.'

'I'm sorry for keeping you,' John said as he got into the back of the car.

'You didn't keep us at all,' Philly answered.

'It's great to get a sudden break like this. You can't imagine what it is to get out of the school and city for two or three whole days,' John said before he settled and was silent. The big Mercedes grew silent as it gathered speed through Fairview and the North Strand, crossing the Liffey at the Custom House, and turned into the one-way flow of traffic out along the south bank of the river. Not until they got past Leixlip, and fields and trees and hedges started to be scattered between the new raw estates, did they begin to talk, and all their talk circled about the man they were going to bury, their mother's brother, their Uncle Peter McDermott.

He had been the only one in the family to stay behind with his parents on Gloria Bog where he'd been born. All the rest had scattered. Their Aunt Mary had died young in Walthamstow, London; Martin died in Milton, Massachusetts; Katie, the eldest, had died only the year before in Oneida, New York. With Peter's death they were all gone now, except their mother. She had been the last to leave the house. She first served her time in a shop in Carrick-on-Shannon and then moved to a greengrocer's-cum-confectioner's on the North Circular Road where she met their unreliable father, a traveller for Lemons Sweets.

While the powerful car slowed through Enfield they began to recall how their mother had taken them back to Gloria at the beginning of every summer, leaving their father to his own devices in the city. They spent every summer there on the bog from the end of June until early September. Their mother had always believed that only for the clean air of the bog and the plain wholesome food they would never have made it through the makeshifts of the city winter. Without the air and the plain food they'd never, never have got through, she used to proclaim like a thanksgiving.

As long as her own mother lived it was like a holiday to go there every summer – the toothless grandmother who sat all day in her rocking chair, her shoulders shawled, the grey hair drawn severely back into a bun, only rising to gather crumbs and potato skins into her black apron, and holding it like a great cloth bowl, she would shuffle out on to the street. She'd wait until all her brown hens had started to beat and clamour around her and then with a quick laugh she'd scatter everything that the apron held. Often before she came in she'd look across the wide acres of the bog, the stunted birch trees, the faint blue of the heather, the white puffs of bog cotton trembling in every wind to the green slopes of Killeelan and walled evergreens high on the hill and say, 'I suppose it won't be long till I'm with the rest of them there.'

'You shouldn't talk like that, Mother,' they remembered their mother's ritual scold.

'There's not much else to think about at my age. The gaps between the bog holes are not getting wider.'

One summer the brown rocking chair was empty. Peter lived alone in the house. Though their mother worked from morning to night in the house, tidying, cleaning, sewing, cooking, he made it clear that he didn't want her any more, but she ignored him. Her want was greater than his desire to be rid of them and his fear of going against the old pieties prevented him from turning them away.

The old ease of the grandmother's time had gone. He showed them no welcome when they came, spent as little time in the house as possible, the days working in the fields, visiting other houses at night where, as soon as he had eaten, he complained to everybody about the burden he had to put up with. He never troubled to hide his relief when the day finally came at the end of the summer for them to leave. In the quick way of children, the three boys picked up his resentment and suffered its constraint. He hardly ever looked at Fonsie in his wheelchair, and it was fear that never allowed Fonsie to take his eyes from the back of his uncle's head and broad shoulders. Whenever Philly or John took him sandwiches and the Powers bottle of tea kept warm in the sock to the bog or meadow, they always instinctively took a step or two back after handing him the oilcloth bag. Out of loneliness there were times when he tried to talk to them but the constraint had so solidified that all they were ever able to give back were childish echoes of his own awkward questions. He never once acknowledged the work their mother had done in the house which was the way she had – the only way she had – of paying for their stay in the house of her own childhood. The one time they saw him happy was whenever her exasperation broke and she scolded him: he would smile as if all the days he had spent alone with his mother had suddenly returned. Once she noticed that he enjoyed these scolds, and even set to actively provoke them at every small turn, she would go more doggedly still than was her usual wont.

'What really used to get her dander up was the way he used to lift up his trousers by the crotch before he sat down to the table,' Fonsie said as the car approached Longford, and the brothers all laughed in their different ways.

'He looked as if he was always afraid he'd sit on his balls,' Philly said. 'He'll not have to worry about that any more.'

'His worries are over,' John said.

'Then, after our father died and she got that job in the laundry, that was the first summer we didn't go. She was very strange that summer. She'd take your head off if you talked. We never went again.'

'Strange, going down like this after all that,' John said vaguely.

'I was trying to say that in the house. It makes no sense to me but this man and Mother wouldn't listen,' Fonsie said. 'They were down my throat before I could open my mouth.'

'We're here now anyhow,' Philly said as the car crossed the narrow bridge at Carrick and they could look down at the Shannon. They were coming into country that they knew. They had suffered here.

'God, I don't know how she came here summer after summer when she wasn't wanted,' John said as the speeding car left behind the last curve of sluggish water.

'Well, she wasn't exactly leaving the Garden of Eden,' Philly said.

'It's terrible when you're young to come into a place where you know you're not wanted,' John said. 'I used to feel we were eating poor Peter out of house and home every summer. When you're a child you feel those sorts of things badly even though nobody notices. I see it still in the faces of the children I teach.'

'After all that we're coming down to bury the fucker. That's what gets me,' Fonsie said.

'He's dead now and belongs with all the dead,' Philly said. 'He wasn't all bad. Once I helped him drive cattle into the fair of Boyle. It was dark when we set out. I had to run alongside them in the fields behind the hedges until they got too worn out to want to leave the road. After we sold the cattle up on the Green he took me to the Rockingham Arms. He bought me lemonade and ginger snaps and lifted me up on the counter and said I was a great gosson to the whole bar even if I had the misfortune to be from Dublin.'

'You make me sick,' Fonsie said angrily. 'The man wasn't civilized. I always felt if he got a chance he'd have put me in a bag with a stone and thrown me in a bog hole like that black whippet.'

'That's exaggerating now. He never did and we're almost there,' John said as the car went past the church and scattered houses of Cootehall, where they had come to Mass on Sundays and bought flour and tea and sugar.

'Now, fasten your seat-belts,' Philly said humorously as he turned slowly into the bog road. To their surprise the deep pot-holes were gone. The road had been tarred, the unruly hedges of sally and hazel and briar cut back. Occasionally a straying briar clawed at the windscreen, the only hint of the old wildness. When the hedges gave way to the field of wild raspberry canes, Philly slowed the car to a crawl, and then stopped. Suddenly the bog looked like an ocean stretched in front of them, its miles of heather and pale sedge broken by the stunted birch trees, and high against the evening sun the dark evergreens stood out on the top of Killeelan Hill.

'He'll be buried there the day after tomorrow.'

The house hadn't changed, whitewashed, asbestos-roofed, the chestnut tree in front standing in the middle of the green fields on the edge of the bog; but the road was now tarred to the door, and all around the house new cattle sheds had sprung up.

Four cars were parked on the street and the door of the small house was open. A man shading his eyes with his hand came to the doorway as soon as the Mercedes came to a stop. It was Jim Cullen, the man who had telephoned the news of the death, smaller now and white-haired. He welcomed the three brothers in turn as he shook their hands. 'I'm sorry for your trouble. You were great to come all the way. I wouldn't have known any of you except for Fonsie. Your poor mother didn't manage to come?'

'She wasn't up to it,' Philly said. 'She hasn't left the house in years.'

As soon as they entered the room everybody stood up and came towards them and shook hands: 'I'm sorry for your trouble.' There were three old men besides Jim Cullen, neighbours of the dead man who had known them as children. Mrs Cullen was the older woman. A younger man about their own age was a son of the Cullens, Michael, whom they remembered as a child, but he had so grown and changed that his appearance was stranger to them than the old men.

'It's hard to think that Peter, God rest him, is gone. It's terrible,' Jim Cullen said as he led them into the bedroom.

The room was empty. A clock somewhere had not been stopped. He looked very old and still in the bed. They would not have known him. His hands were enormous on the white sheet, the beads a thin dark trickle through the locked fingers. A white line crossed the weathered forehead where he had worn a hat or a cap. The three brothers blessed themselves, and after a pause John and Philly touched the huge rough hands clasped together on the sheet. They were very cold. Fonsie did not touch the hands, turning the chair round towards the kitchen before his brothers left the side of the bed.

In the kitchen Fonsie and Philly drank whiskey. Mrs Cullen said it was no trouble at all to make John a cup of tea and there were platefuls of cut sandwiches on the table. Jim Cullen started to take up the story of Peter's death. He had told it many times already and would tell it many times again during the next days.

'Every evening before dark Peter would come out into that garden at the side. It can be seen plain from our front door. He was proud, proud of that garden though most of what it grew he gave away.'

'You couldn't have a better neighbour. If he saw you coming looking for help he'd drop whatever he was doing and swear black and blue that he was doing nothing at all,' an old man said.

'It was lucky,' Jim Cullen resumed. 'This woman here was thinking of closing up the day and went out to the door before turning the key, and saw Peter in the garden. She saw him stoop a few times to pull up a weed or straighten something and then he stood for a long time; suddenly he just seemed to keel over into the furrow. She didn't like to call and waited for him to get up and when he didn't she ran for me out the back. I called when I went into the garden. There was no sight or sound. He was hidden under the potato stalks. I had to pull them back before I was able to see anything. It was lucky she saw him fall. We'd have had to look all over the bog for days before we'd have ever thought of searching in the stalks.'

'Poor Peter was all right,' Philly said emotionally. 'I'll never forget the day he put me up on the counter of the Rockingham Arms.'

He was the only brother who seemed in any way moved by the death. John looked cautiously from face to face but whatever he found in the faces did not move him to speak. Fonsie had finished the whiskey he'd been given on coming from the room and appeared to sit in his wheelchair in furious resentment. Then, one by one, as if in obedience to some hidden signal or law, everybody in the room rose and shook hands with the three brothers in turn and left them alone with Jim and Maggie Cullen.

As soon as the house had emptied Jim Cullen signalled that he wanted them to come down for a minute to the lower room, which had hardly been used or changed since they had slept there as children: the bed that sank in the centre, the plywood wardrobe, the blue paint of the windowsill half flaked away and the small window that looked out on all of Gloria, straight across to the dark trees of Killeelan. First, Jim showed them a bill for whiskey, beer, stout, bread, ham, tomatoes, butter, cheese, sherry, tea, milk, sugar. He read out the words slowly and with difficulty.

'I got it all in Henry's. Indeed, you saw it all out on the table. It wasn't much but I wasn't certain if anybody was coming down and of course I'd be glad to pay it myself for poor Peter. You'll probably want to get more. When word gets out that you're here there could be a flood of visitors before the end of the night.' He took from a coat a large worn bulging wallet. 'Peter, God rest him, was carrying this when he fell. I didn't count it but there seems to be more than a lock of hundreds in the wallet.'

Philly took the handwritten bill and the wallet.

'Would Peter not have made a will?' John asked.

'No. He'd not have made a will,' Jim Cullen replied.

'How can we be sure?'

'That was the kind of him. He'd think it unlucky. It's not right but people like Peter think they're going to live for ever. Now that the rest of them has gone, except your mother, everything that Peter has goes to yous,' Jim Cullen continued as if he had already given it considerable thought. 'I ordered the coffin and hearse from Beirne's in Boyle. I did not order the cheapest – Peter never behaved like a small man when he went out – but he wouldn't like to see too much money going down into the ground either. Now that you're all here you can change all that if you think it's not right.'

'Not one thing will be changed, Jim,' Philly said emotionally.

'Then there's this key.' Jim Cullen held up a small key on a string. 'You'll find it opens the iron box in the press above in the bedroom. I didn't go near the box and I don't want to know what's in it. The key was around his poor neck when he fell. I'd do anything in the world for Peter.'

'You've done too much already. You've gone to far too much trouble,' Philly said.

'Far too much,' John echoed. 'We can't thank you enough.'

'I couldn't do less,' Jim Cullen replied. 'Poor Peter was one great neighbour. Anything you ever did for him he made sure you got back double.'

Fonsie alone did not say a word. He glowed in a private, silent resentment that shut out everything around him. His lips moved from time to time but they were speaking to some darkness seething within. It was relief to move out of the small cramped room. Mrs Cullen rose from the table as soon as they came from the room as if making herself ready to help in any way she could.

'Would you like to come with us to the village?' Philly asked.

'No, thanks,' Jim Cullen answered. 'I have a few hours' shuffling to do at home but then I'll be back.'

When it seemed as if the three brothers were going together to the village the Cullens looked from one to the other and Jim Cullen said, 'It'd be better if one of you stayed . . . in case of callers.'

John volunteered to stay. Philly had the car keys in his hand and Fonsie had already moved out to the car.

'I'll stay as well,' Mrs Cullen said. 'In case John might not know some of the callers.'

While Fonsie had been silent within the house, as soon as the car moved out of the open bog into that part of the lane enclosed by briars and small trees, an angry outpouring burst out like released water. Everything was gathered into the rushing complaint: the poor key with the string, keeling over in the potato stalks, the bloody wallet, the beads in the huge hands that he always felt wanted to choke him, the bit of cotton sticking out of the corner of the dead man's mouth. The whole thing was barbaric, uncivilized, obscene: they should never have come.

'Isn't it as good anyhow as having the whole thing swept under the carpet as it is in the city?' Philly argued reasonably.

385

'You mean we should bark ourselves because we don't keep a dog?'

'You make no effort,' Philly said. 'You never once opened your mouth in the house . . . In Dublin even when you're going to shop it takes you a half-hour to get from one end of a street to the next.'

'I never opened my mouth in the house and I never will. Through all those summers I never talked to anybody in the house but Mother and only when the house was empty. We were all made to feel that way – even Mother admitted that – but I was made to feel worse than useless. Every time I caught Peter looking at me I knew he was thinking that there was nothing wrong with me that a big stone and a rope and a deep bog hole couldn't solve.'

'You only thought that,' Philly said gently.

'Peter thought it too.'

'Well then, if he did – which I doubt – he thinks it no more.'

'By the way, you were very quick to pocket his wallet,' Fonsie said quickly as if changing the attack.

'That's because nobody else seemed ready to take it. But you take it if that's what you want.' Philly took the wallet from his pocket and offered it to Fonsie.

'I don't want it.' Fonsie refused the wallet roughly.

'We'd better look into it, then. We'll never get a quieter chance again in the next days.'

They were on a long straight stretch of road just outside the village. Philly moved the car in on to the grass margin. He left the engine running.

'There are thousands in this wallet,' Philly said simply after opening the wallet and fingering the notes.

'You'd think the fool would have put it in a bank where it'd be safe and earning interest.'

'Peter wouldn't put it in a bank. It might earn a tax inspector and a few awkward questions as well as interest,' Philly said as if he already was in possession of some of his dead uncle's knowledge and presence.

With the exception of the huge evergreens that used to shelter the church, the village had not changed at all. They had been cut down. Without the rich trees the church looked huge and plain and ugly in its nakedness.

'There's nothing more empty than a space you knew once when it was full,' Fonsie said.

'What do you mean?'

'Can you not see the trees?' Fonsie gestured irritably.

'The trees are gone.'

'That's what I mean. They were there and they're no longer there. Can you not see?'

Philly pressed Fonsie to come into the bar-grocery but he could not be persuaded. He said that he preferred to wait in the car. When Fonsie preferred something, with that kind of pointed politeness, Philly knew from old exasperations that it was useless to try to talk, and he left him there in silence.

'You must be one of the Ryans, then. You're welcome but I'm very sorry about poor Peter. You wouldn't be John, now? No? John stayed below in the house. You're Philly, then, and that's Fonsie out in the car. He won't come in? Your poor mother didn't come? I'm very sorry about Peter.' The old man with a limp behind the counter repeated each scrap of information after Philly as soon as it was given between his own hesitant questions and interjections.

'You must be Luke Henry, then?' Philly asked.

'The very man and still going strong. I remember you well coming in the summers. It must be at least ten years.'

'No. Twenty years now.'

'Twenty.' He shook his head. 'You'd never think. Terror how they go. It may be stiff pedalling for the first years but, I fear, after a bit, it is all freewheeling.' When Luke smiled his face became strangely boyish. 'What'll you have? On the house! A large brandy?'

'No, nothing at all. I just want to get a few things for the wake.'

'You'll have to have something, seeing what happened.'

'Just a pint, then. A pint of Guinness.'

'What will Fonsie have?'

'He's all right. He couldn't be got to come in out of the car. He's that bit upset,' Philly said.

'He'll have to have something,' Luke said doggedly.

'Well, a pint, then. I'll take it out to him myself. He's that bit upset.'

When Philly opened the door of the car and offered him Luke's pint, Fonsie said, 'What's this fucking thing for?'

'Nothing would do him but to send you out a drink when I said you wouldn't come in.'

387

'What am I supposed to do with it?'

'Put it in your pocket. Use it for hair oil. It's about time you came off your high horse and took things the way they are offered.' Fonsie's aggression was suddenly met with equal aggression, and before he had time to counter, Philly closed the car door, leaving him alone with the pint in his hand.

Back inside the bar Philly raised his glass. 'Good luck. Thanks, Luke.'

'To the man that's gone,' Luke said. 'There was no sides to poor Peter. He was straight and thick. We could do with more like him.'

Philly drank quickly and then started his order: several bottles of whiskey, gin, vodka, sherry, brandy, stout, beer, lemonade, orange, and loaves, butter, tea, coffee, ham and breasts of turkey. Luke wrote down each item as it was called. Several times he tried to cut down the order – 'It's too much, too much' he kept muttering – then, slowly, one by one, all the time checking the list, he placed each item on the counter, checking it against the list once more before packing everything into several cardboard boxes.

Philly pulled out a wad of money.

'No,' Luke refused the money firmly. 'We'll settle it all out here later. You'll have lots to bring back. Not even the crowd down in the bog will be able to eat and drink that much.' He managed a smile in which malice almost equalled wistfulness.

After they'd filled the boot with boxes, they stacked more in the back seat and on one side of the folded wheelchair. Luke shook Fonsie's hand as he helped to carry out the boxes to the car. 'I'm sorry for your trouble'; but if Fonsie made any response it was inaudible. When they finished, Philly lifted the empty pint glass from the dashboard and handed it to Luke with a wink. Luke raised the pint glass in a sly gesture to indicate that he was more than well acquainted with the strange ways of the world.

'In all my life I never had to drink a pint sitting on my own in a car outside a public house. There's no manners round here. The people are savages,' Fonsie complained as soon as the car moved.

'You wouldn't come in and Luke meant only the best,' Philly said gruffly.

'Of course, as usual you had to go and make a five- or six-course meal out of the whole business.'

'What do you mean?'

'I thought you'd never stop coming out of the pub with the boxes. The boot is full. The back seat is jammed. You must have enough to start a bar-restaurant yourself.'

'They can be returned,' Philly said defensively. 'Luke wouldn't even take money. We wouldn't want to be disgraced by running out of drink in the middle of the wake. Luke said, everybody said, there was never anything small about Uncle Peter. He wouldn't want anything to run short at his wake. The McDermotts were always big people.'

'They were in their shite,' Fonsie said furiously. 'He made us feel we were stealing bread out of his mouth. But that's you all over. Big, big, big,' he taunted. 'That's why people in Dublin are fed up with you. You always have to make the big splash. You live in a rathole in the desert for eighteen months, then you come out and do the big fellow. People don't want that. They want to go about their own normal lives. They don't want your drinks or big blow.'

There are no things more cruel than truths about ourselves spoken to us by another that are perceived to be at least half true. Left unsaid and hidden we feel they can be changed or eradicated, in time. Philly gripped Fonsie's shoulder in a despairing warning that he'd heard enough. They turned into the bog road to the house.

'We live in no rathole in the desert,' Philly said quietly. 'There's no hotel in Dublin to match where we live, except there's no booze, and sometimes that's no bad thing either.'

'That still doesn't take anything away from what I said.' Fonsie would not relent.

Without any warning, suddenly, they were out of the screen of small trees into the open bog. A low red sun west of Killeelan was spilling over the sedge and dark heather. Long shadows stretched out from the small birches scattered all over the bog.

'What are you stopping for?' Fonsie demanded.

'Just looking at the bog. On evenings like this I used to think it was on fire. Other times the sedge looked like gold. I remember it well.'

'You're talking through your drainpipe,' Fonsie said as the car moved on. 'All I remember of these evenings is poor Mother hanging out the washing.'

'Wouldn't she hang it out in the morning?'

'She had too much to do in the morning. It shows how little you were about the house. She used to wash all of Peter's trousers. They never were washed from one year to the next. She used to say they were fit to walk around on their own. Often with a red sun there was the frost. She thought it freshened clothes.'

To their surprise there were already six cars on the street as they drew close to the house.

'News must have gone out already that you've bought the world of booze,' Fonsie said as they drew up in front of the door, and his humour was not improved by having to sit in the car while all the boxes in the boot were carried into the house before the wheelchair could be taken out.

John was getting on famously with the people in the house who had come while his two brothers had been away. In fact, he got on better with strangers than with either of his brothers. He was a good listener. At school he had been a brilliant student, winning scholarships with ease all the way to university; but as soon as he graduated he disappeared into teaching. He was still teaching the same subjects in the same school where he had started, and appeared to dislike his work intensely though he was considered one of the best teachers in the school. Like most of his students and fellow teachers he seemed to live and work for the moment when the buzzer would end the school day.

'I don't want to be bothered,' was a phrase he used whenever new theories or educational practices came up in the classroom. 'They can go and cause trouble with their new ideas elsewhere. I just want to be left in peace.'

Their mother complained that his wife ran his whole life – she had been a nurse before they married – but others were less certain. They felt he encouraged her innate bossiness so that he could the better shelter unbothered behind it like a deep hedge. When offered the headship of the school, he had turned it down without consulting his wife. She had been deeply hurt when she heard of the offer from the wife of another teacher. She would have loved to have gone to the supermarket and church as the headmaster's wife. Her dismay forced her to ask him if it was true. 'You should at least have told me.' His admission that he'd refused the promotion increased her hurt. 'I didn't want to bother you,' he said so finally that she was silenced.

When the two brothers came back to the house, he gradually moved back into a corner, listening with perfect attention to anybody who came to him, while before he had been energetically welcoming visitors, showing them to the corpse room, getting them drinks and putting them at ease. Once Philly and Fonsie came into the house he turned it all over to them. The new callers lined up in front of them to shake their hands in turn.

'I'm sorry about poor Peter. I'm sorry for your trouble. Very sorry.'

'Thank you for coming. I know that. I know that well,' Philly answered equally ceremoniously, and his ready words covered Fonsie's stubborn silence.

Despite the aspersion Fonsie cast on the early mourners, very little was drunk or eaten that night. Maggie Cullen made sandwiches with the ham and turkey and tomatoes and sliced loaves. Her daughter-in-law cut the sandwiches into small squares and handed them around on a large oval plate with blue flowers around the rim. Tea was made in a big kettle. There were not many glasses in the house but few had to drink wine or whiskey from cups. Those that drank beer or stout refused all offers of cup or glass and drank from the bottles. Some who smoked had a curious, studious habit of dropping their cigarette butts carefully down the narrow necks of the bottles. Some held up the bottles like children to listen to the smouldering ash hiss in the beer dregs. By morning, butts could be seen floating in the bottoms of several of the bottles like trapped wasps.

All through the evening and night people kept coming to the house while others who had come earlier quietly left. First they shook hands with the three brothers, then went to the upper room, knelt by the bed; and when they rose they touched the dead hands or forehead in a gesture of leavetaking or communion, and then sat on one of the chairs by the bed. When new people came in to the room and knelt by the bed they left their chairs and returned to the front room where they were offered food and drink and joined in the free, unceasing talk and laughter. Almost all the talk was of the dead man. Much of it was in the form of stories. All of them showed the dead man winning out in life and the few times he had been forced to concede defeat it had been with stubbornness or wit. No surrender here, were his great words. The only thing he ever regretted was never having learned to drive a car. 'We always told him we'd drive him anywhere he wanted to go,' Jim Cullen said. 'But he'd never ask. He was too proud, and when we'd take him to town on Saturdays we'd have to make it appear that we needed him along for company; then he'd want to buy you the world of drink. When the children were young he'd load them down with money or oranges and chocolates. Then, out of the blue, he said to me once that he might be dead if he'd ever learned to drive: he'd noticed that many who drove cars had died, while a lot of those who had to walk or cycle like himself were still battering around.'

From the top of the dresser a horse made from matchsticks and mounted on a rough board was taken down. The thin lines of the matchsticks were cunningly spliced and glued together to suggest the shape of a straining horse in the motion of ploughing or mowing. A pig was found among the plates, several sheep that were subtly different from one another, as well as what looked like a tired old collie, all made from the same curved and spliced matchsticks.

'He was always looking for matches. Even in town on Saturdays you'd see him picking them up from the bar floor. He could do anything with them. The children loved the animals he'd give them. Seldom they broke them. Though our crowd are grown we still have several he made in the house. He never liked TV. That's what you'd find him at on any winter's night if you wandered in on your *ceilidh*. He could nearly make those matchsticks talk.'

It was as if the house had been sundered into two distinct and separate elements, and yet each reflected and measured the other as much as the earth and the sky. In the upper room there was silence, the people there keeping vigil by the body where it lay in the stillness and awe of the last change; while in the lower room that life was being resurrected with more vividness than it could ever have had in the long days and years it had been given. Though all the clocks in the house had now been silenced everybody seemed to know at once when it was midnight and all the mourners knelt except Fonsie and two very old women. The two rooms were joined as the Rosary was recited but as soon as the prayers ended each room took on again its separate entity.

Fonsie signalled to Philly that he wanted to go outside. Philly knew immediately that his brother wanted to relieve himself. In the city he never allowed any help but here he was afraid of the emptiness and darkness of the night outside the house and the strange ground. It was a clear moonlit night without a murmur of wind, and the acres of pale sedge were all lit up, giving back much of the light it was receiving, so that the places that were covered with heather melted into a soft blackness and the scattered shadows of the small birches were soft and dark on the cold sedge. High up and far off they could hear an aeroplane and soon they picked it out by the pulsing of its white nightlight as it crossed their stretch of sky. The tall evergreens within the pale stone wall on the top of Killeelan were dark and gathered together against the moon-light. As if to give something back to his brother for accompanying him into the night, Fonsie said as he was relieving himself in the shadowed corner of the house, 'Mother remembers seeing the first car in this place. She says she was ten. All of them from the bog rushed out to the far road to see the car pass. It's strange to think of people living still who didn't grow up with cars.'

'Maybe they were as well off,' Philly said.

'How could they be as well off?'

'Would Peter in there now be better off?'

'I thought it was life we were talking about. If they were that well off why had they all to do their best to get to hell out of the place?'

'I was only thinking that a lot of life never changes. If the rich could get the poor to die for them the rich would never die,' Philly said belligerently. It didn't take much or long for an edge to come between them, but before it could grow they went back into the house. Not until close to daylight did the crowd of mourners start to thin.

During all this time John had been the most careful of the three brothers. He had drunk less than either of the other two, had stayed almost as silent as Fonsie, and now he noticed each person's departure and accompanied them out to their cars to thank them for coming to Peter's wake as if he had been doing it all his life. By the time the last car left, the moon was still in the sky but was well whitened by the rising sun. The sedge had lost its brightness and taken on the dull colour of wheat. All that was left in the house with the dead man and his three nephews were the Cullens and a local woman who had helped with tea and sandwiches through the night. By that time they had all acquired the heady, vaguely up-lifting spiritual feeling that comes in the early stages of exhaustion and is often strikingly visible in the faces of the old or sick.

In the same vague, absent, dreamlike way, the day drifted towards evening. Whenever they came to the door they saw a light, freshening wind moving over the sedge as if it were passing over water. Odd callers continued coming to the house throughout the day, and after they spent time with the dead man in the room they were given food and drink and they sat and talked. Most of their talk was empty and tired by now and had none of the vigour of the night before. Mrs Cullen took great care to ensure that the upper room was never left empty, that someone was always there by Peter's side on this his last day in the house. Shortly after five the hearse arrived and the coffin was taken in. It was clear that Luke had been right and that most of the drink Philly had ordered would have to be returned. Immediately behind the hearse was a late, brief flurry of callers. Shortly before six the body was laid in the coffin and, with a perfunctory little swish of beads, the undertaker began the decade of the Rosary. The coffin was closed and taken out to the hearse. Many cars had taken up position on the narrow road to accompany the hearse to the church.

After they left the coffin before the high altar in the church, some of the mourners crossed the road to Luke's Bar. There, Philly bought everybody a round of drinks but when he attempted to buy a second round both Luke and Jim Cullen stopped him. Custom allowed one round but no more. Instead he ordered a pint of stout for himself and Fonsie, and John shook his head to the offer of a second drink. Then when Philly went to pay for the two drinks Luke pushed the money back to him and said that Jim Cullen had just paid.

People offered to put the brothers up for the night but Fonsie especially would not hear of staying in a strange house. He insisted on going to the hotel in town. As soon as they had drunk the second pint and said their goodbyes Philly drove John and Fonsie to the Royal Hotel. He waited until they were given rooms and then prepared to leave.

'Aren't you staying here?' Fonsie asked sharply when he saw that Philly was about to leave him alone with John.

'No.'

'Where are you putting your carcass?'

'Let that be no worry of yours,' Philly said coolly.

'I don't think a more awkward man ever was born. Even Mother agrees on that count.'

'I'll see you around nine in the morning,' Philly said to John as they made an appointment to see Reynolds, the solicitor, before the funeral Mass at eleven.

Philly noticed that both the young Cullens and the older couple had returned from the removal by the two cars parked outside their house. Peter's house was unlocked and eerily empty, everything in it exactly as it was when the coffin was taken out. On impulse he took three bottles of whiskey from one of the boxes stacked beneath the table and walked with the bottles over to Cullen's house. They'd seen him coming from the road and Jim Cullen went out to meet him before he reached the door.

'I'm afraid you caught us in the act,' Mrs Cullen laughed. The four of them had been sitting at the table, the two men drinking what looked like glasses of whiskey, the women cups of tea and biscuits.

'Another half-hour and you'd have found us in the nest,' Jim Cullen said. 'We didn't realize how tired we were until after we came in from looking at our own cattle and Peter's. We decided to have this last drink and then hit off. We'll miss Peter.'

Without asking him, Mrs Cullen poured him a glass of whiskey and a chair was pulled out for him at the table. Water was added to the whiskey from a glass jug. He placed the three bottles on the table. 'I just brought over these before everything goes back to the shop.'

'It's far too much,' they responded. 'We didn't want anything.'

'I know that but it's still too little.' He seemed to reach far back to his mother or uncle for the right thing to say. 'It's just a show of something for all that you've done.'

'Thanks but it's still far too much.' They all seemed to be pleased at once and took and put the three bottles away. They then offered him a bed but he said he'd manage well enough in their old room. 'I'm used to roughing it out there in the oil fields,' he lied; and not many minutes after that, seeing Mrs Cullen stifle a yawn, he drank down his whiskey and left. Jim Cullen accompanied him as far as the road and stood there until Philly had gone some distance towards his uncle's house before turning slowly back.

In the house Philly went from room to room to let in fresh air but found that all the windows were stuck. He left the doors to the rooms open and the front door open on the bog. In the lower room he placed an eiderdown on the old hollowed bed and in the upper room he drew the top sheet up over where the corpse had lain until it covered both the whole of the bed and pillow. He then took the iron box from the cupboard and unlocked it on the table in the front room. Before starting to go through the box he got a glass and half filled it with whiskey. He found very old deeds tied with legal ribbon as he drank, cattle cards, a large wad of notes in a rubber band, a number of scattered US dollar notes, a one-hundred-dollar bill, some shop receipts ready to fall apart, and a gold wedding ring. He put the parchment to one side to take to the solicitor the next morning. The notes he placed in a brown envelope before locking the box and placing it back in the cupboard. He poured another large whiskey. On a whim he went and took down some of the matchstick figures that they had looked at the night before – a few of the sheep, a little pig, the dray-horse and cart, a delicate greyhound on a board with its neck straining out from the bent knees like a snake's as if about to pick a turning rabbit or hare from the ground. He moved them here and there on the table with his finger as he drank when, putting his glass down, his arm leaned on the slender suggestion of a horse, which crumpled and fell apart. Almost covertly he gathered the remains of the figure, the cart and scattered matches, and put them in his pocket to dispose of later. Quickly and uneasily he restored the sheep and pig and hound to the safety of the shelf. Then he moved his chair out into the doorway and poured more whiskey.

He thought of Peter sitting alone here at night making the shapes of animals out of matchsticks, of those same hands now in a coffin before the high altar of Cootehall church. Tomorrow he'd lie in the earth on the top of Killeelan Hill. A man is born. He dies. Where he himself stood now on the path between those two points could not be known. He felt as much like the child that came each summer years ago to this bog from the city as the rough unfinished man he knew himself to be in the eyes of others, but feelings had nothing to do with it. He must be already well out past halfway.

The moon of the night before lit the pale sedge. He could see the dark shapes of the heather, the light on the larger lakes of sedge, but he had no desire to walk out into the night. Blurred with tiredness and whiskey, all shapes and lives seemed to merge comfortably into one another as the pale, ghostly sedge and the dark heather merged under the moon. Except for the stirrings of animals about the house and a kittiwake calling sharply high up over the bog and the barking of distant dogs the night was completely silent. There was not even a passing motor. But before he lay down like a dog under the eiderdown in the lower room he remembered to set the alarm of his travelling clock for seven the next morning.

In spite of a throbbing forehead he was the first person in the dining-room of the Royal Hotel for breakfast the next morning. After managing to get through most of a big fry – sausages, black pudding, bacon, scrambled eggs and three pots of black coffee – he was beginning to feel much better when Fonsie and John came in for their breakfast.

'I wouldn't advise the coffee though I'm awash with the stuff,' Philly said as the two brothers looked through the menu.

'We never have coffee in the house except when you're back,' Fonsie said.

'I got used to it out there. The Americans drink nothing else throughout the day.'

'They're welcome to it,' Fonsie said.

John looked from one brother to the other but kept his silence. Both brothers ordered tea and scrambled eggs on toast.

'What did you two do last night?'

'I'm afraid we had pints, too many pints,' John answered.

'You had no pints, only glasses,' Fonsie said.

'It all totted up to pints and there were too many. This wild life doesn't suit me. How you are able to move around this morning I don't know.'

'That's nothing,' Fonsie said. 'And you should see yer man here when he gets going; then you'd have a chance to talk. It's all or nothing. There's never any turning back.'

As Philly was visibly discomforted, John asked, 'What did you do?'

'I thanked the Cullens.'

'More whiskey,' Fonsie crowed.

'Then I opened the iron box,' Philly ignored the gibe. 'I found the deeds. We'll need them for the lawyer in a few minutes. And there was another wad of money. There was sterling and dollars and a few Australian notes as well.'

'The sterling and dollars came from the brother and sister. They were probably sent to the mother and never cashed. God knows where the Australian came from,' John said.

'It all comes to thousands,' Philly said.

'When we used to go there you'd think we were starving him out of the place.'

'They probably didn't have it then.'

'Even if they did it would still have been the same. It's a way of thinking.'

'The poor fucker, it'd make you laugh,' Fonsie said. 'Making pigs and horses out of matchsticks in the night, slaving on the bog or running after cattle in the day, when he could have gone out and had himself a good time.'

'Maybe that was his way of having a good time,' John said carefully.

'It'll get some good scattering now,' Fonsie laughed at Philly.

'Are you sure?' Philly said sternly back. 'It all goes to Mother anyhow. She's the next of kin. Maybe you'll give it the scattering? I have lots for myself.'

'Mr Big again,' Fonsie jeered.

'It's time to go to see this lawyer. Do you want to come?'

'I have more sense,' Fonsie answered angrily.

The brown photos around the walls of the solicitor's waiting room as well as the heavy mahogany table and leather chairs told that the practice was old, that it had been passed from grandfather Reynolds to father to son. The son was about fifty, dressed in a beautifully cut dark pinstripe suit, his grey hair parted in the centre. His manner was soft and urbane and quietly watchful.

Philly had asked John to state their business, which he did with simple clarity. As he spoke Philly marvelled at his brother. Even if it meant saving his own life he'd never have been able to put the business so neatly without sidetracking or leaving something out.

'My advice would be to lose that money,' the solicitor said when he had finished. 'Strictly, I shouldn't be giving that advice but as far as I'm concerned I never heard anything about it.'

Both brothers nodded their understanding and gratitude.

'Almost certainly there's no will. I'd have it if there was. I acted for Peter in a few matters. There was a case of trespass and harassment by a neighbouring family called Whelan a few years back. None of it was Peter's fault. They were a bad lot and solved our little problem by emigrating *en masse* to the States. Peter's friend, Jim Cullen, bought their land.'

Philly remembered wild black-haired Marie Whelan who had challenged him to fight on the bog road during one of those last summers. John just nodded that he remembered the family.

'So everything should go to your mother as the only surviving next of kin. As she is a certain age it should be acted on quickly and I'll be glad to act as soon as I learn what it is your mother wants.' As he spoke he opened the deeds Philly gave John to hand over. 'Peter never even bothered to have the deeds changed into his name. The place is in your grandfather's name and this document was drawn up by my grandfather.'

'Would the place itself be worth much?' Philly's sudden blunt question surprised John. Out of his quietness Mr Reynolds looked up at him sharply.

'I fear not a great deal. Ten or eleven thousand. A little more if there was local competition. I'd say fourteen at the very most.'

'You can't buy a room for that in the city and there's almost thirty acres with the small house.'

'Well, it's not the city and I do not think Gloria Bog is ever likely to become the Costa Brava.'

Philly noticed that both the solicitor and his brother were looking at him with withdrawn suspicion if not distaste. They were plainly thinking that greed had propelled him to stumble into the inquiry he had made when it was the last thing in the world he had in mind. Before anything further could be said, the solicitor was shaking both their hands at the door and nodding over their shoulders to the receptionist behind her desk across the hallway to take their particulars before showing them out.

In contrast to the removal of the previous evening, when the church had been full to overflowing, there were only a few dozen people at the funeral Mass. Eight cars followed the hearse to Killeelan, and only the Mercedes turned into the narrow laneway behind the hearse. The other mourners abandoned their cars at the road and entered the lane on foot. Blackthorn and briar scraped against the windscreen and sides of the Mercedes as they moved behind the hearse's slow pace. At the end of the lane there was a small clearing in front of the limestone wall that ringed the foot of Killeelan Hill. There was just enough space in the clearing for the hearse and the Mercedes to park on either side of the small iron gate in the wall. The coffin was taken from the hearse and placed on the shoulders of John and Philly and the two Cullens. The gate was just wide enough for them to go through. Fonsie alone stayed behind in the front seat of the Mercedes and watched the coffin as it slowly climbed the hill on the four shoulders. The coffin went up and up the steep hill, sometimes swaying dangerously, and then anxious hands of the immediate followers would go up against the back of the coffin. The shadows of the clouds swept continually over the green hill and brown varnish of the coffin. Away on the bog they were a darker, deeper shadow as the clouds travelled swiftly over the pale sedge. Three times the small snail-like cortège stopped completely for the bearers to be changed. As far as Fonsie could see – he would have needed binoculars to be certain – they were the original bearers, his brothers and the two Cullens, who took up the coffin the third and last time and carried it through the small gate in the wall around the graveyard on the hilltop. Then it was only the coffin itself and the heads of the mourners that could be seen until they were lost in the graveyard evergreens. In spite of his irritation at this useless ceremony, that seemed only to show some deep love of hardship or enslavement – they'd be hard put to situate the graveyard in a more difficult or inaccessible place except on the very top of a mountain – he found the coffin and the small band of toiling mourners unbearably moving as it made its low stumbling climb up the hill, and this deepened further his irritation and the sense of complete uselessness.

Suddenly he was startled by the noise of a car coming very fast up the narrow lane and braking to a stop behind the hearse. A priest in a long black soutane and white surplice with a purple stole over his shoulders got out of the car carrying a fat black breviary. Seeing Fonsie, he saluted briskly as he went through the open gate. Then, bent almost double, he started to climb quickly like an enormous black-and-white crab after the coffin. Watching him climb,

The Country Funeral

Fonsie laughed harshly before starting to fiddle with the car radio.

After a long interval the priest was the first to come down the hill, accompanied by two middle-aged men, the most solid looking and conventional of the mourners. The priest carried his surplice and stole on his arm. The long black soutane looked strangely menacing between the two attentive men in suits as they came down. Fonsie reached over to turn off the rock and roll playing on the radio as they drew close, but, in a sudden reversal, he turned it up louder still. The three men looked towards the loud music as they came through the gate but did not salute or nod. They got into the priest's car and, as there was no turning place between the hearse and the Mercedes, it proceeded to back out of the narrow lane. Then in straggles of twos and threes, people started to come down the hill. The two brothers and Jim Cullen were the last to come down. As soon as Philly got into the Mercedes he turned off the radio.

'You'd think you'd show a bit more respect.'

'The radio station didn't know about the funeral.'

'I'm not talking about the radio station,' Philly said.

'That Jim Cullen is a nice man,' John said in order to steer the talk away from what he saw as an imminent clash. 'He's intelligent as well as decent. Peter was lucky in his neighbour.'

'The Cullens,' Philly said as if searching for a phrase. 'You couldn't, you couldn't if you tried get better people than the Cullens.'

They drove straight from Killeelan to the Royal for lunch. Not many people came, just the Cullens among the close neighbours and a few far-out cousins of the dead man. Philly bought a round for everyone and when he found no takers to his offer of a second round he did not press.

'Our friend seems to be restraining himself for once,' Fonsie remarked sarcastically to John as they moved from the bar to the restaurant.

'He's taking his cue from Jim Cullen. Philly is all right,' John said. 'It's those months and months out in the oil fields and then the excitement of coming home with all that money. It has to have an effect. Wouldn't it be worse if he got fond of the money?'

'It's still too much. It's not awanting,' Fonsie continued doggedly through a blurred recognition of all that Philly had given to their

401

mother and to the small house over the years, and it caused him to stir uncomfortably.

The set meal was simple and good: hot vegetable soup, lamb chops with turnip and roast potatoes and peas, apple tart and cream, tea or coffee. While they were eating, the three gravediggers came into the dining-room and were given a separate table by one of the river windows. Philly got up as soon as they arrived to ensure that drinks were brought to their table.

When the meal ended, the three brothers drove back behind the Cullens' car to Gloria Bog. There they put all that was left of the booze back into the car. The Cullens accepted what food was left over but wouldn't hear of taking any more of the drink. 'We're not planning on holding another wake for a long time yet,' they said half humorously, half sadly. John helped with the boxes, Fonsie did not leave the car. As soon as Philly gave Jim Cullen the keys to the house John shook his hand and got back into the car with Fonsie and the boxes of booze, but still Philly continued talking to Jim Cullen outside the open house. In the rear mirror they saw Philly thrust a fistful of notes towards Jim Cullen. They noticed how large the old farmer's hands were as they gripped Philly by the wrist and pushed the hand and notes down into his jacket pocket, refusing stubbornly to accept any money. When John took his eyes from the mirror and the small sharp struggle between the two men, what met his eyes across the waste of pale sedge and heather was the rich dark waiting evergreens inside the back wall of Killeelan where they had buried Peter beside his father and mother only a few hours before. The colour of laughter is black. How dark is the end of all of life. Yet others carried the burden in the bright day on the hill. His shoulders shuddered slightly in revulsion and he wished himself back in the semi-detached suburbs with rosebeds outside in the garden.

'I thought you'd never finish,' Fonsie accused Philly when the big car began to move slowly out the bog road.

'There was things to be tidied up,' Philly said absently. 'Jim is going to take care of the place till I get back,' and as Fonsie was about to answer he found John's hands pressing his shoulders from the back seat in a plea not to speak. When they parked beside the door of the bar there was just place enough for another car to pass inside the church wall.

'Not that a car is likely to pass,' Philly joked as he and John carried the boxes in. When they had placed all of them on the counter they saw Luke reach for a brandy bottle on the high shelf.

'No, Luke,' Philly said. 'I'll have a pint if that's what you have in mind.'

'John'll have a pint, then, too.'

'I don't know,' John said in alarm. 'I haven't drunk as much in my life as the last few days. I feel poisoned.'

'Still, we're unlikely to have a day like this ever again,' Philly said as Luke pulled three pints.

'I don't think I'd survive many more such days,' John said.

'Wouldn't it be better to bring Fonsie in than to have him drinking out there in the car? It'll take me a while to make up all this. One thing I will say,' he said as he started to count the returned bottles. 'There was no danger of anybody running dry at Peter's wake.'

Fonsie protested when Philly went out to the car. It was too much trouble to get the wheelchair out of the boot. He didn't need drink. 'I'll take you in.' Philly offered his stooped neck and carried Fonsie into the bar like a child as he'd done many times when they were young and later when they were on certain sprees. He set him down in an armchair in front of the empty fireplace and brought his pint from the counter. It took Luke a long time to make up the bill, and when he eventually presented it to Philly, after many extra countings and checkings, he was full of apologies at what it had all come to.

'It'd be twice as much in the city,' Philly said energetically as he paid.

'I suppose it'd be as much anyhow,' Luke grumbled happily with relief and then at once started to draw another round of drinks which he insisted they take.

'It's on the house. It's not every day or year brings you down.'

Fonsie and Philly drank the second pint easily. John was already fuddled and unhappy and he drank reluctantly.

'I won't say goodbye.' Luke accompanied them out to the car when they left. 'You'll have to be down again before long.'

'It'll not be long till we're down,' Philly answered firmly for all of them.

In Longford and Mullingar and Enfield Philly stopped on their way back to Dublin. John complained each time, but it was Philly who had command of the car. Each time he carried Fonsie into the bars – and in all of them the two drank pints – John refused to have anything in Mullingar or Longford but took a reluctant glass in Enfield.

'What'll you do if you have an accident and get breathalysed?'

'I'll not have an accident. And they can send the summons all the way out to the Saudis if I do.'

He drove fast but steadily into the city. He was silent as he drove. Increasingly, he seemed charged with an energy that was focused elsewhere and had been fuelled by every stop they had made. In the heart of the city, seeing a vacant place in front of Mulligan's where he had drunk on his own in the deep silence of the bar a few short mornings before, he pulled across the traffic and parked. Cars stopped to blow hard at him but he paid no attention as he parked and got out.

'We'll have a last drink here in the name of God before we face back to the mother,' Philly said as he carried Fonsie into the bar. There were now a few dozen early evening drinkers in the bar. Some of them seemed to know the brothers, but not well. John offered to move Fonsie from the table to an armchair but Fonsie said he preferred to remain where he was. John complained that he hadn't asked for the pint when the drinks were brought to the table.

'Is it a short you want, then?'

'No. I have had more drink today than I've had in years. I want nothing.'

'Don't drink it, then, if you don't want,' he was told roughly.

'Well, Peter, God rest him, was given a great send-off,' Philly said with deep satisfaction as he drank. 'I thank God I was back. I wouldn't have been away for the world. The church was packed for the removal. Every neighbour around was at Killeelan.'

'What else have they to do down there? It's the one excuse they have to get out of their houses,' Fonsie said.

'They honour the dead. That's what they do. People still mean something down there. They showed the respect they had for Peter.'

'Respect, my arse. Everybody is respected for a few days after they conk it because they don't have to be lived with any more. Oh, it's easy to honour the dead. It doesn't cost anything and gives them the chance to get out of their bloody houses before they start to eat one another within.'

An old argument started up, an argument they had had many times before without resolving anything, the strength of their difference betraying the hidden closeness.

Philly and Fonsie drained their glasses as John took the first sip from his pint and he looked uneasily from one to the other.

'You have it all crooked,' Philly said as he rose to get more drink from the counter. John covered his glass with his palm to indicate that he wanted nothing more. When Philly came back with the two pints he started to speak before he had even put the glasses down on the table: he had all the blind dominating passion of someone in thrall to a single idea.

'I'll never forget it all the days of my life, the people coming to the house all through the night. The rows and rows of people at the removal passing by us in the front seat of the church grasping our hands. Coming in that small lane behind the hearse; then carrying Peter up that hill.'

Fonsie tried to speak but Philly raised his glass into his face and refused to be silenced.

'I felt something I never felt when we left the coffin on the edge of the grave. A rabbit hopped out of the briars a few yards off. He sat there and looked at us as if he didn't know what was going on before he bolted off. You could see the bog and all the shut houses next to Peter's below us. There wasn't even a wisp of smoke coming from any of the houses. Everybody gathered around, and the priest started to speak of the dead and the Mystery and the Resurrection.'

'He's paid to do that and he was nearly late. I saw it all from the car,' Fonsie asserted. 'It was no mystery from the car. Several times I thought you were going to drop the coffin. It was more like a crowd of apes staggering up a hill with something they had just looted. The whole lot of you could have come right out of the Dark Ages, without even a dab of make-up. I thought a standard of living had replaced the struggle for survival ages ago.'

'I have to say I found the whole ceremony moving, but once is more than enough to go through that experience,' John said carefully. 'I think of Peter making those small animals out of matchsticks in the long nights on the bog. Some people pay money for that kind of work. Peter just did it out of some need.'

Philly either didn't hear or ignored what John said.

'It's a godsend they don't let you out often,' Fonsie said. 'People that exhibit in museums are a different kettle. Peter was just killing the nights on the bloody bog.'

'I'll never forget the boredom of those summers, watching Peter foot turf, making grabs at the butterflies that tossed about over the sedge. Once you closed your hand they always escaped,' John said as if something long buried in him was drawn out. 'I think he was making things out of matchsticks even then but we hardly noticed.'

'Peter never wanted us. Mother just forced us on him. He wasn't able to turn us away,' Fonsie said, the talk growing more and more rambling and at odds.

'He didn't turn us away, whether he wanted to or not,' Philly asserted truculently. 'I heard Mother say time and time again that we'd never have got through some of the winters but for those long summers on the bog.'

'She'd have to say that since she took us there.'

'It's over now. With Peter it's all finished. One of the things that made the last days bearable for me was that everything we were doing was being done for the last time,' John said with such uncharacteristic volubility that the two brothers just stared.

'I'll say amen to that,' Fonsie said.

'It's far from over but we better have a last round for the road first.' Philly drained his glass and rose, and again John covered his three-quarter-full glass with his palm. 'As far as I can make out nothing is ever over.'

'Those two are tanks for drink, but they don't seem to have been pulling lately,' a drinker at the counter remarked to his companion as Philly passed by shakily with the pair of pints. 'The pale one not drinking looks like a brother as well. There must have been a family do.'

'You'd wonder where that wheelchair brother puts all that drink,' the other changed.

'He puts it where we all put it. You don't need legs, for God's sake, to take drink. Drink only gets down as far as your flute.'

'Gloria is far from over,' Philly said as he put the two pints down on the table. 'Nothing is ever over. I'm going to take up in Peter's place.'

'You can't be that drunk,' Fonsie said dismissively.

'I'm not sober but I was never more certain of anything in my born life.'

'Didn't the lawyer say it'd go to Mother? What'll she do but sell?'

'I'm not sure she'll want to sell. She grew up there. It was in her family for generations.'

'I'm sure. I can tell you that now.'

'Well, it's even simpler, then. I'll buy the place off Mother,' Philly announced so decisively that Fonsie found himself looking at John.

'I'm out of this,' John said. 'What people do is their own business. All I ask is to be let go about my own life.'

'I've enough money to buy the place. You heard what the lawyer said it was worth. I'll give Mother its price and she can do with it what she likes.'

'We're sick these several years hearing about all you can buy,' Fonsie said angrily.

'Well, I'll go where people will not be sick, where there'll be no upcasting,' Philly said equally heatedly.

'What'll you do there?' John asked out of a desire to calm the heated talk.

'He'll grow onions.' Fonsie shook with laughter.

'I can't be going out to the oil fields for ever. It'll be a place to come home to. You saw how the little iron cross in the circle over the grave was eaten with rust. I'm going to have marble put up. Jim Cullen is going to look after Peter's cattle till I get back in six months and everything will be settled then.'

'You might even get married there,' Fonsie said sarcastically.

'It's unlikely but stranger things have happened, and I'll definitely be buried there. Mother will want to be buried there some day.'

'She'll be buried with our father out in Glasnevin.'

'I doubt that. Even the fish go back to where they came from. I'd say she's had more than enough of our poor father in one life to be going on with. John here has a family, but it's about time you gave where you're going yourself some thought,' Philly spoke directly to Fonsie.

'If I were to go I'd want to go where there was people and a bit of life about, not on some God-forsaken hill out in the bog with a crow or a sheep or a bloody rabbit.'

'There's no *if* in this business, it's just *when*. I'm sorry to have to say it, but it betrays a great lack of maturity on your part,' Philly said with drunken severity.

'You can plant maturity out there in the bog, for all I care, and may it grow into an ornament.'

'We better be going,' John said.

Philly rose and took Fonsie into his arms. In spite of his unsteadiness he carried him easily out to the car. Fonsie was close to tears. He had always thought he could never lose Philly. The burly block of exasperation would always come and go from the oil fields. Now he would go out to bloody Gloria Bog instead. As he was put in the car, his tears turned to rage.

'Yes, you'll be a big shot down there at last,' he said. 'They'll be made up. They'll be getting a Christmas present. They'll be getting one great big lump of a Christmas present.'

'Look,' John said soothingly. 'Mother will be waiting. She'll want to hear everything. And I have another home I have to go to yet.'

'I followed it all on the clock,' the mother said. 'I knew the Mass for Peter was starting at eleven and I put the big alarm clock on the table. At twenty past twelve I could see the coffin going through the cattle gate at the foot of Killeelan.'

'They were like a crowd of apes carrying the coffin up the hill. I could see it all from the car. Several times they had to put up hands as if the coffin was going to fall off the shoulders and roll back down the hill.'

'Once it did fall off. Old Johnny Whelan's coffin rolled halfway down the hill and broke open. They had to tie the boards together with the ropes they use for lowering into the grave. Some said the Whelans were drunk, others said they were too weak with hunger to carry the coffin. The Whelans were never liked. They are all in America now.'

'Anyhow, we buried poor Peter,' Philly said, as if it was at last a fact.